AHE'EY

JAMIE LE FAY

ISBN: 1-544-22458-3
ISBN-13: 978-1-54422458-9

BEGINNINGS

PRESENT DAY - 21 NOVEMBER 2014

NEW YORK

A Surprising Reception

"Give me your hand, little Angel," said the one-eyed man softly, extending his right hand to hold the hand of the two-year-old girl who sat comfortably on top of his left arm. The man held the toddler's hand and placed it under the fountain of water that streamed from the eyes of a weeping angel carved out of white marble. The creature's face was lowered into its hands and covered by long hair, its majestic wings pointed towards the sky, the only signal of hope present in the stone statue. The curly-haired baby girl felt the coldness of the water and giggled with delight. She looked back, smiled and touched the face of the man, caressing the silver eye-patch that covered the left side of his face. He held her hand, kissed it and once again placed her tiny fingers under the gleaming stream, much to her delight.

Morgan woke up from her dream as she heard the flight assistant's announcement that the plane was about to land. She wished she could remember the face of the one-eyed man that had haunted her dreams since she was a girl. Morgan placed her hand on her right shoulder and massaged it, attempting to relieve the tension from the long flight. She was exhausted; she'd been travelling for over ten hours.

As she was leaving the baggage claim area of the John F. Kennedy International Airport in New York, she saw a man holding a sign with her name on it. As she walked towards him, smiling, he looked puzzled. She was used to this reaction. She looked quite young for her age; they were expecting an older woman.

The man holding the sign smiled and said, "Ms. Morgan?"

She nodded.

"Welcome, madam. My name is James." He took her luggage, leaving only her handbag.

A group of three men walked towards her. The eldest extended his hand. She recognised him as the mayor of New York, Mayor Jack Dawkins. He had an enormous, open smile and laugh lines surrounding his eyes, presenting a welcoming face.

"Welcome, Morgan. I hope you had a safe trip."

She smiled, humbled by the unexpected presence of such a high-profile figure. She felt slightly self-conscious—he was wearing a formal, and undoubtedly expensive, black suit with a royal blue tie, and his white hair was perfectly combed and very shiny. She attempted to flat out some of the creases on her white linen Indian-inspired tunic with her hands. Her comfortable flat sandals made her feel quite small in comparison to the tall American men that followed the mayor and surrounded her in a circle. Thick, curly hair was half tucked in between her neck and the turquoise scarf that circled her shoulders. She quickly gathered her long dark hair and hopelessly attempted to smooth her curls, running her fingers through the unruly locks that reached her waist. *I might as well try to control a tropical storm,* she thought, amused by her rebellious mane.

A man stood just behind the group, and she couldn't help but notice him. It was clear he was part of the welcoming party, but he didn't look, dress, or act like the rest. He stood at the back and looked directly at her with a kind, warm expression. *Heavenly,* she thought, admiring his lean, strong body. He stood with his back straight, and held his head high, with an elegance from a different time. *I know you.* The rest of the world fell out of focus as she met his eyes. She felt slightly inebriated. She shook her head and blamed the jet lag, while he lowered his eyes, eyebrows wrinkled with some troubling thought. She immediately focused her attention on the mayor, who was explaining that he was going to be travelling internationally that day but that he had wanted to come personally to welcome her and wish her a pleasant stay. She smiled and nodded, processing only half of his words; the room was still spinning around her.

As the mayor introduced her to her appointed driver and her personal assistant, she looked back in the direction of the handsome stranger. Then the mayor finally extended his arm to the breathtaking creature who approached them with a warm smile. His dark hair touched his shoulders; the top part of his hair was gathered in a loose ponytail that left some wide curls waving in front of his crystal eyes. A light goatee perfectly framed his face promising intellectual substance. The mayor put his hand on the back of the younger man.

"Morgan, I would like to introduce you to Gabriel Warren, who will be your host and guide during your visit to New York." Gabriel's eyes, set on her, were like the sea, shifting between blue and green, reflecting the environment around them. He extended his hands to her and held her hand gently in between his for a brief moment.

"Pleasure." The top of her head barely reached his chin. As he talked to her, he bent his head and shoulders, and she looked up to meet his eyes. His voice was reassuring, and his words were sparse but polite. "We should start walking to the car. I'm sure Ms. Morgan is looking forward to getting to her hotel room." His British accent was very pleasing and charming.

The mayor nodded and, as they walked, he continued, "Gabriel's foundation, Ange'el, is a major benefactor to many of our most prestigious New York City venues. They fund the Metropolitan Museum and are involved in a variety of initiatives that support the United Nations and several medical research projects. I leave you in the best possible hands. My flight will be leaving soon. Please enjoy your stay in our wonderful city." He bowed his head to Gabriel, who bowed back.

"Have a safe flight," she said realising she'd barely spoken a handful of words to the mayor.

Carl, the driver, and James, the personal assistant, walked ahead, followed by Morgan and Gabriel. She was still puzzled by the special treatment and the number of minders assigned to her.

"We've made arrangements for you at The Pierre. I trust you'll enjoy your suite and views of Central Park."

"Sounds really delightful," she replied.

Gabriel remained quiet as they walked to the car. She noticed that his shoulders tensed as he scanned the surrounding area continuously. As a man ran in their direction, Gabriel abruptly used his arm to lead her behind him, placing his body in between her and the running man. The man rushed past them, probably late for his flight. Gabriel stepped out of her way, placed his hand on her back, and encouraged her to move forward. He started moving faster, his expression somewhat pensive and preoccupied. Opening the door of the limo, he led her inside.

She felt slightly overwhelmed by his nervous energy and by the proximity of his body. As if on cue, Gabriel relaxed, smiled, opened a bottle of sparkling water and added a piece of lime to it. As he handed her the water, he also placed a plate of fruit—strawberries, blueberries, and green peaches—beside her. She smiled; it was exactly what she needed and what she liked. She was puzzled and grateful for his precision. *What a happy coincidence that my preferences and desires are met so effortlessly.*

She was completely drained of energy, and yet she felt an unusual inner peace. The tension in her neck and shoulders was gone. She ate a strawberry, sunk into her seat, and relaxed. James was at the front of the limo, talking to Carl. She couldn't hear them through the partition that separated the front seats from the back.

"You may want to sleep a little. The traffic at this time is dreadful. It'll take us about an hour to get to the hotel." His voice was calming, considerate, and hypnotic. She closed her eyes and fell asleep.

She woke up as they reached Manhattan; the hustle and bustle of town woke her. It was a warm and bright winter day in late November. The Christmas lights were already up, and the Christmas shopping crowd navigated around the traffic, carrying their bags and packages. As they arrived at the hotel, he opened the doors and gently but decisively attempted to move her and the rest of the group inside the building.

She wasn't sure what bothered her most: the fact that he constantly touched her back and took a clear position of authority or the fact that she was complying with and enjoying it. She rebelled against the captivity of his charm. As he tried, once again, to rush her inside, she stopped, took a step to the side, away from him and started walking slower. He looked at her; brows bumped together in a scowl. She shot him a defiant sideways glance. She was amused by his reaction and happy with herself. He backed off as they got inside the hotel.

Black-and-white marble tiles adorned the floor of the high-end hotel, making a clear introduction to the luxury that was yet to be experienced by its guests. Colourful murals depicting Greek gods adorned the walls of a rotunda that led to a marble staircase. The vivid trompe l'oeil paintings borrowed their style from the Renaissance.

They didn't have to check in and went straight up to the grand suite. Morgan was amazed by the size and sophistication of the suite. She had her own private terrace, a master bathroom bigger than most hotel rooms she'd ever stayed in, and a huge living room that was separate from her bedroom.

"I assume you are too tired to dine out today? I have made arrangements for a light dinner to be served in the suite's living room in a couple of hours. I'm staying in the hotel, and with your permission, I'll join you for breakfast tomorrow morning so that we can discuss this week's plans."

She nodded gratefully. "Good night. Thank you, Gabriel."

He smiled and turned to leave. She felt overwhelmed by his beauty. *Looks are worth nothing,* she thought, dismissing the butterflies in her stomach.

THE INTERVIEW

Gabriel sat in the panelled library of his triplex apartment located on the top floor of The Pierre Hotel in Manhattan. With five bedrooms and seven bathrooms, the Upper East Side penthouse was too large for a man who lived by himself. He turned on his laptop and pulled up the YouTube video that he'd watched countless times. It was a debate organised by Fox News that had aired on mainstream TV three years ago.

"The latest headlines continue to bring us conflicting and confusing information about the gender divide in education. Only this week, two new reports suggest that girls continue to struggle in the so-called STEM fields—science, technology, engineering and math. Female graduates are still significantly underrepresented in these areas, particularly in engineering and computer science. On the other hand, a recent study argues that boys are underperforming in school, lagging behind girls in reading and writing. The study shows that the gap in science and math is closing fast in fields where boys have historically outperformed girls. To help us make sense of this confusing information, we invited two guests who have been active and outspoken on this topic.

"Morgan Lua is the founder of the Hope Foundation, an advocacy group that focuses on the empowerment of girls. Hope has recently secured a staggering two hundred million dollars in funding from five large tech companies in Silicon Valley. They plan to kick off several global initiatives that will promote STEM with young girls and increase the number of female graduates in these areas.

"Walter Zanus is the speaker for the Men's Rights Defence, an activist group with chapters in fifty-five countries in the world. The MRD argues that the women's movement has gone too far and is harming men, particularly boys. Morgan and Walter, welcome to our show.

"Walter, why are organisations such as the Hope Foundation harming boys?"

"The feminisation of the educational system promoted by feminist groups is destroying the future of our young men. Our lads are oppressed by curricula and assessment methods that favour girls. They're forced to sit in classrooms for hours to study or spend time talking about their feelings. We're undermining the power of masculinity. We must let boys be boys. They learn better through physical activity. If you want a boy to thrive, you need to engage his male instinct for problem solving, his energy, competitiveness and physical daring. These are the traits of the men that have led this country to wealth and security throughout history. We need to honour the male heritage."

"Morgan, the data shows boys are struggling in school. Why are you focusing on girls?"

"Boys and girls both struggle with the stereotypes that are passed down to them by society and media. We must evolve our education system to unlock each child's full potential. There is nothing innate, immutable or inevitable about boys or girls doing particularly well or badly in different subjects. Girls in Shanghai outperform Western boys in math, the same boys that outshine the girls in the US. The variable factor is the educational system, the society and the parents. At the H—"

"You haven't answered my question." The tone of the news anchor was somewhat passive aggressive. The smile on his face was tight at the corners as he looked at Morgan.

"Please, let me finish; this topic can't be explained in a neatly packaged media soundbite."

Gabriel always loved to watch the passion with which Morgan asserted her position. Unapologetic and direct, she continued to speak, preventing the unwelcome interruption.

"Our initiatives focus on helping girls overcome the limiting beliefs that stop them from thriving in STEM fields. We set up these programmes as a response to the gender stereotypes prevalent in our society, in our media and in the unconscious or conscious biases of parents and teachers. We create the antidote that can break the glass ceilings currently imposed on girls and women. Soon we'll be launching initiatives for boys as well. We want to ensure that they know that they too can be full-time parents, nurses, teachers and child care workers if they wish to do so. I hope that one day we won't need special initiatives. We need to fix our educational system to abolish all stereotypes and to focus on getting the best out of every young person regardless of gender, race, sexual orientation or aptitude."

"In a moment, she'll be speaking about unicorns and dragons." Zanus adjusted the two or three locks of hair that remained in his bald, shiny head and continued talking. "Look, I don't have time for total political correctness just to appease the feminists and the lesbians. I think it would be foolish to expect that women will ever approach equal representation in a large number of areas simply because their abilities and interests are different for physiological reasons. Science backs me up on this. The brains of men and women are different just like our bodies are different. We have muscles and natural physical ability; they have the babies, and are soft both physically and emotionally. It's that simple."

"Morgan, studies show that differences exist. Why do you fight this God-given nature?"

"Let's leave religion out of this. Differences exist, but they are considerably smaller than those previously reported by pop science. The human brain is highly plastic and adaptable; the experiences and beliefs of each child will shape their skills and behaviours. Our goal is to ensure that the potential of each child is not limited. We debunk generalisations about gender that, frankly, belong to the Middle Ages."

"You sound like you're reading straight from a poorly researched feminist book. Terrible propaganda. Just terrible. All of it," Zanus barked in-between gritted teeth.

"Books, yes. Scientifically validated books. I love reading good books. You should try it sometime," Morgan snapped back at Zanus.

"Nature or nurture: where do you stand on this, Walter?" Asked the news anchor.

"First, let me say that I'm pro-women. I'm the father of two beautiful, sweet, sensitive and very pure daughters. They are my life; let me tell you, if they weren't my daughters I'd be dating them. They are that gorgeous and kind. They make me a better man and remind me every day to protect women so that they can care for the next generation of children."

"Why did you call your daughters pure? Why is this important?" Morgan moved forward in her chair; it was an almost imperceptible gesture, but one that didn't escape Gabriel. He could sense she was impetuous and ready for battle. She was probably aware that both the anchor and Walter were there to undermine her message, and yet she accepted the invitation and was now taking control of the interview.

"Their virginity is the most precious gift that they could give to someone."

"So you reduce their value to society to their looks, sexuality and ability to reproduce?"

"Morgan, we are here to—"

The news anchor lost his varnished Ken-doll composure for just one second. He attempted to interrupt Morgan's confrontational line of questioning, but Zanus snapped, leaning over the table, forcefully placing his red face right in front of Morgan's. He spat his words as he spoke.

"*Look, you witch*; how are things working out for you? You haven't been able to satisfy a man enough to coerce him to put a ring on your finger. Where are all these effeminate men that are ready to care for your babies while you work to destroy the traditional family structure, blessed by God?"

Morgan didn't move; Gabriel noticed her pale complexion turn crimson. Her unruffled exterior carefully hid the frantic pace of her heartbeat. She took only one moment to recover. Morgan held her head high; her demeanour was confident and unapologetic, and her eyes never left the eyes of her opponent. She took a deep breath and spoke.

"*Depulso.*" Her hands danced in front of her body as the spell she'd learned from Hermione Granger was cast on national TV. She giggled, "Well that didn't go as planned." The mischievous response made her relax a little. She composed herself, assuming a serious expression and continued speaking, "Although we still have a lot of work to do, and we haven't mastered sorcery just yet, I'm certain that we've reached a tipping point. There's no turning back now. Change is here and is only going to accelerate." She glowed as if she could vividly visualise the future she was predicting. "The bullies and their boxes will be banished from the face of the Earth by people that refused to be anything else but unique."

"We'll see about that." His finger pointed towards her underlining his threat.

"OK, we're out of time. Thank you, Morgan and Walter, for your time today. What do you think, folks? Are you ready for a world where women wear the pants and men deal with the diapers?" He smiled, showing his bright, over-bleached teeth. "Over to Kelly for an update on today's news headlines."

As she opened the door to let him in, she couldn't help but hold her breath. *Those eyes.* He wore a light blue shirt without a collar and perfectly tailored grey pants. The unbuttoned cuffs of his shirt allowed his sleeves to cover his knuckles. There was no sign of vanity. Everything about him was practical and simple and yet of great quality and taste. *Why do I feel I have known you forever?* He seemed relaxed and smiled when he saw her.

"Good morning. May I come in?"

"Hi. Breakfast arrived just a few minutes ago. This place is amazing. Shall we have breakfast on the balcony? I can't get tired of this view of Central Park."

He smiled and followed her.

She continued to talk as if she needed to fill every moment of silence; her pitch was higher than usual. "It's a bit chilly, isn't it? I hope you don't mind?"

"Not at all."

"Is it true that the likes of Elizabeth Taylor, Onassis and Yves Saint-Laurent used to live at The Pierre?"

"Yes. The Pierre has been a symbol of luxury and glamour in New York City since its grand opening in 1930. Back then, it was popular for its debutante balls, exclusive events and ladies' lunches. The hotel has since attracted the social elite of the world. Many artists and literary icons stay at The Pierre looking for refuge and inspiration."

She hung onto his every word; his beauty was unsettling, his voice and manner hypnotic. His sharp cheek bones and flawless fair complexion reminded her of the androgynous elven people in a Tolkien novel. She'd never seen anyone that beautiful. He overwhelmed her senses, and she found herself having to force her eyes away from him. *Stop it, Morgan.* She shook her head.

"I can imagine all the society ladies wearing their fabulous ball gowns and expensive jewellery in the grand ballroom."

He smiled with his eyes and mouth.

"Unfortunately, some of the ladies didn't manage to hold on to their diamonds. The Pierre Hotel is famous for hosting the largest and most successful hotel robbery in history. Three million dollars' worth of jewellery were stolen from the safety deposit boxes in the seventies."

"Wow. How do you know all this?"

"I'm a frequent guest. I stay at The Pierre every time I'm in town."

"Where do you live?"

"My family . . . owns some land just outside the city," he hedged, looked away.

She pressed him, noticing his vague answer.

"Where exactly?"

"Shall we go over your schedule and make some plans?" She raised her eyebrow, and then she nodded, letting him off the hook. "We planned all your media engagements for Thursday; the interviews will occur just after your speaking event in Central Park. This leaves you two days to relax, enjoy the city and recover from the jet lag before you have to face the masses."

"I have two entire days to enjoy New York City? How wonderful! To tell you the truth, I hate talking to reporters; I'd much rather coach parents and girls directly. But these days I employ a strong team so my job is to be the face and the voice of the Foundation."

"A task you perform rather well," he said graciously. "On Friday you are heading to the UN to finalise the agenda for the Girl's Speak Out conference, and on Saturday, we will drive you to the Catskill Mountains, just in time to spend Thanksgiving with your friend Ann."

Morgan was especially excited to see some of the girls she had mentored in recent years. These young women from all over the world would travel to New York to speak at the United Nations on the eighth of December.

Morgan picked up the suite's complimentary binoculars and looked out to the park. She could see the brown, yellow, and red leaves that covered the ground and a little girl jumping in delight as she experienced the pleasure of stepping on crusty, dry leaves. Morgan smiled, excited by the idea of doing the same. Gabriel stood quietly beside her.

"Your joy is contagious," he said. "I like this time of the year." She noticed she hadn't said a word, and yet he had picked up on her energy.

"Perhaps I will rent a bike and spend the afternoon exploring Central Park," she said with a childlike smile and unadulterated enthusiasm.

She was expecting him to smile and nod in approval, but he didn't. His jaw clenched a little. He was lost in thought for a few seconds and then replied, "I . . . took the liberty of organising an itinerary for today. I would be honoured if you'd allow me to give you a personal tour of the Met, one that few people have had the chance to experience." He stopped, waiting for her response.

She loved art and adored the Met; she visited every time she was in town, so she was happy with the alternative plan. The intensity of his gaze told her this visit was important to him. "Sounds wonderful. The Metropolitan Museum is heaven on earth," she replied. She saw his shoulders relax.

He smiled and explained that she should wear comfortable walking shoes and practical clothes but also pack an evening dress. The Met was hosting an evening party for all their benefactors, and Gabriel would appreciate it if Morgan would kindly go with him to the event.

"Sure," she said, "although the jet lag may make me a dull companion in a few hours."

"I promise to bring you back before midnight," he said, blinking his eyes.

It was difficult for her to look directly into his eyes, particularly on the rare occasions when he smiled. She could easily get lost in them. There was no doubt he was an attractive man, but that was just the tip of the iceberg. There was something special about him, something she was struggling to define. Once in a while, the calm and reserved Gabriel displayed a glimpse of a different side to him. It showed in his eyes, and she was curious about it. *Still waters run deep.*

He raised his eyebrows when his eyes met hers as she stared, and she blushed. She recovered with a question: "Your accent, where are you from? England?"

"My family tree does go back to Europe and, before that, to the Middle East and North Africa, but I was born on a family estate nearby. May I pour you something to drink? Coffee, tea, juice?"

She noticed his hands were on the coffee before she even replied, "Coffee, please."

He filled her cup with coffee and poured some lemongrass tea in his. He kept his eyes on the cup for a little while. "I was wondering if we should change the venue of the event in Central Park. It might rain, and perhaps we could still secure an indoor venue. I have contacts in—"

"Two days before the event?" she said, thinking that it was a very odd suggestion. "And how would we inform the community? It would just generate a lot of confusion."

He nodded, took a sip of tea, and remained quiet and pensive. The sun touched the locks of hair that perfectly framed his face. The wind transformed them into waves of sun-kissed dark chocolate that danced in front of his eyes.

"Before we go to the Met, I must stop by the Angel of the Waters. I always visit when I am in town. It's a tradition."

Gabriel didn't react right away; he kept his eyes on his tea as his long fingers hovered over the rim of the cup. "Sure, I'll take you there on the way to the Met."

He was somewhat assertive in his statement, not leaving much room for negotiation. Morgan couldn't read the man in front of her. One moment, he was smiling and seemed genuinely interested in speaking to her. In the next moment, he was sombre, and his mind was somewhere else.

The food was delicious. The waiter served fresh produce, and reassured her that it was all organic and sourced locally. She had some poached eggs with spinach on a beautiful slice of bread full of seeds and whole grains.

The sun was shining, but the wind had suddenly picked up. Before she realised she was cold, Gabriel had switched on the outside heater next to the table. His ability to predict her needs was both reassuring and somewhat disturbing. Suddenly his eyes flashed to her face, worried brows meeting. He excused himself abruptly, saying he was going to make the rest of the arrangements for the day and would return to pick her up in half an hour. He hadn't touched his food.

Morgan took an unusually long time to get ready. She looked at her pale, tired, and jet-lagged face in the mirror and performed the atypical act of adding some blush to her cheeks. The bathroom suite had all the beauty items anyone could ever need. She observed her features: defined cheekbones, strong dark eyebrows that framed her large brown eyes, and freckles.

She was surprised by her sudden preoccupation with appearance; it wasn't something she normally cared about. Morgan had long ago decided to stop chasing physical perfection. Then she realised the cause of her current anxiety and smiled, making fun of herself. *He's so out of your league, honey.*

Many years had passed since Morgan had felt attracted to someone. She'd given up romantic pursuits a lifetime ago. Morgan couldn't figure out why he tested her peace of mind. He was gorgeous, *so what?* She rebelled against her feelings, washing her face and tying her long curly hair behind her back. She pledged right then and there that she would stop feeding those thoughts. She wore a simple brown dress, a chartreuse scarf, and plain white sneakers. She prepared a bag with an evening gown and a pair of high-heeled shoes. Soon there was a knock at her door.

The power games restarted as soon as they walked down to the reception area. She wanted to walk, but Gabriel insisted they take the limo. He didn't leave room for negotiation, and his tone was firm and authoritative. "It's best we take the limo," he said. As soon as they walked outside the building, she saw James, Carl, and the sedan. The door was already open.

The car went as close as it could to Bethesda Terrace in Central Park.

To Morgan's surprise, all three men got out of the car and walked with her. Carl and James stayed behind, keeping a respectable distance. Gabriel walked by her side. Soon, they reached the fountain. At the top stood a statue of a winged angel, water cascading down into a circular pool. Gabriel fidgeted his fingers, his eyes scanning the small groups of tourists that wandered around that popular location.

Morgan attempted to ignore Gabriel's nervousness. She absorbed, with all her senses, one of her favourite places in the world. She believed in magic—the magic of places, the magic of people, the magic of coincidences, serendipity, and fortune. She enjoyed wandering through the world with the open mind and curiosity of a four-year-old child. In her world the mystical, mythical, and magical inhabited the same space and time as the ordinary and the practical. At Bethesda Terrace, she always felt close to a source of magic and creativity. It was as if she were tapping into the place where dragons, angels, gods, sorceresses, and demons came to life.

"Apparently, Bethesda is blessing the water, giving it healing powers. The lily in her hand represents purity. She assures a pure and dependable supply of water to New York City," she said, trying to capture his attention.

He smiled and replied, "You'll be pleased to know that Emma Stebbins, the sculptor, was the first woman to receive a public commission for a major work of art in New York City."

"One of my favourite moments in television was seeing Bethesda come to life in the series *Angels in America*."

"Do you believe in angels, Morgan?"

"I believe in working towards their virtues—temperance, health, peace and purity." She pointed to the four cherubim that represented those virtues at the base of the fountain. "Well," she smiled mischievously, "maybe not purity."

Gabriel lowered his eyes and frowned. "Yes, the pursuit and preservation of purity can drive prejudice and hate. Many crimes against humanity have been committed in its name. Purity is best applied to water."

She nodded as he spoke. "True. Virtues like modesty or chastity are also related to purity, and are used as an excuse to promote violence against women and girls and limit their rights and freedoms." She paused for a moment, admiring the Angel. "Aesthetically and functionally, I love the idea of winged humanlike creatures masterly carved out of stone and brought to life by magic. Look at her, so perfect; she'll stay there, frozen in time, beautiful, majestic and flawless. If only people could be this perfect . . . ." As she looked into his eyes, she realised that the statue couldn't compete with the splendour of the man in front of her. "Inside and out," she said abruptly, fighting against her shallow feelings. "I wish people could be this perfect inside and out."

"Like the bronze statue of the Angel of the Waters, those who pursue perfection find themselves paralysed by the possibility of flaw, fault or failure."

She saw herself scarily reflected in his words, but she suspected he was introspecting.

"Shall we walk back? I'm anxious to show you my surprise at the Met," he said.

She nodded, hiding her frustration with his need to control every minute of her day.

Thirty-Four Years Ago - 1980

Ahe'ey

Map of Ahe'ey

Sky Falling

Sky saw horror reflected in her mother's eyes as their front door was abruptly knocked down by a sharp blow. She could hear her newborn baby sister crying uncontrollably. The baby was tightly wrapped in the cotton sling that hung over her mother's chest. Ten-year-old Sky tried to control the fast thundering of her heartbeat as four Hu'urei surrounded them.

Sky pressed her lips together and held her breath. She scanned the bodies of the men, observing each sword, dagger, and axe. She waited anxiously for her mother's direction. Gráinne was Sky's world, moon and stars. The girl adored her mum and hoped to become just like her. The fiercest Yi'ingo warrior in the land was a courageous and beloved leader to her people—ruthless and fair in equal measure.

Gráinne was preparing Sky to become the queen of Ahe'ey, a birthright locked in her pure blood. An honour and a curse, a privilege and a burden. Sky recalled her mother's words: "Cherish your loving heart but never listen to its calling in matters of rule. There will be times when you will need to sacrifice the ones you most love for the sake of all our people." Words repeated every time Sky's wild and passionate heart got the better of her.

Gráinne didn't react to the men. The Yi'ingo warrior finished braiding Sky's wild copper hair. Then she placed her fingers on Sky's chin and looked into her eyes. With her gaze, the mother pointed to the open window that stood a few metres from the young girl. Sky stood frozen, processing her mother's silent command. The girl's eyes were wide; her lips squeezed between her teeth as she prepared to run away. Tears streamed down her face as she kissed her sister's head. *I love you; I'll come back for you. I promise.*

Before Sky could react, Gráinne stood up, dagger in hand, carrying her youngest on her chest. The man that stood between Sky and the window fell as Gráinne slashed his throat with a single swipe. Red rain showered on Sky's face. The girl watched nervously; she feared for her mother's life. Gráinne was faster and more accomplished in battle than any Hu'urei in the land, but she'd given birth just the night before. She was weak, too weak to fight three men with a child in her arms.

"*Go Sky!* Fetch help," Gráinne screamed as she placed her body between the rest of the Hu'urei and Sky. The Yi'ingo held her dagger in front of her baby, commanding the full attention of the men. Sky hesitated, watching her mother stumble and nearly faint.

"Leave my home, Iblis, or I will skin you alive." Gráinne's voice quivered.

"Don't kill them. We need them alive," Iblis said, managing the rage of his men, who huffed and grunted at the sight of their dead companion. The three Hu'urei unsheathed their swords.

Sky jumped over the dead Hu'urei and ran towards the open window. She dived straight over the window-sill and rolled on the ground, quickly moving into a standing position. She looked back to meet her mother's gaze. The curls of her blood-coloured hair covered her face and hid the panic in her chestnut eyes. *She didn't want to leave them. She had to leave them.*

"Leave the girl," Iblis ordered, keeping his eyes set on Gráinne, "she's not yet of fertile age." The three men surrounded the woman, Iblis' sword pointed towards her baby. "Yi'ingo, drop your sword or the child will die."

Sky raced as fast as she could, ignoring the blood gushing from a scraped knee caused by the impact of the fall.

"I'll come back for you, Mother."

To leave her family was to abandon her heart. She left in search of help; she was unaware she'd never keep her promise. Guilt would torment her for the rest of her life.

The One Left Standing

Viviane waited as her sister, Luna, caressed the golden hair of her six-year-old son. Bastian was sleeping soundly as his mother kissed his forehead. The two Ange'el women walked together to one of the external pavilions that surrounded the Sacred House.

"I think my Bas will leave Ange'el to become a Ma'asai. He spent the entire day planting melons and squash at the farms. I struggled to clean the clay stuck under his fingernails," Luna said.

"He has a deep connection with nature. Your child is too wild to care about the mysteries, knowledge and crystals of the Sacred House. He will thrive at the farms."

"I can't bear to part with him. He'll have to stay with me for a few more years."

Viviane thought of her own son, Gabriel. She was reassured that, from a very early age, he'd chosen to follow her path. He was destined to become a powerful Ange'el, possibly the most powerful of all Ange'el. His blood was pure, and so was his soul. He was gentle and kind hearted and needed her protection and guidance. She was grateful that he'd stay at the Sacred House with her.

They approached Luna's husband, Lucas, who sat outside on the ground in front of the pyre of fire that burned in observance of the summer solstice. The sisters didn't interrupt his meditation; they sat beside him, attempting to connect with the elders that no longer roamed the Earth.

With her eyes closed, Viviane asked her foremothers for the most precious gift—another child; a pure-blooded descendant of the royal bloodline. A sibling to her son. Another boy to help safeguard and propagate the powerful genes that Viviane and her sisters—Gráinne and

Luna—had inherited from their ancestors. At the age of seventy-eight, she was still young, and she hoped to bear two more royal children.

Deep into her prayer, her mind wandered into the realm of those who no longer had a physical body and, in that state, she didn't see the danger that lurked a few metres away. The largest of the Hu'urei kicked Lucas in the head twice before the Ange'el had a chance to open his eyes.

"Sathian! What are you doing?" Viviane cried as she opened her eyes to recognise the perfect features and poise of her royal kinsman. In his eyes, she saw only madness. Sathian held Luna from behind in a tight embrace. He immobilised her arms, and almost choked her. The man lay her down on the ground by her neck and signalled to another man, who pulled his pants down and spread her legs apart. Viviane wrestled with Sathian's arm, hopelessly attempting to release her sister. He turned to face her, and she looked into his eyes, pleading for mercy.

For one moment, she saw his emerald eyes glimmer with the tears he held back, but a second later, his gaze was dry, cold and empty. He pushed her, and she fell backwards on the ground.

Luna wailed, realising her impending sentence. Viviane felt hopeless; she looked at the unconscious body of Lucas in despair. Inside her head, she could hear her other sister screaming. *Gráinne*, she thought, feeling her sister's agony. Luna kicked the man that approached her in the groin and used a branch from the pyre of fire to stab Sathian in the left eye. Sathian screamed in anger and pain as he placed his hand over the hole that was once his eye.

Viviane gasped. She had the power of foresight, and she saw what was coming. Her world collapsed in front of her eyes and she was helpless. There was nothing she can do. Furious and out of control, Sathian grabbed Luna's tunic with one single hand and threw her on top of the bonfire. Luna screamed in pain as the fire devoured her skin.

"Pull her out!" he ordered as he attempted to recover from her attack, wiping the remains of his eye from his face.

"It's too late." The Hu'urei tried to pull Luna's body from the fire, but her dancing body of pain and despair was now fully consumed by flames. Luna's screams were deafening. Her song of torment and doom came to an abrupt end when Sathian pushed his sword through her heart.

Viviane lay on the ground, crying uncontrollably. She watched the men turn to her. The fear, the shock, and the smell of her sister's scorched body made her vomit. In her mind's eye, she could feel Sathian's feelings—his rage, his madness, his pain, his regret. She denied him compassion. Viviane, the purest of the Ange'el, refused to respond to his twisted torment. In all her despair, she became defiant. She knew what others didn't; she could feel the battle that raged inside him. She looked into his deformed face and quietly waited for her demise. With her mind's eye, she spoke to her son, who slept peacefully in his room at the Sacred House: *"Gabriel, find your cousins and run. Run my dear. Run. I love you."*

One of the men grabbed her long raven-coloured hair, pulling her towards him.

"Don't touch her," Sathian said.

"But—"

Sathian pushed his sword into the man's heart before he could finish his sentence. He kneeled beside Viviane, grazed his fingers along the contour of her face, kissed her lips and said, "You hold everything I love and lost. I leave all my treasures in your hands, Ange'el." He got up abruptly and walked away, followed by the rest of his men.

Viviane stood there, paralysed with fear, weeping, her head sunk into her knees. His words echoed in her mind. She couldn't make sense of them. Like her, Sathian was a royal Ange'el, he was born to bring light to the world—to heal, teach, and nurture. Yet, today, he was the hand of darkness, death and destruction. *"Gabriel, run. Run, my love."* She fainted.

Royal Family Tree

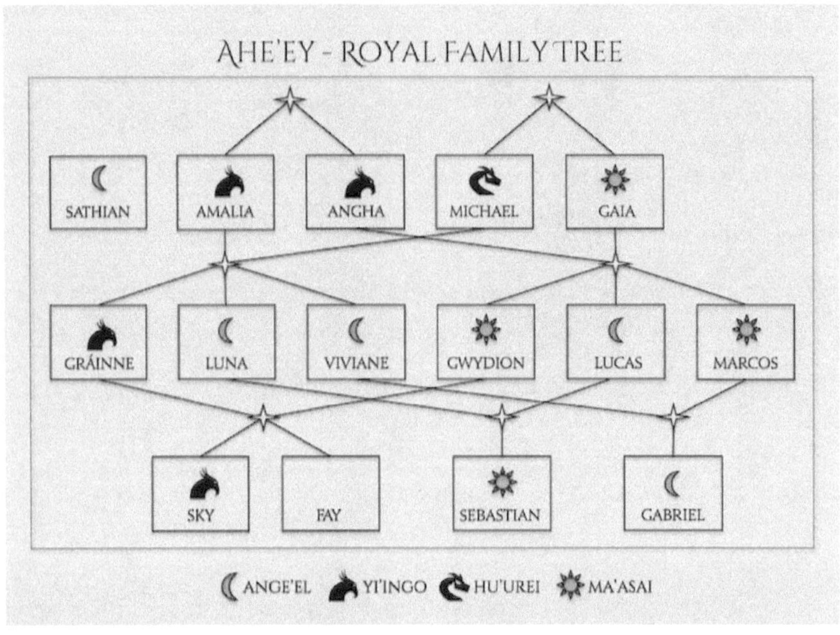

Sky's heart raced, overwhelmed with panic and guilt. She sprinted through the forest, away from the Yi'ingo village. It was the night of the summer solstice, and she knew most of the Yi'ingo warriors and Ma'asai farmers would be drunk, gathered around fires celebrating the fertility of the earth. They engaged in rituals that culminated in the dissemination of their seed. Sky ran in the direction of the Ange'el village in search of her aunts—Luna and Viviane. The girl stopped when she saw the figure of a tall man standing in the middle of the road between her and the village entry.

"Come here," ordered the man.

Sky attempted to fight his persuasion powers, but his skills were too strong. The mind and feet of the strong-willed girl followed the command of the man's smooth voice. As she approached him, Sky noticed that blood covered half his face, coming from a hole that had been recently occupied by a missing left eye. From the left gouge he cried blood, but from the right eye, he cried salty water. He contorted his mouth in pain and grief, and his long dark hair absorbed the briny red river that streamed down his face and neck. As the girl got closer, he lifted her by her neck until her feet were off the ground. Sky gasped for air.

"Who are you?" he asked.

"S . . . Sk . . . y."

He pulled her face closer to his right eye. Sky's mind ordered her legs to kick, but her body refused to oblige. She realised she was under his control, a hopeless slave to his mind's eye.

"The queen's granddaughter. One of four children of the bloodline. A pure-blooded mare." He snarled and released her. She fell to the ground and gasped, attempting to catch her breath.

"Who are you?"

"Sathian. Your worst nightmare, little cousin. The beast who will destroy everything you hold dear." Bitter tears and blood continued to roll down his face into his mouth. Sky could feel autonomy return to her body as the man's face contorted with some inner battle. She got up, cocked up her head and placed her hands on her waist.

"You . . . You monster. You ordered the attack, didn't you?" She looked around for a weapon, a rock, *something, anything* . . . She found nothing.

He spoke to her as if he was speaking to an old companion, to another adult.

"They forced me to do it; do you understand?" he said, looking down at his bloodied hands.

She took a step away from him, testing if she was free from his controlling mind.

"They took everything away from me," he continued, biting his lip and placing his left hand over his missing eye, "and now they will pay, all of them. They'll have a taste of their own poison. Those who value the purity of the royal bloodline will bear impure babies. I'll destroy everything you hold dear, royal brat."

"I'll find you and kill you," Sky shouted as she raced away from him, hoping his mind's confusion prevented him from summoning her back to him.

"No Sky, I *will* find you."

She held back her tears; she had no time to dwell on her feelings. She had to find help, her mother and sister were in great danger.

As she ran towards the Sacred House, she sighed with relief as she saw her cousin—*her best friend*—running in her direction. Gabriel carried their younger cousin, Bastian, in his arms. The little boy slept peacefully. He wrapped his arms around Gabriel's neck and leaned his head against his cousin's shoulder.

"My mum and sister—"

"I know, I'm so sorry, Sky. Our fathers are assembling the Yi'ingo army. They'll rescue them. Come Sky, we must hide in the forest. I must keep you and Bas safe."

"Nooo! I don't need your protection. I must go back and help them."

"Sky, our blood; we must safeguard it. It's our duty. We're the last of our kind."

"I can't just leave them," she said, outraged by his suggestion.

"Help is on the way. Come?" He held onto Bastian with his left hand and extended his right hand in her direction. "Please, Sky. We must run."

"They'll pay. I'll kill them all." She licked the salty tears that coated her lips.

"In due time," he replied patiently.

In any other day, Gabriel's cool, compassionate logic would smooth her solar storm, but today, wasn't any other day. *How can he be so cold?*

"I'll chop them into little pieces and feed them to the dragons." She raised her fist in his direction. He reached to grab her hand, squeezing it gently. She resisted and pulled her hand from his grip. The touch of an Ange'el was nurturing and reassuring. It could heal and relax any creature in the land. She didn't want it; she held on tight to her rage. "And, don't you try to stop me, Ange'el."

The twelve-year-old boy paused for a second, dropping his hand and looking straight into her eyes.

"I won't. I promise. Come, Sky. Bas and I need your protection. You're the warrior, remember? Will you help us? We're lost without you."

He won; he always won. He knew her better than she knew herself, and although she was aware of his ability to steer her will, she couldn't resist his thoughtful influence. She looked at Bastian, then she grabbed Gabriel's hand and led the boys into the forest.

Sathian was drunk with resentment, anger and pain, but it was mainly remorse and shame that stopped him from hurting the girl. He was fighting to keep what was left of his humanity and, tonight, letting Sky go was his small act of redemption. He touched his disfigured face, knowing all too well that not even his royal blood could regenerate an entire eye. He, the most beautiful creature at Ahe'ey, was now forever disfigured. A fair punishment for the necessary violence he had unleashed on his family. *Was it? Necessary?*

"Sathian!" He looked back to see who was screaming his name. It was Lucas running in his direction, sword in hand. There was madness in his eyes and in his face, the type of mania that is only present in those who have suffered tremendous loss. The blonde Ange'el barely knew how to hold the sword that he lifted in front of his chest. He seemed committed to avenging the death of his wife, Luna. Sathian knew Lucas wasn't a warrior, nor had he ever killed any living being, no matter how small. Lucas stopped in front of Sathian, preparing to strike.

"If it's suicide you seek," Sathian murmured, unsheathing his sword, "I'm more than happy to oblige." Sathian rotated his entire body and, in one single blow, decapitated Lucas. As the body of the dead man fell to the ground, Sathian couldn't help but laugh at the battle that was raging inside his head, the maddening cocktail of mixed feelings that intoxicated his mind. Lucas, the son of the love of his life—Gaia— and of his mortal enemy—Angha. To kill Lucas was to torture a woman he loved and hated with equal amounts of passion and conviction. She'd suffer for the rest of her life, and he wasn't quite sure she could endure the punishment he'd unleashed on her. Guilt-ridden and conflicted, he laughed and he cried, leaning further into his madness. *It can't be undone. There's no turning back.*

Sathian walked back towards the Ange'el village, roaming the gardens where he had spent most of his youth. The place remained unaltered, as if time had stood still. The statues he had designed and commissioned together with his dearest love stood above him. Their flawlessness was untouched by the heartaches and misdeeds of their creators. The sculptures represented the perfection, purity, and virtue of the Ahe'ey.

"Lieees!" he screamed as he touched the face of a stone winged angel with his bloodied fingers.

Two Months Later - Ahe'ey

Gabriel watched Sky as the young girl climbed the highest tree in the forest.

"You can do it, Sky," cheered Gabriel.

She planted her feet on the tree and leaned back as her hands pulled a rope that wrapped around the branchless trunk.

"It's too high. I'm going to fall," she screeched, as one of her feet slipped, and her knee scraped the bark. "*Ouch!*"

"Keep going. If you fall, I'll catch you," the twelve-year-old boy said with confidence.

Sky secured both feet in the bark of the tree and yanked her body upwards.

She loosed the rope just enough to move it up the tree trunk. Burned by the friction of the movement, her right hand let go of the rope and she fell backwards. Six-year-old Bastian screamed in panic.

Gabriel reached his arms to catch Sky as she fell. They both hit the ground with the impact of her body.

"I didn't know you could fly," he laughed.

"I told you it was too high," she said punching his chest. "My hand! It hurts." She opened the palm of her hand, red and blue from the rope. He blew on it and kissed it.

"It's just a scratch. It'll heal in a minute. In a few days, you'll reach the top of the tree, and we'll rappel down together," he said reassuringly as he got up and reached under her arms to pull her to a standing position.

"Will you see my mum from the top of the tree? When can we go home?" Bastian whined.

"Luna is within you, Bas. Can't you feel her?" Gabriel placed his hand on the shoulder of his young cousin. A tiny veil of mournful water covered the blue eyes of the younger boy.

Sky lowered her head and bit her lip. Her eyebrows became heavy as Gabriel saw a cocktail of grief and rage emerge in her expression. "We are your family now, Bas," she said. "We won't let you down. They'll pay for what they did. All of them. We'll kill them all."

The young boy took a few steps back, away from the angry girl. Gabriel knew that Bastian was too sensitive and unprepared to deal with Sky's mighty storm.

"The forest is our home. Where else could we go skinny-dipping in the middle of the day?" Gabriel smiled, touching Bastian's cheek. The older boy undressed and ran towards the lake, followed by his two cousins.

"Why do we need to hide away from everyone else?" Bastian asked as he pulled up his tunic over his blonde hair.

"Our blood is special; we need to keep it safe," Gabriel explained.

"But I wanna go hooome!"

The Hu'urei are looking for us; they seek to destroy the royal bloodline. We must stay here, under the protection of the Ange'el."

"Is that why they killed my mum and dad and took Sky's mum and sister?"

Gabriel nodded. "We'll stick together and train a lot. One day we'll join the Yi'ingo army and fight against the Hu'urei. Come, Bas. Join me." Gabriel jumped into the water, attempting to wash away the worries of his young cousins. He showered Sky with cold water as she ran into the lake, chasing him.

Gabriel's light-hearted exterior hid the worries that festered his mind. The two children were now his responsibility. He'd promised his parents that he would do anything and everything to keep them safe and happy. Away from the Sacred House, from his family, and from the comforts and privileges of the royal apparatus, the boy relied only on himself and on the few Ange'el that watched over them. The densest and most remote valley of the Ahe'ey forest was now their home—a haven from the devastating war that ravaged the land.

Sky grabbed his neck and pushed him under water. Bastian jumped on top of his cousins, joining the fun. Gabriel was just a boy—a boy raised to be a king. From him, everyone expected perfection and demanded greatness. He had learned to ignore his needs and to conceal his emotions; he considered his every action and word carefully. Deep inside, he felt flawed and unprepared—he felt human, yet, human was the very thing he wasn't allowed to be. *"Gods are perfect, humans are not,"* they'd told him often at the Sacred House. *"Your blood was designed by Gods and a God you shall be."*

ALONE

Four Years Later: 1984 - Ahe'ey

On her fourteenth birthday, Sky chased Gabriel through the woods with her sword in hand. Her body had blossomed in the four years she'd been living in the forest with the Ange'el. Sky's curves of fertility softened a muscular frame capable of defying and destroying any creature that stood in her way. She climbed, jumped and ran with the ease and ability of a demigoddess.

Her feet barely touched the ground as she followed her cousin up the mountain. He stopped, turned around, and used his foot to roll a large rock in her direction. She jumped to one side, rolling on the ground then straight to her feet. She felt a rush of adrenaline flood her body. She was the hunter and he was her prey. He ran towards her striking her from above with his sword as she defended the blow using the fallen branch of a tree. He rotated around himself pulling the sword away from the branch to strike her on the other side close to her neck.

Gabriel chopped off one of many of her copper braids and stopped the blade just as it kissed his cousin's skin. He laughed as he placed one knee on the floor and picked up the fallen braid. She could feel the blood rush to her face; he'd gone too far, and he'd pay for it. As he stood up, she gripped the hilt of her sword with both of her hands and thrust the blade upwards towards his neck. He jumped back. Sky threw her sword to the side, jumped towards him, spun around and, using the impact of her full body, hit him in the face with her elbow. As he fell to the ground, she placed her knee on his chest.

"I surrender, mighty warrior," he said laughing, pulling her body towards him and wrapping his arms around her. He hugged her tightly as she lay down placing her head on his shoulder. For the first time in her young life, she felt a jolt of desire rush through her body. He looked at the sky as he touched his throbbing jaw. She saw his cyan eyes turn dark as clouds moved to cover the sun. She licked her lips and lifted her hand from his chest to touch his face as he abruptly jumped to his feet.

"Shall we go swimming at the lake?" There was no warmth in his voice. He started walking fast. She got up confused by his reaction and followed him a few metres behind. He looked back to find her and screamed. "Sky, behind you!" He held the grip of his sword, took one step towards her and stopped.

Sky saw four large Hu'urei approach her. She unsheathed her sword and turned to face the attackers that ran towards her.

"The last of the royal wombs. This one is mine," said one of the men as he jumped towards her with his sword above his head.

Sky rolled on the ground and planted her dagger on his gut as another Hu'urei jumped in her direction and pierced her thigh with his sword. She screamed in agony and for a second looked back in search of Gabriel. He stood motionless away from her. *What are you doing?*

"Don't kill the Yi'ingo; she can't have our children if she's dead," shouted Iblis.

Sky stood up, keeping her weight on her good leg. Like her mother before her, she faced men who towered over her and were three times her size. The scars on their faces showcased their rank in society; their bodies didn't regenerate as well as the children of the royal bloodline. They lacked the perfection and the beauty of those who carried pure genes.

Where are you? Sky thought, waiting for her cousin to jump to her rescue, but as she looked back once again, he was gone. Biting her lip to contain the pain in her leg, she jumped between two of the men, using her small size and flexibility in her favour. The Hu'urei turned to face her. She curled her body, rolled to a standing position and jumped high.

The Yi'ingo swung her sword from left to right and decapitated the men. She trembled with the adrenaline that rushed through her body. It was the first time she had killed a human being.

Gabriel, where are you? Tears flooded her eyes as she faced the final Hu'urei, the largest of them all. She recognised him; it was Iblis, the leader of the group that had kidnapped her mother and sister. The enraged man looked at the dead bodies of his companions. He locked his teeth so tight that the veins in his neck promised to burst at any moment.

The man that lay on the ground bleeding from an open wound in his gut screeched like a pig. The high-pitched noise was unbearable. Sky looked up to face Iblis and locked her eyes with his eyes. She then jumped to the left to bury her sword in the heart of the man that lay on the floor. She killed him instantly. The young woman plunged her hand into his wound and licked the blood. Once again, she dipped her hand into the blood and used four fingers to paint stripes on her face. Sky's defiant eyes locked on Iblis. Her enemy took a few steps backwards, shaken by the fearlessness and savagery of the girl. He sheathed his sword and ran in the opposite direction, away from her.

Sky grabbed her stomach and threw up. Her body trembled, and her mind raced. She fell to her knees and lay on the ground between the corpses of the three dead Hu'urei. The young woman burst into tears, shaken by the experience. She felt abandoned and betrayed by the only person in the world she relied on.

Sky and Gabriel never spoke about that event. On that day, Sky's grandmother, Amalia, the queen, took Sky back to Yi'ingo. A year later, the young warrior became their military leader and commander, leading them into battle against the Hu'urei.

On the same day that Sky left Ange'el, Gabriel's parents, Viviane and

Marcus, sent him to New York City. The sixteen-year-old Ange'el emerged from the Bethesda Fountain on the last full moon night of nineteen eighty-four.

45

PRESENT DAY - 22 NOVEMBER 2014

NEW YORK

Morgan's mobile rang. She walked away from the group of men to take the call.

"Morgan, how are you, lovely? Did you have a good flight?" The familiar voice on the other side of the line was Ann Surrey, a distinguished fiction writer and Morgan's oldest friend. Ann had invited Morgan to join her at her holiday home in Woodstock—a haven for artists, musicians, and writers. Morgan would be visiting after she finished with her commitments in New York.

"It was all right. I'm completely travelled out."

"I can imagine. How long have you been on the road with this speaking tour?"

"Over six months. I really need to go back to London and take a few months off. But first I want to see you. I can't believe we'll be together again in just a few days. How's Don Quixote?"

"Sitting on my lap; purring like a diva, demanding to be petted. He's becoming a fat, lazy bum. So, what's new?"

"All is well; the Foundation is finally getting the attention and support it deserves. I'm hopeful we'll start making a greater impact in the coming years."

"I have no doubt, Superwoman. You always achieve anything you set your mind to. I don't know anyone more tenacious and persistent than you. But, how is the love life going?"

"You know I gave up on that a long, long time ago. My high expectations don't match my plain looks." Morgan laughed.

"Nonsense. Put yourself out there, beautiful. At some point, you need to get off your pedestal and make yourself available. Take some risks. I'm getting tired of seeing you drive the good ones away to avoid getting hurt."

"I wish I knew how, my friend. Are you enjoying—"

"Is there anyone that is sparking your interest?"

"No one. Well . . . apart from the broody Greek god that I met yesterday."

"How exciting. What does he do?"

"He's way out of my league. Successful, cultured, pleasant and the best-looking man I've ever seen."

"He does sound a bit intimidating. Single?"

"I don't know. I feel such a strong connection to him, it's ridiculous; we barely spoke."

"Perhaps you could use him to practice getting out there. What could possibly go wrong? A bit of heartache never killed anyone."

"I suspect falling for this guy would be the death of me."

"Oh, just do it."

"You sound just like my mother. She's desperate to marry me off to just about anyone. I rather stay away from London. Her matchmaking efforts drive me insane."

"But you just told me he's perfect."

"I don't know what he is exactly. Probably rich, privileged and spoiled. Looks like that. I bet he's used to having the world at his feet. They have it so easy, these types, you know—the tall, Caucasian, wealthy, handsome men. Doors open, opportunities come knocking. Makes me *so* mad."

"Promise me that you won't close like a clam. Give yourself a chance, darling. You can't walk around teaching girls to practice self-esteem when you have none. Remember to practice what you preach."

"I wasn't talking about self-esteem. And, there are many ways to give and receive love without embarking on romantic relationships."

"Stop quoting from books, Morgan. Those words may be empowering to others, but you don't fool me. Don't hide under that veil of preachy superiority. It's in our nature to fall madly in love and to have mind-blowing sex." Ann laughed.

"That stung a bit, you bully. I don't need it. I have plenty of meaning in my life."

"It stung because you know I'm right. You hide behind books and feminist theory. Give your brain a day off. Can't you fight stereotypes without rejecting your female sensibilities and sexuality?"

"I don't know, and I don't want to talk about it right now. See you on Saturday my dear."

"Do you need me to pick you up?"

"No, thanks; it's all arranged. I'll give you a call when I'm on my way."

"Speak soon."

Morgan lifted her head to look at Gabriel, who stood on the other side of the fountain, observing her attentively. She couldn't help herself; the discomfort in her own skin magnified every time he looked at her. She felt ashamed, unworthy and angry with herself. She was a fraud to her community of girls and young women. She raised her head and walked towards him with a smile. *Perhaps you are indeed perfect*, she thought, absorbing his heavenly glow. *Can I trust you with my flaws?* A shiver went down her spine when she heard his voice inside her head.

Yes, you can.

GRAVITATIONAL PULL

PRESENT DAY - 22 NOVEMBER 2014

NEW YORK

WOMANHOOD

Debilitating guilt crushed Gabriel every time he interacted with Morgan. The Ange'el's affection for the human was weakening his mandate to control her movements and influence her decisions. His task was, once again, to deceive and manipulate. He seemed destined to betray the confidence of those he held most dear.

They entered the Met via a back door. Gabriel led Morgan down a set of stairs and through three access doors that required him to type passcodes and scan his fingerprints. He carried a basket that had been given to him by the Met staff as they walked in the building.

"Are you taking me to the dungeons?" she said with anticipation.

"Yes, indeed. I have conspired to lock you in the safest place in New York. You are a prisoner of the Met, but I hope that soon you'll rejoice in your captivity."

"What's in the basket?" She reached towards it.

"Curiosity killed the cat, Ma'am," he replied playfully, moving the basket away.

He opened the last door and led her into a large warehouse. Golden light filled the room, coming through several small windows protected by steel bars.

"Are these genuine?" Her inquisitive eyes opened wide with surprise.

"Yes, all genuine."

Paintings, dozens of paintings, by Klimt, her favourite artist. Gabriel knew she was deeply passionate about his work. He watched her as she held her breath for a few seconds, processing the burst of colour and beauty that surrounded them.

"Stunning."

She quickly approached *Danaë*, which was on the floor. The painting was leaning against a wooden box that served as the container for transportation to the Met. She kneeled on the ground and, with teary eyes, sat before the great beauty and traced the fine detail of the masterpiece. A vulnerable, beautiful naked woman lay curled asleep, enveloped by her flaming orange hair and golden rain dust that flowed between her legs. She turned to him, pointing to the painting.

"My favourite."

I know, he thought, staying at the door, giving her space to live the moment.

He allowed her to feel joy without having to contain it or to explain it. His eyes never left her. He watched her face light up and her eyes flicker. He found himself holding his breath, waiting for her approval.

She looked back at him. "How?" Her smile filled every corner of the room.

"Ange'el, my organisation, is a sponsor of the Met. When I learned that a Klimt exhibition was opening in a few weeks, I thought you wouldn't like to miss it." She nodded, excited.

They walked together around the room, pausing to observe each piece of art. For each, there was a quiet moment of wonder followed by animated conversation as they exchanged information about each painting. He noticed the joy flowing through her body; it was reflected in the way she almost danced as she moved and the way she almost sang as she talked. Her voice had a higher pitch, and her accent became more noticeable. Morgan's southern European hands endorsed her words with vibrant and graceful gestures.

He shared his knowledge about the history and meaning of each piece with her and did his best to connect his commentary with her work and interests. He mentioned how Klimt's paintings display the multifaceted scope of womanhood, introducing the cycle of life, love, sensuality, sexuality, strength, vulnerability, and death.

He asked why *Danaë* was her favourite, given her small passive role in the original Greek mythology—seduced by Zeus, who visited her in the form of golden rain. She paused for a second, contemplating his question.

"Her vulnerability and sensuality, her perfectly imperfect body and sexual awakening, her cheeks touched by passion," she said, and as she looked into his eyes, she lowered her own and blushed. "I also love *Water Serpents* and *Athena*; they display different characteristics of womanhood."

He was still recovering from her words. She had moved him from the moment he'd seen her speak on TV three years ago—alive, passionate, intelligent, and master of a disarming candour. She used kindness, knowledge, and wit to move mountains. He realised he was staring at her, so he lowered his eyes. He took a step to his right, away from her, smiled, pointing to the portrait of Athena, the war goddess and said, "She reminds me of a dear cousin. I hope to have the opportunity to introduce her to you one day. Sky is a very special woman—a leader, like you." He was unable to hide a tightness in his voice as memories rose.

"I'd be delighted. You know," she continued, "Danaë and Athena are both faces of every woman—vulnerability and power. I wonder when people will stop just valuing women as childbearing and sexual objects. They hunt and lust after youth, beauty and virginity, and then use and discard them, casting them out as old whores. We have such a long way to go to move past these old archetypes and symbols of womanhood.

"The pursuit to preserve the best genes is the puppet master that controls us all. Worth is reduced and simplified to external beauty as everything else is too difficult to measure. The victims fall on both sides of the divide—the ones that have it and the ones that don't."

"Have what?"

"Beauty."

"That's true for women, but not for men."

"That's a rather definite statement," he said, raising his eyebrow.

"I don't see how being handsome can possibly harm a man. It's just another cheap privilege that took zero effort to attain," she replied, distracted at the sight of Klimt's *Goldfish* and *Water Serpents* paintings. He watched her get lost inside the pure femininity adorned in gold, ochre, and red that lay in front of her.

"Perhaps you are being a bit unfair—"

"Am I? Pretty girls are objectified, sexualised, and rarely taken seriously. Handsome men are glorified; it just seems to enhance their other qualities." She suddenly stood up to face him, as if processing her own words. "Well, I mean, you know, it's harder for women. I bet your dashing looks have provided opportunity." Her words were coated in honey as if apologising for her ill-considered outburst.

"I've paid for my looks all my life, Morgan. You, of all people, should know to look beyond the surface," he murmured, walking towards the door, turning his back to her as his eyebrows came down with the weight of memory.

"Gabriel, I'm sorry, I . . . . didn't mean to offend you." She walked towards him, placing her hand on his arm. "I'm a fool, a judgmental fool. I was thoughtless, distracted by all this beauty. Thank you. You're so kind to bring me here. You don't know how much this means to me. Gabriel . . . ."

It took him a few moments to dig himself out of the hole of painful memories triggered by her words. The disgust and fear in the faces of half of the population of Ahe'ey was hard to forget. "I'm sorry. I should be apologising. You have unintentionally hit a raw nerve. Sorry."

"Would you like to share?" she offered, her voice full of regretful compassion. "I'm an idiot."

He took a deep breath and turned to face her with an open smile, recovering his composure. For one brief moment, he unleashed his Ange'el glow—a beaming smile so powerful that washed away her anxiety and regret.

"No, perhaps some other day. Shall we go for a walk? We have plenty of treasures to experience." Morgan followed him happily, still under his Ange'el charm.

Gabriel worked to contain his inner demons. He felt guilty every time he used his powers. He promised never again to use them on her. *I won't be your puppet master, no matter what happens.*

The gifts of the Ange'el were a double-edged sword. The impact of his appearance was nothing when compared with the potency of his mind. He often wondered if the people of Ahe'ey were right; many feared and distrusted him. The Yi'ingo likened him to the monster that had started the war—Sathian, his kinsman and his mirror image. Perhaps his uncanny resemblance to Ahe'ey's worst villain was more than skin deep? He pushed aside the ghost that haunted his nightmares and, with a smile, offered his arm to Morgan who was happy to oblige.

MANHOOD

They went for a walk in the main area of the museum, and once again, Gabriel seemed to know exactly where to take her. They strolled by all the Impressionists, stopping to see *Reclining Nude* by Modigliani and *Two Tahitian Women* by Gauguin. Then they entered the Charles Engelhard Court, a glassed-in courtyard, so that she could enjoy the Art Nouveau architectural elements and the large-scale American sculptures.

She noticed that several of the Met's security guards seemed to be following them from a distance. She assumed it was because Gabriel was so important for them. Once in a while, Gabriel nodded to the guards or stopped by to exchange a few words while she was enjoying the sculptures.

"They've increased security measures since the last time I was here," Morgan commented.

"Yes, they're monitoring every visitor because of the party tonight. We'll have many distinguished guests, including former presidents and diplomats."

"You can assure them that I'm not a terrorist. Although I do have a reputation of asking people for funding in situations when it's difficult to say no." She raised her eyebrows and smiled cheekily.

"I expect nothing less from you."

They sat in the courtyard, enjoying the sunlight that illuminated the room through the glass ceiling and walls. In the basket, there were berries, fruitcake, juice, and a bottle of champagne. He opened the bottle and served her a glass.

"Thank you, this is delightful. Won't you have some bubbles?"

"I'm sorry; I don't drink alcohol, but I'll have some juice." He poured the juice into a champagne glass and toasted her with a smile.

"I guess that'll have to do," she said, rolling her eyes theatrically and then smiling. He smiled back, blushed, and bit his lip briefly.

There was something so genuine and affectionate about this man. The effect she had on him was surprising to her. Most of the time, he appeared guarded and sombre, but beyond that invisible wall there seemed to be a great vulnerability. For a few moments, his discomfort allowed Morgan to relax and set aside her own inner gremlins.

Morgan moved her eyes away from his, to reduce some of the intensity of the interaction. There was a copy of the New York Times on the stone bench and she read the main headline: *November 22, 2014, Walter Zanus announces possible candidacy for President of the United States.*

"I don't know if I should laugh or cry," she said, picking up the newspaper.

"It's no laughing matter. Zanus has gathered an impressive number of supporters amongst the working class and social elite."

"But the man is a complete buffoon."

"A very dangerous buffoon."

"There's no way he'll be successful. I've met him a couple of times. He's an offensive sorta fellow. He'll rub people in the wrong way. He's sexist, bigoted and racist. No one in their right mind will vote for Walter, especially the minorities."

"Don't underestimate him, Morgan. Many, especially men, see the rise of minorities as a threat to their cultural and economic dominance. White men are losing their jobs to women, minorities and people at the other end of the supply chain in third world countries. Beleaguered voters will support him in the hope that he'll restore their vanished status."

"People won't take him seriously. This is the man that said on national TV that a woman's place is in the kitchen."

"That may indeed be his biggest strength."

"Are you serious? I can't believe you are legitimising Walter Zanus."

Morgan placed her glass down on the bench. Her irritated look proclaimed that she was ready for a heated debate.

"I'm not," he said swiftly, raising both hands, palms towards her, "his campaign dares to shatter taboos. Those who think privately what he speaks publicly perceive him as speaking truth to power. And, the journalists struggling with a broken business model are happy to use his sensationalist statements as clickbait. They are selling out in exchange for eyeballs that bring them advertising dollars. It's working in his favour."

"Sure, but progress is everywhere. You have an African American president in office, women and minorities are slowly gaining consumer power, and there are many good, progressive Caucasian men supporting them."

"Some, not all."

"Yeah, I know. But, I don't see how Zanus would ever get a serious shot at the White House. Plus, the jobless working class can't blame the minorities; it's the one percent who're stealing their economic power. And the software, the robots, the artificial intelligence and the value-extraction economics."

"That's not what the clickbait headlines are selling to the masses in the US."

"Do you really think that Walter has a chance of becoming president in two years?"

"Yes, I do. I believe that, in the next few years, we are likely to experience a war between a large population of disenfranchised, jobless, western Caucasian men and everyone else. The status quo is being disrupted, and they don't like it. Don't expect them to give up power willingly. The forces you challenge are dangerous and don't play fair or clean."

They sat there for a while in silence. Morgan was too shaken by the possibility of a future where Zanus was president of the United States. Gabriel broke the silence by talking about art and history. He explained that the Ange'el Foundation spent a lot of its resources on the preservation of artefacts from all over the world. He said that it was sad how much great knowledge from ancient civilisations had been lost. They discussed her favourite sculpture, *The Rape of the Sabine Women* by Giambologna. She talked about the three-dimensional nature of that sculpture and how Giambologna was a master of turning marble into flesh. Gabriel continued to impress her with his knowledge of the things she loved most. He added that the actual Roman story didn't include rape and that the word "rape," in this particular case, was derived from the Latin word *raptio*, which meant "abduction." In return, she showed off her own knowledge of the tale.

"Women were once again both the victims and heroes of the story. The women ended the war by imploring to their Sabine fathers and their Roman husbands. Why are men so cruel?"

"You are full of contradictions, Morgan. Is cruelty really a gendered quality?" he remarked, narrowing his eyes.

She loved the way he challenged her with her own arguments. She shook her head in a gesture of hopelessness.

"Sometimes it's hard to believe in the goodness of men. The two hundred-plus Chibok schoolgirls kidnapped by the Boko Haram are still missing. One day, if they are still alive, they too, may have to plead for their children and kidnapper husbands to their parents. I'm so sick of the violence of men trapped by prehistorical expectations of manhood.

"Manhood is today an uncertain, frail status that is easily threatened. Insecure men attempt to affirm their manliness physically and symbolically. Zanus' appeal speaks to the insecurities of men raised with traditional values; men trapped in a world that is pulling the rug under their feet and challenging everything they believe in.

"We're all to blame; we are teaching our daughters that they can be whatever they wish to be, while our boys are still hopelessly stuck in the man box." The thought of Zanus brought fire to her gut, the type of frustration she struggled to contain. "Sometimes it's difficult to take a peaceful stand when some men only understand the language of violence and war. These people don't want a fairer world; they want power, control and destruction. You don't see women acting like that."

His eyebrows sunk and his eyes focused on the floor. "Women are capable of as much destruction and greed as men."

"Give me one example of a place in the world where that happens."

"Perhaps one day," he murmured and changed the topic. "You won't find the magic of Giambologna here, but I trust you'll still enjoy the sculptures of the American masters."

"Indeed, it's not Florence or the Louvre, but I can assure you it'll do just fine. Unless you plan to fly me to Europe this evening." She smiled, teasing him. He was so considerate and eager to please that she couldn't help but playfully retaliate with light-hearted irreverence.

He blushed. They both struggled to look into each other's eyes, constantly playing a game of hide-and-seek—brief eye contact followed by swift escapes away from the electric charge that rushed through their bodies every time their eyes met.

James appeared with their changes of clothes. "The offices on the top floor are available for you to change in. The party will start upstairs in the roof garden in half an hour, and the canapés will be served at seven in the Sackler Wing, where the Egyptian Temple of Dendur is located."

"Thank you, James," Gabriel said as James gave them the bags and took the basket away.

Soon, she came out wearing a figure-hugging royal blue dress and a pair of high-heeled shoes. It was the best dress she'd ever worn. It perfectly suited the curves of her body and it worked well with her pale skin. She wore her hair down and held a small silver purse.

"You look stunning," Gabriel said softly. His eyes set on her, pupils dilated. She cringed with embarrassment.

"Thank you. Love your suit," she replied casually as she walked towards him admiring his steel-blue fitted suit. He offered her his left arm and placed his right hand over hers. As they walked to the roof garden, they enjoyed fairy lights that were positioned on the stairs and the light sculptures that illuminated the way. She suddenly realised this was a special party. The women were all dressed in the most exquisite gowns, and she recognised many famous faces, including movie actors and politicians.

"I wish I had known how fancy this party was. I would have made more of an effort," she said, a little intimidated as she thought of her pale, makeup-free complexion and absence of jewellery.

"You are absolutely beautiful, Morgan," he spoke in an encouraging tone. He stopped for a second, observing her discomfort. "Will you mind if I leave you for just a few minutes?"

She was puzzled but nodded.

He took a glass of champagne from a waiter's tray, handed it to her and said, "I'll be right back." Gabriel headed in the direction of the two security guards that had been following them all day, exchanged a few words with them, and then he disappeared amongst the crowd.

As she stood on the rooftop looking over Central Park and the city skyline in the distance, she felt quite special. There she was at the centre of the world on a clear winter night with the sky illuminated by a full moon. The outside heaters made the environment welcoming, and although she usually paid no attention to fashion or celebrity, she couldn't help but enjoy a moment in awe of the way the beautiful dresses integrated perfectly with the design of the building and the vivacious light art installations that surrounded her. The vibrant and sparkling environment made her feel alive and grateful—she always remembered her humble beginnings and her journey through life. Morgan never took anything for granted, and today she wanted to experience this moment as if she were Alice in Wonderland.

She saw Gabriel walking towards her. He was stopped several times. Apparently, he was well known and respected by many of the guests. He was perfectly polite and charming. He always wore his cuffs unbuttoned, allowing his sleeves to cover most of his hands. He had the habit of gently squeezing the tips of his thumbs as he spoke, alternating one to the other. *A nervous gesture. Perhaps he is by nature quite shy.* And yet, shy or not, it seemed that the entire world was in line to greet him. He excused himself as he tried to make his way towards her.

"I'm sorry," he said as he finally reached her.

"You're clearly popular, Gabriel."

"It's just another cheap privilege that took zero effort to attain," he repeated her words.

She couldn't detect any hint of sarcasm in his tone. She was about to interject, but he lowered his eyes and took a blue silk box out of his pocket.

"I thought you may like to wear this tonight," he said, his voice trembling.

She panicked, hoping there were no precious stones in the box. She refused to wear diamonds or other precious stones that likely came from places where people were exploited. *But why would I ever doubt his impeccable ability to read my mind?* In the box, she found a necklace and a bracelet made of turquoise, her favourite crystal. They were beautiful, the exact tone she liked, the place where the blue sky met the green sea, the same place that lived in his eyes. The necklace was quite long and the stones small. She could also see some chartreuse glass beads. *Precious.*

"I thought it would complement that wonderful dress well."

"Thank you, it's stunning." Her eyes shined and expressed happiness. She felt spoiled. Everything was perfect. "I'm honoured. But where did you find these?"

"We are at the Metropolitan Museum of Art. Everything is possible." He smiled. He took the necklace from the box and helped her put it around her neck. The necklace was designed so that most of its length would hang at the back; he touched her body as he positioned it at the middle of her spine. He was right; both pieces matched perfectly with the rest of her ensemble.

He looked at her face, which was lit by the full moon. "Are you a child of the moon, Morgan?"

She looked at him, surprised and confused. "Yes. Yes, I guess I am. The full moon fills me with energy and a sense of well-being. It's usually when I'm at my best. It's like magic."

He became lost in her eyes for a second and then lowered his eyes. She felt he was fighting something. He nodded his head and eyes. "We should find our way downstairs and get some food."

The roof garden was now filled with people. Gabriel held Morgan's hand as he made his way through the crowd. He had strong hands and long fingers. Like the rest of his body, his hands walked the tightrope between elegance and strength. He seemed to be overprotective of her, not allowing any man close to her. His possessiveness unsettled her. It seemed contrary to his gentle nature. He used his body and arms as a barrier; she was so small compared to him that she felt engulfed by his body. Morgan was having a difficult time trying to ignore the sense of well-being, peace, and desire she experienced every time she came close to him. *His glow*, that glow he had, seemed to have an effect on her. In any other situation, with any other person, she would have kept her guard up and fought the feeling of wanting to surrender to her desire for him. After all, she barely knew him. But it just felt so right. Everything felt so right. It was as if she'd always known him.

SUBMISSION

Thousands of fairy lights illuminated the Temple of Dendur in the Sackler Wing. In front of it, a band was playing Latin jazz. Many couples were already dancing at the centre of the room on an elevated area where the temple stood. Down at the sides of the platform, people talked and enjoyed extravagant canapés and cocktails. All-light sculptures glowed in different shades of blue, casting a blue tint on their surroundings.

Gabriel scanned the room, looking for any signs of danger, while his companion took a sip of her second glass of Taittinger. She touched the wall of the temple and closed her eyes for a moment.

"It's remarkable what the Egyptians were able to build thousands of years ago. I wish I had a time machine so I could go back in history and explore the great ancient civilisations of the world."

"This is actually a Roman copy of the original Egyptian temple, a model built by Emperor Augustus around 15 BC," Gabriel replied. "It is indeed a shame that so much has been lost, although . . . " He paused for a second, contemplating if he should continue. "I can assure you that humanity is not ready to unveil its full history."

Morgan's eyebrows jumped at the statement and she opened her mouth to ask what he meant.

"Gabriel, how are you?" interrupted a large and loud man walking in their direction.

"Sir William, it's been far too long. I'm well, thank you. How are you? Has your knee recovered fully from surgery?" Gabriel extended his hand to the older man. Sir William's white hair and soft, well-groomed beard reflected the blue hue of the lights. He placed his hand on Gabriel's shoulder and embraced him with affection.

"Fine, I'm walking, but my marathon running days are over before they even began." He had the most effusive belly laugh.

"Let me introduce you to my friend Morgan. She's visiting us from London and is the world leader when it comes to girl's empowerment." Morgan shook her head, smiled and extended her hand.

"Morgan, Sir William is a dear friend of mine. He is the CEO of an innovative biofuel business. He's also my partner in a vital and ground-breaking research project that'll be completed next week. I'm forever grateful for his brilliant mind and friendship."

"We couldn't have done it without the support and scientific insights of the Ange'el Foundation, my friend. How long are you going to be in town, Morgan?"

"Just until the end of the week."

"That's a shame. Next time you visit New York, you are invited to visit our home to have dinner together with our friend here. We miss him, especially my youngest daughter, Karen."

"How is the little one?" Gabriel asked.

"She's great, but she's had little time for me since you introduced her to archery and martial arts."

Gabriel smiled and looked at Morgan. "Karen is eight years old and plans to conquer the world by the age of eleven and a half. She is the poster child for girl power. You two should meet."

"I must go and have a seat. My knee is starting to complain. It was excellent to see you both. Gabriel, please do visit us soon. We miss you, and I do need to give you an update on our shared endeavour."

As Sir William walked away, Morgan began to move her body to the sound of the music that was playing in the background. The band was playing "Águas de Março," a song by Tom Jobim. Gabriel smiled as she mumbled some of the lyrics in Portuguese. He looked at her, held her hand, and led her to the dance floor. There they stood holding each other, her hair whispering against his chin, no words, just a deep appreciation for that moment. She hid her head between his neck and shoulder and let her body move with his.

For the first time in a long time, Gabriel closed his eyes, smelled her hair, and became lost in the moment; a moment where he allowed himself to be just a man falling in love; a moment he would soon regret.

THE ATTACK

Morgan couldn't quite figure out what was happening. First, she saw a man with a knife come straight at them. Although the attacker approached from Gabriel's back, he turned around just at the right moment. In milliseconds, Gabriel turned the knife to face the attacker and pushed it straight into his heart. The man fell to the floor instantly. Morgan stood paralysed. She watched the events unfold in slow motion as her heart raced faster than the speed of light.

Four others came running towards them with knives. She saw Gabriel dance in the air. He used his right elbow to hit one of the men in the face while his left leg hit the head of another attacker. The way he moved—it was incredible. He was graceful and yet strong. Morgan soon realised that the men were trying to attack her. The only thing preventing the success of the attack was Gabriel, who seemed to be a master of some martial art. She walked backwards, away from the men, until her back hit the wall of the temple. She had nowhere to go and her gut twisted with panic.

The two security guards finally came running. Gabriel looked back and shouted, *"Protect her. Stay with her,"* and as he did, one of the attackers wounded his right arm with a knife.

"Gabriel," she screamed, and at that moment she realised how much she cared for him.

Gabriel was now fighting four men simultaneously. He kicked one of his attackers in the head, killing him instantly. The same kick disarmed another attacker; he picked up the knife and threw it at the man, who fell to the floor, motionless.

Who are you? she thought as she watched him move with superhuman precision. She could hear the screams of the people around her. Some of the women fell as they tried to run away in their high-heeled shoes and tight dresses. Glass shattered on the floor as tables were overturned to make way for those trying to escape.

Gabriel's eyes were set on the two remaining attackers. The men stopped, looked at each other and ran away, disappearing amongst the crowd. Gabriel ran towards Morgan and embraced her.

"Are you all right?" Morgan asked holding on to him tightly.

Gabriel nodded. He turned to face the two guards. "Sam. Pursue the attackers and call for backup. I'll follow you as soon as Morgan is safe. Manuel, I want at least six extra security guards at the hotel by the time we get there—two inside Morgan's suite, two at the door, and two downstairs. Sir William," he spoke loudly as he walked in the direction of the older man, "I need to borrow your car. Please don't worry. You are all safe. The attackers aren't coming back."

"I'll call my driver now. He'll meet you with the car at the front entrance . . . ."

"Thank you."

He held Morgan's hand as they both ran swiftly down the stairs. Morgan abandoned her shoes to try to keep up with her long-legged companion. James and Carl were running up the stairs.

"What happened?" James asked.

"Five attackers—three dead, the rest on the run—armed with kitchen knives probably from the Met's kitchen. I need you both to stay here, take care of the guests, and do a post-mortem."

Gabriel and Morgan kept running to the main door. Sir William's driver was waiting for them at the entrance of the building.

"Mark, would you like to join us so that you can bring the car back to pick up Sir William?"

The driver nodded.

"Okay, but I'll drive."

Gabriel opened the back door of the car to let Morgan in. The two men sat in the front of the Porsche Cayenne. Gabriel was driving incredibly fast and seemed to be using back roads.

"Who were those men?" she asked. "Why were they trying to attack me?"

Gabriel didn't reply.

"Gabriel, what is going on?" His silence distressed her.

The hotel was full of security guards who nodded at Gabriel as he rushed Morgan upstairs. "Morgan, I need you to stay in your suite until I'm back. Please don't worry. You're completely safe within these walls."

Before she could reply, he turned around and was gone.

PRESENT DAY - 22 NOVEMBER 2014

AHE'EY

Sky was at the Yi'ingo arena training her novice warriors. She watched Quinn's body hit the ground, rolling on the loose gravel of the Yi'ingo arena. The tiny girl screamed in pain as her knees and elbows, previously scuffed by the same unforgiving surface, bled on impact. Red and blue covered Quinn's milky skin, spoils from a day of intense battle. She jumped to her feet and dusted herself off. The long, royal blue streaks adorning her short dark hair covered her face and Asian eyes. She blew her hair away from her nose with fierce determination.

Sky knew that the fourteen-year-old human was too stubborn to yield to Scout. Quinn's opponent was Sky's most promising young apprentice; Scout's blood was almost pure, and her royal descent made her a contender, one day, for the position of Sky's second in command. Sky had a soft spot for the two stray cats that battled each other in the training arena; their unrestrained fierceness reminded Sky of herself at that young age. Yet, both girls had weaknesses that needed Sky's protection if they were to survive in that land. Quinn was a mere human inhabiting the land of Gods, and Scout's unlawful deviant tendencies could get her killed. Sky's protection gave them a small chance to thrive against all odds.

Quinn used her left arm to clean off the thick mix of sweat and blood that blurred her eyesight. With one flip of her head, blue locks of hair travelled through the air, away from her face. Her menacing eyes locked onto her adversary as she raised her sword in front of her chest.

"Go home little human girl; you don't belong here." Scout played with her sword, waving it in the air, drawing an infinity sign in the space between her and Quinn. "I don't want your royal master to come after me for sending you back to Ange'el missing an ear or a finger."

The purple tips of Scout's white faux hawk trickled down her back, swerving from side to side as her body danced with the sword. Scout was five years older than Quinn. The older warrior was tall and athletic. Her womanly figure was endowed with perfectly symmetrical and proportional curves. In comparison, Quinn was short, thin and flat chested.

"Look who's talking. You're just a lowlife royal bastard. Your blood is as cheap as mine."

Quinn ran in the direction of Scout, her face red, full of fire. The swords clashed in the air several times, unleashing a metallic thunder-like sound throughout the forest. Scout's moves were economical and precise; she blocked each blow using the strength of her core, moving sword and shield just enough to defend herself against the punishing rage of the younger woman.

"I've had it." Scout said on Quinn's fifth strike. The Yi'ingo warrior used the impact of her shield to disarm her human opponent, and kicked her hard in the stomach. Quinn's body was projected backwards, and she hit her head on the wooden fence that surrounded the arena.

"Enough," Sky said, kicking Quinn's sword to the side as the young warrior prepared to pick it up. Her voice commanded the full attention of the dozens of young apprentices that watched the fight.

"I told you, Sky. Humans don't belong at Yi'ingo. I'm a warrior; I don't have time for charity. Look at her," Scout said, pointing at Quinn. "She's weak and fragile. Why are we wasting our time training her?"

"Watch how you speak to me, girl. I'll cut your tongue out."

Sky placed her hand on the hilt of her sword. She didn't need to raise her voice to direct the attention of the group. The cocky purple-crested brat bowed her head to Sky, her unapologetic eyes half hidden under the spikes of white hair.

"I'll make you eat your words in the next Games, Scout," Quinn shouted, still holding her stomach in pain.

"*Enough!* Back to your chores," Sky shouted, pointing to the stables where the horses waited to be groomed. "Quinn, find your sister and take care of those wounds. You're dismissed from your chores for the rest of the day."

"I'm fine, Sky," replied the rebellious young woman as she followed the others in the direction of the stables. "I don't need special privileges."

Sky allowed the girl to leave, even as she noticed the drops of blood that flowed from the back of Quinn's head to her leather tunic.

"Gabriel's human pet weakens this tribe, Sky." Sky turned around to face the older woman. "Scout is right. Quinn has no place in this arena. The creature distracts our warriors. An army is only as good as its weakest soldier. Why do you protect her?"

"I do no such thing, Grandmother. Quinn may lack strength, but she's braver and more determined than most of our novice warriors."

Amalia gathered her long white hair and tied it behind her head, preparing to mount her horse. "She does not belong in this land. Join me tonight for dinner?"

"I can't. We'll be training against the Ma'asai to prepare for the winter solstice Games. We're just three weeks away."

"I don't approve of unnecessary interaction between the Yi'ingo women and the Ma'asai men. A strong army is an independent one, one with no attachments or friendships that could limit their ability to act decisively in the future."

"The Ma'asai have been our allies in war for many years. Bastian is doing an excellent job leading the tribe. I see little danger—"

"You see little danger? So did your mother as she was kidnapped and raped. So did her sister—raped, burned, and murdered. So did your baby sister, dead. Have you forgotten how your beloved cousin Gabriel abandoned you in the forest to fight the Hu'urei alone as he ran to safety? Don't you ever forget why you were trusted to lead this army."

"Even if I did for a second, I have you here to remind me every single day of my life, Grandmother."

"Honour my fallen daughters and granddaughter by not allowing the one who keeps your bed warm at night to make you weak in the knees. Bastian's blind devotion to Gabriel is a threat to Ahe'ey."

"Bas and the Ma'asai will never betray us."

"Bastian is only interested in securing his place at the Throne. You are the last of the royal maidens of Ahe'ey. He wants to woo the best womb for his seed. Bed him, use him, marry him if you will, but don't let him or any other man own you."

With a few words from the Queen Mother, the mightiest of all warriors turned into the abandoned young girl in the woods. The girl that had been foolish enough to trust a man. She bit her lip, processing her grandmother's reminder.

Amalia had lost two of her daughters—Luna and Gráinne—to the violence and greed of men; she had seen an entire generation of women become the target of the most terrible of crimes. The queen mother would never allow history to be forgotten. The perpetrators were dead, their crimes had been avenged, but the defect in the blood of men would forever position them as second-class citizens of Ahe'ey.

"Your attachment to your cousins weakens you. You're a fraud; a pussycat disguised as a tiger. When will you become the fearless warrior queen this land deserves? The influence of Viviane and Marcus is not good for you. My daughter and her husband work to reinstate the status of men. I won't have it." Amalia galloped away. "And get rid of Gabriel's human pets. Quinn and the others are a risk to Ahe'ey's security."

Illicit Lust

Yi'ingo Forest, Ahe'ey

Quinn was practising her hunting skills by following unnoticed a small herd of white-tail deer. She was frustrated that she'd lost the fight with Scout, and she was desperately trying to impress Sky. She lay on the ground hidden by a shrub of Sapote. The animals fled the site as Amalia's voice resonated in the forest a few metres away.

"Disgusting creature!" Quinn heard the old woman scream. "Who do you think you are to disgrace your lineage and waste the few royal genes present in your blood?" Quinn looked around to find the queen mother standing in front of Scout, who was lying naked on a grassy mound with another young woman barely in her teens. Scout jumped to her feet, grabbed her leather tunic that lay on the ground and held it over her breasts. Amalia pulled the girl's purple and white hair and screamed to her face.

"You shame us all with your deviant lust." Amalia punched Scout's jaw so hard that she fell to the ground, hitting her head on the hard rocky ground to the side of the mound. Scout's young companion picked up her clothes and ran away in the direction of the village.

Quinn vacillated; she felt sorry for her young bully, but she was too terrified of Amalia to jump to Scout's defence. She knew that Amalia was unlikely to kill Scout, but wouldn't think twice about killing a human.

"Your body does not belong to you," said the old woman, unsheathing her sword and pointing it to Scout's womb. Blood stained Scout's white hair as she moved back, away from Amalia's sword. She stood up, attempting to cover her body with her hands.

"Please, my queen. We weren't harming anyone; we——" Amalia kicked the girl in the face. Scout hit the ground once again, and the old woman planted her sword in between Scout's thighs leaving an open wound on the inside of the girl's left inner leg. Quinn's heart pounded as she tried to stay still and unnoticed.

"The only reason you will leave this forest alive today is to bear children of royal descent. Do you understand, girl?"

"Men are scum; I want nothing to do with them," Scout spat her words.

"Yes, yes they are. Still, you will hunt the highest-ranking man you can find and take his seed. That is all the interaction you need to have with them. You will do it this year or next time I will not be so forgiving." Amalia pushed the blade of her sword between the girl's legs. "Use your lust to our advantage." The old woman walked away.

Quinn attempted to leave quietly, sneaking away towards the village. She kept her body flat behind the shrubs that stood between her and Scout.

A dagger zoomed past Quinn's ear and stabbed the trunk of the tree that stood in front of the girl. Quinn turned to face Scout who grabbed her, choked her and pushed her body against the tree.

The human girl kicked and screamed, *"Get off me!"*

"If you share a word of what you saw today, I'll cut off both of your ears and eat them." Scout pulled her dagger from the kapok tree, nicked the top of Quinn's ear and disappeared into the forest.

"You deserve your punishment, you bully. *You bastard! You'll eat dirt at the games."* Quinn shouted as she grabbed her injured ear.

USED

Scout was as furious as she was scared. There was no way to escape Amalia's orders; the queen mother never showed mercy for any creature in the land. Scout had some royal blood, but she was still just a bastard, and no one would raise a finger to protect her from Amalia's sword. The thought of laying with a man made her sick; she hated them. She despised the evil that lurked in their blood, but she had no choice; either she obeyed Amalia's command, or she would die.

Scout enjoyed being a warrior, and the thought of a pregnancy was infuriating. *So inconvenient.* The young woman had no motherly instincts and knew nothing about babies. She'd never met her mother; as soon as she was born, she'd been left in the care of the Ange'el at the Sacred House. She was the purest of the impure, a worthless mixed breed, the runt of the litter. Ignored by the pure and envied by the others, she was the loneliest Ahe'ey in the land.

She took a deep breath and convinced herself to get on with the task as soon as possible. Scout walked alone at night along the forest road that connected the Yi'ingo and Hu'urei villages. The Hu'urei used the road in the evenings to seek sexual partners. The builders of Ahe'ey weren't allowed to congregate outside their male-only village since Amalia and Sky had instated martial law. Thirty years of gender segregation imposed by the royal family left the men isolated and sexually frustrated.

Hu'urei men couldn't socialise in groups with members of the other tribes. They were permitted to work outside of their village as long as they walked alone to and from their destination. Some of the men had managed to establish relationships with women when they visited Ange'el or Yi'ingo for work during the day. But most roamed the roads alone at night, looking for company. The Yi'ingo and Ange'el women preferred the charms of the Ma'asai farmers, so only a few visited the road at night looking for sex or looking to make a baby.

"Your name, Hu'urei?" Scout shouted with her hand on the grip of her sword. She gritted her teeth, swung her purple crest of hair from side to side and stamped her feet on the ground. She attempted to look menacing as she faced a man much larger than her.

The Hu'urei was unarmed; he leaned against a tree smoking a long wooden pipe. His rust-red hair was pulled back into one single braid that reached the middle of his back. His face, half hidden under a long beard, expressed glimpses of amusement and disdain.

"What do you want, child?" There was the shadow of a knowing smile underneath his beard. He wet his lips as he appreciated her body. They both knew there was only one reason why Yi'ingo and Hu'urei visited this road at night.

"Your name?" Scout screamed once again, doing a terrible job of attempting to hide her terror.

He offered his credentials swiftly, without apprehension. "Joshua, son of Iblis and Gráinne. Sky's half-brother. Grandson of Sathian, Amalia and Michael, and your equal Scout. Half my blood is royal, just like yours." Joshua's recognition of the young warrior only caused her distress to grow.

"You are not my equal, you scum. You are the son of rape and hate. The descendent of evil himself." She couldn't help her anger as she recognised the leader of the Hu'urei.

He rolled his eyes. "And yet, here you are for my seed. Are you not?" he murmured, looking into the young woman's eyes, reaching his hand over his oversized gut and placing it between his legs. He squeezed the visibly growing bulge that showcased his lust for her.

"Rapists and murderers. All of you."

Joshua grew still as the nervous girl barked at him. "I haven't killed or raped anyone. I'm an honest working man, like the rest of my men. The culprits are long dead. Killed by your warriors."

"Filth of the Earth," she barked.

"You treat us like dogs with rabies. Why do I pay for the crimes of my forefathers?" He took one step towards her; his eyebrows were bunched in frustration even as his eyes continued to wander down her body. "Want my seed? I promise I won't disappoint."

Scout put her hand on the grip of her sword. Her heart raced so fast she forgot to breathe.

"No? Then leave me be. Off you go, young rascal."

Scout ran from the man, unable to fulfil Amalia's command. She was angry with herself. Joshua was a Hu'urei, but he was one of the highest ranking Ahe'ey in the land. His blood wasn't pure, but it was as far up the chain as Scout could hope for. Above Joshua, only Gabriel and Bastian—the first was the devil incarnated and the second, Sky's lover. Every single woman in the land relentlessly pursued the two royal men; women with sexual prowess and desire that she lacked with the opposite sex.

Scout slowed down, sighing, and turned back to find Joshua, but he was no longer there. *This is it. I'm dead.*

DISILLUSION

ALLEGIANCE

Present Day - 23 November 2014 - The Ange'el Sacred House, Ahe'ey

"No."

Gabriel approached his mother knowing full well that her answer was definitive. Her mind's eye could see and hear his request and arguments before he uttered a single word. She knew him better than he knew himself.

"Please, Lady. I beg you."

She turned to face him as he approached her. The glow and the beauty of the Lady of Ange'el were unmatched, and so was her power to command the will of any creature in the land—a gift never abused or misused.

He had travelled to Ahe'ey knowing full well that his chances were slim. She was the queen of Ahe'ey first, the high priestess of Ahe'ey second, and then, only then she was his mother and friend.

"She is not a child like the others. You may not bring a high profile media figure to Ahe'ey."

"Powerful forces conspire to kill her. She needs a haven until I—"

"She is a human Gabriel. She is not worthy of you. In the end, this infatuation will hurt her." Viviane's loving tenderness didn't soften the painful truth of her message, a reality he wasn't prepared to accept.

"This has nothing to do with my feelings Lady." He faced her. Her eyes were filled with compassion, but, on her lips, a tender, knowing smile dismissed his words. He despaired, knowing she was right. "Lady, humanity is at a cross roads. Zanus is attempting to shut down any voice that stands between him and power. If he becomes president, he will pull the plug on genetic research. This man is a creationist, an evolution denier. We don't have much time. We can't afford to lose this battle."

"The battle won't be won from Ahe'ey."

"I need time to protect her."

"She is safe, is she not? Why do you want to bring this woman to Ahe'ey Gabriel?"

"She is—"

"Remember your duty and your legacy. The treasure you hold in your blood cannot be wasted. Romantic whims for humans are beneath you, my purest love."

"They are no different from us." He held her hands, and his clear eyes begged, submitting to the power of her all-knowing, raven black gaze.

"That may be so. And yet, we must preserve our genes. The genes that can help humans survive and thrive. Our blood is the key to their future. Do what you must do, but she is not welcome here." Viviane touched his hand, which was covered with dry blood from the wound on his arm. "The healing power within you must be protected. Have I ever failed you, Gabriel?"

He lowered his head and shook it.

"Then, please, obey my wishes so that they do not turn to commands." Gabriel prepared to reply as Viviane placed her finger on his lips. "Aeslin and Vail reach the peak of their fertility cycle today. Do your duty before you leave us."

Gabriel was empty and distraught as he emerged from the Bethesda Fountain. His physical container didn't leave much room for the being within it. They either craved or feared his looks, his genes, his blood. His body was the claustrophobic prison that isolated his soul. An unwanted privilege that took zero effort to attain. The body—objectified, sexualised, feared, hunted, worshiped—always the body; they adored him or hated him before they ever knew him. The body crushed him; he was its slave. He felt empty, reduced to a soulless thing. He took a deep breath, focusing his attention on the pressing task. He took the phone from his pocket and dialled it.

"Matt."

"Gabriel. Have you found them?"

"No, I haven't. Matt. Listen, I'm calling to resign. I can no longer act on your behalf."

"What do you mean you resign? We have a lot to do here. We need the help of someone with your skills."

"I will continue to work on this case, but my key priority and focus are on Morgan. I won't lie to her."

"Commander, you are certainly aware that that isn't how things work. You cannot simply resign or decide to act independently."

"Sir, with all due respect, there's nothing you can do to stop me."

"Calm down Gabriel. You're an elusive and mysterious chap. I don't quite know where you come from; who you really are, or how you got your . . . unique skill set, but one can't just cut ties with the CIA."

"I'll continue to help you to keep Morgan safe, but I'll be serving her, not the CIA. This is a courtesy call so that you know where my priorities lie."

"You seem attached to this woman. I can assure you we'll protect her." There was a long silence on the other side of the line. "Gabriel. Wait. We can't afford to lose you, son. Your skills and your funds have helped us save many lives. Gabriel? Are you there?"

"Yes."

"Look, I understand and will accept your priorities as long as you continue to help us with this case."

"Sure." He ended the call.

Gabriel felt he let everyone down. Morgan, whom he'd put in danger by indulging in his emotions while he should have been focused on protecting her; Ahe'ey, by showcasing a glimpse of his superhuman abilities in front of hundreds of people at the Met; and the CIA, because he wasn't really acting on their behalf. Morgan's safety and well-being came first. His inability to reveal to her who he was had led to a series of bad judgment calls. He was forced to play by the rules of the Central Intelligence Agency and hide the danger she was facing. The results of these actions were now obvious. It was almost dawn, and it was time to go back to Morgan. He didn't want to lie, and yet, he couldn't share the whole truth.

The Pierre Hotel, New York

Morgan was feeling rather claustrophobic in her hotel room surrounded by security guards. She was still in shock, confused by what had happened, but mostly she was worried about him. *Is he okay? Where is he? Why will no one tell me anything?* She turned to one of the security men at the door of her room.

"Should we call the police? Where is Gabriel?"

"Commander Warren is on his way. He should be arriving at any second now."

"Commander Warren?" She was puzzled by the answer.

"Please don't worry, ma'am. You are safe."

The door opened, and Gabriel walked in followed by four other men. He'd changed his clothes; he was now wearing boots, jeans, and a tight-fitting blue jumper. For the first time, she was able to see the back of his hands, both inked with identical moon tattoos. He looked down avoiding her eyes as she ran to him.

"Are you all right?" she asked. She wanted to touch his face, but there were too many strangers around them. Her heart sank to her stomach, looking into his stern and desperate eyes. *It must be grave indeed . . . .*

"Morgan . . . ." His voice wavered. She noticed the dry blood that covered his right hand.

"Your arm . . . You're hurt," she said as she reached towards him. He stopped her and shook his head.

"I'm okay. Please have a seat."

"Morgan," he continued, "the United States received some intelligence a few weeks ago. The data indicated that a group of fundamentalist men's rights activists were potentially conspiring to kill you."

"A few weeks ago? Potentially?" she repeated, processing the information.

Morgan was aware that, in recent times, she'd become the target of media and online attacks by an extremist group of men's rights activists who were unhappy with the success of her organisation. The backlash increased after a public altercation with Walter Zanus on CNN. Her effective response to Zanus' accusations and gross generalisations had gone viral around the world. The mainstream news mocked Zanus incessantly. This raised her profile with some of the most dangerous conservative radicals in the world. She had received several death threats, but she'd never taken them seriously.

"You knew this when I arrived in New York?" she muttered, incredulous.

Gabriel's jaw clenched, and his eyes closed for a few moments. "Yes, I was appointed to protect you during your stay. We've been focusing on your safety. I can assure you—"

"You knew I was in danger. You withheld this crucial information from me and allowed me to travel to the US? You put my life at risk . . . ," she interrupted him. Her eyes showcased her inner turmoil, her strong eyebrows were lowered, and her fists clenched, the whites of her knuckles showing.

"Morgan," he whispered.

Her mind raced, reviewing the events of the previous days.

"You . . . lied about your identity and the nature of your work to gain my trust. You evidently gained access to information about my habits and preferences. You manipulated me to follow your instructions. Please leave, Commander. All of you, *out*." She was distraught, and she fought to hold back the tears by raising her voice and speaking in an angry tone.

Gabriel stood quietly, his eyes set on her as the others left the room. "Morgan, there is more you need to know about Zanus."

She responded by turning her back to him; she couldn't stand the sound of his smooth, reassuring voice.

"Very well. I'll come back later." He left.

She curled up on her bed, unable to process the information that had been shared with her. An avalanche of feelings went through her mind and gut. She punished herself, aware she was more affected by Gabriel's deception than the threats to her safety. *How dare he? It felt so real.*

Morgan slept for a few hours. James joined her for lunch on the balcony of her suite. She cleared her throat and announced she was ready to be briefed on tomorrow's agenda. James' jaw dropped and his eyebrows rose in alarm. He told her that he was planning to spend the afternoon cancelling all events, in particular, her speech at Central Park.

She spoke calmly: "I'm not going to allow terrorists to stop me from doing my work." James opened his mouth, preparing to interject, but she stopped him with the palm of her hand.

"Okay. In this case, I must go. We have a lot of planning to do. I'll stop by during dinner to brief you on the plans for tomorrow."

It took less than two minutes for Gabriel to knock on her door. "Surely you're not considering going ahead with the outdoor event?" He spoke faster, and his pitch was higher than usual. "It's much too dangerous. We have no way to control the crowd or prevent an attack. I can't allow—"

"You can't what, sir?" she said, raising her voice. She was furious. Her eyes were spears ready to be fired without mercy. "Who do you think you are, to give me orders?"

There was nothing he could say or do. This confrontation wasn't about the event. She needed to show him that she was the agent of her own destiny and that he had no power over her.

"Morgan, don't risk your life for anger and pride." He lowered his voice and attempted to reason with her.

"Great advice from the person who placed my life at risk in the first place. Why don't you go and do your job instead? Aren't you supposed to be leading my security team? Do your job! Neither you nor the MRD will stop me from doing mine. I won't allow manipulation or bullying." Morgan's tone was cutting, almost feral.

"I can't let you risk your life," his mouth twisted; his voice held a cocktail of frustration and desperation.

A second later his expression cleared, he raised his right hand and grazed his index finger in the space between her eyes. His eyes opened wide, and the sea of blue and green flowed towards her.

His glow, his beauty. *I can't breathe.* She felt the desire to heed, to please him, to submit to him.

"No," he murmured, abruptly moving his gaze away from hers. He shook his head and dropped his hand. "I won't . . . ." He vacillated, conflicted with something. His hands always gave away his uncertainty; he played with them, pressing his long fingers against each other. "Very well, madam," he said, underlining every syllable of the word 'madam.' "Have it your way."

He turned his back and walked to the door.

Morgan took a moment to recover from his gaze, confused by the intensity of her feelings. She took a deep breath, attempting to fight the powerful grip he had on her. *His looks, his eyes, those eyes.* She remembered a quote from her childhood.

"L'essentiel est invisible pour les yeux," she murmured to herself, using the line from her favourite book as a shield against him.

He stopped and turned around.

"Indeed, what is essential is invisible to the eye." A tiny drop of his sea of cyan flowed from his eye to the corner of his mouth. She saw him hesitate, leaning in her direction before he turned around. Gabriel left the room and quickly closed the door behind him.

She felt a knot in her stomach every time he looked at her. She was hurt, so upset, ready to put him in his place, and yet . . . she shook her head, trying to keep her feelings at bay. She decided to be proud, proud for having stood up to him, to all of them, no matter the consequences. She lifted her arms hiding her head between them. Why was she so attracted to this man? She wasn't a needy teenager; she wasn't searching for external validation; she wasn't hoping for romantic love, and yet he was stuck in her mind, heart, gut. She struggled to think clearly. A few minutes later, she decided to work on her speech. She reached for the laptop and attempted to type and control her shaking hands.

He left Morgan's room as irresistibly charmed by her strength as he was angry and frustrated by her attitude. He knew what was driving her behaviour; she was too blind and hurt to look at the bigger picture. He had the skill to change her mind, to make her heed, and yet he was incapable of using it to force her to comply. He stopped, looking at the closed door that stood between him and Morgan.

"Your gaze is very powerful, but trust me, it won't open that door," said a familiar voice behind him. Gabriel felt a large welcoming hand squeeze his shoulder. "You all right?"

"Bastian, what are you doing here?"

The tall blonde man smiled openly. "Is this how you welcome your most beloved kinsman?"

Bastian embraced him. Gabriel's younger cousin had grown to become bigger and more muscular than him. The Ange'el was engulfed by the playful clumsy warmth of his dearest friend's body.

"You should have changed." He looked at Bastian's conspicuous kimono-like green-gold tunic, embroidered with the symbol of the sun. The same sun-shaped design adorned some of his large rings and bracelets that rattled as he moved. Bastian wore his hair in a similar style to Gabriel. He had half his hair pulled back in a ponytail, but he showcased a couple of braids on the sides of his head and adorned them with rich golden beads. The Ange'el was tense and stressed, and yet the blonde man couldn't help but smile.

"I need to go, Bas. I need to track some guys." Gabriel turned and prepared to leave.

"Not before you tell me what's going on."

He ignored the Ma'asai and attempted to walk away, but his cousin had a tight grip on his arm. Bastian smiled and, after a moment the Ange'el stopped and nodded. They took the lift to Gabriel's suite.

"Why are you here Bas?"

"Because you clearly need me. Look at you."

"I'm fine. I just need time to think."

"Sage told me you went to the Sacred House and didn't stop by to visit her and the kids. She's very distressed. This is completely unlike you."

"I'm sorry. Will you tell her? Tell her that I'm sorry and that all is well. Please? Tell her I love her and the children."

"Is this about that woman, Morgan?"

"Her life is at risk; she needs protection. She is speaking at an outdoors event tomorrow in front of thousands of people."

"So it's true. Zanus is trying to have her killed." Gabriel nodded. "Just tell her not to do it. Make her. Use your powers; you're justified in this situation."

"I can't." Gabriel let the despair on his face express what he struggled to put in words. Bastian sighed and put his hand on the Ange'el's shoulder.

"What do you need brother?"

"An army."

"The Ma'asai will stand by your side, but you know that Sky will have us both for lunch if I bring my men to Manhattan."

"Thank you." Gabriel's tense shoulders dropped, reassured by his cousin's support. "I'll talk to Sky to try to get the support of the Yi'ingo. If Sky is willing to help, I won't need the Ma'asai."

"Well, thanks for that." Bastian looked at Gabriel sideways and then rolled his eyes.

"You know what I mean. I don't want to cause a rift between you and Sky."

"I should go with you to see her. You two will get—"

"Best you stay out of it. We'll have a problem if she denies me and commands you to remain at Ahe'ey. I don't want you to have to challenge her rule. We have enough problems as it is. You both need to trust each other."

"Hey, irrational and impetuous activities that anger Sky and Amalia are usually my forte. Plus, she likes me, even when she hates me. It's my charm and sex appeal. You know?" Bastian said boastfully.

"Still, I'll try to keep you out of this, if I can."

"I'm here for you brother. Just don't lose your mind too often; one of us needs to be the responsible one." Bastian pointed at Gabriel. "You know, it would be much less trouble if you were willing to bat your magic eyelashes."

"I know. If you don't hear from me, meet me here at dawn. I need thirty of your best men. Hide the swords. And please wear your farm gear. No shiny stuff."

"Now you're pushing your luck," Bastian joked. "Consider it done. I'll be at the farm." Bastian headed for the lift.

"Bas. Thank you."

"I don't quite know what's gotten into you, but let's hope she's worth it."

The Request

Yi'ingo village, Ahe'ey

Gabriel seldom visited Yi'ingo land. At best, the warriors reacted to him with fear and distrust. At worst, hate and anger were present in every expression, every contracted muscle and every thought. The energy projected towards him was as toxic as Venus' atmosphere. A young apprentice walked backwards as she saw him approach the stables where Sky was teaching the girl to saddle a horse. The warrior queen turned to face him. For a brief moment, her eyebrows went up before they sunk low, shading a piercing and distrustful gaze.

"Leave us," Sky said to the girl, who ran swiftly away from the stables.

"Cousin." He bowed his head.

She faced him coldly in silence. He took a step towards her, but she stopped him with her eyes. They rarely crossed paths with each other and barely spoke.

"Sky, I need your help." His anxious tone and disarming candour got through the ice, and a hint of surprise complemented by a pinch of curiosity passed over her face.

She responded with an ironic laughter. "My help? Speak," she commanded, raising her head and one eyebrow.

"Tomorrow, there's an event in Central Park in Manhattan. Thousands of people will attend. The speaker requires our protection. Her life is at risk."

"Why would I risk our anonymity for some random human?"

"She's a light worker. Morgan brings positive change and support for women and girls. Her work is as impactful as the work of the Ange'el Foundation."

"Cancel the event."

"*I can't!*" His voice echoed throughout the forest. He lowered his head, attempting to compose himself.

"You can't?" she repeated with a sneer. "Have you lost the Ange'el gift of manipulation?"

He stood quietly with his head down.

"What do you want from me, Ange'el?"

"Your warriors, they can help secure the area. It's just for a couple of hours."

"*Are you out of your mind?* Has Viviane heard about this? My warriors protect our people from those who threaten our security," she spoke decisively.

He adjusted his tone, trying to reason with her. Silk and honey flowed from his voice and his eyes. "Sky, we were once—"

"Don't you dare. *Don't you dare!*" She leaned in, speaking to his face. Her hand squeezed the hilt of her sword. She gritted her teeth, responding to his silence. "Where were you when we battled the Hu'urei for over twenty years? Where was the powerful prince of Ange'el as my warriors died in the battlefield, crushed by the dragons? Why would I risk the safety of Ahe'ey to respond to the whims of a spoiled coward? Go back to your rich city penthouse Ange'el. You don't belong here." Her eyes and her words were razor-sharp spears.

"Please. Sky."

She mounted the horse and galloped away.

His guilty conscience endured her justified anger and her hate for him. He wore her wrath as a reminder of his weakness, of his betrayal. He gave Sky her rage, and he would suffer it for the rest of their lives. The tension between their roles at Ahe'ey only worsened their frail and fractured relationship. Their agendas were different. She was ultimately responsible for the security of the people of Ahe'ey, and within its borders she was as powerful as the queen and king. She was to be obeyed and rarely needed her mighty army to enforce her orders. Gabriel worked to hide any clues of Ahe'ey's existence from the humans. In parallel, he sponsored and lobbied for technological and political progress so that Ahe'ey's secrets could one day be disclosed.

Gabriel missed the fearless copper-headed girl with the trusting eyes, the one who saw the hero in him. The child he had destroyed.

DIVERSION

Ma'asai village, Ahe'ey

Scout approached the Ma'asai village reluctantly. She would obey Amalia's command even as her entire body rejected the idea with repulsion. The queen mother was known for her ruthlessness, and Scout feared for her life and the life of others like her. She looked for Bastian hoping that she would feel less disgust for the royal Ma'asai leader. Of all the men at Ahe'ey, he was the most trusted by the Yi'ingo. She knew him well. They shared a mischievous sense of humour and love for outrageous practical jokes. Scout risked Sky's wrath by pursuing Bastian, a chance she was now willing to take, as she feared Amalia the most. *It's not like they're married or exclusive. His seed is too valuable to be wasted.*

Within a few minutes, she came across Bastian and his men returning from the fields. The men wore their earth-coloured work tunics, now covered in dirt after a hard day of work. Their voices and laughter resonated throughout the forest. The good humour of the Ma'asai was contagious and welcomed throughout Ahe'ey.

Scout held her breath as she looked at the leader of the Ma'asai; he exuded the confidence of those who win the top prize in the gene lottery. Bastian towered over the others who naturally paid him deference, hanging on his every word. His cockiness was tempered with a kind and generous heart, and a smile that rarely left his face. He saw her coming and waved, his knowing smile was childlike and naughty as if he guessed what she sought. He wasn't the only one presuming her motives; Scout cringed listening to his companions mock him as she approached them. They all knew he was the most prized object of desire of the women of Ahe'ey. He was a willing and welcoming target of both Yi'ingo and Ange'el women.

"I'm not sure Ahe'ey can deal with another one of your bastards Bas. Ahe'ey is full of kids with your handsome face. It's a shame that they also inherit your lack of intelligence. Our species is getting dumber because of you." They all laughed.

Bastian smiled, "Shhh don't scare the girl."

Scout bit her lower lip until it bled a little. She walked towards the men clenching her fists.

"Scout, how are you, fine warrior?" He walked towards her as the rest of the men continued walking to the farmhouse.

She didn't know what to say or do. The panic caused by the closeness of his massive muscled body made her want to escape. She took a deep breath, placed her shaking hand on her shoulder and released the flap in her tunic, exposing one of her breasts.

"You are all business, aren't you?" he laughed, stepping towards her.

She reached to place her hand between his legs, but at that moment she lost his attention. He seemed to focus on something behind her.

"I'm sorry, I must go," he said mindlessly as he walked around her.

Scout turned around and saw Sky standing a few metres away. The warrior queen's eyes spat fire and ice as he walked towards her. Scout pulled up her tunic, covering herself; she bowed towards Sky. She feared the warrior queen but welcomed the interruption of a plan that she was struggling to execute. The young woman prepared to make a swift exit.

"Stay, Scout; this will only take a minute." She held her breath; her body became stiff as Sky approached them.

"What is it, my Sky?" Bastian asked. He looked anxious as he responded to the tsunami of emotions reflected in Sky's face. He placed his hand on her hip, but she slapped it away, with an expression of mild annoyance. His worry turned into a cocky smile. "It pleases me to feel the sting of your jealousy my queen. It helps me deal with the resentment

I have for all those lucky bastards that warm your bed at night."

Scout rolled her eyes at Bastian's overinflated ego.

"Gabriel came to see me," she said, ignoring his antics.

Bastian stood in silence for a brief moment; he cleared his throat before he replied.

"Gabriel? What did he want?"

"He dared to ask me to use the Yi'ingo army to protect some diva during a public event in Manhattan. He'd risk our secrecy; the safety of our people because of some human." Her jaw was tense.

Bastian reached to touch her face. She stepped away from him pacing from one side to the other.

"He must be desperate to come to you for help. Will you answer his call?"

"He's becoming increasingly careless and irresponsible. He must be stopped."

Scout turned to leave.

"Stay," Sky commanded.

Scout sighed at Sky's obvious attempt to prove her indifference towards Bastian.

"He must have a good reason. Will you help him?" Bastian asked.

"I have my kingdom to protect, Hu'urei riots to end and perpetrators to hunt and jail. Civil unrest has increased since Marcus left Joshua in charge of the Hu'urei."

"It's been ten years since the war has ended, perhaps it's time to end martial law and give them back some of their rights."

"They're dangerous; they can't be trusted," barked Scout, appalled at Bastian's suggestion.

Both royals admonished the girl with their eyes. Scout was exasperated by her feeble status; she wasn't allowed to leave and yet she couldn't join the discussion. She lowered her head and crossed her arms in frustration. Her hair fell to her face in a final gesture of solidarity towards the exasperated teen.

"Most of the men were born during the war; they are paying for their fathers' crimes. They rebel against their diminished status at Ahe'ey. They can't walk alone at night without being called rapists. The Yi'ingo lock them up without proper trial, and the ones that get to jail are probably the lucky ones. These men have no rights or privileges. They are angry and they revolt against the system."

"Yes, they are angry. They are the same angry self-entitled men that raped our women and kidnapped my mother and sister. It's easy for a male to take their hate lightly."

"I paid the same price you have Sky. I lost my family, fought the same wars, buried the same companions. Gabriel and I have been talking about reform. We think it's time—"

"You do not have a say of how I rule this land. Under martial law, my word is truth, and only Viviane and Marcus can challenge it. The Hu'urei must earn their rights and freedoms. Why do you side with him? That coward has done nothing for you, for us. Nothing."

"I owe him everything. Don't make me choose, Sky. Because I won't. Will you help him?"

"Has he asked you for your help, because I—"

"Sky, you said this would only take a minute." Bastian pulled Scout towards him abruptly. He caressed the young woman's white and purple crest of hair that hung over her distrusting eyes. His gesture was dramatic as if seeking a reaction. "I have other pressing matters to tend to." He smiled irreverently.

Scout panicked, kicking Bastian in the shin and looking at Sky like a wounded puppy.

Bastian laughed. "Are you jealous my queen? Is that why you are delaying my date with young Scout? Your possessiveness pleases me, my love."

Sky's face reflected the orange-red tones of her hair and the fire in her eyes.

"Don't flatter yourself."

Bastian walked towards Sky placing his hands around her waist as she grabbed the hilt of her sword.

"At least I have a reason to bed others; you have none. I do it happily, but for duty; you do it merely for pleasure. Your duty is to birth my children."

"My duty, when the time comes, is to bear children of royal descent with or without you."

"That's a low blow, even for you."

Scout could hear the hint of annoyance in Bastian's voice.

"You'd have to stop hating Gabriel for long enough to bed him. An impossible achievement on your part." Bastian released Sky, in his face the sulking pout of a toddler.

"You underestimate me, Bastian. Enjoy your duties," Sky said lifting her chin, and nodding her head to Scout.

"I'd never underestimate you." A shadow of sadness loomed over his words.

Sky mounted her horse and galloped towards the forest.

"Why did you feed me to the dragon like that? She'll have my head on a plate by twilight," Scout shouted at Bastian punching him in the chest. He grabbed her wrists and pulled her towards him.

"I'm sorry, warrior; I had to do it. Don't worry; your commander is completely indifferent to my sexual activities. She's more concerned with your needs than mine."

"You're blind," she said wrangling him and releasing herself from his embrace.

"Am I?" A hopeful gleam flashed in his eyes.

"You're the only man allowed to return to her bed more than once and to stay the night."

"Is this true?" The slight waver in his voice gave away the intensity of his feelings. "Tell me. Is it?"

She nodded.

"I have to leave you now; I have some matters to tend to. Come find me tomorrow night," said Bastian.

His absent-minded smile told her he was gone even before he turned to leave. Scout kicked the loose gravel on the ground, defeated by the event. She preferred to face her death at the hands of Amalia than to become a pet at the mercy of the capricious royals.

Greek Gods and Amazon Warriors

24 November 2014 – The Pierre Hotel, New York

Morgan looked at her reflection in the mirror. The makeup team had done a good job. A healthy glow hid her pale complexion, and her cheeks were bright and rosy. Morgan attempted a fake smile; she was pleased with the result. No one would know how she was really feeling. She straightened her head and shoulders, trying to ignore the nausea and panic she felt inside. Her hands were shaking so much that she decided to leave her speech notes behind. *I won't be able to read them anyway.*

She left her suite and walked towards the lift. Her palms were sweating, and her heart raced. Clearly, her emotions were controlling her. *Did I just decide to speak in front of thousands of people, in a public park, knowing that there is a contract on my life? What's wrong with me?* Morgan was tired of people trying to manipulate and push her. She was determined to show them that she was in control of her own destiny. The terrorist threats and the advances of manipulative men wouldn't undermine her commitment to her mission. She was as furious as she was afraid, more than afraid— she was terrified.

She arrived at the lobby, and several security men got up to greet her. She nodded at the men and walked towards the door. She stopped, taking a moment to find her composure before walking outside to face Gabriel. As Morgan looked through the glass door, she noticed the surreal scene emerging outside. She saw three figures. It was like looking at the statues of three Greek gods. *Who are these people, and why do they look so different from everyone else?* Gabriel's silver tunic flowed freely outside his pants, perfectly framing his body. He shimmered in the light, and although he dressed more casually than the two strangers, his natural ethereal glow made him stand out. His jaw was tense and his brows heavy. He took her breath away, and she hated that feeling. She felt that she should hate him.

At his side was a blonde man of similar height, yet he was bigger and more muscular than Gabriel. The two men leaned against the limo, probably waiting for Morgan to arrive. The blonde man wore a brown cape that wrapped around his body. He playfully nudged Gabriel with his shoulder. The two men didn't notice the Amazon warrior princess that approached them from behind the limo. Well, that was what she looked like to Morgan—a tall red-haired beauty with intense chestnut-coloured eyes. Dark braids adorned her long hair, and she wore part of her wild mane up in a faux hawk. The woman held her head high; her eyes flashed, and nostrils flared. She wore leather pants and a leather tunic that hugged her athletic body and full chest. Her cape flowed as she walked, uncovering the sword she carried at her back. She was almost as tall as the two men.

By the time the men saw her approach, she had grabbed Gabriel's tunic by the collar and was yelling something at his face. Her elbow hit his jaw with full power. The blonde man wrapped his arms around her body, pulling her away from Gabriel as she kicked and screamed. Gabriel raised his hands, palms towards her in a pleading gesture. She turned to the blonde giant that towered over her and kicked him in the groin. Gabriel jumped between them, facing the woman, and lowering his head slightly. His companion recovered from her blow behind him. The woman placed her hand over the grip of a small dagger that hung on her waist in a scabbard. Gabriel made no attempt to defend himself. His supplicant eyes surprised Morgan.

Before she could process her actions, Morgan found herself walking towards the door, signalling the guards to follow her. Outside, the strange woman shouted.

"Where are the Ma'asai?"

"At the venue, in the Great Lawn in Central Park. We enclosed the perimeter and created some security checkpoints," said the blonde man.

"You betrayed my direct orders, Bastian."

"I received no such order my Sky. Please! We are already here. It's just for a few hours. We don't want another incident like the Met where he disclosed his skills to protect her. Let me prevent further—" The blonde man stopped talking as he saw Morgan and the security guards approach.

The woman wrapped her cinnamon-coloured cape around her body, fully covering her weapons and her unusual outfit.

How odd. They look like they belong in a sci-fi TV series, thought Morgan.

"Good afternoon," Morgan said loudly. She flashed a theatrical smile, trying to defuse the situation. "Hey, nice outfits. Is this Comic-con weekend? I love Comic-con. Which character are you?" She looked up to meet the eyes of the imposing Amazon. The woman looked at Morgan with an expression of cold indifference.

For one moment, Morgan felt like she was looking into a mirror. She recognised the texture and the fire of that hair. *How strange.* The two women couldn't be more different. Morgan was little and she rarely raised her voice. She had nothing in common with the statuesque, irreverent and athletic woman in front of her. The goddess-like beauty was like a free-spirited, untameable stallion: intimidating, unapologetic and stunning, all strength and power. The security detail stared with large eyes. She was sexy, sensual, and they wanted her despite her evident despise and disdain. For a moment, Morgan wished she was her. The woman transpired self-worth; she was the portrait of complete self-possession.

I bet you aren't fooled by the charms of good-looking men, she thought as she turned to face Gabriel.

"Morgan," Gabriel said, "these are my cousins—Bastian and Sky."

In a heartbeat, Morgan saw him turn from a broken, desperate man to the perfectly charming and composed gentleman she knew. A mask that no longer fooled her. Not even his glow could hide the red and blue marks left on his face by Sky's elbow. However, he smiled briefly at Morgan and turned back to his companions.

"Sky, walk with me to Central Park," said Bastian, pulling Sky by the arm away from the group. The two odd caped figures walked away, and as they left Bastian turned his head to Gabriel, smiled and blinked both eyes reassuringly.

NAUGHTY

"Are you going to tell me what happened?" Morgan asked coldly.

Gabriel looked at the security staff and murmured, "Not now, we're late. You look lovely," he said with authentic, unguarded admiration.

She decided not to acknowledge or react to the compliment.

He opened the door to the car and extended his hand to help her get in. She again ignored his gesture and got into the car by herself. He sat next to her quietly for a few minutes. Her hands were trembling. She tucked them underneath her legs, closed her eyes and took a few deep breaths.

"You have nothing to worry about. I have my best team on the ground. We won't let anything happen to you."

Morgan nodded. She was grateful for his reassurance and encouragement. After all, he had been completely against this activity in the first place. She turned to face him and to look at his jaw. To her surprise, she struggled to find any bruising. A slight yellowish bruise replaced the pronounced blotches of blue and red that had been on his face minutes before.

"Your cousin is a bit intense, isn't she?" she said, raising one eyebrow and offering a tiny glimpse of a smile.

He chuckled and sighed.

"She has a lot of responsibility on her plate, but she has the heart of a lion and wears her authority with grace."

Morgan responded with a quizzing, sceptical gaze.

"Most of the time," he allowed, amused with her expression.

"Perhaps no one will attend the event today. The news probably scared them off." As she spoke she realised for the first time that her actions were putting more than just her life at risk.

"The attack at the Met is not public knowledge. The CIA is controlling the flow of information as this is part of a broader investigation."

She was barely listening to what he said. She felt her jaw falling open and eyes widening with absolute terror. She feared for the safety of her audience of parents and girls.

"Morgan, listen to me," he said firmly and reassuringly, resting his hand on her arm, "It's safe. We've secured the area. There's no danger." His words reached deep into her soul and her body relaxed, hit by a wave of well-being that rippled from his touch.

She shook her head, fighting the bliss. "What broader investigation?"

"Listen, Morgan. For all it's worth, I give you my word that I'll brief you in detail after this event finishes. Right now you have an eager audience waiting for you. Okay?"

She nodded.

"We won't let anything happen to you or your fans." He left the limo and went around the car to open her door.

"Gabriel," she said, looking up to meet his eyes. "Thank you for saving my life." She was expecting a smile. Instead, she got an intense frown.

He shook his head and replied, "It was my fault. Look!" He pointed to the sea of people sitting in the grass at the oval's lawn. She swept her gaze over the scene as they made their way towards the stage.

Entire families gathered around picnic baskets. Playful tween girls and some boys raced around the fifty-five acres of green pasture. A group of girls were on the stage performing "Naughty," a song from *Matilda the Musical.* Black and brown figures lined the periphery of the oval. Some looked like standard security guards while others were enormous, caped men. The conspicuous cloaked giants checked the bags of anyone coming into the great lawn. Their contagious smiles balanced their intimidating physiques.

Morgan walked onstage, and the crowd applauded with delight. Gabriel was there, just behind her. Gabriel's cousins stood at each side of the platform. They scanned the audience with their eyes. Morgan waved at the crowd with a smile and transformed into her public persona—the activist and leader that they had all come to watch. For a brief second, she turned to look at Gabriel, and the events of the last few days flashed through her mind. She decided to go off script and speak from her heart. *These girls don't need perfect, sanitised role models; they deserve sincerity and authenticity.* She walked to the microphone, took a deep breath and repeated some of Matilda's lyrics.

"Cause if you're little, you can do a lot; you mustn't let a little thing like 'little' stop you. Nobody but me is gonna change my story. Sometimes you have to be a little bit naughty."

Gabriel had to take a deep breath at the sight of Sky standing beside the stage. She was watching the crowd, mostly composed of women and girls. With his mind's eye he summoned her attention, and as her eyes met his gaze, he bowed with gratitude. If the fire in her eyes could kill, he'd be long gone; dead, fulminated where he stood, reduced to a pile of scorching ashes by the thunder in her gaze.

The picnic blankets spread around the pasture created a colourful patchwork quilt across the oval. Everyone sat, eating their snacks and enjoying a mild autumn afternoon tempered by the gold blooms of the sun.

"Let's play a game," Morgan spoke to the thousands of smiling faces in the crowd. "Stand up if, today, someone has called you pretty, cute, handsome or beautiful."

About half of the girls in the audience stood up with wide, bright smiles. Some women joined them.

"Okay. Please stay standing. Now stand up if, today, someone you know has made an observation about what you are wearing, the shape or size of your body, or about your hair." Most of the women and girls in the audience were now standing.

"All right. Please stay standing. Now stand up if, today, you've listened or read someone's comment about a woman's looks, either in person or the media." Almost everyone was on their feet.

"Please have a look around you and pause to reflect on the crystal clear message we give to our kids and each other about what we value most. And please, no guilt. As you can see, we are all in this together. We all share the same toxic culture.

"Now only stay standing if someone today has complimented you on your achievements; on how much you have learned; how far you have walked or run; how strong your body is; on the positive impact you've had in the world.

"Stay standing if, today, someone asked you about the books you've read, the meals you cooked or your preferred disciplines at school.

"Stay standing if someone asked you for your opinion about a movie, book or the news.

"Stay standing if, today, someone celebrated the progress you made on something you are working hard to achieve."

Most of the people, maybe around seventy percent of the thousands of people in the audience slowly sat down in a disheartened, introspective silence.

"Everyone, please have a seat. Thank you."

Morgan reached for her purse laying on the floor next to the microphone. She took out a book, opening on a page marked with a crescent moon divider. She read, "'Taught from infancy that beauty is woman's sceptre, the mind shapes itself to the body, and roaming round its gilt cage, only seeks to adorn its prison.'

"This is an old quote from a book written in 1792 by Mary Wollstonecraft; I would like to invite some of you to tell me what this quote means. Raise your hands." Morgan scanned the audience and pointed to two girls who had quickly stood up with their hands up. "Come up girls," Morgan repeated the passage as the girls made their way to the stage.

An African American girl in her teens approached the microphone. She carried herself with confidence, raising her head and clearing her voice before she spoke. "It means girls are taught from childhood that their value comes from their looks."

"Yeah, it's all about the makeup and the shoes and the dresses. Always trying to look prettier than others." The youngest girl stood on her tiptoes trying to reach the microphone.

"Why is this a prison?" Morgan asked, lowering the mic. "And please tell us your names."

"My name is Anita," the eldest said, adjusting the retro frames of her eyeglasses. She wore a t-shirt portraying the face of Ada Lovelace four times. The print borrowed Andy Warhol's pop art colours and style.

Morgan smiled, predicting a clever answer.

"Girls become really unhappy because they can't look like the women in the magazines. That's all they think about. They starve themselves and feel ashamed of their bodies."

The youngest approached the mic and spoke with a slight lisp. "Yeah, my mum told me they're fake. Those girls in *Vogue*, I mean. That the people use the computer to make the photos prettier. Like, it's all about selling stuff: creams and makeup, and sparkling nail polish; it's very bad for the fish in the sea. Like, I do like the nail polish, though, but my mum doesn't let me. Dad says she hugs trees or something," she giggled. "I like trees too, but I also like—"

The audience laughed at the energetic youngster. She played with her dark braid as her pitch increased with her excitement.

"What's your name?"

"Jacinta Melody Jackson, but, you can call me Jax." She smiled widely, revealing a missing front tooth. A second later, she frowned, placed her hand in front of her mouth and squeezed her lips.

"Tell me, Jax, you are clearly a young lady full of girl power; how do you feel about your body?"

"It's strong and healthy. I go to classes—ballet and gymnastics. I'm one of the best in my class."

"Wow, that's brilliant. You look healthy, flexible and strong. But, tell me: do you sometimes have bad days?"

"My mum told me we need to love our bodies."

"I think your mum is right, but we all have bad days, don't we?"

Jax scanned the audience with her eyes. She was met by the waving hand of a tall woman, who nodded at Jax, encouraging her to respond.

"Yeah, I mean, sometimes it's hard. I'm missing my tooth, and I have to wear glasses at school, and my hair is curly, and I want it straight like my friend Nat. Nat is so pretty."

"Thank you for sharing, Jax."

"I wish I had better genes."

"You know, your genes make you unique."

"Sure, but, like, I don't want curly hair, and my mum doesn't let me straighten it. And I want to be a ballerina, but I'm probably going to be too tall, like my mum. And I suck at maths, like, you know?" Her eyes rolled, and her eyebrows tensed.

"Genes control a tiny portion of your natural ability. There are plenty of tall ballerinas, and to be good at maths all you have to do is believe in yourself, work hard and never ever give up trying. Genes are not destiny. They may define some of your physical features and give you a tiny head start on some things, but your lifestyle, your beliefs, and your hard work are much more important. Don't be a slave to your genes Jax."

Gabriel felt the sting of Morgan's words. He looked at Sky, who turned her attention to Morgan, raising one eyebrow.

"I know I shouldn't feel this way. I'm sorry." The girl was morose.

"You feel what you feel. No one but you can legislate your feelings. Give me a hug." Morgan extended her arms and embraced both girls. "Thank you both for your contributions." She spoke a few more words to each of them away from the mic and the girls left the stage smiling.

Morgan turned her head to face Gabriel. She vacillated, hugging her book, taking a deep breath and closing her eyes for a moment. Then, she faced the audience and spoke: "For many years, I've been reminding the women in the community that they are role models. That they should model self-esteem; that they should stop commenting on other women's appearances and throw the beauty mags in the trash. As I do, I must admit that I sometimes feel like a fraud, because on occasions I'm paralysed by a tremendous lack of physical self-worth. So today, I want to acknowledge that we are all works in progress. I want you to know that sometimes it's important to share, to look the monster in the face, to acknowledge its existence. Hiding what we are and projecting what we should be doesn't always keep the monster at bay.

"Together, we are stronger. We work to overcome our upbringings; to outgrow the damaging fairy tales of our youth; to ignore the pressure from entire industries whose profits rely on our self-hate.

"And when you see the monster, remember to look it in the eyes and tell it that every second you lose worrying about your looks is a second you are not learning; it is a second you are not experiencing the world; it is a second you are not contributing to your communities in a positive way.

"When you don't go to the park or to the beach because you are ashamed of how you look, remember the girls and boys that live in war-torn countries that are not allowed the joys of outdoors fun.

"In moments where you focus on your appearance, remember the girls that are kidnapped from their schools in countries where women are denied an education.

"Every moment you are unhappy with your shape or size, remember those who are paralysed, unable to walk, jump, or dance.

"When you starve yourself to reach unattainable standards of beauty artificially constructed by businesses, you are weakening your body and your mind. You are wasting away the precious moments you have and you are giving up your power.

"The obsession with beauty is death by a thousand cuts. Every micro decision is guided by meaningless worry that limits your future, your opportunities and your ability to experience the joys of pleasure.

"Because when you kiss your first boy or girl, you don't want to be so caught up in your lack of self-worth that you forget to enjoy the kiss, that you forget that you deserve the pleasure of that moment. You don't want to be so caught up in your lack of self-worth that you become an object of his or her desire, a grateful unworthy slave to his or her attention.

"Who you are has little to do with how you look. You are what you know, what you can do, the impact you have delivered, and the collection of experiences in your meaningful life.

"More than ever, this world needs your intellect, your cleverness, your resourcefulness, and your passion for making the world a better place for those who are less privileged than you.

"More than ever, this planet needs your kindness and your generosity. It needs those who reject the 'I' and celebrate the 'we'. Those who reject hate, violence, and destruction for the sake of power and financial gain.

"You are the most powerful army in the world; you are the future of this planet. You cannot, you will not spend one more minute of your time looking in a mirror wishing you looked different. And if and when you do, you will have compassion and love for the monster; the victim in the mirror, the helpless slave to upbringing, culture and media. You will be kind to her, and then you will be brave, you will reject the victim, and become the fearless hero this world deserves. And you will reject it again and again and again until the voice inside your head that stands between you and your bright future can no longer be heard.

"Sometimes I need to remind myself that I'm not my reflection in someone's eyes. That what is important; what is truly essential; what really matters about me is invisible to the eye.

"In those days I have to remind myself to live, to love, to laugh, to learn, and to lead.

"In those days remind yourself to live, to love, to laugh, to learn, and to lead."

The audience cheered; mothers and daughters hugged each other with emotion. A man with a young girl on his shoulders held up the flag of Rosie the Riveter and waved it in the air.

Gabriel struggled to take his eyes off Morgan. Her grace, her softness, and her strength all came back. Her magic was back—the ability to move, inspire, educate, and lead people into action. She didn't need to speak loudly because her voice came straight from her heart and her soul. Her eyes sparkled as she talked, and her face was full of expression and empathy. This was the woman who had moved him to tears three years ago when he had first seen her speak on TV. Morgan was a light worker, and on that day, he had promised himself to protect her and support her.

As he scanned the audience, looking for danger, all he could see were the happy faces of girls and parents immersed in her words. They adored her. Even the mighty Sky had fallen under her spell. His cousin's eyes were locked on Morgan, her stance more relaxed, and her face had dropped the unyielding shield it usually wore. He looked at his cousin's face and knew Morgan had won her allegiance. He allowed himself a moment of happiness; he couldn't have wished for a bigger blessing.

Morgan continued to speak passionately, sharing stories of young girls that were driving positive change in the world through their innovation, leadership, and activism. She talked about the challenges that girls faced in developing nations and how, together, they could make a difference.

The audience connected with her passion and candour, clapping enthusiastically as Morgan finished her speech.

"Cause if you're little, you can do a lot; you mustn't let a little thing like 'little' stop you. Nobody but me is gonna change my story. Sometimes you have to be a little bit naughty."

A big line of parents and girls formed to speak to her. Morgan sat on the stage to be closer to them. She answered questions and posed for photos with her audience.

Suddenly, a big man broke the line and rushed in Morgan's direction. He moved decisively as he reached for something in the pocket of his jacket. Morgan jumped, stood up, and walked backwards as he moved forwards. The crowd was surprised by Morgan's reaction; she had dropped their gifts and the book she was signing in her rush to escape.

Some girls screamed, reacting to her panic. Parents pulled the girls away as they searched for the cause of Morgan's anxiety. Sky and Bastian raced in from opposite sides of the stage towards the crowd as Gabriel ran to reach Morgan.

ESCAPE

One Hundred and Forty-Four Years Ago - 1870

Ahe'ey

Forbidden Obsession

The crown of the champion of Ahe'ey adorned Angha's blonde hair as he was carried out of the Games arena on the shoulders of several male and female Yi'ingo warriors. They celebrated his victory as he had, once again, won the Summer Solstice Games, defeating his challengers, Amalia and Michael, the rulers of Ahe'ey, in multiple disciplines. The party at Yi'ingo lasted all night.

Angha did not spend much time thinking about his future, but he hoped to succeed his older sister Amalia, the queen, as leader of the Yi'ingo. Amalia and her husband, Michael, had recently ascended to become rulers of all Ahe'ey. The new responsibilities left Amalia little time to focus on the Yi'ingo warriors.

Angha was a solid military leader: forceful, full of charisma and dominant by nature. The Yi'ingo was a virile young stud, often praised for his strength, physical achievements and muscular body. The most beautiful women in the land warmed Angha's bed, a fact that gave him great pleasure and pride. And yet, he kept a dark passion bottled up—a secret never shared, a wish never expressed.

At dawn, Angha was still drunk and high on the rush of adrenaline that he got from winning the Games. He headed for the sauna at the Ange'el's bathhouse.

"You missed a great party, Sathian," Angha roared as he entered the bathhouse to find Sathian in the pool.

"Congratulations on your victory, cousin. I'm sorry I missed the celebrations. I would rather not enjoy the company of a bunch of sweaty, drunken fools." Sathian's smile was irreverent.

"I missed your witty sense of humour. There was no one around to deliver the cutting remarks and the sarcastic observations that you unleash so effectively."

Sathian left the pool and wrapped a towel around his waist. "I might as well throw pearls at pigs," he laughed.

"One day, someone will take you seriously and rearrange that pretty face of yours, you arrogant fool." Angha grabbed Sathian's long dark hair and neck and gave him a gentle shove. Angha's muscular arm was almost as wide as Sathian's head.

"Let me go, you bull," Sathian attempted to release himself from the stronghold of his cousin. He gritted his teeth, smiled and said, "One can only be offended if one has the intellect to understand the offence. Nature compensated the heaviness of the Yi'ingo's muscles by reducing the size of their brains."

They both laughed. The Yi'ingo found Sathian's humour entertaining, and the Ange'el was always ready to oblige. Angha looked into Sathian's eyes, smelled his skin, and felt a rush of desire shoot through his entire body. He pushed Sathian away from him abruptly and aggressively.

Sathian continued, motivated by his cousin's initial laughter. "Case in point: it seems you are not able to control your animalistic urges, you bull."

Angha's lust and shame left him vulnerable and exposed. "Shut your mouth." Angha grabbed Sathian by the neck and pushed him against the wall.

His cousin laughed and replied playfully.

"Violent . . . check. Dominant . . . check. Predatory . . . check. Unable to control deviant sexual urges . . . check, check, check! Perhaps I will write a case study."

Angha's face was red, his muscles tense, and his hand ready to snap the Ange'el's neck in half. Sathian's expression changed from excitement to fear. Angha took a deep breath. "I'm no animal, Sathian. I'm no bull," he whispered.

Sathian looked surprised and overwhelmed by his cousin's reaction. Angha realised that Sathian's urge to entertain and to showcase his cleverness had led him to make a claim that the Ange'el did not believe in when he first unleashed it. But the truth was out, and there was no turning back.

On that day, Angha attempted to prove to himself that he was no animal, that he was no bull, but a shadow had been cast forever over his relationship with his cousin. Sathian's presence was now a constant reminder of his weakness and shame.

Angha could never decide if his obsession with Sathian had flourished from lust or out of love. All he knew was that his shame was as overwhelming as his addiction to his cousin. Sathian was the most beautiful creature Angha had ever seen. The royal Ange'el had androgynous features that danced the tightrope between male and female energies. He was joyful. There was always a smile on his face and a spark in his emerald eyes.

Young Sathian was flirtatious, titillating, quick-witted, and brilliant. He left a trail of broken hearts across the land as he teased and taunted his victims with his beauty and charm. Both women and men succumbed to his joie de vivre and panache as he was an untypical Ange'el that carried the sunshine in his smile and in his eyes.

Angha knew that his beloved cousin was mostly unaware of the wreckage he caused, as it had been unintentional. Sathian had been an object of adoration from the day he was born. That was all he knew. His nature was to connect, to please, and to seduce. Armed with intelligence and beauty, he was unstoppable.

Immature and insecure, Angha decided to bury any possible doubt anyone could have about his desires by pursuing a romantic relationship with Gaia, the only unwed pure-blooded royal of their generation and Sathian's sweetheart. In a society that relied on the propagation of their pure genes to survive, being queer was a sin worse than murder.

As years passed, his relationship with Sathian deteriorated. Angha's revenge was calculated and Machiavellian as he attempted to disconnect his identity from the image of the animal that Sathian had planted in his mind. He worked to deny the Ange'el everything he most cherished—his woman, his access to knowledge, his status in society, and, above it all, the praise and the love of his Yi'ingo cousin.

Royal Family Tree

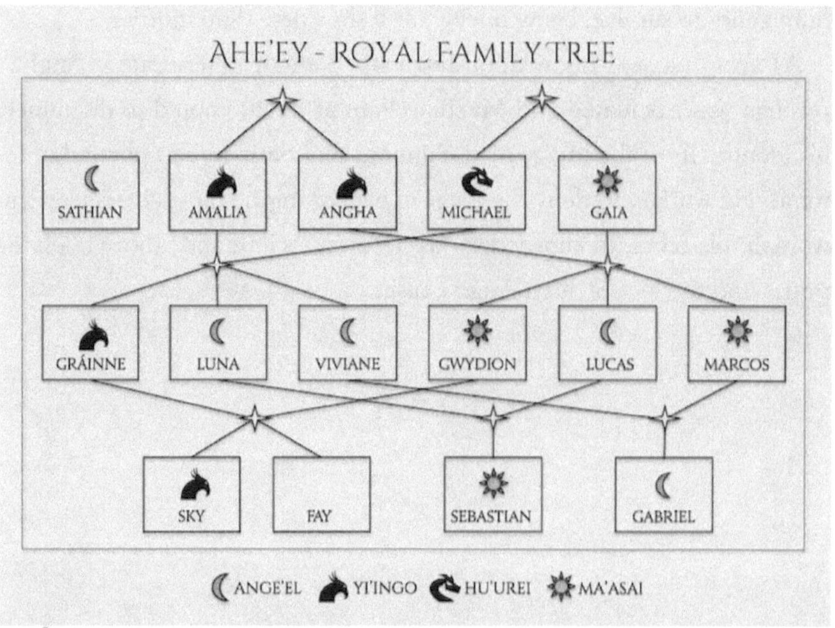

THE ROSE

Gaia was Ahe'ey's most cherished maiden. The last unwed and childless royal lady, a fact she was not allowed to forget for one single moment. Her older brother, Michael, had married Amalia as soon as he entered manhood. They always knew they were destined for each other. The responsibilities set upon them fit them well. They were born to, one day, rule the people of Ahe'ey, and they wore the burden of responsibility with great pride, joy and dedication. The blood of the royal family of Ahe'ey had to be preserved, and with only five royal descendants left, they had little time to lose. They started a family as soon as their young bodies had developed fully.

Gaia was left with the difficult task of selecting one of the two final royal suitors—Sathian or Angha, Amalia's younger brother. Gaia was madly in love with the Ange'el, but a relationship between a nature-loving Ma'asai and a scholarly Ange'el could be quite challenging at times.

Gaia and Sathian had been an item since childhood. While their older cousin, Angha, spent his days learning to fight and hunt, they preferred to occupy their time learning about the history of the world, science, nature, art, and anything else that piqued their intellectual curiosity and creativity.

Gaia and Sathian shared a deep passion for art. They spent many days during their teen years working with the Hu'urei to design and build the statues of the Ange'el garden. They considered each detail, from the tip of the toes of the fairies to the jawline of the female warriors.

As Sathian reached adulthood, he became the guardian of the Ange'el ancient knowledge repository. He was highly intellectual, had a tendency to live inside his head, and loved to debate ethics and philosophy with his students. To Gaia's exasperation, the Ange'el spent his time recovering information from the thousands of small quartz crystals stored in the library of the Sacred House. He revelled as he discovered the mysteries of his ancestors and would spend entire days locked in the library away from everything and everyone.

Gaia looked at her reflection on the silver panel of the library.

"Sathian, I'm a white rose," said the blonde Ma'asai beauty, attempting to conquer the attention of the Ange'el, who sat in front of his desk decoding the secrets of one of the many crystals stored in the library.

"Yes, my flower," he replied without taking his emerald eyes away from the translucent surface that displayed the secrets of the crystals.

She wrapped her arms around his neck and glued her plump rosy cheek to his sharp sculpted cheekbone. His face was softer than hers, clean shaven and scented with a citrusy oil. She moistened her lips with her tongue and kissed it, sliding the tip of her nose to caress his neck.

"A Ma'asai rose requires plenty of light from the sun to bloom." She sat on his lap and attempted to kiss his lips. She smiled as he reached to touch her long hair, but the joy in her eyes vanished quickly as he softly gathered her golden waves in one hand to allow him to view the screen behind her. "A rose needs care, attention and passion from her sun king." Annoyed by his lack of interest, she placed her hands on his face and turned his head to face her. Her frustration escalated quickly when he laughed at her pouty lips and displeased eyes.

"Those who play with fire get burned. Ange'el moonlight does not scorch or sizzle; it nurtures, illuminates, and magnifies your qualities." She rolled her eyes as he continued talking. "Why would you want to be a rose when you can be a ginger root?"

"An ugly and wrinkly ginger root? Is that how you see me?" She grabbed his face and squeezed it with her fingers.

"A plant that detests excesses: sunlight, water, or even wind. It thrives in rich soil, full of nutrients; a root that provides tremendous health benefits to those who consume it." He nibbled on her neck.

"I'm not a root; I'm an exquisite flower—beautiful, fragile and in need of your sunshine. Don't you love me?"

"The flower of the ginger is superb and regal, but if we focus on nurturing the ginger plant to bloom we are unable to harvest its root. Enjoying the exquisite beauty of the plant will prevent us from unlocking its true potential—the nutrients secretly stored beyond the reach of the sun. Why care about trivial matters such as external beauty? What matters lies beneath the surface. What a waste! She is much more beautiful on the inside where she has so much more to give to the world." He kissed her.

"Stop it! Don't you love me?"

"I love you." He adjusted his long hair and raised his right eyebrow. "Do you love me?"

"Look at you, admonishing me and calling me shallow when you are the vainest creature in Ahe'ey."

"What can I do but to accept my stunning body as much as I acknowledge my wisdom and intelligence?" he grinned.

"Perhaps I'll marry Angha and leave you to focus on the splendour of your navel. You can spend your life buried in the library with your crystals."

He laughed, dismissing her threat.

"Your mocking crushes me," said the Ma'asai in tears.

"What do you want from me, Gaia? I love you; you know I do." He lifted her by the waist, and she wrapped her legs around his body.

"Do you mean it, or are you with me because I'm the last of the royal women? Is it me or my blood you seek to marry?"

"I'll marry you and your royal blood. You are my equal and we are meant for each other."

"I can marry Angha and leave you to your other love: feeding your mind with knowledge."

"You won't because you are desperately in love with me." He teased her with his stunning smile. "If you did marry him . . . Amalia and Michael won't allow my seed to be wasted and . . . I would be forced to marry a mixed-breed high-ranking woman." He put her down and lowered his head, fidgeting with his silver and quartz ring. The ring was her biggest competitor—the key that unlocked the door of the library— that made him the guardian of the Ahe'ey ancient knowledge repository.

"They would take away some of your royal privileges. You'd be denied access to the library," she said.

He nodded. "They claim my love and empathy towards an impure wife and children would be in direct conflict with my duties. A stupid, outdated rule. There are at least three dozen impure, bastard children born from my seed in this land. The elders demand I share my genes and expect me to be heartless and cold towards those who I bring to life and their mothers. I won't. I care for all creatures—pure or impure— regardless of marriage status."

"Do you love them? The others?" She touched his ring. "Is this why you say you love me?" Her eyes watered, and her voice quivered with insecurity.

"I love you, Gaia. You know I do. I love you more than anyone else," he murmured, sounding exasperated.

"More than your crystals? If you had to choose between this library and me, what would be your choice?" His right hand moved to cover the ring on his left index finger. A moment of deafening silence, and she felt her insides collapse.

"You and I, our blood, and this library are one. We need each other, and we belong to each other. There is no other way. Until I uncover the mysteries of our genes, the secrets hidden within those crystals, we will continue to be slaves to our blood, rulers and beneficiaries of an unfair civilisation. A system that is completely against the values of our ancient foremothers and forefathers. Our blood should not dictate who rules this land or whom we marry."

"Are you unhappy with your one and only marriage choice?"

"Gaia. We are a dying species. My work is critical to our survival."

"If you reveal the secrets within our blood you won't need to marry me."

He reached to kiss her, but she turned and ran to the door in tears.

Sathian tickled all Gaia's senses and pleased her with fun, intellect and mischief, but he did not, could not, give her what she craved. Gaia only wished that he was as obsessed with her as she was with him, something that was not in his nature. Gaia knew Sathian loved her more than he loved any other living being (except himself). He loved her as much as he could, as much as his wandering and inquisitive mind would allow him to focus on the trivial matters of the heart.

Sathian's self-confidence and idealism made him a pleasurable and interesting companion to Gaia, but he was independent, easily bored, and had the propensity to get side-tracked and distracted by anything that tickled his curious and hungry mind. When it came to love, he was logical. When it came to lovemaking, he was fun and exciting, but he lacked the passion that would ultimately give the object of his affection the certainty that her place was secured in his heart—a fact that pushed Gaia into the arms of Angha.

REVENGE

Two Years Later: 1872 - Ahe'ey

Angha had never paid much attention to Gaia. All he had cared about in the past was demonstrating his physical mastery by winning the Games. His newly found interest in his Ma'asai cousin was fuelled by his urge to keep his deep dark secret safe.

It was easy for Angha to woo the royal Ma'asai maiden away from Sathian. He knew them both well and was aware of the Ange'el's flaws. Angha fully exploited Sathian's lack of skill to make his lover feel significant. The Yi'ingo showered Gaia with gifts, professed his undying love for her ardently and emotionally, and demonstrated his desire in a somewhat predatory way that excited her as much as it terrified her. Starved for attention, Gaia was an easy prey to Angha's hunting activities. Soon, they were engaged, a move that had catastrophic consequences for the Ange'el.

"Why are you doing this to me? You don't love her. I know you don't love her." Sathian's grief-stricken eyes had sunk into his skull.

"What do you know about love? You're too distracted by your own reflection to pay attention to anyone else."

"Is that it? You resent me for not loving you the way you—"

Angha's face flushed, and his jaw clenched so hard that his face deformed under pressure. "Don't flatter yourself, Sathian."

"I love her. You can't . . . can't take her away from me. She's everything to me," Sathian begged. A thin layer of water coated his eyes, and his lips dragged into the sulking pout of a child.

"Everything? Why are you here, Sathian? Why have you come to Yi'ingo after such a long time? For Gaia?" Angha's face was cold. He no longer succumbed to the royal honey of his Ange'el cousin.

"I'll lose everything. They'll deny me access to the library, to our secrets. How can you do this to me? She's nothing to you. You have nothing to lose if you marry someone else."

The Ange'el walked towards Angha and touched his arm. For a moment, Angha felt compassion for the younger man as he watched the tears flood his eyes. Sathian smiled, unleashing all his charm. His watery eyes sparkled, touched by the sunlight. Angha's right hand grazed his cousin's lips. Moving closer, he grabbed Sathian's neck and licked the tears that rolled down his face.

The Ange'el froze; he seemed to be paralysed by a mix of fear, surprise and confusion. He did not move or bat an eyelash, and yet Angha saw it: he saw the disgust in Sathian's eyes, he saw his deviance reflected in his cousin's gaze.

The Ange'el started playing with his silver-and-quartz ring, rotating it nervously with his fingers. Angha placed his right hand over his cousin's hands and squeezed it using the full power of his grip. He felt the warm blood of the Ange'el drip over his hand as the crystal in the ring pierced Sathian's fingers. One second later, Angha pushed Sathian away so hard that the Ange'el fell backwards to the floor.

"Gaia chose the better man. The consequences of her actions are not my concern."

"We were once inseparable. What have I done to deserve this?" Sathian, still on the floor, sucked the blood from his fingers, staining his bottom lip with the deep crimson of his royal blood. Sathian struggled to control his lust.

"You moon creatures need to learn you can't have it all. You taunt us with your mind tricks and your beauty. You think every living being is beneath you and at your feet, ready to love you and to serve you blindly."

"That's not true!"

"You tease us, charm us, make us lust for you. We submit to the lascivious scent of your skin and the sorcery in your eyes. We're slaves. You change us, deprave us, infect our free will."

"*I was born this way!*"

"We become obsessive, forever unsatisfied, craving your touch, your gaze, your body. A curse, a tortuous addiction that defies the laws of nature."

"I've done nothing but love you and be your friend."

"You've done nothing but torture me, you spoiled creature."

"Look who's talking."

"For the first time in your life, you'll be denied everything that is most important to you. I'll break your heart and give you a taste of your own poison. One day you may become powerful enough to seduce me and to conquer her, but that day is not today. Today she's mine."

"She doesn't belong to anyone."

Angha released a hostile laugh, reacting to the irony of his cousin's words. "That is your doom Ange'el." The Yi'ingo relished in Sathian's failure to understand that what Gaia most desired was to be, fully and completely, his.

Present Day – 24 November 2014

New York

Morgan ran towards the back of the stage as she saw Sky and Bastian grab the large man by the arms and lift him up. Then she felt Gabriel's arms envelope her as he placed his body between her and the audience.

Several security guards raced to the stage. Parents embraced their children, trying to make sense of the events that were unfolding. Morgan's ears burned with the panicked screams of the kids. Feelings of guilt, worry and regret overwhelmed her mind and body.

The Ma'asai men, towering above everyone else, scanned the crowd for further signs of danger as Gabriel's cousins immobilised the attacker on the grassy ground.

Morgan's body trembled with the adrenaline of the moment. She felt him place his right hand behind her head, caressing her hair and gently pulling her face towards his chest. His lips almost touched her ear as he murmured, "You're safe Morgan; everyone is safe."

"How . . . how do you know?" She struggled to speak as her teeth chattered uncontrollably.

Bastian approached them, "Just a journalist. All good."

"Can you please ask James to address the audience? He'll know what to say."

"Who's James?"

Morgan pointed towards James and Bastian nodded, heading towards the meek man in the brown suit hiding behind the closest tree.

She was still in shock, frozen where she stood, engulfed by the sanctuary of his heavenly body. Without saying a word he picked her up and carried her promptly to the car. She hid her face on his neck. All she could feel was shame. Shame she'd put her community and her staff at risk. Shame she'd panicked. So much shame.

Gabriel's presence acted like a big magnifying glass. Morgan didn't want him to experience her in this way: so vulnerable, lost, and flawed. When they reached the car, he didn't let go of her. She sat beside him, his arms around her as she rested her head on his shoulder, her nose on his neck. She welcomed the unexpected comfort and familiarity of his body as the sea welcomes the light of the full moon—the tide longing to return to wild heights. The ecstasy of a reencounter that never gets old.

He gently whispered into her ear, "Shhh, you were amazing. I'm so proud of you for your bravery and leadership."

Morgan grabbed his tunic near his chest and couldn't control her tears anymore. He had betrayed her confidence; he was not to be trusted, and yet she desired him. Her life was at risk; she was in a foreign country, and this man was able to bring down all the barriers she'd spent years creating to defend herself from heartache. Morgan didn't suffer fools; she didn't let men in easily, but all she wanted right now was to lose herself in his arms and in his eyes. To trust him, to love him, and to allow him to take care of her. Just those words, "take care of her," were so foreign and dangerous. A bad habit that had been set aside, in the same way she'd set aside sugar or processed foods.

He placed his hand on her face, pressed his lips against her forehead, and then whispered, "Sleep." His index finger touched the space between her eyes.

She felt an intense wave of well-being run through her body every time he touched her. She desperately didn't want him to be in control. She didn't want to sleep.

So she pulled back, looked into his eyes, placed her hand on the back of his neck, and kissed him. His lips were as soft as they looked and tasted unexpectedly sweet. At first, he resisted her, gasping and pulling his face away. His clear eyes widened, pupils dilated and lips parted. His marble face, touched by fire, looked surprised and disoriented as he drew in a ragged breath. She kissed him again, this time fully committing to her desire, and devoured his wavering lips. He closed his eyes as he succumbed to her passion, kissing her back and holding her face and hair in his hands.

For the first time, she experienced him fully out of balance, attempting and failing to control his impulses. The acceleration of his breath had a surprisingly reassuring effect on her. The controlling Prince Charming was hopelessly lost in his desire for her. When he pulled back, they were in front of the hotel. For one moment, he hid his face between her curls, in the nape of her neck.

The car stopped, and Carl opened the back door. Gabriel exited the car and extended his hand to Morgan. She shuddered as she watched the line of people standing at the front entrance of the hotel, waiting for a taxi. She struggled to control her panic. Gabriel held her hand and squeezed it, not letting it go. He helped her get out of the car.

"It's safe; try to relax a little."

They made their way to her suite, and he led her to her bedroom. She sat on the bed, and he kneeled in front of her to remove her shoes. His fingers lightly grazed her toes, melting her worries away.

"Please lie down," he said as he covered her with a blanket and sat beside her. His gracious fingers gently stroked her hand. He looked at her softly, repositioning her hair away from her face. She bit her lip and held her breath, anticipating his next move. She desired the benign energy that emanated from his body. She felt an urge to consume it, to devour it.

Unexpectedly, he closed his eyes and waved his hands over her body, palms towards her, hovering above her from head to toes. Like magic, the stress flowed out of her body, replaced by waves of well-being and peace. Confused and craving his touch, she fought to stay awake and in control.

"No," she murmured.

He opened his eyes, surprised at her response.

"Sleep," he whispered. His index finger skimmed her forehead once again, and she felt her worries drain out of her mind.

"No," she sat back up, pushing his hand away from her.

"I'm sorry Morgan. I didn't mean to . . . . You have a strong mind. I meant no harm. I'll be outside."

He stood up, but she held his hand and pulled him towards her. She put her hands on his face and kissed him, succumbing to the intensity of her desire for him.

He gasped. "Morgan, I . . . I don't want to take advantage. You're in shock. This isn't a good id—"

She didn't let him finish. He was the one who was vulnerable as she kissed him and pulled him to her by his tunic.

"Don't treat me like a child."

"Morgan, I'm not free to love . . . " he whispered, "who I—"

She kissed him again as her hand caressed his finely sculpted torso under his tunic. She felt his desire course through his body, and he was hers. His hands grabbed at her waist, pulling her closer.

His glow, his eyes, his hands, his lips, his neck. How he embraced her and loved her and lit her up from the inside. How he was all man— strong, decisive, and full of desire—his hands on her hips, his hand on her thighs. How he was all angel, predicting her needs, fulfilling her fully with generosity and devotion. How he was all human as he appeared as overwhelmed with emotion and vulnerability as she was. Both engulfed by the strength of their connection. His glow, that glow, his healing touch.

What is this? Am I dreaming? she thought before the act of desire stopped any further reasoning.

Consequences

Gabriel stood outside on the balcony. His naked body was freezing, but his mind was elsewhere. He felt Viviane's calling, and he struggled to fight it and to regain control over his will. He used the cold chill of the night to jolt his nervous system and to defy his desire to surrender. *I'm sorry Lady.*

To all other creatures, his mother's mind was impossible to resist. Once summoned, they quickly made their way to her presence, oblivious of the powerful force that controlled them. The queen possessed all the gifts of the royal Ange'el and, at 112 years old, she had attained the experience to master each one of them. She played every string of her instrument with unmatched precision and mastery. She fully controlled all creatures but one.

Gabriel shared the powerful pure Ange'el blood that ran through her veins. Her grip on him had slowly declined as his command over his capabilities matured. He didn't resent his mother's power, as it was never exploited or squandered. The skills of the Ange'el came from their responsibility and respect for all living things. Their gifts were only fully activated when aligned to the values encoded in their genes.

Gabriel fought to retain control over his body and mind. He punched through the glass table, committing his full strength to the task, and broke it in half. He felt each tear of his skin, watching as his enhanced blood flowed down his arm and stained the stone pavement. The pain coming from his bloodied knuckles and the wounds on his arm was intense and broke through the shroud of her call. *Please, Lady. Stop.*

He had broken the rules, and there would be consequences for him and for the people he loved. He wasn't a victim; he had dreamed of this night for a very long time. As his desire and affection for Morgan intensified, he had carefully considered the repercussions of his actions. Things had precipitated quickly and unexpectedly, but he welcomed the outcome as he couldn't wish for a bigger blessing than to be the object of her affection. *Or was it just her lust? It doesn't matter.* He had been hers for a long time, and now there was a possibility that one day she would be his. He would honour their connection even if he had to fight thousands of years of history and tradition. He felt like a traitor, but a free traitor, no longer a slave to his own blood. He was ready to pay the price for his actions.

As the first signs of dawn showered the clouds in gold dust, he kissed her as she slept and walked towards the lift, nodding to the three security guards that stood outside the suite.

"Are you okay, Sir?" asked the always-sunny lift operator as the door slid open.

"Good morning, Harry. How are you today?" Gabriel knew the young man quite well. Harry and his wife had been employees of The Pierre for the last four years and sometimes served at the Ange'el's private penthouse in the same building.

"Shall I call a doctor, Mr. Warren?" The tall young man pointed towards the blood-stained sleeve of Gabriel's white shirt.

"I'm sorry." Gabriel shook his head, trying to remain present. "It looks like I'm staining your carpet. I'm really sorry. This is nothing, just a scratch." He looked into Harry's eyes and smiled, unleashing the full power of his glowing gaze and erased any quizzing thoughts. The young operator moistened his lips, unable to take his eyes away from Gabriel's eyes.

"Could you do me a favour Harry? Will you ask someone to clear up the mess I made in the terrace of Ms. Morgan's suite."

"Of course, Sir."

"Please don't wake her up." The Ange'el smiled casually, squeezing Harry's shoulder with his uninjured hand. "Thank you."

Gabriel's smile widened, reassuring the young man who blushed, trying to cover the growing evidence of his lust for the Ange'el with his white gloved hands. The Ange'el concealed his right arm behind his back as he exited the lift. He walked outside the building and waited, predicting consequences for his defiance to the queen.

Queen First

The Sacred House, Ahe'ey

Viviane felt it—her son's ecstasy, his love, the elation he was experiencing at that moment. She allowed herself one moment of joy. A second where she was simply his loving mother and the only one who shared with him the unbearable burden carried by the royal Ange'el.

She could feel the power of the connection, the strength of the bond between Gabriel and the human. She understood the significance of what was unfolding. She knew that there was no turning back, that there was nothing casual or fleeting about his actions.

The spark of warmth in her heart quickly disappeared, replaced by the cold and harsh judgment of a ruler of a species on the verge of extinction. His happiness was not her priority, no matter how much she wished it to be. She was the queen first, always and above all else. No one paid a higher price for her crown than her one and only son, her most prized possession and greatest love.

"Lady, have you summoned me?" asked the golden maiden with the clearest of eyes.

"Sage." The queen extended her arms towards the young woman, who rushed to the comfort and delight of Viviane's healing embrace.

"Your heart is heavy with worry, Lady."

"Your mind's eye is becoming more powerful every day my dear."

"What bothers you, my queen?"

Viviane caressed Sage's porcelain cheek.

"My son loves you and the children above all else. He will listen to your pleas before he ever obeys my commands."

"Is Apollo okay?"

"He's fine, but he needs to come back to Ahe'ey immediately. His life depends on it."

The apples of Sage's face turned ruby as her breathing tried to keep up with the pace of her heart. "Is he in danger?"

"He has lost his mind. He risks the secrecy and legacy of the Ahe'ey, and he will be severely punished if he continues to challenge our rules."

"What has he done Lady Viviane?" Sage asked in distress.

"Go to New York and use his love for you to convince him to return to Ahe'ey immediately. Say what you must to bring him back."

"But—"

"Sage, if you fail, I will have to turn my request to Gabriel into an order, and he will obey my commands, willingly or unwillingly. Do you understand? If you fail with love, my niece, Sky, will succeed with force. My son must return to Ahe'ey today." The flustered blonde woman nodded and rushed to the door.

"Find Bastian and ask him to escort you."

PUNISHED

Quinn could hear the crack of Amalia's whip long before she could see it. The lashes echoed all over the forest, followed by Scout's shrieks of pain. Amalia's white stallion reared, mimicking his master's aggression. In front of the horse, kneeling on the ground was the white-and-purple-haired Yi'ingo apprentice. At every attempt that she made to get up and run, Amalia punished her with a lashing that tore the skin of her back right to the bone. The queen mother's horse jumped over the girl who lay where she stood, almost unconscious.

"You will follow our ancestor's rules, or you will die." Amalia's voice was commanding.

"Leave the girl," Sky said, placing her horse between her grandmother's horse and Scout.

Quinn sighed with relief.

"Who are you to defy my orders? I've made you who you are, Warrior Queen," the old woman uttered every word with rage as she cracked her whip in the air. The two horses neighed and snorted, unsettled by the thunderous sound. "Where have you been? I have been looking for you."

Sky's eyes focused on Quinn who stood several metres away, hidden behind a tree. Quinn knew that nothing escaped the hunting eyes of the warrior queen. Sky's signal was almost imperceptible. She looked into Quinn's eyes and then in the direction of Scout. Quinn nodded, acknowledging the order.

"I was in New York. Let's go, Grandmother; we have to talk. Leave the girl; she's half dead. She won't last the night."

Amalia looked at Scout for a moment, eyes narrowed, then nodded.

"New York?"

The two royals galloped away.

Quinn ran to meet Scout and attempted to lift her. The Yi'ingo screamed, "Leave me alone pest." Quinn took a step back, observing the injured girl. She had open wounds all over her back and arms.

"I'll fetch you some water," Quinn said.

"I don't need your help," Scout barked, tears streaming down her face and dripping down her chest.

"Shut up. We need to get ya to a healer in the Sacred House."

"I'm not going anywhere near those witches. I'm . . . a high-ranking . . . warrior; I'll heal." Scout bit her lip, struggling to cope with the pain.

"You're losing a lot of blood you fool," Quinn said, lifting Scout by her armpits and then turning her around to carry the Yi'ingo on her back. "Wrap your legs around me," said the young girl, using all her strength to lift Scout off the ground.

Scout lay unconscious on top of Quinn's back. The human girl walked slowly in the direction of the Sacred House. Her tiny frame struggled to cope with the weight of the Yi'ingo warrior.

"Why are you helping me?" Scout mumbled, half delirious. She attempted to walk, still leaning heavily on Quinn.

"What else would I do? Abandon you in the forest to die?" Quinn's tone was sarcastic. "I'd do the same for a wild boar. Actually, I would probably put it out of its misery and eat it for lunch. Maybe I should do the same with you." She grinned and Scout responded with a weak chuckle. Quinn stopped near a small pond inside the Ange'el gardens. Scout crawled towards the water, dipping her face to cool down her fever.

"Why do you allow her to treat you like this?"

"Who are you to judge me, human?" Scout snapped.

Quinn shook her head, rolled her eyes and turned her back. "Stay here; I'm going to get some help."

By the time Quinn returned with a healer, the Yi'ingo was long gone.

Beauty

It was the first time she'd ever felt fully confident in lovemaking. There was something about this man and the way he looked at her and touched her that left her no space for the self-doubt that had tormented her all her life. Sometimes she thought she could hear him inside her head, putting all insecurity to rest.

They slept holding each other tightly. She woke up in the morning a little later than usual. She tried to determine if last night's events were real or a dream. She looked for him, but he was gone. She could smell him on her skin and a moon-shaped silver-and-turquoise necklace was left on his pillow. She put it on.

Morgan got out of bed, and as she looked in the mirror in the bathroom, she couldn't help but ask herself what he saw in her. She shook her head, trying to overcome these feelings. She thought she had conquered her challenges with her body image. *Why do you do this to yourself?* This had always been her Achilles' heel, the cancer that had lived inside her, festering for years and years. She had worked hard to accept, love, and respect her body. She had healed the broken girl who had once lived inside her.

After a few dramatic ends to romantic relationships, mostly caused by her self-doubt, she had withdrawn herself from the dating scene. She just couldn't cope with the pressure of the male gaze on her, and few men were interesting enough to cause any sense of loss or regret.

Morgan had learned years ago that her past did not have to define her present or her future. She focused on having a meaningful life. She learned to accept her body and appreciate her features and spent little time focusing on her looks. *And now this.* It was confusing to her, confusing that she was so utterly attracted to this man, that he was so out of her league, and yet she felt so sure of his affection. As she looked into her reflection in the mirror, she took a deep breath, held her head high, and smiled, full of pride, compassion, and kindness towards the woman in the mirror.

You are beautiful and strong and accomplished and worthy.

She headed for the shower.

Morgan was eager to see him but attempted to show some restraint by reading the New York Times while sipping her coffee outside. Opening the door to the terrace, she realised the table was missing. She stood by the balustrade of the terrace to admire the view, picking up the suite's complimentary binoculars and scanning the street. She followed a young couple that enjoyed an early morning horse-and-carriage sightseeing tour. The horses pulled up in front of The Pierre, and that was when she saw him, standing outside, pacing nervously.

She saw two people walk towards Gabriel—his cousin Bastian and a beautiful young blonde woman. The woman pulled her long white dress up and rushed towards Gabriel, who received her with open arms. She grabbed Gabriel's face with both hands and kissed him on the mouth. He lifted her up and hugged her. His hand was in her hair, and he spoke to her with great affection. She was probably in her early twenties, and she was a flower. She was graceful, with a flawless and pale complexion. She placed her hands on Gabriel's arm, and lifted his sleeve all the way up. She was clearly at ease with him. She led Gabriel to the lobby of the hotel followed by Bastian.

Morgan stopped for a few moments, frozen by what she had witnessed, trying to find an excuse, a reason, for Gabriel to have such intimacy with another woman. But it didn't take long for a great darkness to invade her thoughts. The intimacy of the scene made Morgan sick. She could hear his words of warning: "Morgan, I'm not free to love . . . ." She remembered all his lies and manipulations, how she was an unlikely match for such a good-looking man. All her fears and insecurities came crashing down on her. She packed her bag frenetically and called her friend, Ann Surrey.

"Ann, it's Morgan."

"Hey."

"Listen, I don't have much time. I'm in a bit of a jam."

"Is everything okay?"

"I need to disappear. I'll explain later. I need a place to stay that's not obvious, where no one can find me."

"I'm not in Woodstock today. I'm spending a few days in a skiing resort near Highmount, farther north in the Catskill Mountains. It was quite a spontaneous last minute decision. Why don't you join me?"

"Thank you."

"Are you all right? Do you need me to pick you up?"

"I'll take a cab."

"I'll SMS you the address. What's going on?"

"I just need some time to think. Listen, don't tell anyone that I'm heading your way."

"That man, James. He emailed me saying you needed to cancel your visit."

"I'm on my way."

"Okay. Safe travels."

Morgan called a taxi. As she was leaving her room, one of the security guards spoke to her. "Ma'am, do you need help?"

"No, thank you. Gabriel is downstairs by the lift, waiting."

She was able to leave the hotel without any trouble. The taxi driver offered to place her backpack in the trunk, but she kept it with her as she only carried essentials. Gabriel appeared outside at the exact moment her car departed. His face was flushed from running; he seemed to be shouting something. She ignored the obvious desperation in his eyes and turned her head away in the opposite direction. Her eyes couldn't be trusted when it came to Gabriel. She knew that any vacillation on her part would lead her straight into his arms, into more lies and manipulation.

DANGER IN THE MOUNTAINS

Catskill Mountains, New York

Morgan headed to the Catskill Mountains, in the southeastern part of the state of New York. *It's the perfect hideaway, too secluded for anyone to find me.* The weather had turned. The sun had vanished behind dark clouds, and she could hear the small lumps of hail as they hit the windshield of the taxi.

The yellow cab crossed the Catskill Mountains on a secondary road, heading to the ski resort.

"A black Jaguar has been following us since Manhattan. Are they with you ma'am?" The taxi driver spoke, meeting her eyes through the rear view mirror. She shook her head. "They're signalling us. Not sure what they want."

"Please keep driving. It's dangerous to stop here; there's no one else around."

Morgan was terrified; she hoped that it was just Gabriel's people. She'd turned her mobile off when he first called her in the taxi. She decided to turn the phone on again. They were driving beside a creek that appeared to be almost frozen. Around them, there was mostly forest and little evidence of human presence. She saw ten missed calls from Gabriel. She tried to call him back, but no one answered.

"This is insane; what the hell are they doing?" The taxi driver panicked as the other car was now beside them, trying to take the taxi off the road. Morgan's heart was racing fast as her body was slammed to one side and pressed hard against the seat belt, which stopped her from hitting the side window. There were four men in the other car. The road was slippery due to the light mix of rain and hail falling from the sky.

The taxi was forced to stop against the fence, but the other car continued at high speed. After a few minutes, both Morgan and the taxi driver left the car, and the driver picked up his mobile to call the police. A motorbike stopped by the side of the road a few metres from them, and the rider ran in their direction with his helmet on.

"*We need to go!*" Morgan yelled as the biker approached. She attempted to go back into the taxi, but the door was locked. "*Let me in!*" Morgan realised that the Jaguar had turned around and was now coming at high speed towards them. Things were happening too fast. The taxi driver frantically got into the car and drove away, leaving Morgan in the middle of the road.

As the Jaguar accelerated towards her, just a few metres away, the biker jumped through the air in her direction, landing between Morgan and the approaching vehicle. *Is he flying?* she wondered. The biker pushed her to the side of the road as the car hit his body, projecting him into the air. The figure landed face down, by the creek. The car lost control, went off the road, hit an oak tree, and exploded.

Morgan breathed a sigh of relief as she saw the Jaguar covered in flames. She waited a moment to see if anyone exited the car. She felt sick with the stench of gasoline and scorched human flesh.

Her clothes were getting wet from the hail, but she ran in the direction of the biker, whose body was half-submerged in freezing water. She pulled him out of the creek, turned him around and took his helmet off.

"*Gabriel!*" she screamed. The cold, blue face of the Ange'el didn't register any sign of life. Morgan attempted to check his pulse, but she could barely feel her hands as the cold temperature of the freezing water burned her skin. "Gabriel!" She pressed his chest gently and placed her face close to his face, listening to his breathing.

He moved his head and opened his eyes, confused. "Where are they? Run, run, Morgan!"

"They're dead, all dead."

"Gabriel, can you move?" He attempted to lift his head off the floor and screamed in pain.

He was barely conscious as he muttered some words: "Lady. I need you."

He seemed to be able to move his left arm and leg, using the left side of his body to try to get up. She grabbed onto his right arm to help him stand up, and he shrieked, rolling onto his left side. His right shoulder, arm, and leg were most certainly injured. The air was freezing, and the ground was covered with hail.

Morgan's mobile was shattered, the screen smashed and unresponsive to her touch. She looked through his pockets to find his phone, but it was wet and dead.

"I'm sorry," she whispered, pulling him by the collar of his jacket and dragging him further away from the water as he screamed in pain. She was sobbing as she released him over a bed of bronze beech sprouts, just beside a low barren bush that was a poor shelter from the hail. His teeth chattered; he raised his head to look in the direction of the blaze and then he fainted. She could barely think as the cold was getting to her. She scanned the horizon and noticed a camping cabin down the road.

"Gabriel. Gabriel wake up." She shook his face, and he opened his eyes. "We have to stand up," she said as she helped him to his feet, avoiding the right side of his body. She put his left arm over her shoulder and lifted him up with his help. She was grateful that she'd always been quite strong and fit. He was able to lean on her, relieving the pressure on his injured leg.

They walked slowly. Each step was agony to him, and he kept whispering a name, "Viviane." Halfway towards the cabin, he fell onto his knees coughing blood.

"Just a few more metres. Come on," she encouraged him.

He was struggling to breathe as blood flowed from his mouth. Morgan ran to the cabin.

"Please help us. Anyone home? *Open the door; it's an emergency!*" She opened the screen door and turned the handle of the wooden door. It was locked shut. She walked around the front porch, picked up a vase from the floor and threw it at the window, breaking the glass. She took off her jacket and wrapped it around her arm. She slipped her hand through the window to unlock it from the inside.

Morgan slid up the window and climbed through it. She flipped the light switch by the main door to discover that there was no electricity in the cabin. In the dark, she scanned the room for a phone, but couldn't find one. She unlocked the door and ran towards him.

"Gabriel, Gabriel wake up." His inert face lay beside a thin sheet of frozen blood. She placed her hands under his arms and dragged his unconscious body through the sandstone gravel and up the wooden stairs.

Morgan found some blankets and pillows on top of a bed. He was heavy; she was unable to lift him onto the bed. She put a pillow under his head on the floor and covered him with a blanket, attempting to make him comfortable.

He coughed again, "Viviane. Lady . . . ." His forehead was boiling as the rest of his body shivered from the cold. Any attempt by her to remove his wet clothes caused him to wail with pain, so she decided to leave his clothes on.

Morgan continued to search for a phone without success. She tried to heat some water, but there was no gas. She used the matches left next to the stove to light the candles that stood on top of the mantel of the small fireplace. She picked up some wood from a woven basket near the heart of the fireplace and a book from the mantel shelf. She lit the paper with a match, eventually got the wood to catch fire, and for a moment let the fire warm her bones. She sat by him and placed his head on her lap. She touched his forehead. He was burning with fever. Morgan despaired and hoped maybe the taxi driver called the police.

"Gabriel, I'll be right back; I'm going to find help. Do you understand?"

"No," he whispered with his eyes closed. His left hand reached towards Morgan, searching for her hand and holding it tight. "They're coming. Don't leave. Please."

"It's safe; they're dead. I need to get you to a hospital."

"*No!*" She felt the strong grip of his hand. "*Wait.*" His voice echoed inside her mind.

She dismissed the command. "You're delirious my love." She placed her hand on his sweaty forehead. Somehow she could feel his pain, and all she could think about was that she wanted to trade places with him. She couldn't bear to see him so fragile and in such agony. Her touch seemed to ease his pain, so she helped him, ignoring her torment, absorbing his pain into her body. She felt sick, but she didn't let go.

"I need to go," she whispered just before she fainted.

Rescue

Viviane placed her hand on her son's neck, looking for signs of a heartbeat. Within seconds she felt each broken bone, and the internal bleeding that was drowning his lungs and draining his life. She felt the human's energy within his body. Deliberately or not, Morgan had passed some of her own life force onto him, and it was that drop of vitality that had kept him barely alive.

The queen's healing energy poured into her son. She controlled it carefully as she needed enough strength to go back to Ahe'ey. A hint of colour returned to his face, and his chest moved up and down once just before he coughed blood. She placed her hand on his upper torso absorbing his pain into her body, concentrating all her intention on his healing. She stopped, overwhelmed with the pain, unable to breathe, losing her sight as her blood pressure collapsed.

"My queen!" Bastian caught her in his arms.

"Bas, take him to the Sacred House." Viviane touched her burning chest, gasping for air. "We will follow you shortly. Sage and the healers are waiting for you at the lake."

Bastian nodded. "Come here, old friend." The Ma'asai carefully lifted his cousin's body from the ground. "Lady Viviane. The human, she's our friend."

"Hurry, Bastian; he is very weak," murmured the queen as Bastian walked out of the cabin carrying Gabriel.

"Will he survive?" Sky asked, her tone cold and detached. She placed one knee on the ground and leaned over Morgan's inert body.

"He's in terrible shape, but he will live."

"Shame," the Yi'ingo retorted, looking through Morgan's body for signs of injury.

"Spare me the lies that blind you, blood of my blood." The queen felt a pinch of guilt as she admonished her niece.

"What do we do with the human?"

Viviane kneeled beside Morgan, placing her hand over the human's hand only to quickly release it with a gasp. The images that flashed through her mind's eye were too painful and familiar to process. They came and vanished in seconds, and as they were remembered, they were forgotten, leaving a trail of unsettling confusion in the queen's mind.

"What's the matter? Is she dead?"

Viviane composed herself, taking a moment to move Morgan's wild waves of hair away from her face. The queen wiped a tear from her eye.

"She's fine. Pick her up; she is coming with us."

"No. I'll drop her at a hospital."

"I'm still Queen of Ahe'ey, am I not?"

"You've ordered me to protect Ahe'ey. She's too high profile; I can't allow it. Your mother will—"

"It's an order Sky." The queen's voice echoed through Sky's body.

BLOODLINE

PRESENT DAY - 26 NOVEMBER 2014

AHE'EY

AWAKENINGS

Morgan woke up as light pierced through her eyelids. She felt weak, as if she'd been run over by a fast-moving train. *Where am I?* She was lying in a large and comfortable round bed, and in front of her was a glass wall exposing the landscape outside. She was in some sort of a pavilion, facing a beautiful garden where nature was alive and vibrant. The sun had just risen, spreading golden light over the landscape.

Around her were white walls and silver surfaces that reflected the light, the sky and the leaves of the trees. The architecture had a minimalistic feel to it. The structure blended with nature without imposing itself. There was a large tree in one of the corners. It was like the room had been built around it to avoid disturbing it. Morgan noticed that the ceiling was made of a translucent material that protected the room from the weather. The leaves of the tree raised and expanded above it, providing natural shade. *Heavenly.* She could hear a gentle breeze outside and the chirping of birds. *Gabriel. Where is Gabriel?*

Morgan was lying on her side. She started to turn her body, carefully making an assessment of each part to ensure everything was okay. Someone was breathing softly just behind her. As she turned, she saw a little girl sleeping. The little girl couldn't be more than two or three years old, and she was snoring in the cutest possible way. The child had shiny, shoulder-length, curly dark hair. The curls were spread around her face and all over the bed. She looked divine.

"Good morning, how are you feeling?" She whipped her head around in surprise at the voice. "My name is Sebastian, but you can call me Bastian. We've met before, remember? I'm Gabriel's cousin."

The man was lying back on a chaise lounge beside her bed. He quickly stood up and gave her a friendly smile. "I'm sorry to startle you and to invade your privacy, but my cousin wouldn't rest until I assured him that I'd be here personally when you woke up." He smiled again and said jokingly, "I even considered knocking him out to stop him from getting out of bed. He came to check on you several times during the night."

"Where is he? Is he okay?"

"He's a bloody mess, but he'll recover if he manages to lie still. He's resting in his room upstairs, in the main building. He has a significant number of fractures on the right side of his body, including his shoulder, arm, leg and several ribs. He's in a lot of pain, and there's some internal bleeding, but please don't worry. Everyone in our . . . family is stronger than your average person."

She frowned, confused. She wanted to see Gabriel and to be at his side, but Bastian continued, "I see you have made some very important friends already," he said, pointing at the little girl.

Morgan smiled and touched one of the girl's curls.

"Aria is Gabriel's youngest daughter. She's usually quite shy, and really only interacts with her family. You should consider it an honour that she has chosen to visit you," he said cheerfully, but by then, Morgan was lost in thought, and her stomach turned.

"Morgan, we got in touch with your friend Ann, your team and a few other people. They know you are safe and staying at a secluded retreat for the next few weeks. The police and the intelligence agency will continue their investigation. In the meantime, you can be rest assured that Ahe'ey is the safest place on Earth."

"Ayee? Is that where we are?"

"Yes. Ahe'ey." He nodded.

"Thank you for your kindness," Morgan murmured, still lost in thought.

Two young women entered the room. Morgan immediately recognised the woman that had kissed Gabriel at The Pierre. A teenage girl with a rebellious look followed the young blonde woman. The teen's short dark hair had some royal blue streaks that fell on top of her dark Asian eyes. She was little but looked quite fierce. The two young women placed trays of food on top of the bed.

"Morgan, my name is Sage. How are you feeling?" The eldest of the two women placed the palm of her hand on Morgan's forehead. "We'll take good care of you," she smiled at Morgan reassuringly, pulling her long sunny hair to one side. Sage's eyes shifted to Aria with surprise and then she looked at Bastian, who shrugged his shoulders.

Morgan couldn't help but feel insecure in the presence of such a young beauty. Gabriel seemed to be married to a noble, enchanting, soft and amazing young woman. There was no place to hide from her light and generosity and Morgan just wanted to diminish and disappear.

It took a few seconds for her to compose herself and smile back. "I feel fine, thank you," she replied with embarrassment.

Sage seemed completely oblivious to Morgan's internal struggle. She sat on the bed, gave her a glass of juice to drink and continued, "You should be fully recovered within the next few days. I'll leave you to have your breakfast with Bastian, but will return a little later to show you where the bathhouse is." Sage helped Morgan sit up and adjusted the pillow behind her back.

Aria woke up. She sat on the bed, looked at Morgan, picked up a piece of what looked like banana bread, handed it to Morgan, and said, "Good foo yuu." Everyone laughed. Then Sage and the teen girl both left the room.

Morgan looked at Aria, smiled, and said softly, "Hi, Aria. Yes, thank you, it must be delicious. Are you sure you don't want to go with your mummy?"

Bastian intervened.

"Aria is not . . . ." He paused for a second as if processing her words. "Oh, I see. I understand now." He moved from the chaise lounge to sit on the bed, gave Aria a strawberry, took a deep breath and said, "Morgan, allow me to tell you a little bit more about my mysterious and reserved cousin."

She nodded.

"Gabriel is the son of the leaders of this land. You may find it archaic, but we're actually a kingdom called Ahe'ey, ruled by a queen, Viviane, and a king, Marcus. In time, you'll understand why monarchy works for us. You see, our bloodline is quite special. The simplest way to put it is that we have some great genes." He smiled cheekily, raised his chin, and winked. "And it's not just the good looks, you know? It gives us some unique capabilities."

"I gathered that much," Morgan said, thinking of Gabriel and how he had fought the men's rights activists and the way he had jumped to save her from the car.

"Some years ago," Bastian continued, "Gabriel offered his unique skills to the US government and the United Nations Security Council. He was put in charge of children's welfare in war zones during specific events. He managed the operations to ensure there was a minimum impact on their lives and also led the on-the-ground rescue missions. Gabriel's groundwork has saved many lives, including the lives of his five adopted children. You have already met three of them today—Aria, Quinn, and Sage."

He stopped for a second to look at Morgan with a bright knowing smile on his face. "They are all children who lost their families in wartime. Our Aria here experienced a lot, and you are the first person outside her immediate family that she has connected with. You must be quite special." He looked at Aria, who was playing with her food as she sat beside Morgan.

Morgan was trying to process all the confusing information. "Sage . . . ," she said tentatively, "is Gabriel's daughter?"

Bastian nodded.

Morgan wanted time to think and to make sense of this new data, and wonder at this incredible, compassionate life that Gabriel was leading, but Bastian continued.

"Gabriel left his role six months ago to spend more time with Aria and to work on another project."

Morgan was confused. "I don't understand. Who are you all?"

"I promise it'll become clear in time, Morgan. I'm just sharing enough information to rest your mind from any doubt about the intentions and values of my cousin."

She could feel embarrassment invade her cheeks with a blush, but was also curious and keen for him to continue.

Bastian put his hand on top of her hand. "Due to his services to the UN and the US government, Gabriel has access to privileged information about national threats, key international events, and so on. The day of your arrival, he received notification of the threat to your life and pulled all strings to be at your side at all times. You were already on your way here. Gabriel has been following your work for years. My cousin is a huge fan of yours. He was forced to play within the rules of the Secret Service, but he was there for only one reason: You."

Sunlight now bathed the entire room. Morgan could see a shape approaching the pavilion. She placed her hand in front of her eyes, trying to create some shade that would allow her to see who was limping slowly in her direction. It was Gabriel. Her heartbeat accelerated as he approached the room. He was supporting himself with a cane in his left hand. He was pale, and his face contorted with each step. Aria jumped out of the bed and ran towards him, who dropped the cane to pick her up with his good arm. She grabbed his face and kissed him on the mouth. It was a mirror of the way Sage had done it at the hotel. Gabriel's face transformed instantly—a gleaming smile replaced a tight, locked jaw. It was the open and happy smile of a devoted father.

"Cousin, you go to much trouble to try to keep Morgan from my charms, but this time, you arrived too late." Bastian said, teasing.

"I am indeed challenged by a worthy opponent." His quivering voice was weaker than usual. It gave away the suffering that he was attempting to hide with his smile.

Bastian hugged his cousin and took Aria from his arms. "Baby girl, Apollo is sick, and we need to be gentle, okay?"

"Geentlee," she repeated, touching Gabriel's face.

Bastian helped Gabriel sit on the side of the bed. "I'll be outside when you need me."

"Thank you, my friend."

"Apollo?" Morgan asked.

"My nickname. How are you?" he asked softly. His eyes were tentative, worried.

Morgan had an open smile and said, "I'm fine. Better now that you're here."

He took a moment to process her reassuring words and her welcoming smile.

"I have a lot to explain—"

She stopped him by putting her fingers on his lips. "Shhh . . . ." Her hand moved up, touching a wound on his eyebrow, and she could feel that he was burning with fever. "All I want to know is that you are here and that you are going to be okay. I'm the one who has to apologise for my foolishness and for putting your life and the life of others in danger."

He shook his head. They were each smiling at the other.

"Will you please stay for a few days?" He placed his hand over hers, and she responded with a nod.

Aria stood on the bed with a piece of bread and handed it to Gabriel. His connection to her was extraordinary. The sombre and mysterious man was immediately replaced by a soft and joyful, a light and mischievous, a playful Gabriel, who made the little girl giggle uncontrollably. Soon, she was outside, singing and chasing butterflies.

"Apollo," Sage said, entering the room with Quinn, "you must rest, my love." She kneeled near him, put her hand on his face and kissed him on the lips. "You can't be walking around on so many broken bones." He hugged her.

"Who's going to practice archery with me now?" Quinn said as she leaned to kiss her father in the same way. "I wanna beat Sky in the Games." It was such a happy moment. Morgan lay back, quietly witnessing the interactions between Gabriel and his daughters.

"I was going to ask Sky to help you, but given your ambitious plans to usurp her, perhaps we should ask Bastian to take my place." He was so happy, present, and vulnerable. This was the true Gabriel, the man who, today, had nothing to conceal and no threat to deal with.

"Well! I'm going to beat Bastian too." Quinn cocked her head, and grinned.

"How can I help you, mighty warrior?" Bastian said as he also re-entered the room. He picked her up and lifted her in the air, above his head.

"*Put me down Bas!*" shouted the spunky girl, annoyed.

Gabriel's white shirt was starting to soak in his sweat. His forehead was wet, and he was making a weak attempt to disguise his pain. Sage looked at him with a frown, and then at Morgan. "Given that you'll both be resting, I wonder if you mind if we move Apollo here to the visitors' pavilion. This way, we may prevent him from continuously walking around. I don't like the idea of him walking up and down the stairs to get to his room."

"Good idea," Morgan said, blushing. "I certainly could use some company."

Sage looked at Quinn, who nodded and left the room to make arrangements.

Gabriel closed his eyes and struggled to sit straight. Sage asked Morgan to support his back while she went to get a basin of cold water and a towel. She poured several oils into the water, soaked the towel, and used it on Gabriel's forehead and neck. Then she removed Gabriel's shirt and continued to use the soaked towel to cool down his body. Morgan admired his back, which was covered with beautiful tattoos. The design was circular; it showed, at the top, a phoenix flying clockwise towards the sun and, at the bottom, a dragon flying away from the sun in the direction of the moon and the stars. The artwork was stunning and intricate but didn't hide the bruises present all over his body.

Quinn made up the second bed in the room next door, and Bastian carried Gabriel and laid him down on it.

"Lady Viviane is on her way. Quinn, please take Aria to the

bathhouse," Sage said. "Morgan, please go with them. Quinn will show you all the amenities. They're just next door. The bathhouse and kitchen are in the main building, called the Sacred House, and the guests' pavilions are set up around it. You won't get lost."

Morgan looked at Gabriel, worrying her lower lip. "I'll be here with him, Morgan. He'll be fine," Sage reassured her.

Morgan nodded and followed Quinn to the bathhouse.

The bathhouse looked like an old Roman spa. It held several pools of water, each with different temperatures, baths, saunas and small waterfalls that served as showers. Colourful murals of sea serpents and women diving into the sea adorned the walls. Morgan appreciated the sensuality of the art at Ange'el. It was everywhere, and it was breathtaking. Small glazed tiles were arranged to represent the bodies of women and serpents intertwined in a passionate dance. The curves of the female form were embraced by the waves of the water creatures.

There were clean robes and tunics available and everything that Morgan needed to refresh herself. Quinn and Aria were both naked, splashing in one of the pools. Aria was lively and happy to follow the commands of her somewhat bossy sister. *Leadership skills*, Morgan corrected her thoughts, smiling.

Sky walked in the room as Morgan was coming out of the shower and putting on a fresh tunic. The warrior acknowledged Morgan with a head bow, took her clothes off, and jumped in the pool. A phoenix tattoo covered Sky's body. The wings of the bird covered her front and back, while the tail went down her right leg. The head of the phoenix stood on her right shoulder, framed by the design of a shining sun. *Stunning*, thought Morgan.

As Morgan dried her hair with a towel, she observed Quinn's excitement towards Sky. She seemed to watch her every move and copied Sky at every possible occasion.

"Where did ya go today, Sky? Did ya fight? Can I go with you tomorrow?" The avalanche of questions didn't seem to bother Sky, who was selective in her answers, but attentive to the girl. Other young women entered the room and joined in the adulation. It seemed that Sky was the local teen celebrity.

Morgan couldn't help but appreciate the beauty of the scene. She'd never before witnessed such a beautiful and fierce group of women. They moved with the confidence and agility of Olympic athletes. They wore chain mail armour over their leather tunics, adorned with tattoo-like symbols. As the women undressed, Morgan observed that there was little diversity in body shapes and sizes. They were all tall and well built, but naturally thin. They had perfect symmetry and proportion, and above all was Sky, who was the ideal balance between strength and flexibility. And yet, in that sea of perfection, little Quinn stood out: much shorter than the others, flat-chested, bruised, and wonderfully beautiful and unique.

Aria ran away from the pool towards Morgan, who picked her up. The little girl hid her face in Morgan's curls.

Sky followed the toddler with her eyes. She got out of the pool and walked towards them. Sky extended her arms to Aria with a smile.

"Kyyee," the little one said, giggling as Sky hugged her and kissed her on the cheek.

"Your speech had heart. You are a good leader of people."

Sky's kind words and approachability surprised Morgan. She seemed different here amongst women and girls, more relaxed and open.

"Thank you Sky."

"Human women have a lot to overcome." Sky stood naked and seemed completely at ease with her body. Morgan adjusted the towel around her body and combed her fingers through her hair, intimidated by the splendid creature that stood in front of her.

"Yes, I suppose we do have some things to overcome. Some days I think we are taking giants steps forward, and other days I feel I'm stuck in the Middle Ages."

"Despite your genes, you must continue to fight and to lead."

"There's nothing wrong with my genes." Morgan was taken aback by the comment.

"You may fool your people. It helps them reach their potential, but in the end, their prospects rely on the code in their blood."

"Genes are switched on and off based on our lifestyle and beliefs."

"You can't regulate what you don't have."

"Studies show that—"

Sky sneered and interrupted Morgan. "Look at me. Flawless, the perfect model of my species."

"Indeed. It must be hard to be so perfect." Morgan attempted and failed to hold back the sarcasm. She could feel her anger rising.

"The beauty you seek; the strength you don't have; the speed and agility you lack; the intelligence you could use when you put your people and mine at risk. I have it all, because it's in my nature, locked within my pure blood, at my disposal to use and abuse. My privilege and my responsibility."

"I'm probably not smart enough to appreciate all your glory. Must be because of my genes. Yes, I'm definitely struggling to appreciate it right now."

Sky's attention wandered towards the pool. Morgan wasn't even sure if the warrior was listening to her. The Yi'ingo looked in the direction of Quinn who sat by the pool with the other young women. "She's the bravest, hardest working and most tenacious of my girls. Like you, she has heart and punches above her weight. But, in battle, she'd be the first to fall and others would fall because of her frailty. There is too much weakness in her blood. Her bruises don't heal; her muscles don't grow. She is a liability to us and so are you."

"You underestimate us Sky, but I'm grateful for your protection during the event. Thank you."

Sky kissed Aria's hair. "Those on top of the pyramid must protect those below with respect, compassion and dignity. Something humans forgot in the way they treat other species."

"Aren't we lucky to have you? Good to know you bestow kindness to all creatures." Morgan retorted, rolling her eyes.

"To those who deserve it." Sky looked at her seriously. "I like you, Morgan. You have potential, for a human. But you don't belong here. Gabriel shames us all. He has refused all his life to perform his duty, to fertilise the wombs of our high-ranking women. And now he brings a human to Ahe'ey. If you become the first he beds, if he loses his celibacy to you, he'll be disrespecting all of us who are working so hard to protect the purity of our blood at all costs."

Was he virgin? Morgan's heart accelerated.

"Bastian and I sacrifice our lives to protect our people and our genes. We bear the brunt of the responsibilities while he mocks our sacrifice with his careless actions. We can't afford to indulge in personal feelings that risk the future of our lineage or the safety of our people. You don't belong here. His seed belongs to them. They, the almost-perfect." Sky pointed at her warriors in the pool.

"Well. I'm sorry for being so flawed and unworthy, but now it's time you stop putting you perfect nose in my business. Understood?" Morgan spoke confidently, leaning forward on her tiptoes, her anger hot.

"He's not your business. He's weak, irresponsible and a traitor to his own people."

Aria became restless in Sky's arms. The warrior caressed the toddler's hair and pressed her lips against the tiny nose of the girl, who responded with a giggle.

Morgan took a deep breath, attempting to empathise with the high and mighty warrior who was testing her temper. "In New York, Gabriel told me that he wished to introduce me to you. We were admiring a painting of the goddess Athena by Klimt, and he told me it reminded him of you. It was difficult for me to imagine what he meant at that time. Now it makes complete sense. You are indeed a powerful and beautiful godlike warrior. He spoke of you with such admiration."

The fire in Sky's eyes eased, touched by a hint of water.

"He said you were quite a special woman, you know? I'm happy to have this opportunity to finally get to know you. I don't know much about this place or your people, but I hope one day you change your mind about my people and me."

"I can't afford it. And neither can he. That's the price we pay. This isn't about you Morgan. It's about our survival."

Sky handed Aria back to Morgan. The Yi'ingo put her clothes on and left.

Morgan felt a tremendous responsibility for Gabriel, the man she had misunderstood, the man who seemed to have a lot on the line. She felt the intense urge to be back by his side.

Morgan, Quinn, and Aria left together. They stopped by the kitchen to pick up cold water in case Gabriel needed it. Aria hid her face on Morgan's neck the entire time. It was a large room with a transparent ceiling and plenty of light. Just beside it, there was a garden full of herbs, fruits and vegetables. The three women in the room smiled at Morgan. They looked more like Sage and less like Sky and Quinn, had peaceful, kind eyes, and quietly peeled apples and pears. They all had moon-shaped tattoos on their hands and wore simple, comfortable cyan tunics. The eldest of the three went to the garden, picked up some crunchy green apples, and gave them to Morgan with a smile.

"Thank you. How did you know that I prefer—"

Before she could finish her words, Quinn replied, "Get used to it.

Around here at Ange'el, they can read your mind."

"Can you?" Morgan asked.

"Nah. Not me," Quinn said, shaking her head, "although Lady Viviane told me I could learn if I choose to. She told me I had potential, but I'm not really fit to be an Ange'el like my sister Sage. I wanna be a warrior like Sky. I'll move to Yi'ingo when Dad thinks I'm ready."

"Do they know everything that I'm thinking?" Morgan whispered, a little overwhelmed by the idea.

"Nah, they don't. Most Ange'el can only sense if you are hungry or thirsty, if you crave a crunchy apple or some chocolate. They sense your fear, excitement, and pain."

Morgan was beginning to feel as if she'd jumped down a rabbit hole since she had met Gabriel.

"How does it work?" she asked.

Quinn looked at her for a moment, then leaned closer to Morgan, keeping her voice low and began, almost like a recitation, "They have developed sophisticated empathic abilities, what you might call intuition. Some Ange'el are a bit more powerful. Each one has their own set of capabilities and level of skill depending on the purity of their genes and their age. Some Ange'el can heal ya. Some can convince ya to do their will. Some know what you're thinking. Some can speak to you using only their minds, and Viviane . . . well, Viviane can do it all." Quinn's eyes opened wide as she whispered into Morgan's ear.

The Queen Healer

Gabriel had been asleep since the previous day. Sage had told Morgan to expect the visit of Lady Viviane, Queen of Ahe'ey, who was also the master healer. Morgan felt the queen's presence even before she entered the room. She seemed to have a magnetic field that expanded way beyond her slim body. She smelled like fresh flowers, wore a blue cloak and appeared to glide as she walked. *Her glow. That glow!*

"My child," the woman whispered as she approached Morgan.

"Hi," Morgan said, confused. Viviane observed Morgan's features in the sunlight and touched her face.

"You have beautiful eyes, Morgan. You remind me of someone I loved."

"Thank you." Morgan felt a rush of desire throughout her body as she looked into Viviane's eyes.

"I am Viviane, Gabriel's mother."

Morgan was surprised. The woman in front of her looked too young to be his mother. *She's probably in her early forties.* Morgan thought.

"Queen Viviane, it's an honour to meet you." Morgan shook her head to snap herself free of the queen's spellbinding eyes.

"Are we treating you well, child?"

"Very well. Thank you for letting me stay."

"It's the least I can do. You saved my son's life."

"I'm afraid I have done nothing but put his life in danger. I'm a dangerous fool." Morgan felt her guilt twist up her lungs, squeezing.

"Come here. Sit by his side." Viviane pointed to Gabriel, who was asleep. "Put your hand on his chest and concentrate on his well-being . . . breathe."

It was easy for Morgan to concentrate on his well-being; just looking at him took her breath away. She wished him the world. She could feel his heart beating; it felt as though her heart was in sync with his. Then she started to feel weak, the pain in her body so intense.

Viviane pulled Morgan's hand from Gabriel's chest.

"You are a natural healer, Morgan. When you touched my son after the accident, you took some of his pain into your own body and saved his life. This is why you became so weak and fainted. You have a rare gift. Few people have such skill without any training."

Morgan was confused, but she'd certainly felt his pain in her own body a moment ago.

"Can I help him? He's in a lot of pain."

Viviane smiled, her eyes bright with Morgan's response.

"You have the gift of service, my dear. You don't yet know how to manage your skill without putting your own life at risk. It is something I can teach you in time if you wish. For now, leave the healing to Sage and I. Gabriel will be fine."

"Lady Viviane, where am I? Who are you people? This place. This world. It's so different . . . ."

Viviane looked into Morgan's eyes. Her face was stern and her lips pressed against each other for a moment before she spoke. "What I'm about to tell you must never be shared with the outside world. Do you understand?"

Morgan nodded.

Viviane and Morgan left the pavilion and sat outside, enjoying the midmorning sunlight. The queen spoke slowly, carefully assembling the history of the Ahe'ey. Morgan closed her eyes as the words and images seemed to flow straight into her mind.

"As you know, one of the costs that *Homo sapiens* have paid for having larger brains is that your children are born dependent on parents and remain that way for many years. The skull and brain are not fully formed before birth. This, of course, led humans to acquire specific roles depending on their sex. The concept of staying at home with the kids, which has been holding back the progress of your women even today, is as old as humankind.

"The Ahe'ey are descendants of an ancient civilisation that organised itself differently from the rest of the *Homo sapiens*. The key differences are that we created an egalitarian society with no class system. From inception, we designed a communal system to look after the children, allowing men and women to have access to all roles in society. This was possible due to two factors: plenty of access to resources such as fertile land, animals, and water, as well as isolation from any other groups seeking to conquer or to steal our resources.

"We were relatively isolated in a big landmass in the middle of the Atlantic Ocean, which meant we experienced little competition for land and resources from any other race. The men and women in Ahe'ey shared all roles in society until about thirty-four years ago, when civil war destroyed the fabric of this great civilisation. But I will leave that story for another time.

"The surplus of resources allowed us to innovate and evolve quickly. We mastered techniques of artificial selection and genetic manipulation tens of thousands of years before the rest of the human race. Nine thousand years ago, the Ahe'ey discovered the ability to engineer cells, the ability to engineer tissues and robotics. We manipulated our own genetics in order to become stronger. Initially, we focused on health—regenerating body parts, delaying aging, curing disease—but soon, we started using our technology to make life easier. We could jump higher, run faster, hear better, and see farther than any other race. We even gave the gift of flight to some of our most-deserving citizens."

"You . . . gave them wings?" Morgan's eyebrow went up. She was starting to doubt the queen's story.

"Almost anything is possible when you fully unveil the magic of biology. We had ethics committees reviewing every activity as we combined the genes of animals and humans to give them the gift of flight, to create self-regenerating skin, and even to survive underwater for long periods of time."

"Fascinating! How long ago did this happen?" *Am I dreaming? Where am I? This is madness.*

"Nine thousand years ago. Every other human race around the world was just moving from hunting and gathering to farming while we had swiftly moved across all metal ages, several industrial revolutions and found ourselves manipulating nature and environment to suit our needs and desires. As we integrated more and more capabilities into our own bodies, there was less need for the material possessions and gadgets that occupy the landfills of Earth as we experience it today.

"We became so advanced in the mastery of the genome that we embedded values into our genes so that only the most virtuous amongst us were able to access these powerful features, such as flight, mind reading, or superhuman strength. These genes expressed themselves only as and when their bearers became worthy of unleashing their power. You could say that the traits for virtue, honesty and general goodness became irrevocably linked to the extraordinary physical traits we had created."

"So you programmed a set of values in your genes? What if there was a bug? Like those we see in science fiction movies."

"Bug?" The queen looked at Morgan puzzled, and then she continued ignoring Morgan's question. "Also, the Ahe'ey were, by the design of their genes, attracted by mates of similar worthiness and, due to that, comparable capabilities or power. This was a welcomed enhancement that helped us find our soul mates, our like-minded and worthy suitors more easily."

"Love coded in the DNA? Unbelievable!"

"Desire for creatures of equal valour."

And yet, he chose me. Did he? Choose me? Morgan tried to ignore the self-doubt that lurked in her mind.

"We took direct control over the evolution of our species and other species. We created dragons to protect our land, large serpents for our recreation, and high-yielding seeds. As we worked to prolong our life expectancy, we genetically limited the number of offspring that the Ahe'ey woman could bear to avoid the overpopulation of our land. We manipulated human and animal traits and created entire new species and subspecies. We, the Ahe'ey, evolved from *Homo sapiens* to *Homo cognatus*—a completely different sub-species.

"We were mighty, and we were perfect. We were an honourable and virtuous civilisation until seven thousand years ago when the earth was stolen from under our feet by the sea in only one day and one night. Our land and most of its people sunk to the depths of the ocean, never to be found again. Ahe'ey vanished, crushed under the sea by the fire-spitting scar at the bottom of the ocean floor. Only a few of our foremothers and forefathers survived."

"So, it's real! The flood described in the religious texts of every culture around the world."

Viviane nodded and continued speaking. "Yes, the few survivors migrated to this island."

"We are on an island?" Morgan asked, puzzled.

Viviane nodded.

"It was a small community of only twenty Ahe'ey. In time, we built this new Ahe'ey in the image of the old one. At the centre, the Temple of Lights and the Games Arena, the places where all Ahe'ey gather for special occasions and celebrations. Around it, four sectors aligned with different roles in society: Ange'el, where the guardians of ancient knowledge, our children, our teachers, and our healers live. Ma'asai, home to our farmers and artisans. Yi'ingo, home to our warriors. And Hu'urei, home to our miners, builders and architects. Until recent times, both women and men lived in the four sectors and performed all the roles.

"As our ancestors faced the loss and doom of their civilisation—their families, friends, possessions, and knowledge—they re-examined their purpose. Most of their external technology had been lost. All that they had now was inside them, in their bloodline and their memories. They were a small community that now faced many difficult questions concerning their future. There were not enough mates to build future generations. They had to decide whether they wanted to 'dilute' their powerful genetic makeup by crossbreeding with other races.

"After much deliberation, it was decided to divide the group into two. Couples and their families would now become the guardians of the bloodline. They ensured that all their descendants would continue to mate only within the bloodline by marrying their cousins. The others were allowed to find partners from other subspecies as long as they brought them into the community so that the Ange'el could raise their children.

"They wanted to ensure that the half-blood children could learn to develop the powers and potential capabilities hidden within their genes and that these would not be misused. They were unsure of the effects of crossbreeding on all the regulatory mechanisms that had been so masterfully integrated into our genome. In fact, the crossbreeding was such an unknown factor that it was decided that only the guardians of the bloodline should keep and have access to certain portions of what was left of the ancient knowledge.

"This decision effectively restructured our society. For the first time, we had a class system that developed swiftly into a monarchy. The guardians of the bloodline became the royal family of Ahe'ey, its key leaders and decision makers. A necessary evil to keep alive the treasures of an entire lost civilisation and to protect them from any potential misuse. The purity of the genes had to be preserved.

"Unfortunately, there were times when high-ranking Ahe'ey left our land to mate with humans and raise families outside our borders. The result to them was catastrophic as the Ahe'ey would hunt and kill the mixed-raced children of those who challenged this new order."

Morgan remembered the words of Gabriel as they visited Bethesda: *"The pursuit and preservation of purity can drive prejudice and hate. Many crimes against humanity have been committed in its name. Purity is best applied to water."*

"The Ahe'ey murdered these children?"

The queen nodded, her face full of sorrow.

"Some may have survived, hidden from the wrath of my ancestors. Sometimes we find the shadow of a shadow of an Ahe'ey in the face and the eyes of some humans." Viviane touched Morgan's cheek, eyes searching her face.

There she was, the queen of a fallen civilisation, the guardian of a lost bloodline, sitting sad and beautiful, the power of her history shining through and around her.

"We soon came to the conclusion that we had to keep a low profile with the rest of the Earth's people. We realised that less-evolved races may use our bloodline and its capabilities in irresponsible ways with serious repercussions. We vowed to help humanity evolve to the point where we could share our knowledge with them so that, together, we could build a world that reflected the values and virtues of our lost civilisation. We kept the focus on our newly found purpose until thirty-four years ago, when Sathian, a royal prince, unleashed the most devastating war on the women of this land."

"Lady Viviane, where exactly are we?" Morgan's mind was spinning. She had many unanswered questions about the Ahe'ey.

Viviane paused, distracted by something, her attention wavering for several moments.

"Morgan, I must leave you now; we will continue this some other time. My husband is leaving on a trip and I must see him off." The queen jumped to her feet and walked swiftly towards the Sacred House.

One Hundred and Forty-Two Years Ago - 1872

Ahe'ey

Sathian sat on the ground, leaning against the base of the bronze statue of a hooded Ange'el priestess. The figure pivoted a large crystal globe around in the air using a piece of cloth. A strong gust of wind forcefully lifted the drapes of her garment, creating ripples of movement around and behind her. Her entire body leaned backwards, attempting to balance the gravitational force caused by the motion of the transparent globe that reflected the rays of the sun. The tension of the cloth that wrapped around the sphere helped provide a sense of twirling motion to the patined bronze and crystal sculpture.

It was a representation of the Ahe'ey and their relationship to knowledge. A balancing act between the insight stored in the crystal and the ability of its navigator to command it and apply its wisdom. It was the last statue Gaia and Sathian had designed together. They had worked on it for months, planning every detail, debating every curve and sharp edge.

"Amalia told you?" Gaia's voice quivered, and her cheeks flushed as she approached him. He nodded, raising his eyes to look into hers.

"The sunlight you seek will burn your white petals and dry the soil that feeds your soul." He stood and turned his back to her, facing the statue and looking at her reflection in the crystal sphere.

"Is it so wrong to want to be spoiled, adored and protected by my future husband?"

"That's not what you're getting."

"I want to be the most important thing in someone's life."

"Yes, indeed. You want to be a thing. You limit who you are—your intelligence, curiosity and potential. You've become a victim of my Ange'el spell. Obsessed by the magnetic pull of my genes, of my beauty and of the sorcery that surrounds me. You want to control it, to own it. As if you could contain an entire ocean in a cup." He slicked his hair back with his hand and his self-important nose raised up towards the sky.

"Don't flatter yourself Sathian."

"You are doing this out of spite. You're letting your ego sabotage our happiness."

"I want to be loved."

"You are loved. I wish you a world of achievements and adventures by my side." He used his ring finger to wipe away the single tear lurking in the corner of his eye.

"I'm not a ginger root Sathian. I'm a rose. The fairest of roses."

"Then let him place you in a glass cage to be admired and desired for all eternity as the *thing* you aspire to be."

"Will you be okay?" she murmured.

He looked at the crystal sphere that gleamed in the sunlight. "You take with you everything that is dear to me." He turned to her, showcasing all his splendid Ange'el glamour. Reminding her that he was the most beautiful and accomplished man in the land. For just one moment, he moved his face towards her and, as she leaned in, irresistibly drawn by his glow, he turned and walked away.

AHE'EY'S SECRETS

Six Years Later: 1878 - Ahe'ey

Sathian sensed that sooner or later he would lose access to the Ange'el ancient knowledge repository. He knew there was no way the rulers of Ahe'ey would allow him to remain celibate. His seed was too valuable and his position at Ahe'ey too high and influential. So he worked day and night to retrieve as much information as he could, excited by the knowledge and the possibilities of what he might discover next. He marvelled at the achievements of his ancestors and still hoped to find the key to the genome of the royal family.

Someone knocked at the door.

"Sathian?" It was Alice, one of the cooks. She was a high ranking Ange'el, but her blood was not pure and due to this she was denied access to the library. Sathian used his ring to open the door and took the tray with the soup from her hands, placing it on the table behind him. He jumped towards her, grabbed her by the waist and lifted her off her feet. He danced around the room, spinning with her with elegance, lightness and happiness.

"Put me down Sathian. I'm not allowed in this room."

"Nonsense. Ignore the silly rules; you deserve to be here as much as I do."

"You changed your tune? What is going on with you today?" She asked. Her fair translucent skin turned rosy with his kiss, and her eyelashes fluttered flirtatiously.

"I found a map Alice. A map of Ahe'ey."

She adjusted her straw-coloured hair as he put her down. "You have to eat; you can't spend all day locked in this room." He ignored her. His eyes and his mind were lost somewhere in the map that was projecting out of a crystal into the transparent surface that stood in front of him. Alice brushed his long dark stray hairs away from his face.

"Look," he said pointing to the map.

"I'm not allowed to look. Do you want to get me in trouble?" She kept her eyes away from the map. "Remember to go out and enjoy some sun darling," she said before rushing to leave the room, closing the door behind her.

The Ange'el's eyes scanned the map as if he was looking for hidden treasure. Sathian's heart missed a beat as he looked at what seemed to be a secret chamber located deep within the Sma'aragdus cave system. Sma'aragdus lay under the slopes of the Ka'alama Mountain, an old extinct volcano positioned on the north side of Ahe'ey, beyond the Yi'ingo village. At more than a hundred and eighty metres high, a hundred metres wide and ten kilometres long, the cave had its own flowing river and a hidden forest that thrived with the little sunlight that managed to infiltrate the entry of the cave. Sathian had visited the Sma'aragdus caves many times but never before noticed the hidden chamber marked on the map. On closer observation, he saw what it looked to be: a human-made well that descended vertically just beside the entry of the cave, straight into the chamber. Beside the picture of the chamber the text read "the Heart of Ahe'ey." He didn't understand what it meant.

His heart was beating fast and his eyes watered with elation. He picked up the crystal and placed it in his pocket, and he ran out of the door in the direction of Ka'alama. His fingers nervously played with the crystal. He was conscious that he was breaking the rules by removing the information from the library, but he didn't want anyone to know of this secret until he could find out more information about the Heart of Ahe'ey. He wondered if the secrets of the genome of the Ahe'ey were stored within it.

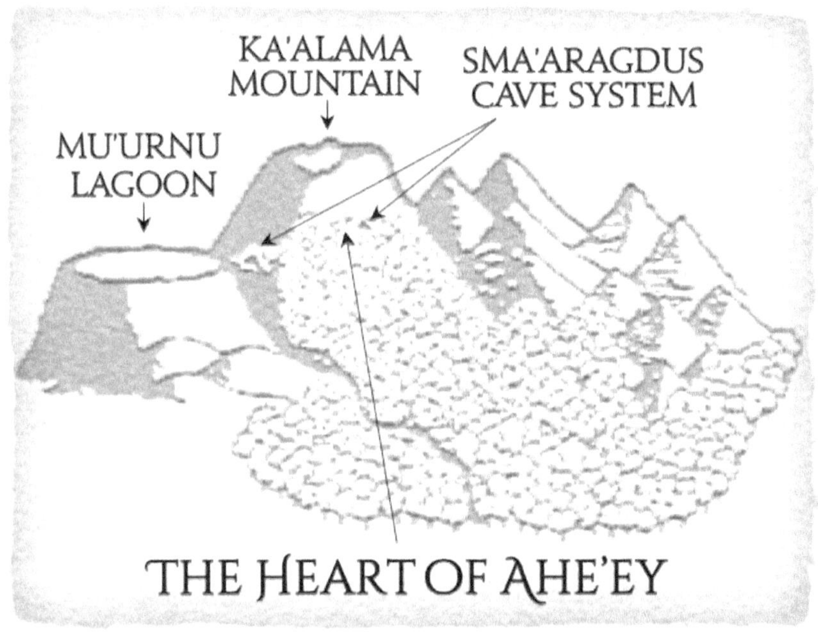

Sathian climbed Ka'alama until he reached the mouth of the cave. He looked down for a moment to enjoy the breathtaking landscape that unfolded beneath his feet. The atmosphere was surreal and magical. The cooler air from inside Sma'aragdus met the hot air from the surface and turned into clouds of mist that rose languidly above the lush forest thriving at the bottom of the cave. The turquoise river flowed from the crater at the top of the mountain between the trees and rocks of Sma'aragdus, emerging in Mu'urnu, a lagoon created by a second crater lower down in the mountain.

Sathian remembered the days he had spent with Angha swimming in the pure rivers of Sma'aragdus and watching the dragons that flew in every morning to Mu'urnu to drink from its pristine waters. The

Ange'el's jaw clenched as he realised that the best memories of his youth had turned bitter since the betrayal of his cousins, the companions of his childhood.

He walked around the mouth of the cave in search of the lost well. He faced west and continued to climb Ka'alama on its steepest side where the bush was almost impenetrable. He knew that this was likely to be the path to the lost well. The Ange'el walked fast, clearing the path with his sword, and ignoring the scratches on his arms and face from tree branches and low bush. Soon, his foot missed the earth beneath it. Sathian lost his balance and grabbed the branch of a tree nearby just in time to avoid a deadly fall. Below him, he saw a deep well sunk into the depths of the mountain. He took a step back and allowed himself a moment of recovery.

Sathian looked down into a spiral of hundreds of stone arches that lined the walls of the well. Through them, he discovered a staircase that descended into the core of the mountain. The well was over ninety metres in depth and twenty metres wide. He searched for the entrance of the staircase and once he located it, he ran down the circular stone stairs as fast as he could, without hesitation.

At the bottom of the well stood a marble statue of a winged angel. The face and hair of the figure were lowered onto his hands, from which a steady stream of water flowed into a small stone basin. Sathian took one moment to admire the sculpture. The marble stone had been masterly transformed into flesh and bone. He could almost see the bouncing of the hair of the creature as it fell down his face. The magnificent wings of the angel pointed upward to the top of the well, and hidden behind them stood a silver door.

Sathian attempted to push the door using the full weight of his body, but it was locked shut. The Ange'el stood back to observe the site more carefully, attempting to find clues about how he could open it. At the centre of the silver portal he could see an engraved circle, in its middle was an arrow held by a pin. The spear raised above the door and pointed downwards. The circle had three lines marked at nine, twelve, and three o'clock. Beside the three o'clock line stood a small symbol picturing a pair of wings.

The Ange'el attempted to rotate the arrow in both directions towards one of the marks, but neither the arrow nor the door moved from where they stood. Anxious for answers, he scanned the well for other hidden passages, but he couldn't find anything else amongst the many stone arches of the well. *You are smart. You can figure this out.* He looked at the weeping angel once again and placed his hand under the stream of water to refresh himself. As his hand touched the water, the arrow rotated to the nine o'clock mark. As he pulled out his hand from underneath the stream, the arrow fell once again to its original position.

He spent hours attempting to unlock the door, but no progress was made. The Ange'el left, frustrated and disappointed. He went back to the library in search of new information that could help him unlock the Heart of Ahe'ey.

Unleashing the Monster

One Year Later: 1879 - Ahe'ey

It did not take long after her marriage to Angha for Gaia to realise that her husband was not as devoted and possessed by her charms as she had been led to believe. Angha quickly moved on. He focused on his athletic and military pursuits and, under the guise of propagating his pure seed, he continued to openly enjoy the sexual favours from a variety of female Yi'ingo warriors.

So Gaia focused on raising her family. She had two babies in two years, Lucas and Gwydion. But the realisation that Angha had manipulated her left her frail and disoriented. Gaia and the children spent most of their time at Ange'el under the care and guidance of the priests, priestesses, and healers of the Sacred House. Angha was a besotted father and treated Gaia and his children with kindness and affection, but he was mostly absent as he worked hard to succeed Amalia at the helm of the Yi'ingo army.

Gaia continued to see Sathian often. He was still single and spent his days at the Sacred House, extracting the ancient knowledge from the quartz crystals stored in the library. In some ways, things had not changed. They were close, too close. The Ange'el settled into the role of friend and confidant. Sathian provided Gaia and the children with emotional support, intellectual stimuli and fun, and soon the two cousins were back in each other's arms. They spent most of their days together until the day Sathian's destiny changed forever.

Gaia and Sathian embraced in her room at the Sacred House. The Ange'el was kissing her neck, holding her long and fair hair in his hands.

"I love you," he whispered.

"I know." Gaia relaxed in the company of her lover, knowing her husband was hunting all day.

The door opened abruptly, banging against the wall. She screamed when Angha entered her room with a bloodied dead deer on his shoulders. He seemed always ready to defy the sensibilities of the Ange'el priestesses.

Angha dropped the deer on the floor, walked towards Sathian, and grabbed him by the neck.

"Get off me, you bull."

Angha pushed Sathian's head down and used his knee to kick him in the stomach and the face. The Yi'ingo reached towards Gaia as she walked backwards and screamed.

"Angha, please stop! I b . . . b . . . beg you."

She put her hands on her stomach as he grabbed her by the waist and abruptly unlaced her belt, using it to tie Sathian's hands behind his back. Angha continued to punish Sathian's body as Gaia screamed in agony. Sathian passed out. Angha gritted his teeth, dropped Sathian on the floor, and walked towards his wife with his fists clenched.

"It was nothing, Angha. A hug, just a friendly hug," she said, sobbing.

Her hands trembled, and her feet stumbled as she walked backwards to escape his rage. He placed his right hand on her neck and squeezed it until her face turned scarlet. She gasped for air. He turned his back to her and placed Sathian on his shoulder in the same way he previously carried the dead deer. He left.

Angha and Sathian disappeared for several days.

In her shame, Gaia concealed the event from her family. The people of the Sacred House were concerned and distressed as their intuition and Sathian's long absence indicated something was not right. Something was, indeed, very wrong.

Afraid for her life and the safety of her children, Gaia would never again speak with the Ange'el, turning her back to him at the moment that he needed her most. She had a secret, a hidden treasure that she needed to keep safe from harm. The well-being of her unborn child was her key priority.

Many years later, Sathian would make her pay for the way she had abandoned him to his gruesome fate. She would die of grief and despair soon after two of her sons perished by the hands of her one and true love.

Punishment

Sathian was dragged by Angha to the Sma'aragdus caves in the mountain, where he was tortured and humiliated for three days and three nights. Angha's punishment was brutal and ruthless. Sathian's flesh was chastised until he was swollen and disfigured, his body assaulted and his mind broken. Sathian's agony led him to the brink of madness. He, the most privileged, loved and spoiled of all creatures didn't know how to cope with so much rage, hate and pain. His screams echoed through the belly of the mountain. His intense wailing attempted to pierce through the cold heart of his punisher without success.

"You can no longer taunt me with that deformed face," Angha barked at one point, after punching Sathian in the face and breaking his nose.

When his torture was done, barely holding on to his life, Sathian dragged himself back to the Sacred House, rolling down hills with many wounds and broken bones. Nothing would stop him as he feared for her life. He searched for Gaia to assure himself of her well-being. But she ran away from him when she saw his bloodied and disfigured body appear in front of her at the Ange'el garden, the same garden that they had designed together in their youth.

At that moment, all that had held Sathian's now fragile mind together unravelled. Sathian succumbed to his rage and his hate. His trademark joy and compassion, his humanity drained from his being, pushed out by the pain and hate he had endured. His royal blood would eventually heal his flesh wounds and broken bones, but the memories of those days would haunt the Ange'el for the rest of his life.

Sathian changed—his youthful idealism, his childish innocence, his joy vanished forever. He was filled with hate and resentment and thirsted for revenge. He became unpredictable, aggressive, erratic. His quick wit was now coated with a gritty layer of sarcasm, cynicism, and spitefulness.

He locked himself away in the library, neglected his students, and avoided royal events. He focused his time on trying to unlock the door to the Heart of Ahe'ey. But for the remainder of his life, until the day of his death that door remained shut. It was indeed his biggest failure and one of a lifetime of regrets.

THE RING

One Year Later: 1880 - Library, Sacred House

"*You will marry Sabine,*" commanded Amalia, who stood by the door of the library.

"*I won't,*" replied Sathian. "I don't need to marry anyone. You need me here, harvesting information from the crystals."

"She is the highest ranking mixed race woman in the land, and almost as beautiful as Gaia. Trust me. She is wonderful."

"I'll give her my seed, but I won't marry her."

"*You will do as I order.*" Amalia's voice filled the entire room.

"Amalia, *please.* I'll bed them all. I'll do whatever you want me to do, but I need to keep this." His eyes begged as he touched his ring.

"You can't. You won't."

"Why?" He hid his hand behind his back.

"You are too unstable and dark to be trusted with such power."

"What have I done?"

"You betrayed your family. You attacked our values and our ways by seducing a married woman."

"I did all that? She loved me. He took her away from me. He. Betrayed. Me."

"She married him."

"And she has no fault in this matter? Who will take the ring? You have no one else . . . ."

"One of the children, in due time."

"We can't wait that long."

"We will. You are no longer trusted with such power. You will marry Sabine. You will honour her and show everyone that you respect the sanctity of family values."

"And I will do all this while you order me to continue to spread my seed? What family? What sanctity? We mock the values of our ancestors with this farce. We need to unlock the secrets to our blood as soon as possible and stop this nonsense. Our slavery to our blood is toxic to all our people."

"Give me that ring." Amalia placed her hand on the grip of her sword.

"Amalia, please. *I beg you.* I'm so close."

"Marry Sabine; replace my husband as the leader of the Hu'urei. Prove to us that you are a leader and a family man, and perhaps one day you will earn the right to return to this chamber." She waited a moment, watching him carefully and then repeated, "Give me the ring."

He gave her the ring, but as he left the library for the last time in his life, he carried the crystal that stored the map to the Heart of Ahe'ey in his pocket.

Present Day - 27 November 2014

Ahe'ey

Morgan watched over her Ange'el. Sage had told Morgan that Gabriel was going to be kept sedated to allow his body to heal. He had seemed overexcited and anxious for the well-being and welfare of Morgan, so Viviane and Sage had decided to force him to take a rest. They left little drops of calming oil between his mouth and nose just after he had something to eat or drink. In a few seconds, he was sleeping peacefully.

Quinn stopped by the pavilion, offering to show Morgan the Ahe'ey grounds.

"Wanna join me? I'm off to Yi'ingo," Quinn whispered.

"I'd love to visit Yi . . ." Morgan was struggling to remember the name of the place. She kissed Gabriel's forehead and left the room with Quinn.

"Yi'ingo. Sky should be training her novice warriors today. I hope to be one next year."

"So, remind me. What exactly is Yi'ingo?" Morgan asked as she and Quinn made their way through the forest to Yi'ingo.

"Ahe'ey is divided into four communities: Ange'el, Yi'ingo, Ma'asai, and Hu'urei. Ange'el is home to our healers, scholars, and priestesses and according to my father, it's the spiritual heart of this land. If you like that sort of thing. Women and children mostly inhabit the Sacred House. Few men live in Ange'el. Marcus and Dad are the exceptions. Viviane is the queen of Ahe'ey, but she is also the high priestess and Lady of Ange'el. Today, we are visiting Yi'ingo, where the warriors live. They protect Ahe'ey and the passage to your world."

"My world? Is Sky the leader of Yi'ingo?"

"Nah, she's not. The ruler of Yi'ingo is Amalia, the queen mother. She's Viviane's mother and Sky's grandmother." Quinn made a signal for Morgan to come closer and whispered in her ear, "Quite an unpleasant and bitter old lady. I shouldn't speak like this of my dad's grandmother, but you know . . . she's really not very nice."

Morgan smiled. Quinn was a spirited and outspoken young woman, quite fun to be around.

"Only warrior women live at Yi'ingo. Some of the Ma'asai join them as warriors on certain occasions, but each man must be vetted by Sky and Amalia before he is allowed to bear arms outside the arenas. Viviane and Marcus chose Sky to lead Ahe'ey during the war. She's Ahe'ey's leader while we are under martial law. Apparently, Ahe'ey hasn't seen war in over ten years. These days, we just experience the rare quarrel between Hu'urei and Yi'ingo or Ma'asai. But Marcus and Viviane have been happy to continue to share the ruling of Ahe'ey with Sky. I think they'll retire soon and want Sky to take their place."

Morgan was distracted by a detail. Sky appeared to be in her mid-twenties; the war had ended ten years ago, and Sky was the leader during wartime. It just didn't add up.

"So how old is Sky?"

"Ahhh, sorry, I forgot you're a human." Quinn's eye roll made Morgan laugh.

"The Ahe'ey can live over three hundred years. Sky is quite young. She is only forty-four years old. Viviane and Marcus are over one hundred years of age, and Amalia is probably twice as old."

"Wow!" She wondered how old Gabriel was.

"I know, right? I wish I had some of their genes instead of just being a human. It's so frustrating sometimes. Did ya know that my dad's broken bones will fully mend in two weeks? I'd probably die or take ages to recover."

"It's reassuring to know Gabriel will recover soon."

"I'm happy to share this with ya. It was confusing to me too when I first arrived here seven years ago. And, ya know, you're a human, and I'm a human, and it's nice to have you here."

"Thank you, Quinn. Go on. I'm curious."

"The Ma'asai are mostly craftsmen and farmers. They produce most of our food. They can occasionally become warriors, but it takes a lot of work and perseverance for Sky and Amalia to allow it to happen. Marcus and Bastian are both Ma'asai warriors. Bastian is the new leader of the Ma'asai. He took over for Marcus a few years ago. The Ma'asai are mostly men, although we are starting to see some Yi'ingo and Ange'el women choose to move to Ma'asai to learn their craft or to stay close to a boyfriend or husband."

"This role segregation by gender is a little surprising for such an advanced civilisation."

"Apparently it wasn't always like this. The separation happened after the war, to keep men from any dominant roles in society. It's punishment for their actions. They're no longer allowed to become warriors or to have access to weapons, and they are also not allowed to learn the mind control skills of the Ange'el."

"Mind control?"

"Uh-huh. Like I said before, some of the high-ranking Ange'el can manipulate you . . . I mean . . . influence you, persuade you. These are dangerous skills in wartime if misused." Quinn looked at Morgan's frown and added swiftly, "Please don't worry. Only royal Ange'el have that kind of power. Viviane doesn't go around reading minds and controlling people. Well, at least not all the time, I hope . . . these are skills used to rule the kingdom, to make decisions when there's a quarrel and, in Apollo's case, to help humans, prevent wars, negotiate peace, and so on."

"Is Gabriel an Ange'el?" Morgan blushed. *Can he read my mind?*

"Yeah, he is. My dad's a legend," Quinn replied, inflating her chest with pride.

"You're adorable . . . I mean, fierce—very, very fierce." Quinn sent a sharp-eyed glance Morgan's way, but let it drop and continued.

"The Hu'urei men are the sons of the war criminals that initiated the war over thirty years ago. They're mostly miners, builders and architects. They have limited rights within Ahe'ey. They aren't allowed to raise children. The kids are all raised at Ange'el, but only the girls are allowed to stay after puberty. The men aren't allowed to wander in groups outside Hu'urei land unless they are doing so for work reasons. And the women they date must report their whereabouts to their tribe leader in order to ensure their safety."

"So these guys are quite dangerous?"

"Not sure. They're angry all the time and tend to have a sharp tongue, especially around the Yi'ingo, but I have met some great Hu'urei boys in the trials for the Games. They are nice to me and don't underestimate me just because I'm human. They're not like the Yi'ingo that treat me like a fragile little doll or worse, a pet. It's infuriating."

"Quinn, are you joining us today?" Sky's voice was like thunder and lightning.

"Morgan, I'll be back in a bit," Quinn said as she dashed, jumping over the fence of the arena and picking up a sword.

Sky looked at Morgan, bowed, and turned her attention to the group of young women in front of her. *A natural-born leader*, Morgan thought as Sky demonstrated sword fighting techniques.

They practised in pairs, but they also learned to fight in larger groups. Sky explained that some of them would never be as strong as a man but that they could level the odds by fighting and defending as a team. She told the young warriors a battle story, of how her second-in-command, Madria, and she had fought twenty-six Hu'urei during the war and killed them all. How they had fought with their backs glued to each other. She explained how Madria, who was quite muscular, used to throw her over trees, taking their enemy by surprise.

"Are you warriors, or are you Ange'el in distress?" Sky shouted from the arena.

Morgan looked at Quinn, so tiny in comparison with all the others and yet completely committed and working hard to keep up. She was sweating and had a few extra bruises on her legs and arms.

"You must be the human visitor," said a cold voice behind Morgan as she walked towards the gate at Yi'ingo.

Morgan looked back and saw a thin older lady with long silver hair down to her hips. She was smaller than the other Yi'ingo. She was only just as tall as Morgan and had large brown eyes. The woman wore a comfortable long maroon dress with a sword hanging from her hip. She stood next to a black stallion, brushing his mane. The animal shared the imposing and somewhat arrogant features of his master. As Morgan turned around, the woman's expression changed. Her round eyes opened wide, and her head moved forwards and then to the side.

"What is your name, child?"

"Morgan. My name is Morgan. How are you?" Morgan couldn't get used to being called a child by the elders of Ahe'ey, but she smiled politely as she faced the gaze of this imposing woman.

The woman looked at Morgan's face as if she'd seen a ghost, her own face gone white. She didn't smile or introduce herself. She just said, "Come with me," and made a hand gesture for Morgan to follow her.

Morgan was getting quite annoyed. "I'd love to, but Sage is expecting me."

"I will send word." The woman's voice was cold but determined. She again signalled for Morgan to follow her.

"What is your name, Lady?" Morgan asked without moving.

The woman's eyes narrowed as her lips turned upward in an incisive smile. She turned to face her and spoke. "I am Amalia, the ruler of Yi'ingo and the queen mother of Ahe'ey. You are in my land."

"Oh! Hello, Queen Amalia. Your great-granddaughter Quinn was telling me all about you this afternoon."

Amalia reacted with indifference or maybe disdain. Morgan was finding it hard to read the ice-cold features of the queen mother.

"Sky is my one and only granddaughter."

This time, she turned around, started walking, and then stopped for a second, waiting for Morgan to follow her. Morgan followed, her steps feeling heavy. They both walked in the direction of the main building, a modern-looking, large rectangular structure made of wood and a glasslike material that sat on top of two huge trees.

Morgan and Amalia stood on a lift-like platform that was operated and guarded by a strong Yi'ingo warrior. Two large blocks of stone slowly made their way down, lifting the three women until they reached the Yi'ingo headquarters. It wasn't a journey for the fainthearted. The platform was completely open, and there was no handrail. Morgan witnessed the agility of the warriors as they slid down ropes to reach the ground faster. She smiled, thinking that they were too fierce and impatient to ride the lifts.

Paintings of women warriors on horseback fighting men and dragons adorned the walls of the wooden building. Each picture used strong reds, ochre yellows, oranges and lines of copper and gold that reflected the sun. The inside of the building was rich and busy, different from the simplicity of the Ange'el quarters, but the Ange'el and Yi'ingo shared their love for light. There were plenty of large windows that brought light and nature into the rooms. Pillows, rugs, weapons, and skins of animals adorned the floor and the walls. A table stood in the centre of the main room, close to the floor. Amalia sat on a pillow in front of the table and gestured for Morgan to join her. Within seconds, several girls came in to serve them food and drinks. They both had a hearty stew. Morgan copied Amalia, soaked the bread in the stew, and ate it. *Divine.*

"What do you make of our land?"

"It's all quite different, surprising, and sometimes a little surreal to be honest. Everyone has been so kind and patient with me."

"My daughter is a fool risking the security of Ahe'ey by bringing you here."

"I'm sorry, Lady Amalia. I can only reassure you that I would never break the trust of Gabriel and his family."

The queen mother made no response to the promise.

"Where were you born, child?"

"I was born in São Miguel Island, on the Portuguese Azores

archipelago."

"I see." Amalia's eyebrows were heavy, and the lines on her forehead deepened.

Morgan stood up and walked around the room, enjoying the colourful art. Women—glorious, beautiful, strong women—battling men and dragons. As she followed what seemed to be a story line across the wall, she gasped and took a step back. In front of her was a picture of Gabriel, wearing black chain mail armour that didn't defend him against the sword that was being pushed through his heart by another warrior. The artwork also showcased a massive dragon flying away from the two men.

Morgan composed herself and stepped forward to take a closer look at the details of the painting. It was Gabriel, she was sure of it, and her heart sank as she looked at the patch of blood on her lover's chest. He wore an eye patch covering his left eye; his head pulled back in pain as the sword went through his body.

"Gabriel!" she gasped, turning to Amalia.

"No, that is not Gabriel; that is my cousin Sathian. The man that brought war into this land."

"He looks just like—"

"Yes, he does. They cannot be trusted. Their minds are too powerful and their hearts too weak. Mark my words child. Gabriel, the last of the Ange'el men, will one day become as dangerous and spineless as that creature." Amalia pointed to the figure of Sathian on the wall.

Morgan bit her lip, stopping herself from jumping to Gabriel's defence. "Lady Amalia, what happened in this land? Who is Sathian? What has he done?"

Amalia observed Morgan's features. The old woman was lost in thought.

"Lady Amalia?"

The queen mother shook her head and quickly arranged her long silver hair in a ponytail. "Yes, I will tell you, Morgan. You should know."

Morgan was confused by the words of the Yi'ingo. She sat in front of Amalia, waiting for an answer.

"In our generation, there were only five royals left: me and my brother Angha, my cousin Michael and his sister Gaia, and our cousin Sathian. Michael and I fell in love at a young age, and Gaia married my brother. Sathian lost some of his privileges when he married a mixed-race Hu'urei. He grew bitter and unfulfilled, contaminating his people, the Hu'urei, with his anger and resentment against the royal bloodline and our privileges, the same privileges he'd lost by marrying Sabine.

"Sathian was too powerful, of a mercurial nature, and quite influential. He was a masterful Ange'el that could plant his thoughts in his people's minds and manipulate their direction and values. Over the coming years, the royal family had to deal with civil unrest. The Hu'urei demanded equal rights and opportunities, inspired by a leader that painted them a vivid picture of the treasures of information that were being kept from them. And yet this was also a man that knew well how risky and possibly catastrophic the misuse of that knowledge could be. But Sathian was blinded by grief, jealousy, resentment, and he was thirsty for power.

"Power or equal rights?" Morgan regretted her words as soon as she'd spoken them. The queen's angry eyes were set on her, scorching her skin from a distance.

"Power and greed. At the time, the royal bloodline was beginning to thrive as both Gaia and I were able to bear three children each. It was perfect. I had three girls, Gráinne, Luna, and Viviane, and Gaia bore three boys: Gwydion, Lucas, and Marcus. As they grew into adulthood and started to raise their own young families, we became hopeful. Our numbers were multiplying, and the bloodline was safe. You see, our pure genes were designed to limit women from having more than two or three children, a way to ensure population control. So the number of pure Ahe'ey tends to remain stable as just enough young are born to replace the old. In contrast, the mixed-race population thrives and grows."

There's a lot of inbreeding in this place. No wonder they are all a bit mad. For a moment Morgan questioned her own sanity. She thought that she might be experiencing a lucid dream. She blinked her eyes, but nothing changed; Amalia was still speaking.

"Sathian was now fully immersed in driving a revolution. He knew that the only way he could dismantle the royal family was to take control of the women. He wanted the royal women to bear mixed-race children. He knew that if and when they did that, they would join him in asking for equal rights and opportunities for their impure babies. He and his son Iblis planned an attack during the night of the summer solstice, the night where warriors would be tired after a day of competing in the Games and the Ange'el would be in deep meditation, plunged into the universal consciousness of the planet.

"Sathian and his men moved on the Ange'el and Yi'ingo; their goal was to kidnap and rape the royal women. My daughter Luna fought bravely, and they killed her and her husband, Lucas. They kidnapped my daughter Gráinne and her newborn girl, Fay. He used the baby to force Gráinne to do his will. Gráinne was kept in captivity and forced to bear a child by Iblis, a bastard boy named Joshua.

"Sathian and Iblis led their armies into Ange'el, Yi'ingo, and Ma'asai, pillaging the land and raping as many high-ranking women as they could find."

"I despair. What's wrong with men? The same tragedy is repeated all over the world. I'm so tired of the violence of men. Tell me about the good men, Lady Amalia." Morgan's outburst allowed her to connect with Amalia.

The old woman placed her weathered hand on Morgan's shoulder.

"I have lost my faith in men in the day I buried my second daughter. There are no good men." Amalia shook her head, her face full of sorrow. Then, she continued her account.

"Women and some men fought side by side against the Hu'urei. Our armies were led by Angha, who was, at the time, the leader of the Yi'ingo army. But a society that had led a peaceful existence for thousands of years was unprepared for the evil that was now roaming the land. Sky's father, Gwydion, together with Angha, Michael, Marcus, and I made many unsuccessful attempts to rescue my daughter Gráinne. She was so afraid for the life of her young daughter that, a year after the birth of her son, she ran to Lake Do'oras and opened the passage to the outside world, attempting to escape from Iblis and Sathian. Without the protection of the moonstone, the toddler drowned, and Gráinne died, consumed by the energy of the portal."

"Outside world? What passage is this? Why did she need a stone to protect her?" *Where am I? Am I ever going to be able to leave this place?*

"The portal that connects Ahe'ey with your world. The moonstone is the key that opens the passage."

"I thought we were on an island?"

"We are."

"This passage, how does it work?"

"We don't know." Amalia's reply was short and sharp revealing her frustration with Morgan's questions. "We have lost the knowledge many years ago."

"Okay . . . so what happened to Sathian?"

"Marcus eventually killed Sathian, but not before the former Ange'el killed Gwydion and my husband, Michael, by unleashing a

Wali'ingooteer dragon on them."

"Dragons? There are dragons in Ahe'ey?"

Amalia nodded. "The dragons were kept in Hu'urei to help with mining and construction projects as they were capable of moving large blocks of stone for long distances. They are extremely strong and can fly. Unfortunately, the use of the Wali'ingooteer in the war caused devastation in Ahe'ey. Angha and I focused all our attention on rebuilding a Yi'ingo army that could crush the Hu'urei and the Wali'ingooteer. Marcus and Viviane ascended to the throne of Ahe'ey, managing the affairs of this land and assuring the safety of the three remaining royal children—their son Gabriel, Sky, and Bastian."

"Gabriel and Sky were raised together?" Morgan was curious about the acrimonious relationship between the two cousins.

"Yes, they were together until the day I took her away to lead the Yi'ingo army and he fled from the war to New York with his tail between his legs."

Morgan tried to ignore Amalia's unkind words towards Gabriel.

"How did you win the war?"

"The odds turned in our favour when Viviane led all the Ange'el in prayer, attempting to connect with the spirit of the Wali'ingooteer beasts. After years of savage killings, the dragons suddenly stopped and sought a new home in the caves of Ka'alama Mountain. The rebels, led by Iblis, fled to the Ju'ug Mountains, where they fought Sky and her troops for many years. They were finally defeated ten years ago, the day Sky killed Iblis, avenging the loss of her mother and sister.

"The dragons were banished from having any contact with the Ahe'ey and only kept alive because of their possible value in defending this land against any external forces. Angha moved to Ka'alama to become the new master of the Wali'ingooteer."

Morgan had gained renewed compassion for the queen who had outlived so many of her children and grandchildren. Amalia had lost her family and experienced great darkness.

Morgan looked again at the picture on the wall; before her stood a being of pure evil, the man that had ordered the rape of an entire civilisation of women, a devil that had perished by the sword of Gabriel's father. *How can the same beautiful body harbour such opposite souls?*

Amalia stood beside Morgan, contemplating the painting. "Their genes are designed to seduce any living creature."

"Whose genes?" Morgan asked.

"The royal Ange'el. Like the sirens in your folk tales, they will enchant you, sing you songs of wonder and delight, make you lose your sense of self, your direction and then, when you have submitted to their will, they will lure you to your destruction."

"He's not like that." Morgan's response was automatic. She bit her lip attempting to hold back her impetuous voice.

Amalia's smile was adorned with pity and superiority. "Foolish creature. You are just one of his pets; another experiment. He will soon discard you, like a used toy. He will break you, and you will wither, drowning in your misfortune and despair. It is our law; he can't waste his royal blood on you. I see a touch of our blood in your features, but you are still unworthy of his seed."

"I'm not a pet, and I don't need anybody's seed," Morgan said before turning around and leaving swiftly. *A touch of their blood in my features?*

BEFORE THE STORM

Danger in the Woods

Present Day: 27 November 2014 - Yi'ingo village

Morgan was deep in thought as she walked back to Ange'el after her meeting with Amalia. She was amazed and confused by all that she'd learned about Ahe'ey and its people. *Am I dreaming?*

"Who are you?"

Startled by the question, she looked around and found a bearded man sitting under a tree by the walking path. He stared at her.

"I have never seen you before. What's your name?"

There was no warmth or friendliness in his deep voice. He stood up and walked in Morgan's direction; his imposing figure blocked the last rays of the setting sun. She took a few steps back, intimidated by the size and manner of this man.

"Hi. I'm in a hurry."

"Keep me company tonight? I'm free."

Morgan noticed the scar over his lip, which gave him a lopsided, mischievous-looking smile. She was so used to the physical perfection of the Ahe'ey that she found herself instinctively judging him as having inferior genes. She admonished herself. *What are you doing? Are you now dismissing people based on their scars?*

"I have other plans," she said, walking faster.

He walked by her side, examining her. "You're different from the others."

"That's what they keep telling me."

"What's your name?"

"Morgan. We're in the middle of a forest, and it's getting dark. I don't know you and am asking you to step away from me." Morgan's voice was commanding, and she settled her face into a stone-cold expression.

"I'm doing no harm. I'm just talking to you." He shot her a glance that made her skin crawl. "Want to have sex with me?" He grabbed her arm.

"*Don't touch me!*" She yanked her arm away and stepped back from him. Her chest heaved with distress, but she was careful to show no exterior signs of panic.

"It's a compliment." He raised his hands, palms towards her.

"Harassment is never a compliment," Morgan said, clenching her fists and turning to face him. She had to look up to meet his eyes.

"You're average looking. Take the offer. I'm doing you a favour."

Morgan rolled her eyes, tired of being called flawed.

"Have you looked in the mirror lately?" She pressed her lips together trying to control her feisty tongue.

Suddenly they were interrupted.

"Step away from her, Hu'urei," Sky roared. "I've told you to stay away from this path." The Yi'ingo strode towards them, holding her head high, looking tall and intimidating. Her hand was firmly on her sword. "Go back to your village *now!*"

Morgan was relieved to see Sky; she immediately felt safe as the powerful warrior placed herself between Morgan and the man.

"Relax, Warrior Queen. I'm just talking to the weird one. Howza man supposed to get some fun these days? Maybe you'll join me tonight? We'll make impure babies together." His eyes twitched, and the disdain was plain in his face as he looked at Sky beneath lowered lashes.

"*Step away from her!*"

"I'm not breaking the law. You have no right to interfere. You've killed my father and my uncle. You take my children. What else do you want?"

"Get near her again, and I'll arrest you or kill you, depending on my mood."

Sky was now standing face-to-face with the man. She was as tall as him, but he was twice as big. There was no fear in her face. Neither his words nor his build seemed to faze her in any way. "Follow the path of your ancestors, and you'll have the same fate, you useless scum."

"She's alone at twilight in these woods. She's asking for it. She can speak up and fend for herself."

"It's not my responsibility to defend myself from you. You shouldn't invade my personal space," Morgan spoke, peeking her head out from behind Sky.

"Walk away scum," Sky grunted.

"Watch your back, Yi'ingo, or you'll share the fate of your mother," he yelled, moving even closer to Sky, who stood firmly in the same place. Her hand was on her sword, waiting for his next move. "Or perhaps I'll go after that little blue-haired human that you love so much."

Her elbow hit his face like lightning hitting the earth, and he fell on his back, holding his broken nose in between his hands. She kicked his stomach twice, pulled up her sword, and pressed it against his neck.

"You touch any woman on this land, and I'll hunt you down, then kill you slowly and painfully." She kicked his groin, and he screamed at the excruciating pain.

"Your brother will hear about this."

Her eyes raged fire and water simultaneously. "I have no brother."

Sky and Morgan walked away, leaving the Hu'urei curled up on the ground, delirious with pain.

"You okay?"

"I'm fine. Thanks, Sky. That guy was a freak."

"It's in their nature. They're aggressive, violent, and vile."

"You know Sky, saying it's in their nature actually excuses their behaviour and takes accountability away from them."

The Yi'ingo looked down at Morgan as if it wasn't worth her time. "It's in their blood. Quinn should have warned you—the Hu'urei use some of these roads at night to seek sexual partners. Since we instated martial law and segregated the men, they roam the roads at night looking for sex."

"Sounds like you have a lot of sexually frustrated citizens."

"Yes, it's not a high priority in my long list of problems. I'll walk you to Ange'el."

"Thank you. Although . . . you are making my life difficult with all this life-saving business." Morgan looked at Sky sideways with a cheeky and defiant look. "Just so you know, I'll continue to challenge your pretentious supremacist nonsense."

"If you had my blood you wouldn't need saving. You'd be smart enough to stay away from these woods, and you could fend for yourself," Sky retorted with a half-smile.

"I was doing just fine before you arrived."

"Sure you were. Here. Take this." Sky unsheathed her sword and handed it to Morgan. "Learn how to use it."

Morgan raised an eyebrow and looked at the sword. "This won't help me. I don't think I could ever wave this thing around. Violence isn't the answer."

"Is this why I keep having to come to your aid? Take it. Who knows, you might like it. If . . . you are strong enough to lift it, weakling. That blood of yours makes you too weak."

Morgan's eyes narrowed, and she snapped the sword from Sky's hands.

"That pedestal seems awfully high. Watch your step, or you might just fall on your flawless face."

They both laughed. Morgan dragged the sword as they walked together to Ange'el.

The Test

Marcus climbed Ka'alama by foot. He wanted the time to finely craft his request to his father. He needed to carefully consider every word, every phrase, every expression of his face and voice. Once in a while, he could see the eyes of the dragons glowing in the dark, reflecting the light of the moon. The creatures watched him from a distance, attentively guarding their lair and their master within it.

Marcus refreshed himself jumping into the Mu'urnu lagoon. He cleared his mind, and attempted to suppress his worries. As he entered the cave, he had to adjust his eyes to the darkness and dampness of the place. He walked through the gloomy corridor, following the light several metres in front of him. The passage led into the colossal Sma'aragdus cave that opened to the skies above it—the entrance for the giant winged lizards that slept within it.

Angha's home was carved into the rock wall. Marcus entered a series of rooms connected by carved staircases. Each room was stocked with expensive furnishings that expressed the colours and sensibilities of the Yi'ingo. Red, copper and gold artwork adorned the walls, depicting battles and hunting expeditions. The mighty Yi'ingo warriors held swords and bows. Their postures showcased all the strength and beauty of their perfect and highly functional bodies. The largest frame portrayed Marcus, the only Ma'asai warrior present in the artwork. In it, Marcus pushed his sword into Sathian's heart.

"This memory of your heroism warms my heart in the cold and dark solitude of my existence. My youngest son avenged us all." Angha approached his son and placed his hand on his shoulder.

"I'm lucky to be alive. I still don't understand why he spared me."

"He didn't spare you. You killed him in battle against all odds." Angha abruptly removed his hand from Marcus' shoulder.

Marcus observed the painting, reliving the battle, and finally decided to tell his father what had really happened that night.

"We were fighting Sathian and a group of twelve Hu'urei when the dragon flew in. Michael died immediately, when the beast used his tail to pierce his chest. Gwydion and ten other Yi'ingo had to stay back and fight the dragon while I went in pursuit of Sathian. I could not pin him down. He was so fast and agile. My armour could barely cope with the power of his blade and I failed to defend myself against several of his blows."

"You fought bravely."

"When I took my helmet off so that I could follow his rapid movements, he wounded my left leg. I thought I was going to die."

"You took your helmet off?"

"Yes. The Wali'ingooteer had killed all the Yi'ingo, including my brother, and was now flying in my direction. But Sathian lowered his sword. He looked at me and then at the dragon. With my leg wounded, I knew I couldn't escape the beast, so I decided to attempt to kill Sathian before the dragon could kill me. I had resigned myself to die. As I moved to attack Sathian and the dragon jumped to attack me, I saw Sathian raise the palm of his hand, sending the dragon away. I pushed my sword into Sathian's heart as the dragon flew to the skies."

Angha's face turned—eyes focused on Marcus like sharp spears, lips creased with tension, and fists clenched, triggering the muscles in his arms and neck.

"I assumed Sathian wanted to kill me himself," Marcus finished.

"Why are you here Marcus?" Angha barked.

"Father, how are you?" Marcus was puzzled by the old man's reaction.

"Surprised to see you here."

"I came to ask for your support."

"Speak."

"Sky's strength, courage, leadership, and charisma have elevated the Yi'ingo into power and brought peace to our land. But, today, Ahe'ey is divided, and the factions are becoming more and more aggressive towards each other. The Hu'urei haven't caused problems in over ten years, but they feel there is nothing they could ever do or say that would re-establish their status as full citizens of Ahe'ey."

"They are traitors and murderers."

"They are young men, casualties of war, still paying for their fathers' misdeeds. Joshua is a good man and a natural leader. He deserves a voice at the court; after all, he is Sky's half-brother and Gráinne's son."

"She was raped!"

"Not his fault. The Hu'urei feel they are outcasts—unable to take part in society—and unless we reach out to them, there will be a full rebellion."

"Your friendship with Joshua makes you weak and too accommodating to the needs of the bullies that destroyed this land."

"We must end this hate against all men. You must speak to your sister."

"I will talk to Amalia and Sky and ask them to start receiving some of the Ma'asai boys at Yi'ingo. Sky should marry Bastian soon."

"It's not enough. We must mend the rift with the Hu'urei. But the Yi'ingo will never initiate this."

"The Yi'ingo must rule. Without us, you would have perished in the war."

"The Yi'ingo are thriving and have protected this land and its borders quite well for many years, but that focus has left them disengaged from the key reason of our existence. The focus on Ahe'ey meant they lost interest in contributing to the overall well-being of humankind and this planet. They have lost their connection with humans."

"Humans need to be ruled by us. They are destroying our planet."

"That's because we no longer know how to guide, teach, and influence the affairs of the world. We are struggling just to bring order and peace to Ahe'ey."

"Humans and Ahe'ey don't need guidance; they need a leash. Amalia and Michael made the wrong decision to crown Viviane. No Ange'el should ever rule this land. And you . . . you are soft under the influence of your wife. This planet and all its people need to be ruled with an iron fist."

"No. We have one, and it's not working. Sky had to make hard decisions, unfair decisions in some situations. The conflict between Yi'ingo and Hu'urei will not heal while Sky is in power, and while Amalia guides her hand. Even the Ma'asai struggle with Sky's disdain and distrust for men."

"What are you proposing?"

"I want your support to place Gabriel on the throne of Ahe'ey. Gabriel must be king. Amalia and the Yi'ingo will accept him if you support him."

"You have lost your mind! Sky must rule. It's time for the Yi'ingo to take the throne. No Ange'el male should be given such power. They are weak and dangerous. Sathian's hate still lurks in the minds of the Hu'urei."

"My son is honourable, fair and a leader. He will never abuse his power. He understands the outside world and can bring our tribes together."

"I haven't seen him since he was a child. Is this not the boy who abandoned Sky alone in the forest? The coward who refused to fight in the war? I hear that he doesn't care about our land, that he prefers the company of humans and the skirts of the Ange'el. Your son is a coward. Blood, not essential oils should stain his hands."

Marcus had prepared for this moment. He knew what he had to do. For a second, he vacillated, overwhelmed by guilt. He heard the voice of his wife inside his head.

Be strong Marcus. We don't have any other choice. We are running out of time.

"Let me prove to all Ahe'ey that Gabriel is strong and brave enough. That he deserves the throne of Ahe'ey. Please, Father!"

"How?"

"I need your most powerful Wali'ingooteer."

"For what purpose?"

Marcus took a deep breath and forced his mouth to speak; his lips resisted at every word. "To fight my son."

"Are you insane?"

"Let him prove his valour to you, to Ahe'ey. Allow him to fight your strongest dragon."

"Gabriel will be crushed, Marcus. Do you wish his death?"

"Please. I beg you."

"He is unfit to rule. Amalia tells me he wastes his royal seed by refusing to lie with our women and to take their fertile wombs."

"Then you have nothing to lose with his death." Marcus' tongue burned. He felt the desire to pull it out and feed it to the dragons.

"You sentence your son to a most terrible demise. Is Viviane aware of this?"

Marcus inhaled deeply before responding. "My wife and I speak as one. If he defeats the dragon, he will be king."

"He will not Marcus. Your son will descend to the depths of hell as Sky ascends to the throne."

"Your answer?"

"Sky must take the throne soon. Viviane's sentimentality brings weakness to Ahe'ey. We need a strong hand to control the Hu'urei and the humans, and to defend our pure blood. If I need to kill Gabriel to make Sky queen, so be it."

Marcus bowed his head. His heart sank into his hands and he squeezed them tightly.

"Marcus, remember this day. The day you and Viviane murdered your son."

Many Tender Smiles

28 November 2014 - Ange'el village

Morgan was awakened just before dawn by a scream. Aria ran into the pavilion, crying. The little girl appeared to be distressed as she ran barefooted straight towards Gabriel's room followed by Morgan.

"*Apollooo!*" she cried. "Losss hombres . . . los hombres mataronn . . . hurt."

Gabriel sat up in bed. "Shhh, it's only a dream, mi amor. Solo fue un sueño," Gabriel whispered as he held her in his arms. "I'm here, remember? You're safe." He stroked her back, and she immediately calmed down and began playing with his hair. Soon, she was asleep again. He placed his lips to the child's head in a prolonged kiss and then laid her down beside him.

The corners of his lips jumped upward at the sight of Morgan. "I'm sorry," he said, "we didn't mean to wake you up."

"Is she okay?" she asked, standing by the door.

"She'll be fine." He adjusted his body assessing his state.

"How are you feeling?"

"Okay," he said. "Was I sleeping for long?"

"Three days. It's the twenty-eighth of November," Morgan answered.

He attempted to get out of bed, but his face contorted with every movement. Black bandages wrapped his leg, arm, shoulder, and torso. He wore a dark blue sarong tied around his waist. She walked towards him, sat on the bed, placed her body under his left arm and helped him up.

"Have you been looked after?"

"You have a wonderful family, Gabriel." She looked up, still holding onto him, feeling the warmth of his body and enjoying the citrusy scent of his skin. He smiled, took a step away from her and picked up the cane that lay on the floor next to his bed.

"I hope they have been welcoming. I wasn't expecting to be down for so long."

"Sage forced you to take a much-needed rest."

"I'll have words with the lady in question." His threat was warm and playful.

She realised that they had lost the intimacy they previously shared. His politeness was somewhat distant and guarded. His eyes, expression, and words were as kind and assuring as ever, but he seemed extra cautious. He respected her space and made no attempt to re-establish physical contact. She realised that he probably had no idea why she'd run from him in New York or that Bastian had spoken to her.

"I'm going to have a shower." He left the room, using the cane to support himself, keeping the weight off his right leg.

When he came back, it was already daylight. Morgan was reading a book and lying on the chaise longue.

Gabriel was barefoot; his right arm tied in front of his chest. He wore comfortable white slacks and a white tunic. The white material had a translucent quality to it. She peeked over her book admiring the contour of his body showered by the morning sunlight. *Beautiful.*

"Is that Sky's sword?" He raised his eyebrow and pointed to the weapon leaning against the wall—a long gold-plated sword with a phoenix on its grip.

"Uh-huh. A gift from your cousin."

"You spoke to her?" He looked somewhat puzzled.

"Yes, I did. She's still a bit intense," she said, "but very . . . helpful. I've also met your mother and grandmother." He frowned, and she changed the subject swiftly to avoid worrying him with the encounters of the previous day. "Why do the Ahe'ey still use swords? Aren't you supposed to be a more advanced species?"

His eyes opened wide. "You seem to be quite well connected and informed, lady."

"Yes. I am," she replied lightly. "Why would anyone use swords in this day and age?" She put her book down.

He picked up the sword with his left hand, raising it in front of him as he spoke, "To be a warrior with a sword in your hand is different from being a warrior that holds a gun or the remote control of a drone. There is nothing fearless, brave, or honourable in killing from a distance. Killing from a distance changes the nature of war.

He turned to face the garden.

"Taking a life should be the last resort. It shouldn't be painless or effortless. You must feel it. Live it. Suffer it. The least you can do is to stand face-to-face with the person you are going to kill. There is honour in doing so."

His words and idealism moved her.

"The Ahe'ey chose a long time ago to keep things simple and honourable. Produce and consume only what we need, cause minimum impact to nature, and deliberately and consciously deal with matters of the life and death of all creatures, removing the desensitisation and trivialisation that you experience in your world. I don't mean to romanticise war. Killing with a sword is as terrible as killing with a gun."

Morgan walked towards him and embraced him, resting her head on his back and caressing his flat stomach over the bandages and under his tunic. He turned to face her, taking a step backwards away from her. She saw confusion in his eyes.

"Shall we go for a walk?" he asked, leaning the sword against the wall. She realised that she had no right to touch him so intimately after everything that had happened. She was embarrassed by her unusual forwardness. Her desire for him seemed to, once again, cloud her best judgment.

They walked side by side quietly. The pace was slow, as he was still quite weak and in pain. They followed a stone path through the trees. The surrounding landscape was beautiful. The main building, the Sacred House, was positioned at the centre of a large garden. Around it were several pavilions for visitors, a fishpond, an edible garden, a rotunda, and many statues of lean human figures that looked like fairies, female warriors and angels.

"Morgan," he said as he played with his thumbs, looking straight into her eyes, "you must allow me to explain why—"

"Bastian spoke to me when we first arrived here," she said reassuringly.

He processed the information with an almost imperceptible nod. "May I ask you—why did you run away? Did I hurt you or upset you?"

She could hear the angst in his voice. Morgan shook her head.

"I want you to know that what happened between us wasn't a lie. I . . . I care for you . . . ." He spoke with such softness, his head and shoulders leaning towards her, compensating for their difference in height. His willingness to be so open and vulnerable surprised and relaxed her.

She raised her fingers and gently caressed his face. She replied courageously, "I was running from myself, from my demons." She stopped for a second, gathering her strength. "I saw Sage kiss you and . . . ."

He closed his eyes and threw his head back, "I'm sorry. I can only imagine how strange we all are to you."

"I should learn to trust you, and to accept my worth," Morgan replied. "I'm a work in progress. Flawed. Very, very flawed."

"Listen Morgan. This place is different . . . and I'm different."

"I know."

"I want you to be able to take the time to get to know me. To really know me, beyond this . . . ."

"What?"

"Never mind." He rushed his hand through his hair. "I know this is all a little peculiar and that you'll have many questions. I don't want you to feel pressured. I want you to enjoy every moment of your time here with us at Ahe'ey." He kissed her forehead. "I'm really looking forward to showing you my strange world."

She placed her hand on the back of his neck, pulling him closer so that she could kiss him on the lips. He pulled back gently and kissed the palm of her hand. She took a deep breath, trying not to read too much into it. She had doubted Gabriel too many times already, the man that had almost died because of her foolish insecurities.

She remembered the attack.

"Gabriel, who's trying to kill me? Why is the CIA involved?"

"We believe Zanus is behind a plan to assassinate over two thousand people—high-profile socially progressive types from around the world. Leaders that speak about the environment, equal rights and other left-leaning agendas."

"He wouldn't dare," Morgan was shocked by the revelation. "So why don't they arrest him?"

"All attacks are led by Muslim Americans. They leave behind incriminating evidence towards Arab terrorist organisations, setting up the perfect storm. He is at the helm of a sophisticated campaign to drive fear, to push people into the arms of the conservative right and place him in power. It's an elaborate plan to lead up to the 2016 presidential elections—kill the people that speak against them in the media, quiet their peers with fear of further attacks and blame Muslims."

"I need to get back and warn these people. I need to speak up against this monster."

"Morgan, the CIA is working on this."

"Have people been killed?"

He nodded. "To my knowledge, at least twelve."

"Then we must speak up. Face him publicly with these accusations. We can use the power of social media to spread the word. We can't let people continue to die."

"We're working on it. Social media is a dangerous tool."

"Why?"

"Governments and corporations are listening; it's not safe."

"Says the guy who comes from a place where the rulers can read minds and manipulate people."

"It's not the same; we are driven by values coded in our genes."

"Was Sathian guided by the same values?" His head dropped and she felt as if she had crushed him with a large boulder such was the intensity of his gaze. "I must go back, Gabriel. If I accuse him publicly, he would be too busy defending himself to continue his plan."

"And we'll lose the chance to gather proof against him and put him in jail. Morgan. Please. I just need a few more days to heal. Stay here with me, and we will leave together in a few days— a week tops. Will you do this for me? Trust me just this once?"

How could she deny him after all he had done for her? She nodded.

Gabriel and Morgan sat on the grass in the shade of a tree in the garden so that he could rest his leg. Once in a while he gasped for air, reminding her of the real extent of his injuries. After a while, they heard some voices approaching.

"Why did ya pick a fight with her, Ollie? I'm the one who'll need to live at Yi'ingo in a few months' time. I don't need more enemies there."

"I won't be quiet while they humiliate us. They needed a lesson."

"And exactly what lesson did you teach them by getting beaten up by a girl two years younger than you?"

"At least I do something. Everyone else ignores it. I'm sick of it."

"Morgan, meet my son, Oliver. You already know Quinn," Gabriel said as the two young people passed by them.

"Oh, hi . . . ," Oliver said. He had big brown doe eyes and dreadlocks that pointed in all directions.

"Hi, Oliver, it seems that you need to have someone look at that eye," Morgan replied.

Oliver tucked his face down, hiding his eyes beneath his hair. His chocolate skin concealed some of his bruises, but the swollen eye and the scratches around his eyebrow were quite evident. He responded with a cold stare.

Quinn punched her brother in the shoulder. "It's okay, Morgan. Ollie's just awkward, that's all," Quinn replied with her usual sassiness.

Gabriel stood up to have a look at Oliver's eye, but the young man pulled away.

"It's nothing." He stroked his hand through his tousled hair. "How are you, Dad?"

"I'm okay. What happened?" Gabriel asked. Both Oliver and Quinn stood in silence for some time. "Well?"

"Some of the Yi'ingo apprentices were . . . teasing us in the training arena," Quinn bit her lower lip.

"I told you both that I don't want you there without Bastian or me or another adult present. You're still too young."

"I'm almost fifteen, and we went with Sky," Oliver retorted.

"What were they teasing you about?"

The teens looked at each other and then lowered their heads and looked at their feet almost in sync.

"Apollo, we'll chat some other time," Quinn replied with a forced smile.

"Quinn, it's fine. Morgan's a friend."

The girl kicked the gravel on the ground nervously. "They said you were a coward for not participating in the Games, that you are afraid of Sky. That you deserted from the war," Quinn said and then she raced to Gabriel and gave him a hug. "We know it's not true, Apollo. We know you. Don't worry."

Gabriel kissed Quinn's hair and looked at Ollie, who remained where he was with his head down. "Why did you fight, Ollie?"

"Someone has to defend our honour. Sky certainly doesn't. She stays silent while others taunt us."

For a brief moment, Gabriel's eyes closed as his eyebrows collapsed over them. He recovered and replied calmly, "Honour? Are you defending my honour or your pride?"

"*Why don't you fight?* I've seen you—you are the bravest of them all. When you rescued me, you were . . . amazing. You could beat any of those Yi'ingo freaks with a hand tied behind your back. Why don't you take part in the Games? Why don't you show what you are really capable of? *Why do you let us down? Do you want us to be ashamed of you?*"

Morgan noticed the large waves of unconfined emotion spewed by Ollie's face and body. His sister rolled her eyes, crossed her arms, and gave him a dirty side-stare.

Gabriel took some time to speak. "Ollie, there will come a day when you will understand that there are more important things than purposeless demonstrations of bravery. There are more important things than my pride or your pride. I can't make you not be ashamed of me. I hope that, in your heart, you know better and that my actions—past, present, or future—never lead to real dishonour in this family. What others think of me isn't my concern. I'm truly sorry you had to go through this but ask that you never again fight to defend my pride."

Ollie was holding back his tears. "Why does Sky . . . ."

"Never mind Sky. She has a lot of responsibilities. She has no time to think about such small matters."

"Why do you always defend her? She hates you."

The boy has a point, thought Morgan. For one second, she saw Gabriel turn his sombre gaze towards her as if he'd read her mind.

"Ollie, please, let's go and have a look at that eye before the swelling starts obstructing your vision."

The two teens walked in the direction of Ange'el. Gabriel and Morgan walked behind them.

"Are you okay?" asked Morgan.

"How could I not be when I have you here with me?" His eyes betrayed his words. His jaw was clenched, his eyebrows heavy, and his arms crossed in front of his chest.

"Do you want to talk about it?"

Gabriel shook his head.

Morgan couldn't take her eyes off Gabriel. She had so many unanswered questions about the sweet, broody Ange'el. The man who had jumped in front of a car to save her life was believed a coward in this strange land. *It just doesn't add up. How can anyone think he's a coward?*

Ollie was sitting on a bench in the healing room of the Sacred House. Gabriel was beside him, cleaning his wound and applying some healing gel. His long hands were so gentle—how could these be the same strong hands that had fought for her at the Met? Morgan recognised Gabriel's expression and gestures. She had seen the same practices being used by Viviane and Sage when they were taking care of Gabriel. *You're a healer too*, Morgan thought as she observed the Ange'el. Gabriel closed his eyes; he seemed to be absorbing his son's pain into his own body.

"I'm okay, Apollo. You don't really need to do that. It's not like I'm weak or anything," said the teenager.

"Let him," Quinn said. "After all, you're only human."

Gabriel opened his eyes and looked at Quinn, who was standing near Morgan by the window. He tapped on the bench. "Come sit here, Quinn." The girl sat beside her brother. "Being human is a wonderful thing. There's nothing 'only' about it."

"Yeah, I know, but we don't have the same . . . superpowers . . . y'all have. Look at ya, already up and about."

"Remember, Quinny, many of our skills can be learned. Notice how Sage is becoming such a great healer, you are becoming such an extraordinary warrior, and Ollie is one of our best produce growers."

"We'll never be as good as you or Sky and Bastian, and . . . " she paused.

"Yes?" Gabriel asked.

"Even within the human species, we seem to be the wrong race," Quinn said, wincing and shoving her hands in her pockets.

"Wrong race?" Gabriel asked. He seemed genuinely surprised.

"Yeah," Ollie continued, "you don't see Africans or Asians in this land. Clearly there is something special about being Caucasian that made you evolve faster as a race. It's annoying for the rest of us, you know?"

Gabriel put the gel and the cloth down, walked towards the window, and paused for a second. He turned around to face his children. "The Ahe'ey race is all white due to geography and chance. The land inhabited by the Ahe'ey twelve million years ago turned out to be the most fertile land, also populated with the few animals that could be domesticated. The surplus allowed us to focus on other things, innovating and creating new technologies. Caucasians were just at the right place and at the right time."

"But look at the so-called first-world countries today. They are also mostly white." Quinn said.

"That's changing fast. Biological differences within the human races are negligible. Other non-Caucasian races have experienced the same acceleration towards an evolved civilisation during particular times in Earth's history."

"Too many coincidences if you ask me—the Ahe'ey, the western world —all Caucasian." The girl shrugged her shoulders.

"All the capabilities that the Ahe'ey have acquired that humans don't have are genetic manipulations," Gabriel explained patiently.

"The result is still the same, Dad. You're all white, and you're stronger, smarter, and faster. You read minds and heal. And, there lots of stories of Caucasian gods and guardian angels in old books," Ollie said.

"There are stories of mythical creatures from all races. Perhaps we can read them together on the internet?" Morgan said as Ollie and Quinn glanced at each other looking confused. "You have internet, don't you?"

Gabriel shook his head.

"Just wait until humans find out about the Ahe'ey. They'll connect it with the Aryan race theories of the Nazis; the entire world will become even more racist," Ollie said.

"If someone like Zanus learned about the Ahe'ey . . . ." A shiver went down Morgan's spine.

Gabriel walked towards his son and placed his hand on his shoulder. "This is one of the many reasons why we sought refuge in this land, where we can access the world to help humans evolve and yet maintain anonymity and discretion. Humans are not yet ready to meet us or to make use of our technologies responsibly. There is too much division and hate."

"It's not much different here. Is it?" Morgan responded, feeling the need to defend her people. "Have you spoken to Amalia or Sky lately?"

Gabriel frowned, but he didn't reply directly to Morgan. He leaned down slightly and looked straight into Ollie's eyes. "The good news is that you and Quinn are part of the transition team, and I hope you can recruit more human leaders of all races. But please remember that most of the skills of the Ahe'ey can be learned. All you have to do is practice."

Quinn looked at Morgan and then at the floor, shoulders hunching as if she were taking on the blame for all the problems of the world. "I heard Amalia tell Sky that the fall of the Ahe'ey started on the day they decided to mate with humans. That it has weakened who you are, affected your virtues, and led to war and hate."

Gabriel's response was assertive, passionate and decisive. His voice echoed throughout the room and commanded attention. "The demise of the Ahe'ey started the day we designed an unequal society, where some had more privileges than others. Our demise started when the Ahe'ey lost their virtues and values, assuming that their perfect bodies and increased capabilities trumped your humanity. As for who is braver in the arena—the naturally muscular Yi'ingo warriors that heal fast or the human girl that has half their strength, is half their size, and yet is of equal valour? Who is braver, more courageous, more determined, and more hardworking?"

Morgan interrupted, quoting Shakespeare: "Though she be but little, she is fierce."

Gabriel smiled and continued talking. He controlled the room— unleashing his glow and charisma. His words seemed to flow straight into the minds of his captive audience.

"Our demise started when our noble pursuit to protect our past led to elitism and racism. Sathian, who led the revolution, was an evil man. His actions should be condemned, and his damage will never be forgotten, but he was just the voice of a growing dissatisfaction that had been lurking for thousands of years. Never ever undermine your race, but it's most important that you never dismiss your uniqueness and your value. The only limitations you will encounter are the ones you accept without questioning, as they will become your own sad reality. Your sky, your limit!"

And yet, you just showed us a glimpse of your extraordinary power. A power we will never have, Morgan thought.

"But is it not important to protect your genes?" Ollie said.

"Yes, it could save many lives. We need to make it available to the rest of the people of the Earth. We just need to find better ways to do it." Gabriel's eyes were set on Morgan. "Off you go, and stay away from Yi'ingo, both of you."

"But I have to train with Sky," Quinn interjected.

"We will train together in a few days."

"That's soooo unfair! See what you did, Ollie?" The teens rushed out of the door.

"Ollie, I'll see you soon at the farm," Gabriel said softly. The boy never turned to respond.

"Your family—Sky and Amalia—they don't quite agree with you," Morgan whispered in his ear.

"I know. My kids will prove them wrong."

"It's a lot to ask of such young people."

"I thought that if anyone were with me on this, it would be you."

"Just remember that they aren't experiments." She immediately regretted her words.

"No, they are *young people full of potential. Remember?*"

Never before had she seen anger in his eyes. She knew she had offended him and she was irritated and embarrassed that she was arguing for the side of nature and repeating Amalia's words. She attempted to defend her views even though she didn't want to be right.

"I *do* remember, but then I look at you and Viviane and Sky and Bastian with all your skills and perfection. How can I reject nature, when she shines all her glory on you? It's hard. I can't. The kids must feel it too. It's a tough ask Gabriel."

His silence was deafening.

"That annoying symmetry drives me crazy with desire," she said with a smile, trying to lift the tension between them.

"My kids will prove them wrong," he repeated sombrely.

"Do you understand that everyone in this place is telling them otherwise?"

"Not everyone." Compassion returned to his gaze, and he kissed her hand.

Morgan struggled to hold on to the ideas that she had championed so passionately for so many years. The Ahe'ey were challenging everything she believed in, weakening her self-worth and presenting a deterministic reality that she had always rejected. *I'm not a robot; I'm much more than the code in my DNA.*

"Yes, you are," he replied to words that she hadn't spoken out loud.

"My mother is calling me," he said abruptly. "We must go."

Morgan looked at the Ange'el, puzzled. She hadn't heard anything. She followed him as he rushed across the long corridor of the Sacred House. Gabriel was limping badly, but that didn't stop his sense of urgency. Morgan saw a little red-haired girl sitting on the floor outside a room with her face between her hands. The child stood up and ran to Gabriel, who picked her up with his good arm. Tears ran down her freckly cheeks. She looked to be six or seven years of age.

"Riley, what's wrong?"

"Dad! We were climbing the mulberry tree to pick the best berries for my pie. Maya fainted high up in the tree and bumped her tummy on the branches as she fell." Gabriel kissed Riley's ruddy cheek, put her down, and entered the room, followed by Morgan and the girl.

"The baby. This is beyond our skill," Viviane said, who came to meet him at the door. Morgan could see Sage sitting near Maya, who was lying on a bed by the window.

"She is with child. The baby is weak. I can't feel him anymore," Sage said as her father approached them. Morgan could hear Riley weeping quietly at the back of the room.

Gabriel sat on the bed and placed his hands on top of Maya's hands. He picked up a wet cloth and used it on her forehead. He touched her face and her hair gently. The Ange'el closed his eyes and sang in a language that was unknown to Morgan. His hands massaged her belly softly. Morgan could feel in her own body the waves of well-being emanating from the Ange'el prince. After a few minutes, he looked at Riley and signalled for her to join him. She stood between her father's legs, he held her hands, and they both touched Maya's stomach.

When this happened, Sage and Viviane smiled. Morgan looked at Sage, confused by the sudden change in the moods of the Ange'el.

Sage whispered in her ear, "Apollo must know the baby will be fine. This is how he encouraged me to become a healer and built my confidence. He always brought me in to help him once he was sure things were going to be okay."

Riley copied her father, closing her eyes and singing. Suddenly, she giggled, and a few seconds later, she gave a little squeal of joy. "The baby is kicking inside the belly!" She hugged Gabriel with a victorious look on her face. He smiled.

"We need to be quiet, my love. Maya needs to rest."

Maya's eyes were open, and she looked at them both with tears in her eyes. "Thank you," she said. Gabriel kissed her hand and left quietly.

Outside the room, Morgan could hear the excited little girl talking to Sage. "I'm going to be a healer just like you and Dad, but I'm also going to save human children and bring them here like Apollo does, you know? I'll need to learn how to heal and to fight. I have to go and tell Quinn about how I saved Maya's baby. She'll be proud . . . and maybe a little jealous." Sage nodded as the girl dashed away with a spring in her step.

They are young people full of potential. Morgan recalled his words. *The power of belief can move mountains.*

He looked exhausted as he sat on a bench on the second floor of the inner courtyard of the Sacred House. Morgan put her hand on his shoulder and he pressed his lips to it. Viviane approached them with some tea and gave it to Gabriel.

"My son, the most powerful healer in this land."

"I had the best teacher, Lady. I have yet to master many of your other skills. I wish I had your power of sight," he said with a smile.

"It will come. Your mind's eye gets stronger every day. Please drink,

Gabriel. You need to nourish your body. You shouldn't be healing others in your current state, yet we had no alternative but to call upon your skill."

"I'm fine. You must excuse me, ladies. I'll need to get some sleep." His forehead was wet. He limped slowly to his room just a few metres away.

Morgan and Viviane walked through the inner courtyard of the Sacred House. High up, at the centre of the courtyard, above the building, stood a giant crystal globe held by a frame made of a silver-coloured material. It was an impressive and imposing sight.

"The Eye of Ahe'ey is an energy-generating globe that harvests the power of the sun and the moon," Viviane said. "It is also where all the knowledge of our ancient civilisation is stored. Thousands and thousands of years' worth of data and history, inaccessible to us as we lost the technology to read it when our home was engulfed by the sea. Now we only have the tools to read some of the thousands of small quartz crystals that are stored here at the Sacred House. The Eye is a constant reminder of all that we have lost. It is a window to our past and to our future that remains locked to us until the day humankind reaches the technological advancements that will enable us to unlock its mysteries."

The high priestess was wearing a translucent white gown that reflected the light of the Eye. Her long hands danced as she spoke, painting her words in the air, and her eyes reflected the sadness in her heart as she recounted the great loss.

Morgan was grateful for the trust of the queen; after all, she was just a stranger to Ahe'ey and could, in theory, betray the secrets of Ahe'ey and sell them to the highest bidder. But then she remembered that Viviane could read her heart and her mind, and could discern that she was trustworthy.

"So sad. How close are we to developing the technology to read the Eye?"

"Close, about fifteen years away. Gabriel and the Ange'el Foundation are working with several universities and businesses around the world to help speed up technological innovation. We work tirelessly to recover our knowledge and our past." Viviane played with a silver and quartz ring on her middle finger as she spoke.

"So, some humans know about you?"

"No. No one outside Ahe'ey knows the truth. Gabriel's team at the Ange'el Foundation is only told that our mission is to invest in the future and protect the past. We fund projects that drive technological and social progress, and we retrieve, store or erase evidence of our existence. Gabriel has capabilities that allow us to contain the information."

"What do you mean?"

"He manipulates memories as necessary to keep our secrets safe."

"That's terrifying."

"Terrifying would be to see our knowledge in the wrong hands. Gabriel and the Foundation have spent a lot of time preventing humankind from finding clues and proof of our history and existence as, unfortunately, men are not yet ready to uncover our mysteries."

"How do they cover all of this up?" Morgan began to sense the enormity of this work.

"As clues of our existence are found throughout the planet, they fabricate information that removes the credibility and validity of its source. Most of the time, they try to take preventative action by concealing historical and archaeological sites and removing artefacts. But sometimes matters escalate and get to the press and social media before they can contain it, and in this case, we use misdirection to neutralise the problem."

"Give me an example." Morgan wondered how many times she had heard about discoveries that were related to these people, only to dismiss them because of Gabriel's work.

"Do you remember the pyramid that was discovered near the shore of your birthplace, the Azores islands, only to be dismissed by the Portuguese coast guard as natural seascape? We produced fake hydrographical surveys showing natural mountain ranges—by doing so, stopping any further investigation or media enquiries about that story."

Morgan remembered this event well. She had been born in the Azores, a Portuguese island group not too distant from the Strait of Gibraltar in the Atlantic Ocean. She'd left Portugal when she was very young but still followed the local news on an ongoing basis. The discovery of the pyramid had received significant international media coverage until the moment when the Portuguese coast guard dismissed it.

Viviane looked into her eyes and continued, "Power comes with great responsibility. Every day, Gabriel makes difficult choices about how he uses his power to benefit humankind. It's his burden to carry, and a task that is getting increasingly hard because of the internet. Information is spreading too fast and soon even Gabriel and I won't be able to contain it."

"Are you going to erase my memories?" Morgan asked flippantly.

"We will see."

"You . . . *you have no right!*"

"Morgan, you are our guest. We will respect you as long as our privacy is not compromised."

"*You don't own my mind!*" Morgan flinched away from the idea of someone tampering in her head.

The queen stood still, unfazed by Morgan's distress.

Trust me, Morgan heard inside her mind. She stiffened and shook her head.

Get out of my head. "I would never betray Gabriel's confidence."

"Trust me. Knowledge is power and power corrupts even the most virtuous. I am your friend, Morgan."

Morgan struggled to stay upset. Viviane's ethereal beauty and tone of voice dissipated her anxiety, and Morgan lost her battle. She wondered at the power of the Ahe'ey. "Your people seem to have delved into eugenics with astonishing success."

"I prefer the term genetic engineering. We did not engage in the negative eugenics practices developed by the Nazis."

"Are you the Aryan race that Hitler was trying to emulate?"

"Possibly. The dividing line between truth and fiction disappears the further we attempt to travel back in time. Footprints of the Ahe'ey can be found throughout your religious, fiction and history books."

"Yet you didn't stop at curing disease. I wonder if you have had unexpected consequences from tampering with your genes."

"We had some dark times in our history. We made mistakes . . . mistakes that, we hope, we can help prevent being repeated by humans as you start playing with the building blocks of life. You are so close to discovering gene-editing technology. Soon you will be playing God and may destroy all that nature has created in millions of years."

"Gene editing?"

Viviane nodded. "You are about to experience the Renaissance of biotechnology. The risks are tremendous."

"So are the benefits."

"As I said before, knowledge is power, and power in the wrong hands can bring chaos to the world. I continue to retrieve all the knowledge we can get out of our crystal archives. It is a slow and arduous process, but incredibly rewarding. Every day, I learn more about our past—our successes and mistakes. Gabriel and I are a team. He works outside Ahe'ey, and I work within it. Together we uncover and protect our knowledge."

Morgan was suddenly reminded of Amalia's words. She remembered that Sathian had been banished from accessing that knowledge when he married outside the royal lineage. Morgan felt her heart sink as she thought of Gabriel. Viviane looked into Morgan's eyes, probably reading her thoughts. The queen provided no reassurance or response. She bowed and continued on her journey, leaving Morgan paralysed by the stream of thoughts and worries running through her head. *"I'm not free to love"* he had told her once as she led him into her bed. Morgan thought of Sathian, the Ange'el prince that fell into darkness after being separated from what he valued most—knowledge.

The Map

Thirty-Two Years Ago: 1982 - Ahe'ey

Viviane felt her sister's despair, and she predicted the worst. She woke up in the middle of the night and ran to the lake, barefoot and in her nightgown. It was madness, but there was no one to stop her going to the aid of Gráinne. Marcus was away fighting the Hu'urei together with the Yi'ingo army.

Gráinne, stop, my dear sister. You need the moonstone to open the passage. In Viviane's mind's eye, she could see her sister holding her little daughter Fay in her arms. Gráinne was kneeling and touched the surface of the water, attempting to open the portal. The light emanating from the lake enveloped both mother and child.

Lake Do'oras was a passage between the two worlds. Ahe'ey was protected by a hexagonal force field that shielded its presence from the outside world. Humans were unable to see the large island that stood between the Caribbean and Bermuda.

The new Ahe'ey Island was an old outpost of the ancient Ahe'ey civilisation. Thousands of years ago, the mainland had been connected to several outposts through a series of passages that enabled the Ahe'ey to travel around the Earth quickly and with minimum environmental impact. These portals, made of pure water surfaces, allowed them to visit other species while causing little disruption. Throughout the millennium, the Ahe'ey had connected with humans, providing them with useful knowledge and resources appropriate to their evolutionary state.

The Ahe'ey were devastated every time they had to hopelessly watch a great human civilisation crumble due to the overexploitation of resources or disconnect between the short-term greed of their leaders and the long-term survival of their people. One after the other, the Ahe'ey had witnessed the doom of large communities that had substantial and yet unfulfilled potential. They had sometimes tried to intervene, but like many exasperated parents, they had learned quickly that there were lessons that needed to be experienced first-hand if learning was to occur.

Each passage had a guardian who ensured travellers exercised the utmost respect and compassion for all living creatures and that humans who found their way through the passages could be redirected back to their world as quickly as possible.

The most honourable and virtuous members of Ahe'ey, usually the elders or rulers of the land, could open and close each passage. They were called the gatekeepers.

The energy required by the gatekeepers to open a portal was such that many used the aid of a unique device, a moonstone ring that was passed from generation to generation. The ring acted as a magnifying device, multiplying the power of the gatekeeper and unleashing it to open the passage. Viviane was the current ring bearer, and she was the only one able to open the portal, which had been closed for many years.

There had been times in history when the portals were deliberately kept closed, the most recent one due to a Nazi crusade to find the origins of the Aryan race and the lost city of Atlantis. Hitler had become obsessed with the myths and stories that echoed the distorted history of Ahe'ey. In his eyes, Atlantis was the mythical homeland of the Aryan race.

In 1935, the leader of the SS had gathered a group called the Ancestral Heritage Society, composed of scientists loyal to the Nazi Party. Their mission had been to uncover and manufacture evidence to support the racial theories of the Nazis, theories that claimed that they were the descendants of a superior race. Hitler's master plan had been to eliminate all other races considered inferior by him and his followers.

The Ahe'ey had assembled to discuss what to do. Many had wanted to intervene, but they did not have the numbers to face the Nazis, and the risk of being exposed and used by Hitler for his own purpose was too high. Amalia and Michael had made the difficult decision to close the passage, abandoning humankind to face one of the darkest periods of its history.

The passage was closed and, without the moonstone, any attempt to open it would be suicide. The energy of the portal was likely to consume even the purest and most powerful of all Ahe'ey. Gráinne was not an Ange'el, she had no experience in controlling power fields and, without the ring, the energy of the portal would most certainly destroy both mother and daughter. Viviane felt the despair in her sisters' heart as Gráinne tried to get away from the control of Sathian, Iblis and the Hu'urei.

As Viviane's feet touched the sandy beach, she saw the body of her sister face down in the water, and she screamed. She ran towards Gráinne as another figure emerged from the forest running in the same direction. Viviane turned around her sister's body and searched for any signs of life, but the light had consumed and extinguished Gráinne's vitality. There was nothing Viviane could do but mourn the loss of another sister. She held onto Gráinne's body, crying uncontrollably as the figure standing just behind her screamed, *"Fay! Fay!* Where are you, my love?"* She recognised the voice that echoed in the forest, as Sathian dived into the lake and swam up and down looking for the girl. Viviane could hear the devil sobbing as he emerged for air.

"Ange'el!" he said, looking at Viviane with the only eye left on his scarred face. As he walked in her direction, Viviane gasped in anticipation of her demise. She could feel his darkness in her body. She experienced hate and repulsion for the murder of her family; the type of feeling that did not belong in the mind and body of an Ange'el, a feeling that made her feel sick to her stomach.

"Ange'el!" he repeated as he approached her. "Where is the girl?"

Viviane did not have the physical strength or the fighting ability of her late sisters. She was a child of the moon, and her body and mind were fully at the mercy of the realm where all beings are connected, where all things have a place and a purpose. The place where chaos and confusion turn into clarity. Three pillars—insight, knowledge and wisdom—supported her so she could serve her people the best she could. Her strength and power did not come from muscle mass in her body and at that time, the power of her mind's eye could not compete with the mastery of the dark Ange'el that stood in front of her.

"*Answer me!*" he screamed, still sobbing.

"Far away from your claws you monster." Her voice wavered.

A large group of Hu'urei ran towards the beach and surrounded the two Ange'el.

"Stand down," he said to his men.

"But Father—" Sathian placed his hand in front of the man's face before he could finish his objection. Iblis backed off.

Sathian reached and grasped Viviane's right hand. He looked at her jewellery— the moonstone and the quartz rings. He touched the quartz ring that was placed on her middle finger and forever locked to her genes; the ring that opened the door to the ancient knowledge repository; the key that, once lost, could not be reobtained as it imprinted on the genes of the current owner and rejected the genetic material of previous bearers. The key that belonged to the guardian of the ancient knowledge of the Ahe'ey was now Viviane's.

She raised her hand proudly and defiantly in front of his eye.

"Kill me if you wish, but *this* will never be yours again." The hate in her body and tongue was unnatural and offensive to her mind, yet she unleashed her grief on him. "May you burn in hell, Sathian."

"I envy you young Ange'el; everything you hold was once mine."

Viviane turned her face away from him. Gruesome memories inundated her mind as she cried and caressed Gráinne's hair—the images of Luna's body in flames. Two years had passed, but she could still smell the sizzling flesh of her sibling and could hear Lucas screaming as he woke up to find the charred, lifeless body of his wife lying beside him.

"May you experience the pain, rape and despair that you have unleashed on my family."

"*I have!*" He shared his life with her in one single second. The sad and violent images flashed through her mind in the form of a plea for help and demand for redemption. Viviane fought the compassion that attempted to conquer her heart. She held her sister's hand and allowed her grief to speak.

"Neither your past nor your future will ever redeem you from the evil you have released in this land. Suffer in hell for eternity."

Sathian turned his head and scanned the lake once more. He kneeled on the sand with his hands in his face. He stood there quietly for a few minutes and then he reached into his pocket and took something out. He opened his hand and offered it to Viviane.

"The Heart of Ahe'ey: find it and unlock it. Save our people from this slavery, from this madness," he said.

Viviane looked at the crystal that stood in the palm of his hand.

"*Take it!*" he roared.

Her right hand trembled as she reached to pick up the crystal. His eyes were still set on the ring that adorned her finger. She took the crystal from his hand and before she could pull her hand away he held it and pulled her towards him.

"I see why he likes you, Ange'el. You are pure light and love, everything I was supposed to be. Remember to touch the tears of the weeping Ange'el." Sathian walked away as she fell to her knees broken by fear.

"Death to any Hu'urei that come close to the royal Ange'el and her son. Stay away from them; they are not to be harmed."

HEAVEN

Present Day: 1 December 2014 - Ange'el village

Morgan had never been this close to heaven. Ahe'ey was stunning. The four villages were set up as fully sustainable living areas mindfully designed to reduce their ecological footprint. The Sacred House looked like a series of crystal boxes stacked on top of each other, pointing in many different directions. The structures were accentuated by clean, round white walls and silver-coloured pillars. Some of the roofs and external walls were covered with vibrant green gardens and waterfalls.

The exterior walls of the Ange'el buildings were made of a transparent crystal-like material that was able to harvest the energy of the sun and the moon and store it for future use. The crystal surfaces reflected their surroundings, mirroring the nature around them, vanishing from sight, and giving privacy to the people within the buildings, who could experience the nature around them in total seclusion.

The interior spaces were simple and full of light. Trees and plants were integrated within the structures that worked around nature instead of imposing on it. The rainwater was captured by the vibrant gardens on the top of the buildings. Fruits, vegetables, and flowers took what they needed before the remainder of the water was filtered by the building's structure and stored for consumption.

The Ange'el loved statues of women's bodies. They were everywhere —angels, fairies, circus performers, ballerinas, warriors. Ange'el was a tranquil and beautiful place where the twilight burst into a thousand colours as water and crystal reflected the changes in light.

Morgan's arm was red due to the many times she'd pinched it during the day. She didn't know what had blessed her to have the privilege of being the object of his affection, to be able to experience his world of wonder and magic. She expected to wake up from this dream any minute. The people of Ange'el seemed to be able to predict her every need and desire, and Gabriel, in particular, kept delivering experiences that were straight out of her dreams. They visited Bastian at the Ma'asai farms, swam in the lake, picked fruit from the garden with the children, and ate it by a small waterfall in the forest.

During the evenings he always retired early to the separate room in the pavilion. The knowledge that he was severely injured didn't stop her from slightly resenting his decision as she desperately longed to be near his body.

Morgan and Gabriel were both resting at the Ange'el garden near her pavilion. Morgan was leaning against a tree, reading the poem "Invictus" out loud. Gabriel was lying with his head on her lap; she played with his hair and used her fingers to discover the features of his face. She grazed the almost imperceptible marks around his eyes, shadows of smiles and good times. She loved the way his expressive eyebrows moved to show curiosity, compassion and empathy, and how they perfectly framed the crystal water inside his eyes.

Morgan could hear Amalia's and Sky's words echoing in her head. *How could anyone hate this man?* she thought as she explored his face, attempting to read his heart. He looked content, and his eyes mirrored a lagoon by a tropical island, a peaceful turquoise haven of tranquillity.

She was wilful and impatient when it came to getting to know him. She was hungry for any information that allowed her to unveil the layers of her highly complex lover as much as she craved his body. This was as close as she had ever been to obsession, consumed by a lover who was capable of showcasing the innocence, sweetness, and playfulness of a child, the shyness of a languid teenage boy, the courage and leadership of a war hero, and the broodiness of Austen's Darcy. She was impatient to know his innermost fears and desires. She experienced the same kind of anxiety that often made her read a great novel throughout the night, unable to sleep, eat, or move until she had reached the end only to mourn its loss as soon as she finished the last page.

He held her hand and whispered, "I was yours from the first moment I saw you over three years ago. You spoke straight into my heart, and from that moment, I vowed to love you. I kept track of your work, wishing you well in all your activities, and waited for the opportunity to meet you. You have enchanted my mind, body, and soul. Never doubt my love for you, Morgan. Every moment away from you tears me apart. I'm utterly spellbound, bewitched, and enchanted by your light." His unguarded words always surprised her. Never before had she met anyone so willing to wear his heart on his sleeve.

"I wish I'd known I had such a handsome and adorable admirer back then. I'd have rushed to New York much sooner. I may not be able to live one single day away from you."

"You won't have to as I am right here and refuse to leave your side." His eyes sparkled in the light. "I don't know what the future will bring, or how you'll feel about me, this land and its people. But as you discover us and our history and make your decision, please never ever forget how much I love you."

"May I decide now?"

"No, my love, you may not—not until you fully understand who we are, our purpose, our flaws . . . and my flaws." He kissed her, and she kissed him right back.

Her hand moved down his chest as she licked and then bit his lips gently. He pulled away, sitting by her side, breathing heavily. Her heart dropped.

"You don't desire me?" Her words were barely audible as she uttered them from a sulky pout. "I guess I don't look like——" He kissed her passionately, devouring her lips and seizing her hips with his hands. When he finally pulled back, they were both out of breath.

"Morgan. You are all I desire. Never doubt that. Please."

"Do you fear my desire for you?"

"I know this sounds ridiculous and affected, but I've been the object of lust all my life."

"Sounds like a good problem to have," she said flippantly, immediately regretting her words. "Your physical appearance is just a tiny part of who you are."

"And yet, few can see past it. They love me or hate me based on nothing else than appearance."

"Hate you? Because of Sathian?"

"Who told you?"

"It's not important."

"According to some, my appearance is a reflection of the purity of my genes, the code that holds the best of the Ahe'ey's values, virtues and capabilities. But Sathian looked exactly like me, and believe me; he was the worst of the worst."

"It goes to show that genes aren't the be-all and end-all and that who you are is not defined by how you look. You know this."

"And yet, you and I know that genes matter to some extent. Whatever I hold in my genes could save many human lives."

"Hey handsome," she smiled, "I want to know everything about you. Will you tell me? Everything? I want to see you. Really see you."

He kissed her neck.

"Was I your first?" she whispered after a bit.

He nodded. "Does it show in my lack of skill?" he laughed nervously. He ran his left hand down her back, and she jolted with desire.

"You tease me. Gabriel, why now? Why me?"

"You looked beyond the surface, beyond the Ange'el glow. You rejected it. You searched skin deep to find my weakness, my darkness, and still you chose me."

"What darkness? Being around you and your family is the closest I've been to heaven."

"Look beyond it. Take your time. The power I hold is dangerous, and it's mine in the best and the darkest of days. Always there, available for me to use and abuse in a moment of weakness."

"Have you? Abused it?"

"No. I don't think so, but others have fallen before me. Sathian, the most virtuous, the purest of the Ange'el turned into a monster."

"I trust you. What is your most ardent desire?" She attempted to focus his attention on something positive.

"You are, my love." He smiled.

"What else?"

"To release my people from the slavery and injustice imposed by the quest to preserve the royal bloodline."

"So you are resigned to the imminent extinction of your genes?

"No," he responded abruptly. "Your people and mine could benefit greatly from my genes."

"You are contradicting yourself," she said, confused.

"Not necessarily." She waited for further explanation but saw him vanishing within himself and his thoughts. She changed the subject.

"How much will you have to give up to keep me in your life?" Morgan looked into his eyes, silently asking him to give her a candid answer.

He searched her face for the missing context and kissed her forehead.

"I don't know. I've not discussed it with my parents. Things have changed since the war. There are only three royal descendants now. The dynastic guardianship of Ahe'ey's treasures has its days counted. I'm working on new solutions. I promise you that our love will not compromise the future of Ahe'ey or the future of humankind."

"But will it hurt you? Will it impact your role at Ahe'ey?"

"If it does, it will be a low price to pay to have you in my life."

"Were you supposed to marry Sky?"

"I'm the last person on the planet that Sky would agree to marry."

He didn't answer my question.

She gathered the courage to tell him about her conversations with Sky and Amalia, and their unkind words towards him. He fidgeted with his fingers as he listened to her account.

"They're not your biggest fans are they?"

"They . . . have their reasons," he whispered.

The Ange'el lowered his head, and Morgan decided to let it go for the time being.

PREDATOR AND PREY

It didn't take long for him to return to her bed. Their connection was wholesome and multidimensional. The physical attraction trampled over any attempts at restraint or delayed gratification. No guilt or second thoughts entered his or her mind, for it felt as right as the night that follows a day.

She watched him—the nape of his neck, his chiselled cheekbones, the contour of his jaw. She watched him—his exquisite body, the elegance of his hands, the length of his legs. She watched him—his curls dangling in front of his eyes, protecting the world from the power of his gaze. She watched him—his joyful smile that illuminated even the darkest corner of the world.

As a little girl, she'd devoured stories of princes and monsters and heroes and villains that would save or take the damsel as their prize, tales where men consumed, and women were consumed, fables where men were the predators and women the prey.

Due to nature or nurture, or both, women aspired to be taken. The game of desire was a dangerous, unbalanced game: a game where the virgin became the whore, where the prince became the monster, the vampire, or the werewolf, unable to control his destructive nature. He would succumb to his instincts. There was nothing he could possibly do; after all, it was in his nature . . . or was it? Stories that told boys that being predatory was in their blood and fables that told girls they were meant to be taken, ravaged, and destroyed. These archetypes shaped the dreams and desires of human beings, shaped behaviours and values. "Boys will be boys" excused violence and rape. "Sugar and spice and all things nice" encouraged passiveness. Nature or nurture. Nurture or nature. The only thing she knew for sure was that when people take things for granted, they stop searching, growing, exploring. They become trapped in a belief system that defines them and shackles them into what society expects of them.

Who was the predator? Who was the prey? Never before had she felt such an intense desire to consume, to devour. She was the predator and the prey. They were equals in their lust as they were in their love. Their desire came from light, not darkness. It was nurturing, alive, and joyful. They were both agents of pleasure and delight, strong and vulnerable, passionate and caring. Perfect chemistry, delightful mischief, spiritual connection, and above all, love.

FALSE PRIDE

4 December 2014 - Ange'el village

Morgan wandered through the inner courtyard at the Sacred House, soaking up the sun and daydreaming. She was on a rollercoaster ride of emotions. A week had passed since she'd arrived at Ahe'ey, and the outside world seemed to be a vague memory of a distant past as she succumbed to the magic of this enchanting land and its people. She cared deeply about her foundation; she adored her mother; she had amazing friends and colleagues, and yet she felt totally at home at Ahe'ey as if these people were her family. She loved them. Every time she thought of Gabriel, she smiled. She'd spent so many years fearing this kind of love—the kind that overcomes one's sense; the kind that leaves you unable to function properly, an obsessive love where there is no escape. Her guard was down. She was smitten. He was her world, and she was okay with it.

"Be careful, child," Viviane whispered, appearing behind her. "Don't get so absorbed by my son's light that you forget and forgo your own."

Morgan turned to face the glow and the wonder of the Ange'el.

Like her son, Viviane carried light, beauty and wonder in her eyes. "There will come a time when he will need you, where the destinies of both of you will rely on your own strength and ability to make decisions. Don't allow your love for him to weaken your sense of self."

"It's not that easy, is it?" Morgan understood the well-meaning words of the queen. It was obvious to anyone around her that she was madly and desperately in love with Gabriel.

"No, it is not. A time will come when you will need all your strength to make the right decision for you both. Without your true north, you will be guided by despair, self-pity, pride, and jealousy. You will dwell in a sea of unvirtuous emotions in the name of love. Emotions that, at every moment, are acting against it and ignoring what truly matters. Love him deeply and passionately with all your heart; trust that love, but stay true to yourself."

"You are scaring me, Lady. Sky and Amalia warned me against the Ange'el men as if they were predators—"

"You do not understand, Morgan. We are not the predators; we are the prey. They hunt us for our beauty, light, virtue, intelligence and influence. They want to use us; they battle to control our bodies and our minds. The gifts that we were born with, that are coded in our genes by our ancestors are our biggest blessing and our darkest curse." Viviane's voice echoed as she replied swiftly to the accusations of the Yi'ingo. The Ange'el's distress was quickly controlled under a veiled smile bursting with the sweetness and healing properties of Manuka honey.

"I wish you well, Morgan. I see false pride as your biggest enemy, the mountain that you will have to climb on your way to enlightenment. The pride that is not grounded in confidence but worn as armour to hide vulnerability. The artificial golden façade that is the most loyal companion of insecurity and self-doubt. In the moments of self-doubt, when your pride is tested, remember to choose love. Love for yourself and love for him. Trust love above all else. Remember that there is strength in vulnerability."

"They seem like contradictory goals, self-determination and love for another."

"They are one and the same as you cannot truly love another without loving and accepting yourself first. You know this, but now the stakes have been raised a thousand times."

"To be honest, I'm struggling to find a balance. Love is such an addiction. When I look at him and experience how wonderful he is to his family and to me . . . it's so easy to get lost in his wonder; to want to follow him blindly. I'm a fool in love. I used to be so independent, but I must admit he tests my strength with his perfection."

"The ultimate proof of love is the ability to add value and to truly and wholeheartedly accept the object of your affection, including its shortcomings. Blind submission is the opposite of that. You should want to share and contribute with your own experiences, knowledge, and point of view. You should want to enrich the world you share together with your own colours and textures. Gabriel is not perfect—no one is. Only statues are to be kept on pedestals, and even statues are unable to maintain their immaculate perfection forever. An unbalanced relationship leads to resentment as flaws emerge, and it contributes nothing to the loved one or to the relationship. Flaws will emerge.

"Very few amongst us know the truth; that the war that raged this land was fuelled by a man and a woman that loved and lusted after an Ange'el. Mad from their obsession and need to control him, they pushed him to his limits."

Morgan had her head down, like a little girl being admonished by her mother. Viviane placed her fingers on Morgan's chin. They were long like the fingers of her son, and they raised Morgan's face, making her look in the eyes of the queen. "Morgan, you are strong and a leader in your world. I know you are just enjoying being in love. These are magic days that you should savour with the carelessness of a child. It is not easy for anyone to love an Ange'el prince without being consumed by it, but I believe you can. I believe in you, and when the time comes, you will be tested, and at that time, remember this moment and trust your friend, the Lady of Ange'el."

"How come you don't have the resentment of Amalia and Sky against men?"

"I am surrounded by good men, the best of men, but I don't judge the resentment or anger of my kinswomen as it has kept us safe in moments where my skills as a healer and spiritual leader were insufficient for the stability and safety of this land."

Morgan nodded. "When you work in the area of women's and girls' rights as I do and you see the crimes raged against them every day, it's difficult to have a balanced view of men. You spend your days working towards the welfare of women and hoping to find some good men ready to stand up and work by your side, but the numbers are much smaller than they should be, and the progress much slower. I have tried to keep my faith in men, but I had many moments of doubt until the day he came along."

"There are as many shades of women as there are shades of men. The trick is to realise that we are all one and the same. We are part of the same organism striving to keep its balance. At Ahe'ey, we learned a long time ago that education is everything. The day humankind stops having different expectations, values, and teachings for boys and girls is the day you will achieve an equitable society."

"I know this, I do."

"Nurture can destroy nature."

"Or . . . nurture can overcome nature. I wish I knew which was true." Morgan paused for a moment, processing Viviane's words. Foreboding was beginning to curl in her stomach. "You know, Lady, he loves me as ardently as I love him. The blind devotion is mutual."

"I know, and that love for you has the potential to destroy him. Your love will soon be tested by the harshest of storms and the coldest of all winters. My son will need you and your strength. Will you be there for him when the time comes? Will you overcome your ego and your fear?"

Gabriel smiled and turned around to face his cousin before Bastian was seen or heard.

"Hey!"

Bastian walked into the pavilion and immediately filled the room with his large body and sunny disposition.

"Bas, come in. How are you?" The two men hugged, right shoulder to right shoulder. Gabriel winced as his cousin slapped him in the back over some of his broken ribs.

"Happy to see you spend so much time at Ahe'ey. We've missed you."

"I visit all the time. Three, four times per week."

"Your children at Ange'el maybe, but you have been neglecting some of us."

"I'm sorry."

"So?" Bastian raised his eyebrows.

"What?"

"Oh, come on Ange'el, aren't you supposed to be able to read my mind? Don't play dumb. Did it finally happen? Was it wonderful?"

Gabriel nodded with a smile that he felt with his whole body. "I love her so much Bas."

The Ange'el was engulfed by the arms of his cousin. "You look different, so happy and relaxed. Now you know what you have been missing out on."

"Bas. Stop. Broken bones. Remember?"

"Sorry."

"How are you and Sky?"

"She won't see me, since New York. Two Yi'ingo warriors now guard the passage at Lake Do'oras. I had to get a special permission from

Viviane to leave to New York to take care of your affairs. And, apparently, Amalia has been looking for me. That won't be a pleasant meeting."

"I'm sorry to drag you into my mess. I can speak to Amalia and fall on my sword."

"She'll lock you up, you fool. What's done is done. Anyway, Amalia won't punish me. I'm good with her as long as I'm the breeding stallion of the Yi'ingo. Of course, Sky is not happy about it. I can't win."

"You don't have to have sex with all those women, Bastian."

"It's my duty. One of us has to do it." Gabriel caught the pinch of censure in Bastian's tone.

"I'm sorry Bas."

"Never mind. I enjoy it . . . most of the times. Sky keeps her bed well stocked with my men and my friends so at least this way I don't feel the sting so much."

"Of course you do, and so does she."

"You know, we are well matched, Sky and I, if we are matched at all.

"Sky will come around. She loves you."

"I don't think Sky knows what love is. We've grown apart lately. She refuses to move on, to accept that the war is over. She holds on to her rage and hate for men."

"Her rage is her power and her shield Bas. She's just doing her job. Without her, we would have lost the war."

"The war is over."

"I know. Give her time; she'll come around."

"I just can't get through."

"You don't need to get through anything. You are everything to her, I promise."

"She has a strange way of showing it."

"Trust me."

"I do. You and Sky are my family. Oh, by the way, you have a letter from Sir Charles." Bastian handed the letter to Gabriel. "I'll leave you to it and see you tonight at your mother's party."

"Party?"

"Yeah, the queen has organised a dinner for all of us tonight, and tomorrow there is going to be some announcement. The four tribes are gathering at the Temple of Lights at noon, and you and I are supposed to meet your father just before the event."

"No one has told me about this."

"That's because it was my job and I was in Manhattan. Your mother told me explicitly that you are not to leave Ahe'ey before the event tomorrow."

"Where is my father?"

"I haven't seen him in days, but we'll certainly see him tomorrow. Speak later."

Gabriel opened the handwritten letter. The Ange'el stayed away from email and the internet. The digital channels of the humans were neither private nor secure.

"Gabriel, my friend. Where are you? This is not the time for you to vanish. I have some news about our venture. The project is complete, but unfortunately, we have some challenges to deal with that require your skills. Our servers have been hacked, and some data has been stolen. Our project's data is safe and offline in cold storage, but I'm wondering why we are the target of such sophisticated attacks. Is this related to the incident at the Met? We need you. Contact me as soon as you can. Yours truly, Sir Charles H. Mathews."

Gabriel felt his heart race. Someone was on his tail, most likely Zanus. The fight at the Met had exposed some of his skills, and Sir Charles had been seen in his close company. He took a breath, attempting to control his heartbeat and to quiet his mind. He knew Viviane would pick up his thoughts if she felt his panic; he had to keep his venture secret from his mother at all costs.

"Gabriel," Morgan said arriving at the pavilion, "we need to talk. Gabriel?"

"Yes, my love." He smiled, projecting his glow to hide his worries and putting his arms around her. She frowned and pulled his hands away.

"I need to get back to New York."

"Okay," he replied, surprised by her hostility.

"I need to deal with the situation with Zanus and to get back to my foundation." She seemed determined and unusually sombre.

"Is everything okay? What happened?"

"Nothing. I just need to get on with my life. I have one, you know?"

"I do. Know." He was confused; his mind was still processing the letter. "We'll leave tomorrow afternoon. My parents ordered me to stay at Ahe'ey to attend some announcement tomorrow morning."

"You don't have to come with me. I can leave today, and you can meet me later when you have the time."

He held her hand. "What's going on? Who were you speaking to? My mother?"

His loving gaze managed to elicit a weary smile from her.

"I forgot about my life, Gabriel." She pressed her head against his chest. "This place, you . . . you make everything else vanish. I need to find some balance. I'm not a pet. You know?" Her words pierced his heart.

"I understand." He released her hand, but she grabbed it back and squeezed it.

"I love you so much. I just can't let it consume me. Do you understand? I need my life back. In this place, I feel like an impostor, a lesser being."

His pained gaze slowly raised to meet her eyes.

"Who made you feel like that?"

"Look, in my world, it's easier. I walk into a boardroom, full of middle-aged white guys, and I know I deserve a seat at that table. It's hard; they all speak the same language; they all share the same interests, and I feel like a foreigner. And my irrational self takes over, and I feel unworthy, undeserving, no matter how long is my list of achievements. Because I know their bar is modelled on them, not me, because I know some of them are thinking they had to lower the bar. Whether they try or not to welcome me, I feel like I don't belong, but I persevere. I get on with it because my voice is needed at that table; I owe it to others.

"I'm the face of change, of what needs to happen in the world, the equality and diversity that must have a seat at that table. I do it for the chocolate-skinned girl in Congo. And, I have good days and bad days, moments where I'm able to be me, and other moments where I find myself copying them and trying to be them. But I keep at it, even when it's awkward and soul crushing. But here, I . . . I can't compete with you or your world. I have little to offer. At best I can simply love you, at worse, I could go insane in self-doubt and destroy us both. I . . . don't want to be an impostor."

"Are you saying that Sage is an impostor? Ollie, Quinn, Riley, Aria. Are they impostors?"

"*No*, of course not."

"Why do you see it in them and fail to accept it in yourself?"

"What?"

"Possibility. Potential. Power. Perfection."

"I've done it all my life Gabriel, but now—."

"Now what? Remove the rose-colour glasses. I need you to see the human in me."

"I need some time, some space, away from here, away from you."

"Very well. We'll leave together tomorrow, and you'll have as much space as you need away from me. I promise. I also have . . . some urgent business in New York."

He would have preferred to leave today, but challenging his parents' orders would only make matters worse. The stakes were too high, and he had to ensure that he didn't bring unwanted attention to his activities or whereabouts. He had to stay away from the Yi'ingo's sword and his mother's mind's eye.

Morgan looked into his eyes, worry pulling her eyebrows together and lips down. "Will Viviane erase my memories when I leave?"

"I promise that you can leave Ahe'ey whenever you wish and that no one will ever manipulate your mind. No one. You have my word."

BETRAYAL

Viviane wanted the party to be a special occasion for her family. The following weeks were going to be difficult, and for just one day, she wanted to be the mother, the grandmother, and the aunt, instead of the queen and the high priestess. She wanted to indulge in the company of all her dear children without the weight of Ahe'ey's destiny on her shoulders. No one else would ever know why this occasion was so special. No one would ever suspect that this might well be the last time that they all dined together. She missed Marcus, who was away initiating a series of events that would forever change Ahe'ey's history. He was summoning a necessary storm.

Viviane had the perfect excuse, a party to welcome their new guest, Morgan. Tables and chairs were set up at the Ange'el's garden, and the cooks had spent the day making the most popular recipes. They knew which treats excited the children and the favourite dishes of each one of the adults. The air smelled like sweet bread, chocolate cake and apple pie.

Ahe'ey didn't need electricity during the evenings. Light-absorbing particles covered the pavements and buildings. The surfaces harvested ultraviolet rays from the sun during the day and dramatically lit up like a starry sky at night.

The Ahe'ey applied the same beads of light on their hair, clothes and even their skin during celebrations and special occasions that deserved a bit of sparkle. Each tribe used them differently. The Yi'ingo tended to go for strong colours, like red, orange, and yellow. The Ange'el preferred white light, blue, and cyan, and the Ma'asai inclined towards the greens and browns.

As the sun set, Ahe'ey was transformed into the magical world of fairies. Sage organised special lanterns to hang in the trees. Each had different colours that perfectly matched the eclectic collection of multi-coloured glasses and bottles on the tables. The glasses didn't match in shape or size, but somehow, together, they created the perfect ensemble.

The children arrived first: Oliver came along with Riley and Quinn, who was carrying Aria. It was going to be a challenging environment for the little girl due to all the guests, so Sage placed her in the corner, safely surrounded by her sisters and brother. Aria was wearing a cute red dress, and Oliver made a point of calling her a sweet strawberry. The baby repeated "Sweeeet strawbryy" while playing with his dreadlocks. Viviane smiled; she was fond of her adopted grandchildren.

The guests started to arrive—the kinswomen and men from Yi'ingo and Ma'asai joined the Ange'el hosts on this special occasion. The Yi'ingo brought their own fresh meat, which they had hunted that morning and prepared in advance. This was a common practice as the Ange'el were mostly vegan and refused to touch animal meat. The fire was ready for cooking so they didn't waste much time with courtesies. The Ma'asai brought fresh fruits from their farms and a collection of alcoholic beverages; there were few occasions where the latter were allowed in the Ange'el village.

Edible petals and herbs adorned each plate, and the tables were full of a diverse selection of colourful vegan dishes. It was a rare occasion that the Ange'el's quarters were so full of colour, exuberance, and noise. One could hear the loud laughter of the Ma'asai combined with the strong, commanding voices of the Yi'ingo from miles away.

Bastian arrived alone. Viviane inwardly rolled her eyes and smiled, amused at the vanity of her nephew, who wore a vibrant kimono-like chartreuse tunic adorned with white light beads. He kept his hair away from his face with a ponytail. Surprising Sage, who was bringing some bread to the table, he picked her up and twirled her around.

"You're looking gorgeous, little Ange'el fairy. I'd steal you for my own if I didn't fear your father. He'd chop me into little pieces and feed me to the Wali'ingooteer."

"Stop it, silly man." She gave him a loving hug and took him by the hand to a seat beside Viviane.

"Lady Viviane," he said as he bowed.

"Come, Bastian, have some food. You are starving."

"I enjoy the Ange'el power of sight when it means having all of my needs fulfilled. I spent the day hunting with the Yi'ingo and reviewing the crops, and I somehow forgot to eat. How are you, my lady?" he asked while adding some deer and sweet potatoes to his plate.

"I am well; happy to have all my children in one place for a change."

Gabriel and Morgan arrived soon after. Viviane held her breath, looking at the shadow of the shadow of her past. Morgan wore one of Sage's dresses, a beautiful and simple long white gown adorned with silver and light beads. Her hair was out of her face, held by just a few braids and joined at the back, and her long curls had a touch of sparkling sand. On her neck was a moon-shaped turquoise stone. She glowed with happiness and wonder. Morgan held onto Gabriel's arm as one holds a most valuable treasure.

As Viviane looked at her son, her heart sank thinking of what was to come. His distant and sombre gaze vanished as all his children left the table to kiss him. Aria came running. "Apollooo, my looove." He picked her up with his left arm and she squealed, "Geeentle!"

"Hello, my love," he replied.

Aria grabbed Morgan's face and kissed her on the lips. Morgan blushed as she had since discovered that it was a gesture from children to parents, and everyone laughed at the girl's innocent candour. Morgan held the little girl in her arms.

"It seems you have Aria's blessing, cousin," shouted Bastian, laughing. "What are you waiting for?"

Gabriel smiled and walked towards Bastian and his mother. Morgan followed Gabriel with Aria in her arms.

Gabriel kissed Viviane and sat in front of her after holding the chair out for Morgan.

"Apollo, it's a party," Sage said, almost singing. Her eyes were set on his plain white tunic. "You could have made more of an effort." She pulled a cyan and silver scarf from her neck and wrapped it around his, then she worked to add a few braids to the sides of his hair. Gabriel's quiet smile didn't fool Viviane. She could feel that something wasn't right, but the others remained unaware. Riley joined the fun. She scraped beads of light from her arms and ran her hands through his hair, making it sparkle.

"There," Riley said, victorious.

"Your father doesn't need any help in the glowing department," Viviane said, then turned to Morgan. "How are you, Morgan?"

"I'm well, Lady Viviane. What a wonderful event. I really love all the light and colour; this place is magical. I've been here for a week, but this is the first time I've ventured out during the evening." She looked at Gabriel and then blushed a little. "The bugs, trees, plants, and even the water lilies in the pond glow in the dark. It's like magic."

"They've been genetically modified by our ancestors. Infused with luciferin, a light-producing substance found in jellyfish," Gabriel explained. Morgan began asking him about other feats of their ancestors, and they quickly became distracted.

They ate and talked about the crops and gossip coming from the different tribes. Bastian bragged about his hunting skills to Morgan. "The head of the deer was, at least, this big—it was a magnificent animal." Bastian was loud and proud.

Gabriel amused Viviane; he stood just behind Bastian and was copying all his gestures but reducing the sizes of the beasts that Bastian was describing by half. The Ange'el prince was relaxed in the company of his loved ones; he became more joyful and fully present. Viviane appreciated her son's tender nature. She could see how vulnerable, loving, and open he was when his family surrounded him. He wore his heart on his sleeve and savoured every moment with the joy and appreciation of a man who takes nothing for granted.

One of the Ma'asai had picked up a guitar and was playing and singing in the background. Quinn got up, holding Aria, and they both danced together, followed by Riley, who pirouetted around the fire. Aria was becoming more trusting and relaxed. She wasn't speaking to any strangers, but she wasn't hiding from them either.

"Aria is making great progress," Viviane commented.

Gabriel just smiled and kissed Morgan's hand.

"How is Oliver adjusting to the Ma'asai life?" Viviane asked Bastian. Oliver was sitting by the musicians.

"It's still early days. I think he misses his sisters, and he's struggling with the food. Finding good vegan food at Ma'asai is hard. But he's a natural farmer and loves it. Plants grow twice as fast when he speaks to them. He's a quick learner, and I expect he will become my right-hand man in no time."

"I will have one of our cooks teach him how to prepare his own vegan meals at Ma'asai. What happened to his eye? I am seeing that it was a somewhat distressing event for him."

"He had an argument with a young Yi'ingo apprentice; he'll be okay. It won't be an issue going forward," Gabriel replied.

"It is unwise to expect so much of these children in such a hostile environment," Viviane said.

Morgan's nod was almost imperceptible, but it became evident to Viviane that her guest empathised with the children's experience.

"They are doing just fine," Gabriel said with a pinch of defensiveness in his tone.

"You may be a powerful Ange'el and a dedicated father, but you will never truly grasp the impact of discrimination on their young minds. You will not be able to shield them for much longer, my love."

"You underestimate their resilience and potential."

"No, I don't." Viviane decided to change the topic as she could feel the tension rise around the table.

Viviane was used to her niece's grand entrances, but even the Lady of Ange'el was surprised by Sky's show that night. The Yi'ingo arrived late by horse, jumping the fire where the meat was being barbecued. She leapt off the horse with the elegance of an acrobat, landing on her feet with her head held high. Her faux-hawk added to her height and contributed to the majesty of her profile. She wore a two-piece copper outfit that perfectly matched the colour of her hair and hugged her figure. Her top had a phoenix embroidered on the sleeve with gold light beads. Viviane's niece was set on making an impression and accomplished her goal within seconds of her arrival.

The Yi'ingo strutted in the direction of Viviane, kissed her, and sat beside her.

"Is my mother joining us?" Viviane asked.

Sky shook her head. "No, she told me that she disapproves of parties in times of war."

"We are not at war."

Sky shrugged her shoulders, looked at Gabriel and Morgan, and bowed her head slightly. Then she focused her attention on Bastian, who sat on the other side of Viviane.

"I heard you let a wild boar escape this morning, cuz. Gettin' old?" A smile dangled on the corner of her lips. It usually took less than a few minutes after being in each other's company for the two to engage in a somewhat cutting exchange of pleasantries. But Viviane knew they genuinely enjoyed each other's company in an aggressive and mischievous way. Sky's tone was always somewhat defiant and sarcastic, taking a stab at Bastian's overconfidence and self-importance.

"I was being generous, my dear cousin . . . giving your warriors a chance to shoot. Clearly, the Yi'ingo are losing their reflexes. What's happening? Too much time spent trying to look pretty?" Everybody laughed. "Look at all those braids, feathers and golden beads in your hair. Did you spend the day in front of the mirror?"

"I wore the same feathers and braids when I beat you at the last Games. Not a single strand of my hair fell out of place as your pretty face hit the ground. Black and blue suit you quite nicely. Particularly around your eyes and jaw."

Bastian's laughter echoed throughout the forest. His self-belief was bulletproof, and he was happy to engage in good fun with anyone, especially with Sky.

Viviane observed her three heirs. She knew them all so well—their struggles, fears, aspirations, and desires. Each had been raised to fulfil a particular purpose for the future of Ahe'ey. They were all so different and unique, and she wished that this night would never end. They all benefited from the attention and the love of everyone around them. The young Ange'el apprentices paid them deference by keeping their plates and glasses always full.

Gabriel was graceful, reacting to the attention with kindness and humility. He always smiled and thanked them, and yet he sometimes was genuinely unaware of their attraction to him. He showed interest in them, discussing their achievements, but things always came to an end quite quickly so that he could return his attention to his family.

Bastian was quite different. He saw every interaction as proof of his irresistible charm, felt entitled to all the attention and tokens of interest and flirted shamelessly with every young single woman around him. The girls kissed him, sat on his lap, and organised encounters for later in the evening. Bastian was never alone in bed for long. He was like a big kid in a candy shop, and no one could admonish him as he showed no sign of malice or manipulation, just a great deal of enjoyment for the finer things in life. There was only one that he favoured above all others, one that always got his undivided attention when she wanted to, but she never stayed for long.

Sky reacted to male praise and attention with disdain and arrogance. Few had the confidence and courage to pursue her, but she was so stunning and accomplished that some could overcome their fears, motivated by the possibility of such a magnificent prize. The boldest and the bravest were sometimes welcomed to her bed only to be led outside as soon as she was done with them.

Viviane turned to Sky, her heart full of guilt from the events that would soon unfold. The queen placed her hand on top of her niece's and whispered in her ear, "I want you to know that I love you as a daughter. I love you as much as I love my son." Sky looked at the queen sideways quizzically and then nodded with a smile.

4 December 2014 – The Pierre Hotel, New York

Maria Diaz walked into her boss' penthouse at The Pierre Hotel as she'd done every day for the past five years. The CEO of the Ange'el Foundation cleaned her sweaty palms on her blue pantsuit and tried to shake off the stress with a quick neck stretch.

"Gabriel? Sebastian?" she called out. "Gabriel?"

Maria always felt tiny as she walked across the large living room with twenty-three-foot-high ceilings. The light coming from the large windows flooded the room with the rays of a hopeful autumn sun. Sebastian had told her earlier in the morning that Gabriel was away, but things had changed significantly in the past few hours and her deep anxiety was making her grasp at straws. She desperately needed to speak to him.

"Gabriel?" She sped up her pace as she looked for him in room after room, going up and down the central marble staircase that connected the three floors of the penthouse.

"Dónde estás, corazón?"

There was no response. The place was empty.

Maria settled in the panelled library filled with the historical artefacts that they had recovered over the years. She particularly enjoyed the crystal sphere that, when she held it in the palm of her hand, made her feel like she was having a deeply spiritual experience or was under the influence of some hallucinogenic drug. She stayed away from the globe now; she had no time for out-of-body experiences, no matter how much she needed them right now.

Maria sat at his desk, kicked off her shoes and cursed. She was used to his disappearances—the times when his mobile didn't work, when he would vanish from the face of the earth for several days. But, today, she needed to talk to him; she was desperate, and she couldn't wait. There was only one thing she could do—leave him a letter that he could read upon his arrival. She felt hopeless and frustrated. She opened the wooden box that stored the paper and pens, took a deep breath and began writing:

"Corazón, some urgent developments need our immediate attention. Your cousin told me you are sick and that you will take a few more days to recover. I'm sorry to disturb you, but unfortunately, we can't afford to lose any time. Please contact me as soon as you get this message.

"Last night, Muriel Chapman, the editor of Vogue, *posted a video on her Facebook page. The video shows you in a fight at the Metropolitan Museum. In her post, she thanks you for protecting the party attendees from the terrorists and slams the CIA for asking everyone at the event to keep the attack confidential. The video has gone viral on YouTube and has now been watched by three million people worldwide. Walter Zanus appeared on Fox News an hour ago demanding answers from the CIA."*

Maria pulled up her phone and replayed the recording, transcribing it.

"I quote, 'We must protect our gracious women like Ms. Morgan from extreme Islamic terrorists. The attempt by the CIA to keep this attack a secret is an act of betrayal to our great Nation and our God abiding citizens. I call for an immediate review of their actions and question their intentions as they fail to warn us of this great danger. I've been told by my trusted sources that the CIA has covered up several assassinations of prominent figures over the past weeks. Islam is raging a war on Western liberties. We must unite and fight back. It is time to rise against evil and return this country to its former glory. I'm working with my people to find the man who showed such a great deal of courage during the attack. I want to thank him personally for protecting our fragile women from being raped and murdered by Islamic fundamentalists. We need more men like him, ready to kill the brown-skinned criminals that immigrate into this country to destroy our fine nation.'

"I kid you not, this insufferable clown is using the event at the Met to advance his

agenda of hate and division. What happened at the Met? Was it really terrorism? Why are they after Morgan? Are you ever going to tell me anything?

"Sorry . . . Gabriel, the media is putting a lot of pressure on the CIA, and they are conducting a frantic hunt for any information that will lead to your and Morgan's whereabouts. It won't take long until someone identifies you. Muriel and everyone at the Met knows who you are. The foundation will soon be flooded with media requests. I need your clear direction on how to deal with this crisis. I'll be at the foundation waiting for your call. Needless to say, we will go dark until we hear from you. Besos, Maria

"P.S. There is also talk of footage of some other event in Central Park, where a large group of unusual cloaked figures apparently protected women and girls from terrorists. The KKK has released a statement placing a bounty on any information about these 'Protectors of the Nation.'"

THE LIONESS AND THE DEER

Ange'el Village, Ahe'ey

Morgan and Sky exchanged a smile across the table. Their last encounter had brought them closer, and Morgan was increasingly curious about the warrior. She was puzzled by the arrogant and bigoted woman who gave Gabriel such a hard time. Morgan didn't know why, but she wanted to know Sky better.

Sky flashed a brief, mischievous smile as she used her dagger to place a piece of deer on Morgan's plate.

"Thanks," Morgan replied with a tentative smile.

"Good to know you don't eat only bird food like the rest of them," Sky spoke, pointing the dagger in the direction of Gabriel and Sage.

"I haven't been able to switch to a vegetarian diet, though I've tried many times. Instead, I try to pick organic, ethical meat. I like to know that the animal had a happy life and didn't suffer in death."

"At Yi'ingo, we only kill what we eat, and we hunt animals that roam free in the forests. Most are instantaneously killed, but we do have the odd accident when we are teaching our apprentices to hunt." Sky looked sideways at Viviane. "According to my aunt, this practice stops us from attaining a higher spiritual awareness and connection to the earth, but what we lack in insight, we gain in courage and bravery." She shot Gabriel an unrelenting stare, and the Ange'el's brows sank over his eyes.

Bastian's eyes set on Gabriel's face before he jumped in. "Yes, it's true," Bas said in a mocking tone. "The Yi'ingo show all their bravery by killing baby deer and cute squirrels."

The dynamic between the three cousins is quite . . . interesting, Morgan thought as she took a bite of the delicious deer. "Yes, it's a narrow definition of bravery," Morgan replied as she caught Oliver's annoyed look. The boy had approached the table to pick up some food but quickly left to rejoin the musicians.

"It may be narrow, but when you expect young women to fight and kill to protect their people from pillage, rape, slavery, or murder, it's good practice to ensure they are capable of killing even the most innocent of animals."

"It's sad that, to defeat evil, we sometimes need to match its actions. I wish there were another way," Morgan replied with sadness, thinking of Zanus' group.

Sky's eyes, narrowed to slits, stayed on Gabriel, "Some people walk through life refusing to look evil in the face and stand up for what is right. No amount of positive thinking can stop violence and hate. Some of us haven't been blessed with the opportunity to choose to keep our hands clean." Sky's voice was resentful.

"Once you use that sort of power—the power that comes from violence and fear—how do you know when to stop? It's such a fine line."

"You can either be the lioness or the deer. The lioness decides whether or not to stop; she owns the line. The deer can only run or fall. Either way, both paths are more honourable than the life of the hyena—the scavenger that feeds on the remains of deer killed by lions. I despise the cowards who stay silent while others suffer and fight." Sky's eyes were set on Gabriel.

Morgan was surprised by Gabriel's silence. He was so different around Sky; he just fidgeted with his thumbs under the table as he listened to the discussion. Morgan grabbed his hand and squeezed it before she spoke. "I'm grateful for your protection, Sky. I do wonder at how hate and fear can change people and sometimes even stop them from seeing the truth. Last week, distrust blinded me and clouded my judgment. I made mistakes and people got hurt. I regret it. I just hope your warriors keep their hearts open to the good around them."

The mightiest of warriors looked down at Morgan. "Hearts blind us; they are dangerous in times of war."

Morgan looked at Bastian, who proceeded to attempt to cheer Gabriel with some light conversation. The Ange'el responded with a lacklustre smile; there was no light in his eyes. Morgan couldn't help but feel for Bastian. He was like the child of divorced parents, trying to fill the awkward silences and tense moments. This was a different approach to that of Sage, who frowned at Sky. Morgan had never seen the tender, loving Sage express anger before.

"Sage, shall we join Ollie and delight our audience with our amazing voices?" Gabriel smiled as he got up, exiting the loaded atmosphere. The Ange'el picked up the guitar and tested if he could move his right hand and fingers enough to play. Soon enough, Riley, Quinn, and Aria also joined them. Sky crossed her arms in front of her chest, clearly uncomfortable as Viviane watched her, eyes full of admonishment.

Morgan walked around the table and whispered in Sky's ear: "And yet, we both know you have one."

"Have what?" Sky asked, puzzled.

"A lioness' heart." Morgan smiled, squeezing Sky's shoulder. "You're okay . . . for an Ahe'ey," she said before she walked in the direction of her lover.

As Gabriel sang with his children, Viviane's Ange'el released some sparkling multi-coloured lanterns shaped like angels, dragons, birds, and serpents. Morgan felt as though she was dreaming. Nothing this beautiful could exist in the world.

Morgan enjoyed Bastian's company away from everyone else. She knew she could trust him and that he was her friend. Bastian's blind loyalty to his cousins reminded Morgan of a big grizzly bear protecting her newborn cubs. It was endearing to watch. She was grateful that Gabriel had such an amazing friend.

"What happened between those two? Why does she hate him so much?" she asked.

"I'm sorry, it's not my place to tell that story." His gaze was steady.

"That's okay. I'm just curious."

Bastian shot a glance at Sky from the distance.

"Don't hate her; she has her reasons."

"Yeah, that's what I keep hearing."

Morgan toyed with the idea of talking to Bastian about something that had been on her mind for some time. Finally, she gathered the courage to proceed.

"I really don't understand why you can't just harvest your DNA and keep it safe."

"We've been storing the blood of our royal family for several generations. We use the methods that become available as human technology evolves. It was a project started by Sathian in his youth. We store these samples at the Sacred House under strict security." Bastian's eyes waited for her next question.

"So why are you still forced to marry within the bloodline?" Morgan attempted to maintain a casual tone, but deep inside, she was desperate to understand the chains and shackles that were keeping Gabriel bound to these ancient dynastic traditions.

"Unfortunately, there are still degradation and contamination issues with the methods humans have developed to store DNA long term. We run the risk that when human technology is finally ready, we'll find that the DNA we have stored may be 'dirty' or 'degraded' and will not perform well in the sequencing process."

"Okay, but we have recently sequenced the human genome in its entirety. Surely, we could use the same technology to map the DNA of the royal Ahe'ey?"

"Yes, genome sequencing is now possible, the technology is evolving quite rapidly. But, it's still difficult for us to have access to the machines and bring them to Ahe'ey unnoticed. And, it's strictly forbidden to move samples of royal blood outside Ahe'ey under the penalty of death. In recent years, the Yi'ingo have executed several Hu'urei that tried to take samples of royal blood to the outside world to be analysed."

"Death sentences? Why?" Morgan sighed. *And they call themselves a great civilisation.*

"Amalia and Angha wanted to ensure that it doesn't happen again as it exposes the bloodline to the potential risk of misuse."

"Fear won't take you far," Morgan whispered. Bastian didn't react to her words and continued with his explanation.

"A few years ago, Gabriel wanted to use a team of human scientists outside Ahe'ey to sequence our genome. He believed he could keep the project secret by trusting just a few human collaborators. He discussed it with the royal family. Gabriel's proposal was vetoed by Amalia after she consulted with Angha in the mountain. The risks of the information ending up in the wrong hands were too big. The social networks are a huge threat to us, and since 9/11, the US National Security Agency has significantly increased its information technology capability to monitor internet and cell phones. Human privacy is as extinct as the dinosaur or the dodo bird. We can't afford our secrets ending up in the wrong hands."

"Surely you can find some trustworthy human partners," said Morgan.

"Humans lack the moral and ethical framework to handle the truth."

"You know, Bas, you all spend a lot of time pointing out the flaws of my people as if the Ahe'ey don't have their own issues," Morgan said, irritated with the constant undermining of the moral values of humans. Bastian laughed nervously, reacting to Morgan's annoyed face. But she looked up and stared straight into his eyes and the giant winced and became sombre.

"I'm sorry, Morgan. You're right. Believe me; I'm aware of our flaws. Well, not my flaws, I'm perfect," he chuckled, trying to lighten the mood. "I assure you that I get astonished every day by news of the great deeds of some of your heroes and leaders."

"Perhaps you should stop being so astonished. It's who we are. Like the Ahe'ey, we have the potential for both good and evil. Your astonishment denotes privilege and prejudice."

"I apologise, Lady. I didn't mean to offend you. I . . . I guess you're right—"

"You know, Bastian, we humans do the same thing you guys do. We go to poor countries full of good intentions. We want to end poverty, disease and violence. We ignore their culture, their history, their knowledge and their wishes under the pretence that we know better, that we are better. We bring science and resources, but we also bring a sense of superiority that stops us from listening to their unique solutions. We forget that what works in a particular context doesn't necessarily work in other conditions. We forget to ask them what they want and need. The 'white saviour industrial complex' is alive and well in my world and I would hate for the Ahe'ey to take the same path."

Bastian stared at her for a moment, then a small smile tilted his lips.

"We're blessed to have you here with us to guide us, my friend." He kissed Morgan's hand.

The Devil Was Once an Angel

Viviane was watching events unfold with amusement. The bench she shared with Sky was shaking vigorously; her niece's foot was restlessly stomping on the ground. Sky became increasingly annoyed as she watched Bastian flirt with a young Ange'el woman who sat beside him. Maheeka wasn't much older than Sage, probably in her mid-twenties and was clearly excited to have the attention of the great Ma'asai prince. They whispered in each other's ears and exchanged naughty glances. The young woman blushed as much as she smiled. It was uncommon for an Ange'el to be this forward with anyone but it was the first time the young woman had drunk alcohol.

"Sky, I was hoping you could help me improve my aim while Apollo is recovering. I really want to enter the archery competition this year." Quinn was sitting beside Sky, doing her best to imitate the Yi'ingo's posture and attitude.

"Sure, Quinny, how about we start right now?" Sky jumped to her feet and picked up one of the bows leaning against the main building.

"Hey, Bas. Follow me and bring some apples, will you?" He shot her a sideways glance and then followed them to a tree nearby.

One by one, Sky shot five apples off Bastian's head while explaining the technique to Quinn. "And of course, if you really want to hurt them, aim for the groin," Sky said loudly, changing her target for a few seconds and making everyone laugh.

"Groins. Yes, yes, I got it," Quinn said, imitating Sky's tone of voice and keeping her nose high.

"Careful, ladies, the royal bloodline needs those . . . assets," Viviane said, joining the fun.

Suddenly, the mood changed and a wave of silence spread throughout all the tables. Joshua, the leader of the Hu'urei, had arrived. Joshua was a few years younger than Gabriel, but the lines on his face and his roughened appearance made him look much older. He was a big, imposing man, yet he was clearly uneasy as he stood waiting to be invited to sit.

Everyone was surprised by the presence of the Hu'urei. Viviane had asked him to join them. After all, he was her nephew and a cousin of the royal heirs to the throne. Gabriel got up and limped in the direction of Joshua, while the others looked on suspiciously.

"Joshua! Glad you could join us. Let me introduce you to our guest of honour, Morgan." Joshua looked at the Ange'el with distrust and made no effort to respond to Gabriel as he walked beside the Ange'el in the direction of the main table.

"Lady Viviane." He bowed as he reached the table.

"Welcome, Josh, I am happy you could make it. You will be glad to know that today we have more to offer than fruit, grains and vegetables."

"The smell of barbecued meat prompted me to walk faster," he replied, a slight hint of humour in his voice.

"This is Morgan. Her humanitarian work is praised across the world. We are honoured to have her as our guest," Gabriel said.

"Is it wise to expose Ahe'ey to more humans?"

"Morgan is a trusted member of this family. Josh, have a seat and eat something," Viviane said.

"The Hu'urei should be part of any decision that puts our people at risk, Lady."

"And what gives you the right to make such claim?" Sky roared, heading towards the table in the direction of her half-brother. Sky and Joshua faced each other, heads held high. Her hand clasped the hilt of her sword tightly.

"*Sky! Joshua!*" Gabriel raised his voice. "This is not the place, and this is not the day to have such discussions," the Ange'el spoke assertively.

"I take no orders from you," Sky hissed in Gabriel's direction, looking straight into his eyes.

"I mean no disrespect to you, Lady Morgan," Joshua said. "I'm honoured to meet you, but they should trust me to take part in these decisions." Morgan smiled and nodded, accepting his explanation as he kissed her hand.

"Trust is a funny thing," Sky said. "Our human guest should know this better than anyone else. Their devil was once an angel, just like ours." Sky turned her back and left, followed by two other Yi'ingo warriors.

Gabriel lowered his eyes, took a deep breath and spoke, "Joshua, this is my daughter Quinn. Soon, she'll be the greatest Yi'ingo warrior in this land. She plans to take the title in the next Games and usurp the unbeatable Sky. The champion isn't aware of her plans though; we want to take her by surprise." Gabriel's voice was pleasing and jovial; Quinn inflated her chest as she walked over to greet Joshua.

The Hu'urei leader laughed loudly, disarmed by the feisty posture of the girl. He composed himself and shook Quinn's hand. "Let me know if you want me to help you with sword fighting or survival skills. I'll do anything to see Sky fall on her mighty arse. I was disappointed that my own daughter chose to join the Ange'el instead of the Yi'ingo. It would have been fun to teach her to fight. Where is my Muriel tonight?"

"Muriel made a vow of silence this week. It's a shame she can't join us, but if you wish to see her mother, Selene, she's helping in the kitchen tonight," Sage replied.

"Selene doesn't care for my company. She was only after my seed," Joshua replied, his words unfettered by politeness and self-censorship. Sage blushed.

"This is Sage, my eldest daughter," Gabriel said. Joshua looked at Sage's face and softened his tone.

"I'm sorry. I have poor manners. Yes, I remember your name, Lady Sage. My daughter tells me your healing abilities are exceptional, a great feat for a human."

"Thank you, sir. I do have the best teachers. My father and Lady Viviane have taught me very well."

"There's nothing minor about being a human. The bloodline is overrated," Gabriel said. "Sage is a natural healer and the kindest Ahe'ey I know."

Joshua continued to avoid direct eye contact with Gabriel. Every time the Ange'el spoke, Joshua's jaw locked tightly and his eyes filled with distrust. The kindness of the Ange'el towards him was coldly received and never reciprocated.

"So how's my daughter, Lady Sage? Is she doing well at Ange'el?"

"Very well. She's an excellent teacher."

Joshua's expression softened as his eyes admired the fine features of the golden maiden.

"Josh," Viviane said, "I expect all your men at the Temple of Lights tomorrow."

"Of course, Lady. The king told me there may be some news," the Hu'urei responded without moving his eyes away from Sage.

Viviane was fond of Joshua; he was rough and clearly defensive after years and years of distrust and accusations by so many at Ahe'ey. He had developed a layer of coarseness that played into the character that was expected of him, and yet deep inside, he was a good and fair man. During the war, Marcus had killed Joshua's grandfather, Sathian, while his father Iblis and the rebel Hu'urei troops had taken shelter in the forest where they then battled the Yi'ingo and Ma'asai armies for years.

Marcus had taken a close interest in Joshua, guiding him to rebuild the village and lead his people in a time of great distrust for any Hu'urei. Joshua was a casualty of war as much as everyone else in Ahe'ey. Viviane wished that one day Sky and her Yi'ingo could reconcile with Joshua and the Hu'urei now that peace was once again flourishing in the land.

Viviane felt her mother's presence before Amalia came into her room at the Sacred House. The Ange'el tried to remain calm. She knew this was going to be a difficult conversation and that she would have to be careful not to disclose any of her plans. Amalia had a way of triggering strong emotions in her daughter. The queen mother had become bitter and aggressive during the war as her family had perished and her dreams had collapsed. She had become obsessed with creating an unbeatable army of women warriors and rebuilding her royal lineage. Because of this, she had put tremendous pressure on Viviane and Marcus to have more babies, which they had tried desperately to do without success. Amalia needed another girl to ensure the royal bloodline did not vanish with Sky, Bastian, and Gabriel.

Viviane had felt useless, unable to fulfil her mother's wishes, and was also pushed into the role of queen of Ahe'ey due to the death of her older sisters. She had been the least suited to the role. She was a spiritual being who sought connection with all living beings and was highly sensitive to the world around her. Her soul was compassionate and nurturing at a time when Ahe'ey needed strong and decisive leadership. Marcus had been her rock and a natural-born leader, but after years of rapes, pillages, and slavery, no woman wanted a man to be the ruler of the land, not even the man who had killed Sathian. So, Amalia and Viviane had shared the leadership of the Ahe'ey with the support of Marcus. The queen mother had become the ruler under martial law, while Viviane and Marcus had focused on rebuilding Ahe'ey. As Amalia got older, Sky replaced her at the helm of the army. Women were safe and vindicated under a matriarchal regime which was supported by the good men who had fought beside them during the war.

Thirty-four years had passed since the beginning of the war and Viviane was now a seasoned leader. Beloved by her subjects, she was working on healing the scars of her people and creating a better Ahe'ey. She knew her mother's hate towards men was one of the strongest blockers against her plans. Stuck in the past, Amalia had poisoned the minds of her Yi'ingo, especially her granddaughter, making them both a liability to Ahe'ey and humankind. Viviane and Marcus had a plan, a path forwards that needed to be concealed until the right time had come, but omitting information from Amalia would not be an easy task. While Amalia was not an Ange'el so she couldn't read people's minds, she knew her daughter very well.

"Your sisters are turning in their graves." A shiver went down Viviane's neck as her mother spoke. "I mourn the day my daughter invites the head of the Hu'urei to a royal party."

"Joshua is my nephew and your grandson, and he's an honourable man."

"A bastard of rape, the reason why your sister is dead. How can you betray her memory? Why do you continue to feed the cancer that plagues our land?"

"It is time to move on and reform. We must rebuild the ties between all our tribes, and embrace peace and prosperity."

"That is exactly what they want. As soon as we relax our guard, they will betray us once more. They seek power."

"What power, mother? What would they seek? The royal bloodline will stop with the daughters and sons of our children. It is time we give all of our citizens equal rights and opportunities."

"Over my dead body. Your liberal ways will put the safety of our people at risk."

"You design your own self-fulfilling prophecy. Every time we treat

Hu'urei as different, every time we limit their rights, we are awakening the Sathian within them. The same is happening when we tell our spiritual boys they cannot be an Ange'el or when we don't trust our men to serve in our armies. By keeping power away from them forcibly, we fail to teach them how to use it responsibly. We fail to inspire them to be the best leaders they could be because it is something that is denied to them. Some may comply, but I promise you that, soon, we will have an uprising on our hands."

"So you accept that there is a Sathian within each one of them?"

"There is a Sathian within all of us, and the systems we created during a time of need are now fuelling the worst in our people. I see the aura of our land, the colours of our shared consciousness, and they are dark with the frustration and the unspoken anger of so many. We need reform, and we need your support and Sky's support. It is not just the Hu'urei that are frustrated. We claim to defend our women as we take control of their wombs. Is this much different from Sathian's plan? He took them by force. We take them by the rule of law, controlling whom they marry and with whom they can reproduce. We must reform our land or civil war will rage upon us again."

"That is never going to happen, not on my watch, and you better keep a close eye on your son and his activities. It is clear whom Sky will choose to be at her side while she rules. Look at your son; he is a mirror of Sathian, every feature, every expression. What will prevent Gabriel from becoming the next Sathian?"

"How dare you!" Viviane seethed. "Only you and I know what happened and how that monster came to be."

"It does not change the fact that he turned into one. It does not excuse his actions."

"No, it does not. But he is not the only monster in this land, is he?"

"Leave my brother out of this. He is old and has fought bravely in war."

"The dragons are in the wrong hands."

"The dragons are our insurance against evil. Gabriel has long shown that he solely cares about his own self-preservation. Why are you allowing him to raise an army of humans in our land? You know he carries Sathian's blood, his sickness."

"I'm devastated by your hate, mother. You never once made an effort to know Gabriel or the children. Gabriel is your grandson. I want you to go now. Enough."

"He is also the grandson of the man who murdered my daughters. Have you told your husband?"

Viviane shook her head, her heart sinking, "It would destroy him."

"If Angha ever finds out . . . "

"Mother, we must appoint another minder for the dragons. He is too old and unstable."

"I trust him. I hope you are still trying to have more children. Why don't you do that instead of polluting this land with human brats? I had you when I was a hundred and forty-two years old. You still have time."

Viviane began sobbing. She had been trying and failing to have more children for many years. Her mother and some of her people saw her as a failure, as she was unable to fulfil her obligations to preserve the royal bloodline.

Amalia continued, "Perhaps Angha's seed can still—"

"*Enough!*" Viviane yelled, disgusted by her mother's suggestion.

Amalia stopped but quickly moved onto her next order of business. "I am here because of Morgan. You took a great risk in bringing her here."

"She saved my son's life."

"What do you know about her? What do you see with your Ange'el heart? I am certain she is a distant descendant of Ahe'ey. Her features, they are flawed and impure; she is too fragile, but they remind me of—"

"Leave." Viviane was relieved Amalia had given her the perfect excuse to cut the conversation short. *"Leave now!"*

Incoming Storm

Marcus was back from the mountain. He entered his room in the Sacred House and embraced Viviane, who placed her hands on his face and looked into his eyes. His face was pale, reflecting the heaviness of his heart. He struggled to hold back the tears that flooded his conscience.

"It is done," Marcus said, knowing words were wasted as the Ange'el could read his mind and his heart. They both held each other tight. They had designed the most ambitious revolution ever attempted—a plan that could prevent another civil war; a conspiracy that, at best, would place their son under tremendous pain and distress and, at worst, would lead to his destruction. He who was the most precious treasure that they had ever created together. Today, and from that moment onwards, they were a queen and a king before being a mother and a father. Today, they would have to leave their emotions behind and execute the plan without hesitation. Today, but not right now.

Right now, they cried and consoled each other, damning their fate. The farmer and the priestess were about to shed the last vestige of the idealism they had shared in their youth. They were taking the destiny of their people into their own hands, and their tools? Manipulation, misdirection, and propaganda worthy of Machiavelli himself.

The Royal Mandate

5 December 2014 - Ange'el village

Gabriel and Bastian walked up the stairs of the Temple of Lights, the central building that united the four quarters of Ahe'ey. The tribes were coming together in this venue in one hour to listen to an address from the rulers. It was a rare occasion that fuelled both anxiety and excitement amongst the people of Ahe'ey.

Gabriel was limping and still in a great deal of pain, but he climbed two steps at a time, leaning on a walking cane. He looked forward to seeing his father. Gabriel adored Marcus; their relationship was strong, based on love, mutual respect, and admiration. Due to historical and political reasons, they weren't able to see each other often. Gabriel lived between Manhattan and Ange'el, while Marcus was currently spending most of his time at Hu'urei, mediating between them and the Yi'ingo. The last time Gabriel had seen Marcus had been over four weeks ago when the king and the queen had renewed their marriage vows in this same venue.

As the Ange'el looked up, he saw Sky sprinting down the stairs. Her face was flushed, and she didn't stop to speak to her cousins. The Yi'ingo's shoulder brushed against Gabriel's injured shoulder with enough strength to leave him dizzy with pain.

"*Sky!*" Bastian shouted, but she was already out of reach. The men looked at each other, puzzled, and continued. The Ange'el felt Sky's anger in his mind's eye and knew something serious had happened.

Gabriel saw Marcus as soon as they entered the throne room. The king patted Bastian on the back with affection and embraced his son tightly for a few moments.

"Don't break him, Marcus; your boy is a bit frail at the moment. Even

Sage could beat him at the Games," Bastian said with a smirk on his face.

Marcus looked at Gabriel and said, pointing at Bastian, "The last time I saw your cousin fight, he was having his face rearranged by Sky at the summer Games."

Gabriel and Marcus smiled, and Bastian replied, "She beat me by three points. Next time, I'll hands down win the Games. Marcus, my dear uncle, I'm afraid that by the end of this year you won't be the only living Ma'asai to have won the Games."

"We shall see about that."

Marcus had short dark greyish hair and light green eyes. He was tall and well-built and sported the same light goatee as his son. Although he was 134 years old, he looked like a man in his mid-forties. He wore a deep green and gold tunic adorned with a pendant that featured the sun. After a moment, he became sombre and looked down to the floor to gather his thoughts. By the time he looked up, the light had vanished from his eyes.

"Is everything okay?" Gabriel asked, feeling the tension and apprehension in his father's mind.

Marcus focused his gaze on Gabriel and spoke, "Many years ago, I put the safety and prosperity of this land above your interests and happiness."

Gabriel nodded as his father put his hand on his shoulder.

"At that time, I told you I would have more to ask of you in the future. This is the day, and this is the place."

Gabriel remained calm and attentive; after all, his parents had always been outstanding leaders and mentors. Everything they had asked of him over the years had ended well. "You have my life and my allegiance, my king."

Bastian frowned and crossed his arms in front of his chest. "He's done enough, Marcus."

Gabriel looked back, feeling the presence of his mother as she walked in the room.

"Oh, this is serious," Bastian said, bowing to Viviane who looked unusually sombre.

Marcus continued, "We need to put the war behind us, bring our tribes together and focus our attention on helping humanity."

"Agreed," Gabriel replied, wondering what he would ask of him next.

"This won't happen while Sky and the Yi'ingo are in power."

Both Gabriel and Bastian interjected at the same time.

"That's not fair," Bastian said.

"Sky won't ascend to the throne. She will never be Queen of Ahe'ey." Marcus' tone was commanding and definitive.

Gabriel's eyes were wide; the turn of events surprised him. He pulled away from his father. "Sky has been tireless in her quest for peace."

"Security, not peace," Marcus replied.

"They are one and the same," Bastian interjected, his brows pulled down together.

"No, they are not. The pursuit of security can fuel war. Security divides; peace unites."

Gabriel continued, "At a tender age . . . when we most needed her, you gave her temporary rule under martial law, and now . . . now, you are telling us that she may not be the next queen of this land?" His surprise turned into frustration on behalf of his cousin. "She has worked so hard and sacrificed so much. Sky is the worthy ruler of Ahe'ey."

"She was never meant to be a ruler in times of peace, my dear," Viviane said as she walked closer to the group.

"You used her in war and now discard her in peace." Bastian's fists clenched.

"Sky is and always will be a leader and the protector of Ahe'ey, but she will not be its ruler." Viviane's eyes turned to Gabriel, cutting. "You are the only one who can unite our tribes and lead us to fulfil our mission to guide humans and protect this planet."

Gabriel shook his head in disbelief and exchanged a glance of incredulity with his cousin. He was angry as he began to understand why his parents had summoned him. "I will not betray my cousin . . . my cousins. In a few years, I hope and wish Sky and Bastian will rule together." He looked at Bastian, as he knew he was saying something that had never been spoken, but that had always been assumed by everyone; after all, Sky and Bastian were lovers, the last royal lovers of Ahe'ey. "I'll do everything in my power to support them, but I won't betray them."

"I have no aspirations to the throne, but Sky expects and deserves it," Bastian said.

"There is nothing to betray," Marcus said, raising his voice. "The conviction and courage that Sky demonstrates on the battlefield are different from the skill set required to bring our tribes together and to guide humankind. She is belligerent, as she should be. She is the finest warrior Ahe'ey has ever had. Don't expect or ask a tiger to change its stripes. We informed Sky today that we want you to be the next ruler of Ahe'ey."

"What have you done?" Bastian's nostrils flared.

"She's not a tiger; she's a queen, and you broke her heart . . . again." Gabriel finally understood the pain he had seen in Sky's eyes a few minutes before.

Viviane placed her hand on Marcus' forearm and continued, "Marcus and I are not young anymore, my dear love. We've lost touch with the outside world—how they speak to each other, what they care about. Like Sky, we have been focused on our own land, and now we have two options—we can fully reject our purpose and close Ahe'ey to the outside world, or we can place the right leader on that throne, one who can bring us back to our original goal."

Marcus placed both hands on Gabriel's shoulders. "Son, if we keep the passage open, without the right ruler, we risk being found before humankind is ready. We have spent too much time not supporting humankind's evolution due to our internal problems while simultaneously risking humanity by leaving our portals to this land open. It is simple—either you take the throne, or we will close the passages forever."

Gabriel panicked. He was now pleading with his father, desperate, scared, "You can't close those portals. They need our help. I'm raising leaders that will bring light to humankind—their leaders, not ours, their children, my children. I'm working on . . . ."

"Yes! Yes, you are," Viviane spoke, at first vehemently, then her tone became gentler. "Yes, you are, my love."

Gabriel lowered his head and closed his eyes, trying to make sense of his parents' decisions. He grieved for Sky, who had sacrificed so much for so long.

Bastian sighed. "Cousin, your parents have a point. You . . . You are the right leader for this land, one I'd be honoured to serve." Gabriel could feel his cousin's inner conflict, but after another moment, Bastian sighed and continued, "I love Sky. I . . . I adore her. But, a ruler can't hate half her subjects. My men suffer under her rule."

The growing chorus of voices didn't convince the Ange'el prince to take Sky's future as his own. "She'll change in time. The rage, the hate . . . these aren't who she is; they are what she has become. You punish her for being precisely what we needed her to be." Gabriel wouldn't conceal his internal struggle.

Viviane raised her hand towards her son. "Gabriel, I will close the passage indefinitely if anyone but you takes the throne. I have no other choice. That is my final word."

Gabriel couldn't allow it. There was too much at stake. He'd been working so long, and so hard to, one day, share their gifts with humankind.

"Mother, I beg you. Don't. I can continue to work from the outside and collaborate with Sky and Bas."

"Sky will never work with you unless she is forced to serve you," Marcus said. His mouth was set, firm in his conviction.

"Listen to what you are saying. You can't force Sky to do anything. In her eyes, I'm a traitor. That will never change."

"At the end of this journey, she will respect you."

"How is that possible? I'm not well known in this land. No one here will respect me as much as they respect Sky and Bastian. The Yi'ingo and Hu'urei will never agree to this, and even the Ma'asai will have their doubts about my worth. Sky is intelligent and kind. She will evolve to serve all her people. Sky and Bas, together, are the perfect team."

"You're assuming we are an item, cousin. That's far from certain, and I have no aspirations to the throne," Bastian said, his brows low, still troubled over Sky.

"Gabriel," Viviane said, "you are loved and adored by many. Your rescue work with children, your diplomatic work, your kindness and your knowledge are celebrated in this land. Yes, some will doubt that you have the courage and strength to rule." She paused, and the silence was deafening as they waited for the words she was about to speak. "Therefore, we ask you to fight the Wali'ingooteer tomorrow to earn your crown."

There was a breath, the slightest moment of pause in between the uttering of the statement and the settling of its implications.

"You can't be serious, my queen!" Bastian shouted, placing his body between Gabriel and the rulers of Ahe'ey. "You can't expect Gabriel to fight against a dragon in his current state. It's suicide."

"Please, Bas, stop," Gabriel murmured as he considered his mother's eyes, which were unblinking and unapologetic.

"Have you no faith in your cousin?" Marcus replied to Bastian in a firm voice.

"I have all the faith in the world, but this is madness. I won't let Gabriel become a sacrificial lamb in your political games. Let me fight on his behalf. I'll take his place in the arena." Bastian shook his head; distress and shock showering his face and body.

"Is this what you would have me do?" Gabriel asked. He knew his parents would never ask him to risk his life if it weren't critical to Ahe'ey's future.

"Yes, son, it is," Marcus replied biting his lip.

Sky was in Gabriel's heart and mind as he replied to his parents, resigned.

"Very well, you have my word. Is there anything else?"

"Yes." Viviane said, "Yes, there is."

The queen's eyes flickered in the light. She vacillated for a second, and Marcus prepared to take over, but she stopped him, straightened her head, and continued, "Our gifts and our wonders are locked in our blood, our genes, passed from generation to generation and unveiled only to those who truly deserve it. You, my son, Sky, and Bastian are direct descendants of the first Ahe'ey, designed to strengthen humanity. You have the purest blood, and we cannot afford a ruler of this land to pollute your body's enhanced building blocks of life."

Gabriel's voice quivered as he whispered, "Don't do this, Mother.

Don't ask me to—"

"Also," Viviane interrupted, "a man cannot rule Ahe'ey without a female counterpart. The Yi'ingo would never accept it, and of course, they expect you to select an Ahe'ey ruler as far up the bloodline as possible. If you defeat the Wali'ingooteer, we expect you to select a queen from amongst the high-ranking Ange'el and Yi'ingo. Scout—Angha's bastard child—has the purest blood after Sky."

Gabriel's heart hit the floor and shattered into one thousand pieces. "I won't. I can't hurt her. I can't live without her."

"You have no choice if you want us to continue to work to guide her people," Marcus said.

"Why would you want a loveless royal wedding? Why do you keep repeating the same mistakes? Ahe'ey needs reform."

"You are all love. You will love again, Gabriel. You will care for anyone in your care as you always do. Once you are established as the ruler of Ahe'ey, you are free to drive the much-needed reform," Viviane answered. "We are on the same side, but change does not happen overnight."

"I'd rather die than hurt Morgan in this way," he said in despair.

"If you die, you will hurt her, your children, and your people. You will miss on the opportunity to drive change in the world." Viviane closed her eyes and touched her moonstone ring. When she opened them and spoke again, her tone was resolute. "The portal is now closed and will remain so until all our conditions are met."

He was gone, cornered into submission with no escape route, broken. His knees went to the floor, his left hand followed, resting on the cool ground, his eyes lowered and he quietly mourned the events that were soon to unfold. "I won't . . . I can't . . . ."

Marcus kneeled in front of his son. "Have I ever let you down, son?"

Gabriel shook his head, eyes still on the floor. "Trust me just once more."

Gabriel said nothing.

Marcus continued, "Gabriel, look at me. I ask you that you give me your word that you will marry one of your kinswomen. In return, if you win this fight with the dragon, you will become king, we will reopen the passages, and you can continue your work and start to reform Ahe'ey."

"I beg you to change your mind." His voice was barely audible.

"We won't. This is our final word. Answer your father, Gabriel." Viviane's voice was the voice of a queen, and there was no trace of his mother in it.

Gabriel was empty, numb, his wings clipped. He was trapped in the gilded cage of a lost, dying dynasty. Gabriel nodded, resigned.

"Please allow Morgan to leave."

"The passage is closed," replied Viviane before she left the room with Marcus.

The Announcement

As the two rulers made their way to the amphitheatre at the Temple of Lights, Gabriel remained in the same place on the floor. Bastian put his hand on his shoulder, and he started to get up.

"Are you okay?" Bastian asked.

Gabriel nodded, struggling to speak.

"Why are you going along with this? They're insane." Gabriel was pale, his light had completely vanished; he couldn't find anything to say to his cousin. They moved towards the temple's exterior plateau and stood behind the king and queen who had been joined by Sky and Amalia.

Gabriel could see the crowd arriving and taking their place in the stone amphitheatre that surrounded the temple. All four tribes were present, but they were mostly separated from each other. Each group huddled together with people from their own clan. While there was some engagement between Ange'el, Ma'asai, and Yi'ingo, the Hu'urei kept themselves isolated from the others.

As Marcus began speaking, Gabriel looked at the statuesque Sky, now wearing her full Yi'ingo regalia—a golden chain mail armour dress adorned with a body plate, decorated with the symbol of Yi'ingo, the phoenix. Her helmet showcased two wings, the symbol of an Ahe'ey guardian. There she stood, in all her glory, showcasing all her power, dressed as the guardian of her people, sending a clear message to all that she was their leader. Her eyes expressed the intensity and rage of a thousand solar storms.

Sage, Morgan and the rest of Gabriel's children arrived and stood downstairs in front of the large crowd and just a few metres away from the royal family. The Ange'el's eyes were set on Morgan; the darkness in his gaze conveyed his unspoken sorrow. He communicated directly into her mind, "I'm sorry." She looked at him and her quizzing eyes searched for answers.

Marcus spoke: "Ten years have passed since the war ended. Our society has found peace under the protection of our brave Yi'ingo warriors. Our soil is fertile and rich due to the hard work of the Ma'asai. Our homes and venues have been rebuilt to their former glory due to the mastery of the Hu'urei. The Ange'el have provided our children with a solid education system and have supported our spiritual and physical well-being. Our land is flourishing. We are ready to let go of our recent past and refocus again on the mission of our founding foremothers and forefathers.

"We are prepared to take the last steps to fully reintegrate our tribes and allow every citizen to take part in all roles and to enjoy the same rights and opportunities." The Hu'urei cheered. The men had some level of trust with Marcus, and his words were welcomed with enthusiasm.

"This will enable us to focus on our fellow earthlings, to help them evolve beyond the mindless greed that threatens Earth and all its living beings. Viviane and I have served you the best we could through a dark period of Ahe'ey's history. We could not have done it without the support and leadership of Sky. Together, we have focused on ending the civil war and rebuilding our land in partnership with our citizens. It is time for reform, and it is time for a leader who can help us connect with the outside world. Due to the tragedy of war, we only have one more generation before the purity of our royal bloodline is lost forever. The clock is ticking, and we need a leader who will help us prepare humankind to receive our most precious gift."

The audience became more excited and hopeful. Viviane took over from Marcus. "In two weeks, on the day of the winter solstice, we plan to hand over the throne of Ahe'ey to a new ruler, a leader that we are confident can unite us all and guide us to pursue our destiny."

The Yi'ingo cheered in expectation of what was about to be announced.

Viviane continued, "Our son, Gabriel."

The crowd's surprise was evident. A gasp propagated through the thousands of people in the audience. Many Ange'el and some members of the Ma'asai expressed enthusiasm. The Hu'urei mocked Sky, uttering sounds of those who had been avenged, while the Yi'ingo expressed rage and anger on behalf of their warrior queen. Amalia's face was twisted in disbelief.

Gabriel looked at Sky, who was trying her best to show dignity, but her eyebrows, jaw, shoulders, and hands showcased the rage that was burning inside her. Bastian had walked towards her and stood by her side.

"He didn't want this," Bas murmured in her ear.

Gabriel remembered the little girl that used to swim in the lake and run in the forest with him. It had been a time of carefree smiles and trust, almost forgotten, and now forever buried in their past by layers of resentment and distrust. And yet he loved her like a brother loves a little sister, and he wished he could take the sting away. She looked him straight in his eyes, and in them, he could feel her hate, rage, disapproval, disdain, resentment, and pain.

Viviane continued swiftly. "Since he was a young boy, we have asked Gabriel to focus his work on humankind. He has spent most of his time outside this land, and due to this, we understand that many of you do not know him well."

"He's a coward, unfit to rule," Amalia spat her words in his direction.

The Yi'ingo cheered, stomping their feet and shouting unpleasantries. Gabriel stood quietly; he was numb, resigned to the expected backlash.

He didn't react to the disdain of the Yi'ingo; his mind was far away, with Sky, Morgan and his children.

"*Place me in charge!*" Joshua shouted from the front of the crowd; he stood up and climbed midway up the stairs of the temple as the Hu'urei cheered him on. "We don't need another Sathian. I'm ready to rule."

The Yi'ingo laughed. Sky jumped down to the flight of stairs, landing a few metres above Joshua. She placed her hand on the hilt of her sword and several Yi'ingo and Hu'urei stood up.

Viviane continued, unfazed by the chaos that surrounded her, "Although we have no doubt of his valour, courage, virtue, or leadership ability, we have asked Gabriel to fight the strongest of the Wali'ingooteer tomorrow, in the main arena. In doing so, he will showcase both his courage and skill, reassuring you of his claim to this throne."

The energy of the public shifted with the news of the upcoming battle with the dragon. A wave of chatter travelled within the crowd, many reacting in the same way Bastian had done, predicting the result, and already mourning or celebrating his loss. Amalia looked appeased by the news, probably predicting Gabriel's death and the rise of Sky to the throne.

Sky looked back at Viviane in shock and surprise. "Suicide," she shouted, and she turned back to Gabriel to meet his eyes, but they were no longer on her. He was looking at his children, attempting to reassure them with a forced smile. He winked at Quinn, who was trying to make sense of the news.

The crowd's whispers turned into loud conversations. Groups gathered to express surprise and disbelief. Viviane raised her voice and continued, "Once Gabriel defeats the dragon, he will select a queen from within the Ahe'ey people, and they will both be crowned king and queen. He will honour the wishes of our foremothers and forefathers in keeping the royal bloodline as pure as possible."

Morgan closed her eyes for a few seconds. Gabriel's eyes were set on her, despairing, wanting to take the pain away, feeling her pain as his own, double the pain of one heart breaking. The news of the upcoming wedding, should Gabriel survive, had little impact on the audience. The upcoming battle made everything else irrelevant. In their minds, he was already a dead man.

Sky shook her head and spoke, "This is a waste of everyone's time. If you want to kill your son, you should just get on with it and do it today."

Viviane continued, "It is our belief that Gabriel is the only ruler who can connect us with humans. The passage to the outside world is now closed and will remain so until Gabriel ascends to the throne. If Gabriel loses the battle with the Wali'ingooteer, the passage will remain closed, as the world is a dangerous place full of greed. If our gift ends up in the wrong hands, it could be exploited and lead to a catastrophic result."

Most of the public listened with detachment; years of war had disconnected them from any virtuous goals to help the outside world. Sky turned her back and left, and with her went all the Yi'ingo.

As the people dispersed, Gabriel walked down the stairs, limping in the direction of Morgan and the children. His mind's eye was set on them. He reminded himself that these were the people he was willing to lose so much for.

Sage's face was as pale as snow as she kneeled in front of Riley who was crying uncontrollably. Aria picked up on her siblings' energy and sobbed. Sage wrapped both girls in her arms, attempting to reassure them. Quinn came to her rescue.

"Apollo is the strongest and bravest Ahe'ey I know. He'll defeat the Wali'ingooteer easily," she said with certainty.

"I sure will," Gabriel replied with a glowing smile. That was enough for the little ones to nod and clap.

Ollie stood with his arms crossed in front of his chest, his shoulders slumped over his body. Guilt and worry inundated his eyes. "You have nothing to prove, Apollo. You really don't," he whispered.

"Look at me Ollie." Gabriel placed his hand on his son's chin and lifted it, feeling his love for his children like a wonderful ache. "This is not your doing. Everything will be just fine. Will you believe in me?"

The boy nodded.

"I need you to be strong and support Sage with the children. Do you understand? Will you do this for me?"

Ollie hugged Gabriel.

Gabriel and Sage looked at each other; no words needed to be spoken between the two Ange'el. He silently showered her with reassurance and love and asked her to be strong and a role model to her siblings. She kissed him and guided her brother and sisters back to the Sacred House.

When he finally reached Morgan, he was lost for words. There was nothing he could say or do. His eyes said it all.

"This fight—"

"It'll be fine." He projected a false confidence with his voice. "I'm superhuman, remember?" He forced himself to smile.

"You can barely walk. I can't do this . . . ." In her mind, he saw confusion, worry, and grief. She didn't say anything about the royal wedding he had agreed to.

He reached towards her, placing her face between his palms. "Listen, Morgan—"

She pushed his hands away. "I want to go home. Is that possible? Will you help me go back to New York?"

He lowered his head for a brief moment and then he nodded. "I gave you my word, remember?"

Morgan was stunned, mindlessly following Gabriel, who was walking unusually fast given his injuries. She wanted to stop him and ask him why, to demand an explanation, but his eyes and his body told her that he had none to offer, that there was no way back. She could see his pain but was unable to overcome her own grief in order to provide him with any comfort or reassurance. She felt scared, humiliated and betrayed.

They stopped at the pavilion. She changed into her own clothes, and he picked up a bag. Then they walked to the stables, and he whispered, "Do you know how to ride?" His voice choked.

She shook her head.

He walked in the direction of his horse, who was restless, probably feeling his master's distress. Gabriel took a minute to calm the animal before he helped Morgan mount and then mounted behind her. As he wrapped his arms around her, she closed her eyes for a second, reassured by the feeling of his body.

They galloped through the woods in the direction of Lake Do'oras. She sunk into his arms, enjoying the warmth of his body behind her. She loved him; there was no way to ignore it. As she looked at the bandage on his right arm, she remembered the price he had paid the last time she refused to be vulnerable, the last time she refused to reach out to him, the last time that pride had got in her way. She picked up his hand and kissed it. She reached behind her to touch his face and felt the tears that ran down his face as he kissed her hair.

They continued riding, feeling each other's presence, embraced in an intimacy that they were about to give up forever. He whispered in her ear, "I didn't—"

"I know," she interrupted, touching his leg. "I know, my love . . . .

Come with me, leave all this behind. Please."

"I can't. I wish I could, but I can't."

"You can't fight in your condition—"

"I have no other choice."

Sky bolted into the forest with her head held high. The fire in her gut was so intense that she could taste it in her mouth. She'd been serving the queen and king her entire life, working to save her sisters, to make Ahe'ey safe. That was all she'd known, and it had cost her blood, her sweat and the tears that she'd never allowed herself to cry. There was no one worthier and more qualified to rule Ahe'ey. What had happened today had been a betrayal to her and to the women of Ahe'ey.

"Sky. *Sky!*"

She ignored him. Bastian was the last person she wanted to see.

"Please stop."

She picked up pace. "Leave me alone. What do you want?"

"To be with you at this moment."

"Not now. Go back to your king."

"Are you ever going to let me in? Are you ever going to let anyone in?" He grabbed her arm, stopping her from walking away.

She turned to him, yanked her arm away and gritted her teeth.

"Are you here to laugh and gloat?" she spat the words, ramming her face so close to his that their noses almost touched. His betrayal, more than anyone else's, stung. "I saw you going with him into the hall. You could have stopped him. You could have taken my side and opposed this insanity."

"He wasn't the one that needed stopping. We would never betray you."

"We? You and him? Above everyone else. Always . . . no matter what. You're a pet. Nothing but a pet. Too weak to see beyond his glow."

"I see beyond his glow just as I see beyond your rage. Always have. Perhaps I am a pet, but I'm your pet as much as his."

"Go." Her eyes were wet, her jaw clenched and her muscles contracted in fury.

"No. You're my queen. The strongest, bravest, most courageous warrior in this land. I'm not going anywhere."

"What do you want?"

"Sky, I'm not the best at this, but I love you, and I, for one, need to share with you more than just your bed. You're hurting, and I'm here for you. Accept it. Accept me."

"Why do you follow me? I'm of no value to you anymore."

"What are you talking about?"

"I've lost the throne. The royal bloodline won't survive another generation."

"Is that what you think of me? Is that what you thought this was about? The throne? The bloodline? Really?" He shot her a disheartened glance.

He turned around to leave when she pushed his chest hard with the palm of her hand until his back crashed into a tree. She didn't want to talk, cry, or be vulnerable; never vulnerable, never again. She grabbed his face and pulled it towards hers, kissing him hard and moving her hands decisively over his body. He tried to stop her, grabbing her wrists and pushing them away from him.

"Talk to me," he begged just as she bit his lip until it bled.

She pulled him down to the grass, wrapped her legs around him and bit his neck. He surrendered to her power. They were two forces of nature caught in passion, matching each other in energy—aggressive, wild—trying to numb her inner pain.

The raw sexual ecstasy cleared her mind and tamed her rage. As she got up to leave, he held her face with his two hands and kissed her. She refused to make eye contact.

"Did you support his claim to the throne?"

His eyes fell to his feet, and she had her answer. "Sky . . . your hate for men . . . is—" Her elbow hit his face, and she walked away. "Sky, you must understand, I . . . must serve my men."

For the first time in years, she cried as she ran through the forest. She decided to go to the gate and tell the Yi'ingo guardians that they could leave their posts. Now that the queen had closed the passage between the two worlds, there was nothing to safeguard. Only Viviane and her moonstone had the power to reopen the passage at Lake Do'oras.

Sky was going through Bastian's words in her head. She had the scent of his skin on her skin, and her heart told her to go back into his arms, so she ran fast, away from him. How could she ever know if he truly loved her? She was doomed to have Gaia's faith, always doubting the love of the man by her side because of her genes and her royal status.

Bastian and Sky had lost their parents at the same time during their childhood. They had both been rescued by Viviane and Marcus, then taken to an Ange'el hideaway in the forest. Bastian was four years younger than Sky; she had always tried to look after him when they were little. A few years later, she had to leave Ange'el in order to go back to Yi'ingo to eventually lead the army into battle. She had lost all contact with her young cousin.

When Bastian was old enough, he had decided to join the Ma'asai army to support the Yi'ingo in their fight to secure the land. As brother- and sister-in-arms, they had fought many battles side by side, saved each other's lives numerous times, respected one another, and they never forgot that, before they were warriors, they were homeless children who had lost everything they had and ended up together as refugees. They knew one another beyond the masks they wore today. They were the two kids who had followed Gabriel through the forest as he welcomed them both as brother and sister during the darkest times of war.

The actions of Sathian, the murder of her mother, and the loss of her sister would have been reason enough for Sky to distrust and despise all men, but she still remembered the moment that had sealed her heart from men forever, giving her the beliefs she held so strongly today: the day her beloved cousin Gabriel left her to fend for herself against the Hu'urei in the forest. The day he had turned his back on her in the moment she needed him most.

The hero of her childhood—her cousin, brother, father, mentor— turned out to be nothing more than a coward and a traitor, and she hated him for it just as much as she used to love him. Today, Bastian had finally picked a side, and she would never forgive his choice. *Never.*

Ahead of Morgan and Gabriel stood two large capsule-shaped buildings sheathed in translucent crystal. He dismounted the horse, placed his hands on her waist and helped her down.

"Where are we going?" Morgan asked.

He held her hand, guiding her into one of the buildings and waited for the crystal sliding door to close behind them.

"To a place where my mother can't hear us."

"Viviane can't read our minds here?"

"Objects hold memory, particularly artworks like paintings, sculptures, and books. They hold the energy of their creators—their intentions, fears and aspirations as they engaged in their creative process. The Ange'el are quite sensitive to it because the vision and emotions of artists are powerful and pure. This capsule stores thousands of artworks. This place overwhelms our Ange'el senses, and it shields our conversation from my mother's mind's eye.

Morgan held her breath as she scanned the large rectangular building. Around her stood thousands of artworks—statues, paintings, tapestries— each portraying men. The figures were fighting, hunting, holding trophies, and lying in sensual and sexual poses. The beauty and intensity of the experience made Morgan dizzy, and she felt as if she were hallucinating. She experienced desire, elation, and surprise. The light that came into the building had a soft quality to it as if the harshness of the sun was filtered and transformed to best serve the purpose of illuminating the art.

Morgan and Gabriel were surrounded by the bodies of men in their prime, proudly showcasing the purity of their genes in the perfection of every line of their physique.

"Where are we?" She held his arm, attempting to stop her head from spinning.

"Twenty-five years ago, Amalia decided to erase the history of men from Ahe'ey. The pain and anger caused by what Sathian and the Hu'urei had done were such that the women of Ahe'ey needed to let go of their love, devotion and celebration of the half of the Ahe'ey population that had committed the most deplorable crimes. Amalia believed that the best way to recover and move on was to erase that memory. So, every statue, every painting and every crystal that instilled feelings of love, lust, devotion and celebration of men was banished to this place, the graveyard of men's history.

"But I've seen paintings of your father at Yi'ingo."

Morgan looked at the naked male bodies, some made of stone and others of bronze. Their manliness visible, provocative and sometimes obviously erect challenged her ability to concentrate. She blushed, realising the power of the art and she was curious about a culture that had once portrayed women and men as equal in their power but also in their ability to be an object of lust. She wished she could have known them in their prime, before the war. *Even Michelangelo would have blushed in this place.*

"Those paintings don't celebrate my father's achievement in war, they show Sathian's demise. You'll find some art outside this place where men play supporting roles, but it's a rare occasion. Bastian is the exception. His achievements in war and games are celebrated all over Ahe'ey. They have been preparing the minds of the Ahe'ey for an upcoming marriage with Sky.

"That level of propaganda and control sicken me."

"You have to understand, Morgan, most men followed Sathian. They perpetrated despicable crimes. The women of Hu'urei tried to stop them; they begged for their sisters. Sathian's wife, Sabine, committed suicide upon hearing the crimes unleashed by her son and her husband. Overwhelmed by grief and shame, she hanged herself as the men discussed their next attack in the Hu'urei town hall."

"I understand, but erasing people out of history is a crime."

"You can compare it with the denazification of post-war Germany. Amalia ordered the removal of the physical symbols of hubris and male achievement. The goal was to humiliate and shake the followers of Sathian, the ones who didn't commit a crime but instead stood silent as evil roamed the land. The offenders were killed, but there was still the need to instil collective guilt and contrition in the hearts and minds of those who allowed it happen."

"So the history of men was simply deleted? Is it taught at school?"

"Not much, although they know that we had an equal society, and they know about the war. They mainly learn about the women leaders in history and very little about the men. Any Ahe'ey in their thirties or younger see men as second class and as distrusted individuals."

"How do you feel about this?"

"Listen, I was a boy when Sathian and his men killed and raped my people. I feel deep shame and regret for what happened. Every day I remember the evil that spread in this land, and I pray never to be afflicted with the weakness of my ancestors."

"How can you even compare yourself—"

"But, I also feel tremendous responsibility for our men and boys, and I want them to feel proud of who they are, to aspire for greatness, and I want them to see and read about role models that look like them. I want them to know that they aren't monsters. But . . . "

"But what?"

"What happened wasn't supposed to happen. Maybe there is a defect in our genes."

"How can you say that? Someone very smart once told me that we must accept in ourselves the potential we see in others."

"At the Met, you said that you sometimes doubt the nature of men."

Remembering her words, Morgan winced but continued, "Sure, I have bad days where I get frustrated with all the violence in the world, but you and I know it's mostly nurture, not nature."

"Not here Morgan. Ahe'ey pre-war was an equitable society when it came to gender. All children had the same education and opportunities."

"Amalia told me that Sathian's powerful mind manipulated the Hu'urei," she said. "Perhaps it's not men's fault, but a weakness in the blood of the Ange'el. Either way, I'm both."

He grabbed her hand and guided her down the corridor. She could feel his hand shake. The intensity of experiencing the art left her exhausted. The artworks spoke to her, the stories and emotions overwhelmed all her senses as if she could hear, see, taste, smell and feel them.

And then she saw them, two lovers made of marble, naked, wrapped in each other's arms. His hand rested on the meatier slope of her hips, fingers pressed against her flesh. Her hands were on his face, pulling him closer as her lips raised to steal a kiss. *Gabriel*, she thought for a second before she realised who he was.

"Look at the love in his eyes and in his body."

She blushed as she saw the stone arousal between his legs.

"Touch them, Morgan, feel their love locked in the stone. Their intentions towards one another forever frozen in time. Do you feel it? Their love?"

She closed her eyes as she touched the cold surface of the stone. She felt love, desire, idealism, hope, loyalty and tenderness. There was no hate or pain. She nodded, heart throbbing.

"Is this Gaia?"

"Yes."

Morgan realised what he was trying to tell her. The energy emanating from the statue wasn't different from the connection she shared with Gabriel. It was pure love.

"How did he change so much?" She looked at the reflection and the essence of her lover in that statue. She felt a sting of jealousy for Gaia.

"He changed. He betrayed everything he was, everything he believed in at this moment in time."

"You need to let this go, Gabriel." She couldn't contain her grief anymore. She sank her face into his chest and sobbed. "I . . . I can't leave you. I need to know you are alive, that you survived the dragon. I don't care who you marry; I need to stay here by your side—"

"Listen, Morgan. There's a reason I brought you here, to a place where my mother can't hear us. I need your help."

"Tell me."

"I have committed a crime punishable by death. A necessary crime."

"What is it? What have you done?"

"I've been sequencing the Ahe'ey genome together with Sir Charles. He completed the project this week."

She felt her eyes go wide at the implications of what he was saying. "This changes everything. Why don't you tell them?"

"Because they will kill me. No one at Ahe'ey can know of this, or I'll be trialled and executed."

"Your mother and father would never allow it."

"It's not that simple. During a trial, each member of the royal family votes, and it takes only two royal votes to condemn someone to death."

"Amalia and Sky?"

"Or Angha. I plan to tell them, but the timing must be right."

"Come with me."

"I'm able to get you out of Ahe'ey, but I won't be able to make it out."

"What do you need?"

"I need you to work with Sir Charles. Destroy the sample of DNA and keep the sequence of our genome safe and away from the internet. I suspect Zanus is digging around for information about me. Sir Charles may become a target. If, for some reason, the passage doesn't open in two weeks—"

"What do you mean?" A wave of distress and pain travelled through her entire body. She knew what it meant.

"Morgan, listen. If I don't contact you in two or three weeks, you're responsible for the safekeeping of our genome and will need to decide when humans are ready to receive our gift."

The implication behind his words slammed into her, leaving an aching wound in her chest.

"Run away with me Gabriel. Please."

"I wish I could; I fear for your safety in New York. But, if I leave, I'll never be able to come back. I won't see my kids. The passage will be closed for many centuries; humans will self-destruct and take the entire planet down with them. There's too much knowledge and potential at Ahe'ey; we need to unleash it. I need to fight the dragon so we can have the hope of guiding this world to safety."

"Do you stand a chance?"

"There's always hope." He smiled, but she could see through his glow. "I'll be fine. As soon as you reach Manhattan, you must seek the protection of the CIA. Zanus is dangerous. I wish I could be by your side as you stand against him."

"Zanus' days are numbered," she said, wiping her teary eyes and giving a pathetic attempt at a wink. "We'll slay both dragons and save the day. Yes?"

"Yes." Gabriel embraced her. "Listen, once we leave this capsule, I need you to stop thinking about the genome. Put it out of your mind until you reach Bethesda."

She nodded.

Morgan looked once again at the statue of the royal lovers. For a moment, she wished that she could trade places with them and stay there with Gabriel, frozen in an embrace for all eternity.

"What's in the other capsule?" Morgan asked as they mounted the horse.

"Another part of our history, erased by my ancestors when the sea destroyed our land."

He said no more and they galloped in the direction of the lake.

The Confrontation

Sky approached the gate that led to Lake Do'oras. A silver wall surrounded the lake and adjacent forest. Scout guarded the only road that led to the lake. The young warrior stood between the two large pillars that marked the end of the walls on each side of the road.

"*Scout!*" Sky shouted.

Scout bowed. "All is well, my queen."

"Viviane closed the passage; you can leave your post," Sky said, noticing that something happening behind her was distracting Scout. Sky turned around, and saw Gabriel and Morgan riding in the direction of the gate. The Yi'ingo lowered her head and looked up through her lashes, her eyes set on him like spears. Her tense body and clenched jaw announced to the world that she was ready to pick a fight. She stood in the middle of the gate, blocking it.

"The passage is closed. No one is allowed in or out of Ahe'ey," Sky barked without moving.

"Get out of the way, Sky," Gabriel replied impatiently.

"Unless you're the king of this land—and, clearly, you're not and never will be—you have no right to challenge the rules and no power to open the passage," she said, putting her hand on her sword defiantly.

"Get out of the way, Sky." His tone was unusually menacing and aggressive.

She reacted to it: "And who's going to make me? You?"

Gabriel dismounted the horse, pulled up his sword and limped in the direction of Sky. The Ange'el's response surprised the Yi'ingo.

"Gabriel, what are you doing?" Morgan asked. She dismounted the horse and followed him.

Scout unsheathed her sword and ran towards the Ange'el.

"Stand down, Scout," said Sky, raising her hand towards the young warrior. "He's mine."

Sky pulled up her sword and waved it defiantly in front of her body. Her gritted teeth and tight lips warned him that she was serious and prepared to fight. But once again, he surprised her, advancing rapidly towards her and attacking first. Their swords clashed three or four times.

"*Sky, Gabriel, stop!* What are you doing?" Morgan screamed as Scout used her body to block Morgan from interfering with the battle.

Gabriel's body was evidently broken and couldn't match Sky's strength, but he was surprisingly fast, and able to predict her every move. His body moved from one side to the other like the wind. He was still the skilled fighter Sky remembered from her youth. She bit her lip as the memories flooded her mind, again feeling the sting of his betrayal. However, while his show was impressive, he failed to fully commit to each blow.

"Weak? Poor you," she snarled. In the next few moments, Sky raised her game. She knew exactly where to hit him, using her elbow against his right shoulder. He screamed in pain, and she delivered another blow in the same place and a third one to his broken ribs. She responded to her inner conflict by inflicting blow after blow on his broken body. Every time she felt compassion for Gabriel, every time she felt his pain, she punished him over and over again, unleashing hell on the Ange'el.

"Sky, please stop; he's injured. I beg you," Morgan screamed, wrestling with Scout. The young Yi'ingo pushed her so hard that she fell backwards.

"Stay back Morgan. Scout, don't hurt her," Sky ordered.

Gabriel went down on his knees, trembling with pain, and spewing blood from the corner of his mouth. He turned his head and set his eyes on Morgan, taking a deep breath. In just a few seconds, he used his injured leg to trip Sky onto the ground, and the tip of his sword was on her chest. He stood there, looking straight into her eyes. His cyan water met her crimson fire, yet the blaze in her eyes only grew stronger. He bowed, sheathed his sword, turned his back to her and walked away in Morgan's direction. Sky jumped to her feet, wearing her anger in her heart. She followed him, pulled him back by his hair and placed her sword on his neck.

"*Do it, Sky!* For mercy's sake, end my torment," he challenged her in a husky, pained voice. He grabbed her hand and pushed her sword farther into his neck, until it bled.

She dropped the sword, confused by his reaction, and watched him and Morgan mount the horse and gallop towards the gate. They crossed the two pillars coated in silver and headed across the forest towards the lake.

Sky didn't have time to worry about her pride. She quickly realised his plan—it was suicide. Her mother had perished attempting to do just the same thing.

She turned to Scout, "Take the horse, find Bastian and tell him to meet me at the lake as soon as possible. Gabriel is planning to escape the fight with the dragon. He's going to try to open the passage without the moonstone."

Sky ran in pursuit of Gabriel. Without a horse, she feared she would be too late, but she knew only Bastian could change Gabriel's mind. *The coward is going to die and kill Morgan in the process.*

TWO DRAGONS

"You all right?" Quinn sat beside Bastian under the shade of a tree. She'd been trying to appear strong in order to calm her brother and sisters, but the gravity of the situation was starting to get to her.

"So-so. You?" Bastian replied.

"A bit worried," she winced.

"Yeah, me too." He placed his arm around her shoulders, and she slumped into him.

"You think Dad will be okay?" She was hoping for some reassurance.

"We'll make sure he is, right?"

"Right!" Quinn said, looking up to meet his eyes. "He's strong, but I've seen a Wali'ingooteer once; they're *huuuge* . . . and he's still recovering. What are we going to do?"

"We wait and see Quinny. We wait and see."

They sat in silence for several minutes, simmering in their own thoughts.

"Bas."

"Yes."

"Why didn't he fight in the war?"

"You should ask him."

"He won't tell me. He gets super silent and weird when I ask, so I stopped asking."

"I'm sorry Quinny. I'm sure he will one day."

"It's all right Bas. I know he's brave."

"The bravest. Like Sky."

"Yeah. Like Sky." Quinn allowed herself to relax a little.

"*Bastian!*" Scout shouted as she galloped in their direction. "You must come with me, *now!*"

"What's going on warrior?"

"Sky's orders. The Ange'el is taking the new human to the lake. He plans to open the portal without the moonstone. The coward is fleeing Ahe'ey."

Quinn and Bastian looked at each other, jumped to their feet, and ran in the direction of the stables.

"*My dad is no coward!*" Quinn shouted, desperately holding to that belief.

Gabriel and Morgan reached the lake. It was a peaceful, ethereal place. The forest gave way to sand, sand gave way to water, and water gave way to a mist so thick that it kept the eye guessing at what could be beyond it. The warm and sunny morning had quickly transformed into a somewhat chilly and grey afternoon. The sun was glowing behind the clouds, but it was just strong enough to paint the sky and water with shimmering silver light.

Gabriel looked at the crystal water, hoping he was strong enough to complete the task. When he had been sixteen years old, Viviane had asked him to reopen an ancient passage to Ahe'ey. The portal was situated at the lake in Central Park, New York. The rulers of Ahe'ey had been attempting to engage with several influential bodies in Manhattan and needed a quick way to access the city. Viviane had given the boy her moonstone; she had known that he was virtuous enough to successfully open the portal. Gabriel had accomplished his task, given the ring back to his mother, and soon after, he'd initiated his work outside Ahe'ey.

Gabriel had some idea of the power required to open the portal without the ring. He knew he had it within him to open it for just long enough to get Morgan out of Ahe'ey. He just needed to summon all his strength to keep the passage open for a few seconds. His potential death during the battle with the dragon could mean that she would be stuck in Ahe'ey forever. He had to find a way to get her out, and he desperately needed her help outside Ahe'ey.

Gabriel dismounted and then helped Morgan down. The Ange'el winced as he reached up to her. His body ached from the battle with Sky, and he was struggling to breathe. He could taste blood in his mouth. They faced each other.

"Gabriel, are you okay?" she asked as he gasped for air.

He nodded, "I'm so-rry you had to wit-ness . . . ," he struggled to speak.

She placed her hand on his chest and closed her eyes.

"I'm okay, Morgan." He held both of her hands, kissed her right one, and spoke. "Once I open the passage, all you have to do is walk into the lake, set your intention to Bethesda and follow the light. When you reach Manhattan, you'll find yourself inside the fountain; if you leave quickly, following the light, you won't get wet. It's the middle of the day so someone might see you. Just keep walking; avoid cameras and phones and don't speak to anyone. The mist will protect you for a few moments."

Morgan's face suddenly changed with a realisation. "Sky's mother, she died attempting to open the portal."

"She was a Yi'ingo; I'm an Ange'el. It's different," he lied, unleashing a confident smile. "Here's a bag. It has money, a credit card, and a mobile phone. Put this long coat on and walk to The Pierre; I own a penthouse there. The key and the details are in the bag. You can stay there for as long as you need. I leave you the contact information of Sir Charles, the CIA, and Maria Diaz, the CEO of the Ange'el Foundation. There are letters addressed to all of them inside the bag, ensuring that they will provide you with any assistance you may require."

"Do they know who you are?"

"No, they are all on a need-to-know basis. You can trust Maria and Sir Charles but avoid disclosing too much; it's dangerous for both them and us. Be careful with the CIA. Tell them nothing about Ahe'ey."

"I love you," Morgan said, touching his torso.

He felt her love, and faltered for a moment.

"I'm . . . I'm just a flesh-and-blood machine, nothing else. Designed with a higher purpose, a purpose that I must now fulfil. The rules that were programmed by my ancestors into every cell of my body are meant to bring the world knowledge and salvation when the time comes. As the heir to the throne of Ahe'ey, I'm no longer free to love whom I love. This path wasn't my choice, and it was hidden from me, but it is, unfortunately, one I must follow." He struggled to continue as his eyes flooded with grief, but he blinked it back and spoke, "I'm but a puppet of my blood. It's my responsibility to ensure that no one else suffers my fate. If you love me and wish to see me happy, please go and be as happy as you can be. Find love. Your happiness is my happiness."

Morgan sobbed, but Gabriel couldn't afford to let his feelings take control. He wiped her tears, kissed her, and kept talking. "I need you to start walking towards the lake. In a few seconds, a white light—a passage—will appear in front of you. Walk towards it and never look back. Promise me you won't look back."

She agreed with her eyes.

"You must walk fast, as I can only keep the passage open for a few seconds."

"I love you," Morgan repeated, using her fingers to wipe the dried blood off the corner of his mouth. Her face was overwhelmed with sorrow collapsing on itself with sobs.

"Morgan, please," he said. He kissed her, looked straight into her eyes, and, for the first time, gave himself permission to unleash his Ange'el powers of persuasion on her. He raised his index finger and touched her forehead between her eyes. "Go."

She started walking towards the water. Gabriel put his left knee on the ground, lowered his head, and touched the sand, which was coated by the cool water of the lake. "I love you too," he said, just before he closed his eyes.

Sky looked back and saw Bastian approaching her as she ran to the lake. He was galloping as fast as he could, followed closely by Scout and Quinn. Without stopping, Bastian leaned his body towards the side of the horse, helping Sky jump on his back as he pulled back to a sitting position. As they approached the lake, they were almost blinded by the intensity of the light that emanated from a winged creature kneeling in front of the lake.

She saw it, the creature with two white wings glowing on its back. "Gabriel?" Sky called out as she struggled to see beyond the light and the thick mist that had descended over the shore.

His hair was longer and flowing in the wind, white as snow. He looked like one of the statues in the Ange'el garden—perfectly sculpted, flawless, ghostly, ethereal, pure light. She saw it; they all did—a glimpse of his true potential, of his ultimate form, the most authentic expression of his genes. His spirit flourished through his virtue, love, and sacrifice.

But he's flawed. So flawed. How is this possible?

At Ahe'ey, there were many legends of the twelve Ahe'ey citizens who had managed to unlock the power of flight through their noble deeds thousands and thousands of years ago. Ange'el women and men who had gained a godlike status with their people; demigods who had moved through all stages of learning and growth and could tap into the collective consciousness of the universe. The cosmos, a single and dynamic organism that shared common energy and information with all its beings.

They were creatures that could act as individual beings and also as part of a larger collective and compassionate whole. They were connected to a universal consciousness, approached the world holistically, and could use both logic and intuition to advance their work. They were leaders that championed cooperation and facilitated alignment between opposing forces. They were healers, filled with light, love, knowledge, virtue, and strength. Many Ahe'ey now doubted that they had ever existed as no one had attained such status since the sea had engulfed the ancient land.

How did he earn his wings? The Yi'ingo saw Gabriel's aura flicker. It was becoming weaker and diminishing, replaced by a deep darkness. Without the protection of the moonstone, anyone attempting to open the portal would be consumed by its power.

At the lake, a white mist assembled in front of Morgan as she walked towards it. *"Morgan! Stop, you'll die!"* Sky shouted. Bastian and Sky galloped towards Gabriel, but the magnetic field around the Ange'el made the horses rear and then bolt. Sky and Bastian hit the ground, paralysed and overwhelmed by the energy around them. They were helpless as they watched the energy consume the Ange'el.

A tunnel of light surrounded Morgan. She stopped.

"Come back, Morgan," screamed Sky, desperate.

Sky saw Gabriel raise his head and look at Morgan. He was translucent. His eyes were the only splash of colour, and his white hair flowed in front of his pallid face. "Go, Morgan. Please go. Do it now." His voice was ghostly and low. Sky could see the energy consume him; his life force was being sucked from his body. She realised that Morgan's indecision was killing him. "Go, my love," he murmured.

The thick mist was intensifying. The human was but a shadow under a veil of light and clouds.

"Come back, Morgan." Quinn galloped in Morgan's direction.

"Quinn, come here you fool," Scout screamed, following close behind the younger girl. Their horses reared, refusing to continue, and they both jumped to the ground. Quinn ran into the tunnel, followed by Scout. Morgan placed her hand in the water as Quinn grabbed her by her jacket. The tunnel closed, and the three women disappeared.

Sky and Bastian attempted to stand up, only to fall back on the ground exhausted, unable to fight the force field around their cousin. Sky's eyes scanned the water in search of the three women. Her heart raced when she realised they were all gone. *We've lost them.* She wondered if they had reached the other side of the passage. She cursed Gabriel for placing them in such danger.

A figure emerged from the fog behind them. She wore a blue cloak and appeared to be floating above the sand due to the surrounding mist. She rushed towards Gabriel, cutting straight through the force field.

Viviane took off her cloak and used it to cover her son and contain his energy. Gabriel fell in his mother's arms, frail and unconscious. The queen touched his face, looking for signs of life. His skin was cold, his lips were blue, and his face was pale as snow. With complete concentration, she placed her hand on his chest, transferring some of her own vitality into his body, until he pulled his head back and opened his mouth to take a breath. She kissed his forehead.

"You will be fine," Viviane whispered in her son's ear.

She turned to Bastian, "Help me with Gabriel."

The Ma'asai kneeled and took the unconscious body of his cousin in his arms.

"Open the passage, Lady," Sky urged.

"No," the queen replied.

"Quinn, Scout, and Morgan are—"

"Sky, in two days, there will be a battle between my son and a dragon. I need everyone in Ahe'ey to be present, from every tribe, including your grandmother and the elders. Please go and ensure this happens."

"You can't just abandon the—" Bastian stood beside Sky, facing the queen.

"Enough! Do as I say. Now."

"I cannot believe you are going ahead with this charade," Sky bit out as she bowed. The Yi'ingo took a glance at the lake looking for any signs of the women, mounted Gabriel's horse, and disappeared.

RITA HAYWORTH

Central Park, New York

As Morgan walked into the lake, she pictured the Bethesda Fountain, the place she always visited when she was in New York, the stone angel that had been so dear to her, that had sparked her inspiration and imagination for so many years. Now, it was obvious to her why she had such an attachment to that magical place, the portal to her lover and to a strange and magical world. She wondered if part of her had always known her life would lead here.

Morgan was afraid that she was about to wake up from a dream, that as she stepped into Central Park, she would realise that dragons, sorcerers and warriors didn't exist, that it was all an illusion, her most special and personal dream. To calm herself, she pictured the image of the one of the four cherubs featured on the Bethesda Fountain, the one that represented peace.

After the third step into the lake, she could no longer feel the wetness of the water; it was as if she was walking above it. On the fifth step, she couldn't see the lake or the shore. She was surrounded by a mist so thick that she couldn't discern her own hands, even when she placed them right in front of her nose. Two more steps and she saw the contour of a chubby, naked child. She extended her hand to the figure, only to feel the cold, solid surface of stone. Above her, a pair of wings eclipsed the light of the sun. She suddenly realised where she was as she stood facing the statue of one of the cherubs of the Bethesda Fountain and above her stood the angel of the waters.

She was somewhat amused as she realised that she was standing on the middle platform of the fountain. *My sorcery days are numbered. This didn't go exactly as I planned.* She shook her head. *I wasn't even supposed to get wet.* The amusement was replaced by a frown of apprehension as she noticed that it had snowed recently and that a coat of white fluffy snow had replaced the usual pool of water. She had completely forgotten that it was winter in New York. Morgan knew she'd have to jump into the freezing pool and her body shivered at the thought. She took her tote bag off her shoulder and used the handles to tie a knot, sealing the contents inside.

A thick mist surrounded the fountain; she couldn't see beyond it. She sat on the stone plate and jumped, landing on her feet, immediately sinking into the white snow and reaching the frigid water beneath it. She moved as fast as she could, and managed to lose one of her flat shoes in the freezing mush. As Morgan exited the fountain she couldn't feel her legs; her body shivered so badly that she struggled to have any rational thoughts. She heard some voices behind her.

"Where the hell are we?"

Morgan turned around to face the Yi'ingo warrior, who had appeared from nowhere. She recognised the woman that had wrestled with her at the gate to Lake Do'oras and took a few steps away from the warrior. Scout was as tall as Sky and cut a pretty menacing figure.

"New York. We must be in New York," said a familiar voice, coming from the thick mist.

"Quinny?" Morgan asked, surprised.

"Yeah, I'm here Morgan," Quinn said with excitement as she emerged from the water. Morgan noticed that both young women had managed to avoid getting wet. "Don't be afraid. We'll protect ya. This is Scout. She's a bit sour, but a pretty good warrior."

Scout's eyes, hidden under her purple crest of hair, looked down at both humans with manufactured indifference. Morgan took a moment to make sense of the situation; she hadn't expected company.

The mist dissipated, Morgan could see a few tourists wandering about, confused by the fog.

"We need to get out of here fast," Morgan said, as Scout prepared to walk back into the fountain.

Quinn grabbed Scout's cape and pulled her backwards. "The passage is closed you fool." Scout's hand went straight to her sword.

Morgan noticed how out of place these two were. "You two; hide your swords under your capes and follow me. And, don't make a scene."

Quinn immediately acquiesced to Morgan's firm tone, while Scout stood still, with her hand on her sword.

"*I said follow me!*" Morgan held her head high, and looked up to face the scorn of the Yi'ingo. "This is *my* world. If you want to remain anonymous and keep your people's existence a secret, you follow me *now*."

After a moment, Scout wrapped her cape around her body and followed Morgan, who shivered with cold. Quinn threw a sideways glance at Morgan and smiled with her eyes. "Nice work," murmured the teen. "Did you see Dad's wings? Sooo rad!" Morgan was too cold to try to make sense of the girl's words.

They ran to the lower passage of the terrace, to the tunnel that stood in between the granite staircases. Every step was excruciating for Morgan, and her shoeless foot was turning blue. "I ne-ed… to stop for a mo-ment," she said.

"Do you need help angel?"

An old woman sat against the wall; two blankets—torn, dirty and grey —covered her. She sat on a couple of large sheets of cardboard that provided her with a weak insulation from the cold stone floor. She had a kind, weathered face; each skin crease told a story of poverty, sadness, and struggle. "Take this before you freeze to death. Your tiny bones will break if they continue to shake like that." The old woman removed one of her blankets and extended it to Morgan.

"Th . . . thannk y-youu," Morgan said, struggling to form words between her chattering teeth. The old woman moved her body, making space for Morgan on the cardboard surface. Morgan sat down and wrapped the blanket around her legs and feet, massaging them with her hands, trying to dry herself.

Scout and Quinn stood back, wrapped in their capes observing the odd stranger with some suspicion.

"Where's the young man? The other angel with the sweet magic eyes? I haven't seen him in a while. He brought me chocolate chip cookies the last time he visited." The old lady's breath smelled like rotten eggs and whisky, and the four remaining teeth in her mouth were brown as she smiled openly, possibly remembering Gabriel. "Such a charming creature. He always reminds me of Gregory Peck. Don't you agree? It's that natural glow he has."

Morgan's heart skipped a beat as she thought of Gabriel. Only at that moment did she realise that she had been under his spell. "He . . . he needs help. I'm here to help him." Morgan wasn't sure why she trusted this stranger with such information, but she always relied on her instincts, and this woman had shared what little she had with her. "We must go now. Thank you for your kindness." Morgan gave the blanket back to the old woman and stood up.

"Wait! What is your name darlin'?"

"Morgan, my name is Morgan."

The woman took a pair of old leather boots out of her bag. "Take these or you won't get far." The boots were so large that Morgan had to fill the extra space with paper.

"Thank you so much; what's your name?"

"People call me Rita. Like Rita Hayworth," she replied, full of sass.

"When I was younger I was as pretty as her. I was prettier actually, but I don't want to sound too full of myself, you know?" She smiled again, flicked her long grey braid and put her hand on her hip.

"Rita, I'll be back soon to repay you for your kindness." Morgan placed her knees on the cardboard and gave Rita a hug. The old woman appeared surprised by Morgan's gesture.

"Decaying humans. They sicken me," Scout murmured. Rita's laughter echoed across the tunnel. The old woman released an effusive belly cackle followed by a loud snort. She seemed amused as she listened to the Yi'ingo.

"Human generosity. It inspires me," Morgan retorted without looking at the Yi'ingo.

"Perhaps one day you can take me with you to the land beyond the fountain?" Rita's tone of voice had a lot of honey and a touch of whisky, revealing the sweet sass of Hayworth.

"Perhaps one day." Morgan nodded with a smile.

"Angel!" Rita called again. "Use the private entrance to the suite. Stay away from The Pierre's lobby."

"Who are you?" Morgan frowned, suddenly curious, and turned to face the old lady.

"Just an old vagabond and a friend," she pulled a bottle of whisky and raised a toast to Morgan before she drank it.

Morgan started running towards The Pierre, trying to keep herself warm. She was followed by the two caped figures. They observed the world around them with wide eyes and open mouths.

"These humans seem to occupy a lot of space," Quinn murmured as they left the park and ran through the streets of Manhattan. "Where are the animals and the trees? This place is horrible."

"They're a plague," Scout replied. "You're a plague."

"I love you too, Scout," Quinn replied promptly without flinching.

Morgan sunk her head into her hands as she read Maria Diaz's letter to Gabriel. *It's all my fault. We're doomed.* She looked through the instructions that Gabriel had left for her in the bag and dialled Maria's number from the landline.

"Corazón, where have you been?" said the voice on the other side of the line.

"Maria?"

"Oh. Hi. Yes. Who is this?"

"My name is Morgan. Gabriel asked me to contact you."

"Hi Morgan, I've been following your impressive work. Is everything all right?"

"It's best that we speak face to face. Could you meet me at The Pierre? I'm staying at Gabriel's place."

"Sure, I'll stop by shortly. Did you speak to any of the press at the lobby?"

"No, we used the private elevator at the back."

"Great, please stay out of sight. I'm on my way."

Morgan found Gabriel's laptop on the desk and switched it on. She was surprised that the device wasn't password protected, but then she realised he had nothing to secure as he never stored anything online.

She googled her name, and an avalanche of results appeared on the screen. Some of the stories related to the event at the Met and many others were associated with the hashtag #ProtectorsOfTheNation, and these linked to video and photo coverage of Gabriel and other Ahe'ey.

The KKK's generous bounty had uncovered worldwide footage of some of the Ahe'ey's interventions in war and global affairs. The white nationalists had used emerging facial recognition technology to spot

Gabriel in any footage on the internet. They had leveraged the reach of social networks to gather evidence of the existence of what they claimed to be the "perfect Caucasian men with superhuman powers". Morgan's heart ached as she witnessed the bravery of her lover in videos from times of war.

A lot of emphasis was being put on the race, gender and features of the "protectors". The clearest photos and videos were taken in Central Park during her speaking event and featured Gabriel and the tall, and mostly blonde, Ma'asai men. Sky didn't feature in the leaked footage. *It didn't fit with their propaganda,* Morgan thought with disgust.

Sensationalist websites were jumping on the story, using clickbait headlines to drive traffic to their sites and profit from the advertising. The conspiracy theories were wild and the white supremacist agenda was evident and unapologetic.

Morgan watched several interviews with some of the people that appeared in the footage. They all said the same thing: they had no recollection of Gabriel, or of the events that had unfolded. She suspected that the Ange'el had cleared their memory, but unfortunately had been unable to delete the digital footprints captured by CCTV cameras, mobile devices or satellite footage. No one would have looked for it, but the events at the Met and Central Park, the interest by Zanus and the KKK, and the technological progress of AI and social media had culminated in the perfect storm.

Fox News was the only mainstream broadcast news channel paying attention to the story. At the centre of their coverage was Walter Zanus and his sophisticated campaign to distort the truth about her attack and create fear and division.

Digital tabloids picked up on the story from a different angle; they focused on the handsome, rich philanthropist turned superhero. "Forget

Marvel's Wayne and Stark, Warren is the real-life superhero," read the *Daily Mail*'s headline.

The internet was on fire with photos, videos and stories about the most desirable bachelor in the world, and, of course, it didn't take long for the interest to turn into an obsession. The top trending fandoms on Tumblr were no longer posting about Marvel, *Hunger Games* or Sherlock actors. Videos of Gabriel had been turned into animated GIFs, dissecting every expression, gesture, and every part of his body. Gabriel's heroism, beauty and glow had gone viral with teenagers, and they were unaware that, with it, they were passing on white supremacist propaganda designed by the worst people in the world.

Morgan was overwhelmed by the enormity of the problem. *What have I done!* She got up and paced back and forth across the room as the two young warriors, slouched on the leather sofa, exchanged puzzled glances. Morgan looked through Gabriel's mobile contacts until she found Sir Charles' phone number. She rang him and walked into one of the bedrooms so that she could have some privacy.

"Hello my friend, I've been desperate to hear from you."

"Sir Charles! It's Morgan, Gabriel's friend."

"Morgan, where is Gabriel? I need to reach him urgently."

"He's going to be away for a little while. I have a letter for you from him, and I need to speak to you about your project. I was tasked to take every copy of . . . of . . . the results and destroy the original sample."

"He shared the project with you?" His voice was incredulous.

"Yes, I'm acting on his behalf. Listen, I have a letter from him that hopefully explains everything, but we need that sample destroyed ASAP and to protect the data at all costs."

"I understand. I'll destroy the sample now. I have a couple of copies of the results; one stored in three CDs and the other on an external hard drive. They are safe for now, but we've experienced several incidents of hacking and theft. We must relocate them."

"Once you read the letter, if you trust me, I'll take them off your hands."

"Okay, but you're a bigger target than I. And, I'm afraid that us meeting may cause more scrutiny over my association with Gabriel. The entire world knows who you are and are looking for you both."

"I can send two young friends that no one knows and no one can track to Gabriel or I. Is this line safe?"

"Nothing is safe right now, but the security team at the Ange'el Foundation has cleared this device, and I know Gabriel's home is checked regularly."

"At this time, no one knows where I am, and no one would expect me to be carrying that sort of data. I'll work to keep the data safe. Are you attending any public event at a place full of young adults? A University conference, maybe? A mall or a public place where my friends can go unnoticed and blend in?"

"I'm escorting my niece to her international debutante ball tomorrow evening at the Waldorf Astoria."

"That's perfect."

"Listen, it's quite an expensive and exclusive affair, but I'll pull some strings to add them to the guest list."

"It's the perfect cover."

"What names should I use?"

Morgan was silent for a while, and then she replied, "Tatiana and Anya Allabergenova, from Tashkent, Uzbekistan. They don't speak any English."

"Please spell that last name for me."

"A-L-L-A-B-E-R-G-E-N-O-V-A."

"How will I find them?"

"It's going to be hard to miss them; one has white and purple hair, the other black and blue. They are quite the conspicuous pair."

"Try to get them to fit in; buy them some white ball gowns. The ball is held in the Grand Ballroom. They should arrive late after all the debutante presentations. I'm sorry to say this, but I'll need them to hand over Gabriel's letter first. I need to read it."

"Of course. Thank you."

"Is my friend well?"

"He needs our help, Sir Charles. We have a hurricane heading our way."

"Is there anything else I can do to help?"

"I'll let you know, thank you. For now, I just ask you to continue to exercise absolute discretion."

"Of course. Goodbye."

"Bye." Morgan took a deep breath, trying to quiet her racing mind. She walked back to the library to join Quinn and Scout.

"Ladies, I have a task for you. You're going shopping. I need you to buy two white ball gowns for a party you are attending tomorrow night."

"I'm not going to any party," Scout crossed her arms.

"Scout, Ahe'ey's secret information is at risk of being disclosed to humans. I need you and Quinn to fetch this information from an ally at a party tomorrow."

"What kind of information?" Scout asked, full of suspicion.

Morgan vacillated for a few moments and then replied, "Some time ago I stole some of your blood. I've used human technology to finally decipher the composition of your DNA."

"That's against the law. I'll kill you!" Scout unsheathed her sword and moved towards Morgan as Quinn jumped between the two, sword in hand.

"It's done. There's no going back," Morgan said, standing her ground. "Once you retrieve the information from Sir Charles, and the passage to Ahe'ey opens, you will take it back to Queen Viviane." Scout moved forward as Quinn and Morgan retreated. Morgan continued, "If you kill me, the information will not get back to Ahe'ey. I'm on your side."

Scout took some time to think and then she sheathed her sword, her eyes still suspicious. "So now we need to clean up your mess."

Quinn turned to face Morgan. "Sure Morgan. We'll do that. Is shopping close by? What's a ball gawn?"

"You . . . don't remember, Quinn?"

The girl shook her head.

"Oh for heaven's sake," Morgan laughed and then blinked at the girl, "I forgot you are an Ahe'ey. A gown is a dress, like the long ones the Ange'el wear, and a shop is where you get the dress."

"Right, we can do that. We can go *gawns* shopping."

"Scout, look at me." Morgan's voice was confident. She had realised that the young warrior responded better to firm orders. "Sky, above everyone else, would want to keep this information secret. Do you understand? I need you to work with me." Morgan had Scout's full attention. The young woman was listening carefully behind a detached and scornful façade.

It took some time for Morgan to explain the task at hand. The girls huddled around the laptop, looking at the international debutante ball website. There were lots of questions and some eye rolls, but things got practical quite quickly. They replaced their leather tunics with tops and jackets from Gabriel's wardrobe. The girls reluctantly put their swords away but kept the daggers hidden in their Yi'ingo boots. Morgan called some designer stores, explaining that two foreign debutantes were on their way, and that the girls were a bit shy. The budget disclosed by Morgan bought all the attention, patience and discretion they would need. They were handed a map with instructions and learned how to use the credit card.

"Come here Scout." Morgan pulled the tie off her own hair and reached to touch the Yi'ingo's high crest. Scout grabbed Morgan's wrist in a defensive manoeuvre. "I'm not going to hurt you. We just need to make you look a bit more normal." The Yi'ingo didn't let go of Morgan's arm; the warrior seemed to suffer from chronic distrust. Morgan softened her expression and smiled. "Scout, you are so beautiful and tall. Everyone is already going to look at you in the street. We need to tone down the hairdo, just a little. Okay?" Morgan noticed that the young woman blushed and released her hand.

She's just a kid. A very tall, strong, stubborn and beautiful kid. "Come darling. Sit here." Morgan tapped the desk and Scout leaned against it. Morgan used her fingers to brush Scout's hair, and arranged it in a tight, purple bun. The Yi'ingo's expression changed; the suspicious warrior melted away to Morgan's touch. The human used her index finger to clean some dark smudge off Scout's eyebrow. "There. That's better," Morgan said softly with a smile. Scout's entire face turned crimson before she jumped to her feet and walked away.

"Try to fit in, will you girls?"

"Sure, we'll be very discreet," Quinn replied, jumping backwards and doing a no-handed cartwheel. Scout grabbed Quinn by the collar of her jacket, pulled her up and moved towards the door, dragging the younger girl along with her, "Let me go you . . . you impure bastard," Quinn screamed, batting at the hands that held her.

"Quinn, that's not nice," Morgan admonished.

"Hey, it's only fair; she calls me human all the time."

"You *are* human, and so am I."

"And she's an impure bastard," Quinn replied, matter-of-factly.

"We'll talk about this when you're back."

As the girls left, Morgan sat in the most expensive penthouse in the world, thinking of ways to contain the damage she had caused.

A Dying Wish

Sacred House, Ahe'ey

Sky wasn't sure why she was there or how she had got there. She had walked to the Sacred House on autopilot. The warrior just knew that she had to see him before the fight, but she wasn't sure what she was going to tell him. He was in his room on the second floor of the building. The door was open and he was standing by the veranda, looking out at the moon. The moonlight lit his face and hair. He was serene, and she was surprised to find him on his feet.

She walked in, and he turned around to face her. "Sister," he said with genuine affection in his eyes. Sky hadn't heard him call her that since their youth. She stayed at the door, frozen. She'd learned many years ago not to show emotion. Emotion was her weakness, the only hole in her armour that could be exploited, and so in situations where she felt vulnerable and emotional, the best defence was an ice-cold face and a marble-like posture. Frozen by fear, but no one on the outside would ever know that . . . unless they were a high-ranking Ange'el with the power of sight. Unless they knew her better than she knew herself.

"Thank you for coming. I wished to see you and to speak to you."

She suddenly realised that he'd summoned her here. He was indeed Viviane's son and heir. Her jaw tightened, and her face flushed with red anger. She was furious with him. Gabriel walked in her direction, threw his walking cane on the bed, and held both her hands. No man in the world, apart from Bastian, had the courage to proactively touch her; she remained frozen.

"I'm sorry," he said, looking into her eyes. A close look at his face uncovered how fragile he really was; he was gaunt, pale, almost transparent. The energy had been sucked out of his body. There was a deep sadness in his eyes. He was grieving, hurting both physically and emotionally. "I'm deeply sorry," he repeated.

Is he talking about our fight yesterday or events in the distant past? What does he want? Why am I here? She panicked. She didn't want to feel compassion, connection, or love. It was too easy for her to love her cousin, her brother, the hero of her youth, the best man she ever knew—a reality that she didn't admit to herself often. But she couldn't forgive his flaw, his lack of courage and bravery in the moments she had most needed him. She didn't move her hands, and she avoided looking into his eyes as he spoke.

"I'd give my life to take away the history that has kept us apart, but I can't. We've both paid the highest price for it. There's nothing that I can do to change it. I've betrayed you. I have no right to ask you for anything, and yet, today, I have something to ask of you."

She released his hands and walked to the veranda. After a moment, she turned around, leaned against it, and said calmly, "Speak." She felt in control—he wanted a favour.

He limped slowly to the veranda, looked down for a second, and then faced her. "Humankind is struggling; the environment is collapsing, and violence against women and girls is pervasive. Divisive politics drive racism and hate. The focus on the gross domestic product as their measure of success is going to destroy the world and will be the end of this cycle of life on planet Earth."

"Your humankind is full of rats that don't deserve our time or energy."

"And what about humans like Aria, Quinn, Ollie, Sage, and Riley? What about Morgan? I know you have been busy looking out for our own people, Sister, but please don't forget who we are and why we were given these gifts. Their destruction is our failure, and it's the doom of millions of human beings just like my daughters and son. In the end, it will also be our doom."

Gabriel was pleading. She had never seen him beg like this, and she was unsure of his objective.

"What do you want from me? Your parents have chosen you to lead this kingdom. You're unworthy of the throne but you'll have it. I'm bound to serve you and will honour my king the best I can, regardless of my views on the matter. What do you want, my permission? A brave leader doesn't ask for permission. At some point in time, you should start displaying some courage."

His face showed that he was in no mood for her attacks. He turned his back to her for a moment and when he faced her, his expression was calmer.

"Think of me what you want if it suits you, Sky. Wear anger as a shield if it keeps you alive and our people safe but do not abandon them. Don't turn your back on humankind as an act of rebellion against me. I'm nothing. Forget me.

"Tomorrow, I may well be dead, and you'll be queen. I'm standing here, begging you to focus on opening the passage and moving forwards with our purpose. You have people that could be your allies in activities that are less suitable for a warrior. My daughters, my son, Morgan and Bastian can replace me, and there are many others out there. Please work to mend the rift with the Hu'urei. It's time we reintegrate all tribes and refocus on our purpose. Human civilisation is now facing the perfect storm of ecological and social problems that is being driven by overpopulation, overconsumption, and environmentally toxic technologies. They're on the brink of collapse, and they'll take us with them. We can't let that happen." He kneeled in front of her, begging.

She finally understood. He was sharing with her his dying wish and his goodbye. *He thinks he'll be dead by tomorrow.* She looked at his broken body and his exhausted face. She realised he was probably right; he had no chance against the beast. *You don't deserve to be sentenced to death by your own parents.* But she didn't dare think about it any further.

"The beast has a weak spot behind its ears. No bone." The words came out, despite her resistance to feeling pity or sorrow for him.

"Promise me, Sky, please."

She looked down at him, and she nodded. The Yi'ingo was struggling to maintain her cold exterior. Her emotions were complex, conflicted and intense. She needed to get out of there, to move away from him. He got up slowly and she turned around, preparing to leave. He held her hand by the tips of her fingers; his grip was gentle and yet she stopped without turning to face him.

Gabriel whispered, "Bastian adores you. He's more vulnerable than he appears to be when it comes to his feelings for you. Don't punish him for my crimes or the crimes of our ancestors. He doesn't deserve it. For your sake, don't push him away." She pulled her hand from his grip and left without saying another word.

As she left his room, she met Sage, who was bringing some food. Sage's body stiffened. The frown was evident on a face that never frowned and never exuded any other feeling but kindness and empathy.

"I wish you had stayed away. My father needs to rest. He has enough on his mind without being the target of your hate. You're not welcome here."

Sky looked at the young woman. A human with all the qualities of an Ange'el, demonstrating that she could be feisty and brave as she attempted to protect her father. Few dared to speak to Sky in that tone. The Yi'ingo warrior had no hard feelings or harsh words for the gentle dove. Sky lowered her eyes and left.

Marcus was resting at his farm in Ma'asai. In his head, he was reviewing the events of the past few days. The king was on edge. Things were unfolding as planned, but he knew that the worst was yet to come. If he could take Gabriel's place, he would do it in a heartbeat.

Marcus came to Ma'asai every so often, particularly when he needed some privacy. The rooms at the Ange'el's Sacred House were all set quite close together. Marcus did not always favour communal living when he was burdened with Ahe'ey's affairs. Some days, he needed the space of the farm, the familiarity of the wooden houses, the direct contact with the land and all its living beings, and the distraction and escapism of Ma'asai's training arena. Sometimes he needed the privacy of a place where no one could read his mind.

The home of a Ma'asai was a celebration of Earth's life. The walls featured vertical gardens used to germinate seeds until they were ready to face the outdoors. Containers held recyclable goods like eggshells full of calcium and other micronutrients. The sunlight, moonlight, water, and the wind were preciously harvested and used as required. The Ma'asai shared their homes with birds, bees, plants, and some other small animals. The senses were spoiled as one experienced the colours, scents, and sounds of nature inside a farmer's home. Their acute understanding of the fabric of life and their sensitivity to nature allowed all living things to thrive under their protection.

The ecosystem of the land was in perfect balance; it was a self-sustaining environment rich in biodiversity and was highly productive. The farmers had a deep connection with the land and all its life. They understood that the interdependency of species could be nurtured to lead to agricultural sustainability. They farmed both land and animals, taking just enough of what they needed, with minimal intervention.

The Ahe'ey knew that they were just one species amongst many in a way that humans did not, because although humans had experienced the Darwinian revolution, they continued to act as though humankind was set apart from other species by its consciousness. Blinded by their self-claimed superiority, they had artificially separated themselves from nature, objectifying it, destroying it.

Due to the length of their lives, the Ahe'ey had more time to go through additional stages of learning. They evolved from the primal need for self-preservation and the pursuit of safety and power to a heightened awareness and connection with the consciousness of all beings.

Marcus had once been the leader of the Ma'asai before he married Viviane and, by her side, ascended to the throne of Ahe'ey. It was not easy for a farmer to see his green fields burned by the rage of war, to watch helplessly as the women of the farmer's tribe abandoned their homes to seek the refuge of the Yi'ingo and Ange'el sanctuaries.

The farmer became a warrior and then a king. A ruler toughened by the war and responsibilities of the throne, and yet deep inside, he was a Ma'asai, a nurturer of life, and he was at peace when he could hear the bees and the birds at work, spreading new life throughout the land.

He was distracted by his own thoughts, leaning back on a daybed, when Bastian came in the room. He was not his usual good-humoured self. He stood sombre and silent by the door, looking straight at Marcus.

"Bastian, what an unexpected visit," Marcus said warmly. He loved his nephew and considered him a son. Marcus had spent more time with Bastian than he had with his own son Gabriel, who had spent a lot of time out of Ahe'ey. A few years back, Marcus had mentored Bastian to become the leader of the Ma'asai and they had become close.

The king was no Ange'el but he could read Bastian's mind as his thoughts were written on his face. He waited until Bastian finally spoke.

"Cancel Gabriel's fight with the dragon," he pleaded. "No one has ever survived a one-on-one battle with a Wali'ingooteer. Gabriel is in poor health. Please stop this madness."

"You know Gabriel needs to win this battle if he is to be king." His words burned his tongue as he spoke them. He was consumed with guilt and worry.

"No. I don't. It's your doing that people aren't aware of his valour and virtues. It's your doing. So tell them. Tell them the truth and end this charade. I've seen him sacrifice too much already."

"I wish it was that easy, son. People will need to see it and experience it with their own eyes."

"In that case, delay the battle. Why are you setting this up when he is so weak? Why are you so committed to planning your son's death? He won't survive with half his body broken."

"For all our sakes and for the sake of humankind, he must survive."

"Is that it? Are you gambling your son's life on a high-risk game? Is that all he means to you?"

Marcus got up, walked straight to his nephew, and grabbed his tunic at the chest. His face was close to Bastian's, angry, lips quivering. The younger man did not flinch. Marcus turned his back and left.

Extraordinary Circumstances

The Pierre Hotel penthouse, New York

"Morgan!"

Morgan heard the Hispanic accent and walked to the living room to meet Maria.

"Maria?"

The woman nodded, "Hi Morgan, have you spoken to anyone?"

Maria's tone and expression demanded both attention and urgency; her olive skin was pasty, and the dark shadows under her eyes reflected the stress in her body.

"Just Gabriel's partner, Sir Charles. Gabriel asked me to reach out to him."

"The world's gone mad. They're looking for you and Gabriel. This place is surrounded by media."

"I know; I've checked the internet."

"Where is Gabriel? I need to speak with him."

"He won't be available for a few weeks."

"What do you mean? I must speak to Gabriel. Now." Maria's voice echoed in the room and the stress in her eyes turned into emotion. "We are under tremendous scrutiny. Where is he?"

"At home, with his family. He's appointed me to be his representative. You can work with me." Morgan's tone was reassuring and friendly.

"With all due respect, I don't know you—"

Morgan responded to Maria's intensity in a calm and considered manner, "Maria, please don't shoot the messenger. I have a letter for you from Gabriel."

Morgan led Maria to the library and handed her the letter. Maria picked up the letter, sat on an upholstered chair and read it. Her eyes filled with tears, "He says he may never return . . . ."

Morgan had to gather all her strength to reassure the woman. "He's dealing with some trouble, but you and I know that he can handle anything. He'll be fine," Morgan said, trying to believe in her own words.

The letter seemed to reduce Maria's reservations about Morgan. The CEO of the Ange'el Foundation softened her expression, walked towards Morgan and placed her hand on her arm.

"We need a plan. I'm running blind here, Morgan. I've been protecting Gabriel's family secrets for a while, and I've been made aware of some of his special capabilities, but what I saw in those videos . . . it's amazing. It's also gone viral; I don't know how we can possibly contain it."

"Let's break the problem down. They are trying to find Gabriel or any other of these men they saw in the footage. It won't happen. They won't find them."

"Surely, anyone can be found."

"No, for the next few weeks Gabriel and his . . . people . . . are safe. We do need to ensure that we hide any artefacts. Sir Charles' company has been under attack; I assume the same is happening with the Ange'el Foundation?"

"Yes, but we have nothing. Gabriel takes everything away, and our records are clean. We have been subject to break-ins and some hacking, but all they have or will find are records of philanthropic activity. Our people know nothing, and even I have only a shallow understanding of what's really going on."

"How can you work in these circumstances?" Morgan was curious how it was possible to work so blindly and trust so fully.

"Morgan," Maria smiled, her tone sweet and her eyes bright, "you've met him, how can you not trust him? It's impossible. Isn't it?"

Morgan felt a burst of fire emerge in her cheeks as she lowered her eyes and nodded.

"We go out of our way to make him happy. Gabriel es un ángel."

Morgan wondered if Maria loved him. *How can she not?*

Maria continued, "I read somewhere that a few days ago the Hope Foundation was also the target of hacking attacks."

"They won't find anything. For now, I prefer to leave them in the dark. This place, do we need to worry about anything here?"

"Nothing much. A lot of expensive artwork, sculptures that seem to come alive when you touch them, and a few strange artefacts, but nothing that any scientist or art historian would pay attention to. They are ancient objects that look like modern day designer objects. Also, I'll dismiss the house staff so that no one knows you are here."

"Okay . . . so . . . first, we stop Zanus and the KKK from using Gabriel and his family to spread their hate campaign."

"Plus we need to stop this attention and scrutiny by the entire world. I was interrogated by the CIA for two hours yesterday; it was horrible. It was the first time I was relieved that Gabriel tells me so little." Maria flashed a small smile.

"So how do we stop the white supremacist campaign? Zanus is lying. Perhaps I should just go to the media and tell them the truth. Explain that the CIA believes that Zanus is behind the attacks on progressive leaders around the world."

"Is that so? Jesús, the man is running for president."

"Gabriel believes it's true."

"Ay Dios mio! Tú . . . You are well regarded; I'm sure I can organise a press conference with some of our key contacts in the mainstream media —the *Guardian*, the *New York Times*, and some of the new media companies that reach the younger audiences. You have a large footprint on social media, right?"

Morgan nodded.

Maria continued, "I'll also connect with Democracy Now and the Real News Network."

"Maybe this isn't a good idea. Going to progressive media will only place a brighter spotlight on Gabriel and . . . his family. We need to focus on shutting down the KKK's propaganda first."

"But, these networks can help us spread our message."

"No, we would only be preaching to the converted. We wouldn't reach the far right audiences because of the internet filter bubbles. And, even if we did reach some extreme right people, they would immediately dismiss a story from liberal media. It would backfire."

"Bubbles?"

"Yeah, people only see news that reinforces their opinions, what they already like. Let's release a statement to Fox News, far right websites and to the KKK. We will organise a live broadcast on the web, and invite them and Zanus to watch."

"*Estás loca!* Are you insane?"

"Possibly, but extraordinary circumstances demand extraordinary action."

"Why would they pay attention? What will make them come?" Maria touched the pendant that hung from her neck. She unconsciously caressed the wing of the silver angel.

"We'll tell them exactly what they want to hear." Morgan's heart raced; she could hear it pump like a wild horse refusing to be tamed.

Grieving Warriors

Bastian was unleashing his anger in the training arena at the Ma'asai village, fighting Magnus, the tallest and largest of all Ma'asai.

"Bastian, my friend," big Magnus said as he used his shield to protect his body against Bastian's attacks, "you're taking the training too seriously today. I'm starting to think you actually want me to lose my head. I give you my word; I didn't date your girlfriend . . . this week." Magnus laughed, his eyes pointing to Sky, who was approaching the arena. Magnus was breathing heavily and struggling to keep up with a determined Bastian, who, for a change, had no smile or jokes to retaliate with. Bastian saw Sky and stopped the onslaught.

"Yes, perhaps we should call it a night," he said, patting Magnus on the back. Bastian was sweating and recovering his breath. He looked at Sky suspiciously. She didn't often step on Ma'asai land.

Sky picked up a sword, and she continued where Magnus had left off. No words exchanged, no explanation given. It was a mighty battle—muscle against muscle, strength against strength, power against power. They matched each other in their rage, a dance worthy of being witnessed by gods.

The Ma'asai men gathered, coming from every direction. It wasn't every day that they could see such an affair. What Bastian had in pure muscle strength, Sky matched in flexibility, determination, and speed. The two warriors knew each other well and could predict the other's each and every move. They were used to fighting beside and against each other.

To the audience, it looked like a high-stakes battle as Sky launched her body forwards, sword in hand, pointing towards Bastian's head, just to see him dodge at the last minute and swing his sword close to her neck as she jumped back to avoid it. However, to the cousins, it was just a well-synchronised dance because in the arena, as in bed, these two forces of nature understood each other deeply. The battle lasted an hour, until Sky just stopped by throwing her sword and shield to the floor. She walked away and then stopped for a second, as if asking him to follow her. He did.

They walked together to his farm. As she moved closer to him, he took a few steps back. He wasn't in the mood to be used tonight. She seemed unfazed by his reaction; she looked him in the eyes and offered him her hand. He took it and she pulled him to her. Then the unexpected happened. Sky put her head on his chest and burst into tears as he held her in his arms. They stood comforting each other, both feeling angry and hopeless. There was nothing to say. It was the first time that there had been no psychological barriers between them.

In the morning, they both woke up early at Bastian's farm. Sky went back to Yi'ingo so that she could dress formally. They reunited with each other at Ange'el to escort Gabriel to the arena. Although weapons were forbidden for those watching the event and they never mentioned it to one another, Bastian noticed that, like him, she had her sword hidden beneath her cape.

Escorting Him to Battle

6 December 2014 - The Sacred House, Ange'el

Bastian helped Gabriel get ready for the battle. The Ange'el remembered six-year-old Bastian, the orphan boy that was devastated by the loss of his parents and found shelter under the wings of his Ange'el friend. Young Bastian had been so afraid of losing more people from his life that he had always attempted to fill every silence and to engage those close to him with an endless array of attention-seeking tricks designed to enrapture the ones he loved. In so many ways, he was still that boy. Under all the muscle, the good looks, the arrogant smile, and the illusion of confidence that he projected to others, there was still just a young boy trying to fill the hole he carried in his heart. Only Gabriel knew how to soothe that pain, as the bond the two men had with each other reassured Bastian that he wasn't alone, he was never alone, and yet, *soon, he may well be*.

"I've something important to ask of you, Bas."

"Anything, brother."

"Watch over my kids, please. They are fragile and insecure in this land. They'll need support. Work with Sky to open the passage, find Quinn . . . and Morgan. They are in danger."

"There's no need for such talk—"

"Bas, please."

Bastian's lips twisted at the supplication, unhappy, but accepted it after a moment. "Consider it done. If something happens to you, I'll care for your children as you've cared for me, my friend. They are my family. I'll protect and support them."

Sky started talking as soon as she entered the room. Her body was tense, and she avoided eye contact with the Ange'el. "I brought you the lightest chain mail armour I could find at Yi'ingo. It's the finest in the land. We coated it silver and organised new chest and shoulder plates with the Ange'el insignia. It's quite light, and it won't limit the mobility of your arms." She continued with a grin, "Not that you have any arm mobility at the moment."

"Thank you, sister."

Sage fitted an exoskeleton around his chest, arms, and legs. The lightweight, honeycomb-like external structure made up for the weakened inner bone structure and was perfectly moulded to his body.

"We should cover all of it with a long tunic. We don't want the dragon to find the sensitive spots," Sky said.

Sage nodded with enthusiasm. "I'll go get it."

"As you are using your left hand to fight, we designed a shield that will slot straight over your right arm. This means you'll need to move your right arm less to defend yourself." Bastian demonstrated the technique with his own arm. The shield and the chest plate had the design of a full moon and four stars.

"We're trying to keep you as light as possible. Agility will be indispensable to dodge the three tails of the Wali'ingooteer. The faster you can cut them off, the safer you'll be. At least for two minutes as they regenerate themselves quite quickly," Sky continued. "Remember, their skull is open at the back of their ears, so it's the best spot for a mortal blow."

Sage helped Gabriel put on a royal blue tunic and the chain mail armour over it and Bastian helped fit his chest and back plates. Gabriel was adorned in shimmering silver which showcased his Ange'el insignia. He was ready for his test, and he was as calm as ever. There was no sign of fear in his face. Sage braided his hair on the side, tied it at the back, and placed a moon-shaped amazonite stone pendant around his neck.

Then, she went to fetch Ollie, Riley, and Aria, who kissed their father goodbye.

"All I can promise you is that I'll do everything in my power to return to you alive, but if I don't, I want you to know that you made my life beautiful and worth living and that you have the most amazing family surrounding you. I'll be watching over you and loving you every single day of your life."

The young girls remained optimistic, none of them contemplating any other future than the return of their dear father. Ollie was trying and failing to hold back his despair. He had tears in his eyes as he looked at his father.

"Stay," the boy begged.

"I wish I could, my son." They embraced, and Gabriel whispered in Ollie's ear, "I love you." Oliver nodded as Gabriel kissed his head. Ollie and the girls stayed behind as Bastian, Sky, and Sage escorted Gabriel to the arena.

Gabriel took Sage's hand and kissed it. "My Sage, I don't want you to witness this. You don't need to be here. I apologise for the weight that was placed on you these last few weeks. I didn't mean to leave so much on your shoulders, although I'm in awe of the way you rose to so much responsibility with such grace."

"You gave me everything, Apollo. I wish I could do more for you. I want to stay. I'll stay." He hugged her and kissed her forehead. Ollie appeared behind her, and Gabriel nodded, signalling that he could stay.

"I wish Quinn was here with us," Ollie murmured just before Gabriel entered the arena.

Bastian placed his hand on the Ange'el's shoulder and said, "You know, this would be a good time for you to unleash those wings of yours." Gabriel looked at his cousin, confused, just as the crowd welcomed him with a roar.

Gabriel took a deep breath and closed his eyes for a moment. He was a spiritual man, one who rejected meaningless acts of violence. He didn't seek glory or adulation. The Ange'el went through the list of reasons why he'd accepted the battle and had to win it. He opened his eyes and entered the arena. The energy of the place overwhelmed him—the minds and voices of the Ahe'ey demanded blood. His blood, the dragon's —to the crowd, it didn't matter. They were there to get some closure, delivered by the bloody death of Ange'el or dragon.

MISDIRECTION

The Pierre Hotel penthouse, New York

"Where is Commander Warren?" The director of the CIA skipped all the pleasantries as he burst through the door of the penthouse at The Pierre. "Do you both understand the impact of your actions? We have the eyes of the public and the media on us, and you disappear, just like that. Where is he? I don't appreciate being summoned without any explanation. My place is with the top man, in Washington, not here."

"Calm down, sir; have a seat," Morgan said, ignoring the arrogance and self-aggrandisement of the old man.

"Where have you been?"

"At the Catskills, hiding." Morgan had rehearsed her story and was ready for the questions.

"Nonsense. We found the four burned bodies; we've cleaned up the mess and looked for you both everywhere. You are going to tell me who he is and where you have been or I'll have you arrested and taken for interrogation." The director's tone was cutting and aggressive. He dared to grab her by the arm. His grip was firm, and he pulled her towards him as he spoke.

Her eyes narrowed; she yanked her arm from his hand and spoke decisively. "Gabriel and the Ange'el Foundation have been an important ally to the intelligence community of this nation. His message for you is quite simple: either you collaborate with me, under my conditions or neither you nor your employers will ever again benefit from the funds, intelligence, technology or covert action provided by Ange'el. One mistake and they'll vanish forever. Is that clear? If you touch my team or me, if you try to deceive us, or betray us, you *will* regret it."

"The pussy . . . cat has claws. How do I know you are truly speaking on his behalf?"

"One more misstep and Ange'el is out," Morgan said, unfazed by the crudeness and aggressiveness of the man. She'd now seen his true colours; she knew where she stood. Morgan handed Matt a letter from Gabriel. The man shifted in his seat and unbuttoned his collar as he read the letter.

As Morgan observed the man, Viviane's words popped into her head: "*We use misdirection to neutralise the problem.*"

"What do you want?" he asked, abruptly.

"Can you manipulate photos and videos?"

"Of course. Are you coming to the United States to engage in psychological warfare and deceit? How odd; you're profiled as a left-wing tree hugger. Not so nice after all, are you?"

"Are they good enough to endure rigorous scrutiny?" she continued calmly.

"It's easier with photos. We can beat most qualitative tools used by media and mainstream digital forensics. They won't pass a detailed perusal from the top experts, but we control most of those."

"How fast?" Morgan was encouraged by Matt's replies; her plan was coming together quite nicely.

"What do you need?"

Unfair Advantage

Sky felt the rush of adrenaline that she always experienced when entering the Games Arena. All ten thousand citizens of Ahe'ey packed the venue. Every single citizen was present to witness the unusual event. The tribes were mostly segregated, dividing the arena into four distinct patches of colour. The Ange'el wore their simple tunics in shades of white, cyan, or blue. Some of them had their eyes closed, setting their intention on their beloved prince and praying for his success.

The Yi'ingo's side of the arena looked like a patchwork of leathers, reds, oranges, and coppers. Their leaders were adorned with gold that shined in the sun. Amalia had selected some of the Yi'ingo warriors to maintain peace and order during the event. They were strategically placed around the arena and at each gate, and yet every Yi'ingo in the audience carefully observed the behaviour of the Hu'urei. They weren't comfortable with such an unusual and large gathering of builders. The men never attended the Games in such great numbers, and they kept mostly to themselves. Seeing them all come out in force as requested by the queen was unsettling for the guardians of Ahe'ey. Sky scanned the crowd, locating the notorious troublemakers and making a mental note of their positions in the audience.

The loud and boastful Hu'urei stood out due to their dark tunics and long beards. The builder's sense of architecture and design was expressed in the way they were dressed. The tunics were simple but featured asymmetric details that were perfectly balanced and clean. Layers of black and grey fabrics added structure and texture. What their outfits lacked in colour, they gained in pure art and design. The border between the Hu'urei and the Ange'el was a curious place. Half the Ange'el seemed to enjoy and connect with their dark neighbours—black, cyan, and white mixed in areas of the audience. In return, the Hu'urei became less loud and more courteous next to their spiritual lady friends. Sky distrusted the intentions of the Hu'urei and censured the foolishness of these women. Some of the Ange'el appeared to agree with Sky, moving to a different location as more builders arrived at the arena.

The Ma'asai mingled with some of the Yi'ingo. Some of the farmers wore their brown work tunics, others their formal green kimonos. Green and brown could be seen sprinkled amongst the women warriors at the fringes of their area of the audience.

The quiet nature of the Ange'el and the distrusting posture of the Yi'ingo were replaced by smiles, laughter, and the general good disposition of the farmers, who shared drinks and jokes as they waited for the event. Drinks hadn't been allowed at the venue on this day, but their tunics made the perfect cover for smuggling a bit of stress relief into the arena. Some of the Hu'urei joined them in the fun. With her eyes, Sky signalled one of her warriors to confiscate the drinks of the builders.

A circular golden cage was now rising from the ground, separating the audience from the fighting ring. The cage was raised above the floor by a second structure with the same round shape but it was made of a strong, transparent material. The crystal lower half of the tube was designed to stop the audience from interfering in the fight by projecting swords or arrows into the arena, and it was tall enough to prevent anyone from climbing over it.

The audience stood up as the king and the queen sat on the thrones that were set on a stage just above the area where the Ange'el were seated. Viviane and Marcus were loved and respected by all, a difficult feat in a land that was so divided and scarred by war. Amalia sat just beside them along with several other Ahe'ey elders. Angha was the only royal not in attendance; he rarely left the belly of Ka'alama. Sky, Bastian, Sage, and Ollie stood in silence by one of the entrances to the arena, near the transparent wall that separated them from the fighting ring. At four metres in height, the impenetrable wall stood over twice as high as Bastian. Their faces were sombre, and their bodies echoed their feelings; a quiet hopelessness was present in their posture and their eyes.

A gong resonated over the arena, and a door slid across the floor of the ring, allowing the creature to emerge. The audience gasped. They hadn't seen a Wali'ingooteer in over ten years and the creature was as beautiful as it was frightening. It had the body of a sea serpent, long and flexible, giving it the ability to move fast. The body split at the end into three distinct tails with sharp spikes that could pierce the most robust armour. The creature was covered with blue and green scales that looked as soft as feathers but were as strong as steel. Its arms and legs were short but allowed it to stand and handle items as its hands and feet were shaped like claws and had opposable thumbs. The claws were large enough to wrap around a person. Sky shook her head, trying to get rid of the gruesome memories of the war.

The dragon's scales shimmered in the sun as it turned and stood up to look at the audience. Its head was as high as the height of the transparent wall, but not high enough to reach the top of the cage that stood above it. Its huge red eyes observed the audience with curiosity. The wings were so large that there wasn't enough space in the ring for it to extend them. It looked like the transparent cage had been built to measure, to keep the creature grounded. The dragon's body occupied two-thirds of the ring.

The faces of the warriors reflected their fear and hate for the beast. They had seen companions fall in battle, crushed by the vicious attacks of the powerful and deadly creatures.

Sky had never seen such a large dragon; its mouth could snap Gabriel in half in a single bite. "What are they doing? They're going to kill him," she said, looking at the queen and king. She felt a knot in her stomach.

The Wali'ingooteer had the intelligence of a six-year-old child. They could live up to one hundred years. Based on the size of this beast, Sky estimated that the dragon was at least sixty years old. It was probably used during the war and had been responsible for many deaths. The dragons had self-regenerating properties that were even more developed than the Ahe'ey bloodline. If one was to cut off one of their tails, it'd grow back within minutes.

"It's not the first time they've sacrificed their son. Only this time they seem determined to end his life," Bastian murmured.

Sage had tears running down her face as Bastian embraced her. The gong echoed once again, and the sliding door opened on the floor of the ring. Gabriel emerged without a cane to help him stand; the exoskeleton gave him the supporting structure he needed to walk without limping. As Gabriel climbed up the stairs, he glowed. The cyan and silver of his Ange'el armour enhanced his aura. He looked calm as he faced the creature that stood in front of him, twice as tall and a hundred times stronger.

Hooded Clan Power

Morgan was sitting at the desk trying to write the press release when Quinn walked into the library. The teen wore the dress she'd bought the previous day over her leather clothes.

"How can people wear this, it's so impractical and painful." Quinn adjusted the gown's bustier over her flat chest, her face scrunched. "I can't breathe with this on. Why are there wires inside this thing?"

Morgan laughed, "Tulle and ruffles? I didn't think that was your style, Quinny."

"We need skirts big enough to hide the swords and long enough to cover the boots. There's no way we're wearing those pointy torture devices that humans call shoes."

"You're not taking your swords to the ball."

"You said we had to protect a package. We need our swords."

"Where's Scout?"

"She's sitting on the balcony, sulking. Ya know how she is. What are these for?"

Quinn asked, pulling two silicone bust boosters out of a bag and looking at them, puzzled.

Morgan giggled. "They're dangerous tools used to make women feel bad about their bodies," she responded.

Quinn dropped them on the floor. "Why would they do that?"

"Go fetch Scout. I need to speak to you both."

The young woman lifted her large and puffy petticoat off the floor and left the room. Morgan noticed the sword strapped to her leg under all the ruffles.

"You're not taking your swords tonight," she repeated as Quinn shuffled away.

Morgan refocused on the task at hand, searching the internet for the right language, going through white supremacy sites and reading each word with trepidation and disgust. Footage of Gabriel killing her Eastern-looking attackers was being celebrated all over the sites. She took a deep breath and typed:

PRESS RELEASE

A few weeks ago I was subject to a horrific attack at the Metropolitan Museum; an assault that showed me the truth, that made me stand against those who attack our Western liberties. I was lucky to be in the company of a man who is part of a global community of guardians trained to protect those who are most exposed to the worst evil in the world, the sub-humans. This community, which has been named by the Internet as 'The Protectors of the Nation' is indeed quite extraordinary. I've spent a few weeks with them, watched them train in martial arts and learned about their mission. I have decided to join their movement and have been given permission to share what I've learned and to introduce you to some of their leaders.

The Protectors of the Nation—their identity preserved by hoods; their anonymity a sacred right that allows them to guard us against those who challenge the natural order of the world. The supremacy of our great values is under threat, and the guardians are rising once again to purify this land through fire. Their virtuous ideology will rise again; their hooded power will protect those who are worthy from those who are not. Those who seek to disrupt our social order will fall by the hands of our siblings. Devotion to our own will make us stronger, and we will not give up until our virtue, our morals, our values, messages and views are law.

Our Knights will ensure that the eternal light rises again. Our circle and clan is bound by our special blood, the superior genes that unite us. The right to the supremacy of the children of the sun is our civil right.

Join me tomorrow at an online event where I will share more with you about The Protectors of the Nation. Details to follow shortly.

Morgan - Founder and CEO of the Hope Foundation

"This is horrific," Maria said as she joined Morgan in the library. She read the briefing over Morgan's shoulder.

"Depends on the lens you use to read it. Our goal is to attract the worst of the worst to our online event, and no one else. This language will hopefully achieve that."

"And then what? What are you going to tell them?" Maria's forehead wrinkled with worry and disbelief.

Scout and Quinn walked into the library wearing their Yi'ingo outfits. Maria's eyes showed some recognition of the symbols embroidered in the warriors' clothing.

Morgan replied to Maria, "I'm still working on that part of the plan, but I have some . . . assets. Can you work on the logistics? We'll need broadcasting and recording equipment, an online conferencing platform, a website—"

"Excuse me; I need to take this call. My wife is calling," Maria said, picking up her mobile and walking away.

Scout raised her eyebrows and turned to Morgan. "Women can marry women here?"

"Yes, in some parts of the world they can. We are fighting hard to make it possible everywhere."

"Disgusting," Scout said, crossing her arms in front of her chest.

Quinn rolled her eyes and shook her head as she shot a sideways glance at her grumpy companion. "Hypocrite," she murmured. Morgan raised her eyebrows, but decided to let the girls work through the new idea on their own.

Scout seemed to ponder over what Morgan had said for a while and then she asked, "You fight for women to marry women?"

"Yes . . . No. We don't fight with swords. Instead, we work to change the laws so that women can marry women and men can marry men."

"You want to marry a woman?"

Morgan shook her head.

"So why do you fight to have the rules changed?"

"Because everybody should be able to marry whom they love."

"But they can't have children . . . "

"Quinn, who's your father?"

"Gabriel, the future king of Ahe'ey," replied Quinn proudly. Scout dismissed it in a single scornful glance.

"It's not natural; it's a sign of a defect in the blood."

"No, Scout. Different doesn't mean broken. It just means different," Morgan replied gently.

"Why would you fight for someone who's different?"

"When we protect those who are different, especially the ones that are most vulnerable, we are protecting all of us against those who use hate and fear to divide us in order to obtain control and power. Today they may target others, but soon they will come for us. So we stick together, all of us. We embrace our differences and find ways to try to understand each other."

"But, not everyone has the same worth. That's just a fact," Scout retorted. Quinn's lips tightened.

"Is that right? Some people don't care about bees, yet most of what we eat relies, directly or indirectly, on the bees doing their job. Diversity is life. It strengthens the ecosystem. Listen, Scout, we don't have time for this today, although I do hope you'll see past your bigotry one day."

"What's bigotry?"

"Prejudice." Morgan changed the subject as she had other pressing matters to deal with. "Ladies, I have an important task for you."

"Another party? No more dresses, pleaaase," Quinn said, kicking the silicone breast enhancer that she'd previously dropped on the floor.

"Nope, this time you will need your swords and your boots."

Impossible Odds

Games Arena, Ange'el

Bastian placed his hands on the shoulders of Sage and Ollie and pulled them closer to him. The Ma'asai boy smelled of a familiar scent.

"You smell like flowers, Ollie," Bastian pulled up the boy's cape to uncover his secret. "Good plan," Bastian said, reassuring the boy.

They watched Gabriel bow to the creature, whose fiery eyes were set on him. In a surprising move, the creature bowed back and screeched so loudly that it made the audience gasp in fear. The gong sounded for the third time. Gabriel unsheathed his sword and jumped over the tail of the dragon, which had been unleashed in his direction. The tail hit the wall like thunder, and the entire arena shook as if hit by an earthquake. The Ange'el was still in mid-air when he rotated his body to cut the attacking tail of the dragon. The tail fell to the floor as the creature squealed in pain, and the audience cheered with renewed hope.

The Wali'ingooteer immediately unleashed its other two tails against Gabriel. The Ange'el dodged the spikes using his speed and flexibility. The audience was witnessing Gabriel's skill for the first time. The surprise on their faces reminded Bastian that few had experienced Gabriel's physical mastery. The Ma'asai prince looked at Marcus and Viviane, angry, and yet he could see how pale and worried they were as they watched the fight that was unfolding in front of them; Marcus squeezing Viviane's hand.

Gabriel struggled to find safety in the small space. The creature attacked with his mouth, his tails, and his wings. It would only take one blow to kill the heir of Ahe'ey. Gabriel jumped on top of one of the dragon's wings and used it to thrust himself towards the tail of the beast. He managed to swing his sword and cut another one of the dragon's tails. The Wali'ingooteer released a piercing cry and used its wing to hit Gabriel and throw him against the crystal tube. The Ange'el hit the wall with the right side of his body, just above where Bastian, Sky, Ollie and Sage stood. Sage ran towards him, touching the wall where Gabriel's face was. The Ange'el reassured his daughter with a weak smile and got up. His pale face showcased the agony he felt throughout his entire body. He was drunk with pain, confused, still trying to get his bearings.

Bastian screamed, "*Turn around! Turn around!*"

Gabriel turned just in time to see the head of the dragon coming towards him. He used his sword to pierce the dragon's mouth. The Wali'ingooteer moved its head in pain but hit Gabriel with its wing. The Ange'el rolled on the floor, onto his feet, and then screamed in pain as the exoskeleton that secured his right leg had been shattered by the dragon's attack. Gabriel was unable to put his leg on the floor without recoiling in excruciating pain.

Outside of the wall, Sky looked at Bastian and her eyes landed on his hands and then on the top of the circular structure. The Ma'asai agreed with a single blink of his eyes.

Gabriel put all his weight on his left leg as he continued to fight the tail of the dragon. The Wali'ingooteer seemed quite frustrated by Gabriel's ability to dodge its strikes. The Ange'el took a deep breath and ran on his broken leg in the direction of the dragon. He jumped onto the back of the beast. The creature attempted to shake him by aggressively crashing its large body against the wall. Gabriel tried to reach the dragon's neck. He gasped for air, holding on to the Wali'ingooteer with his left hand and fighting with his broken arm, which barely had the strength to lift the sword. The Ange'el raised his sword to strike the dragon in the neck but the beast's tail slammed Gabriel against the wall. The exoskeleton around his body and arm snapped as Gabriel hit the ground and screamed. As he attempted to stand, the dragon's tail stabbed him in the right shoulder. The Ange'el was pinned to the crystal wall, a gush of blood pouring down his arm.

The queen cried out in despair, and the crowd stood up and screamed. Viviane closed her eyes, using her mind's eye to see and hear better. She battled her motherly instincts, fighting her burning desire to use her powers to help her son.

In a matter of seconds, Sky and Bastian handed their swords to Sage, who looked confused at the gesture. Sky ran away from the arena towards the door, while Bastian moved to stand just beside the wall. The dragon pulled back its tail, and Gabriel fell to the ground, dizzy with pain and blood loss.

Ollie jumped to his feet, pulled a bunch of yellow flowers from his pocket and proceeded to punch the crystal wall with the flowers in his hands.

Sky came running towards the ring. She jumped onto Bastian's interlocked hands, and he used all his strength to propel her up in the air, high enough for her to hold onto the bars of the golden cage that stood above the transparent wall.

The dragon headed in the direction of Ollie, throwing its mouth against the transparent surface that separated the creature from the boy. Ollie pressed the flowers to the walls with his hands, unfazed by the thrusts of the creature.

"What are you doing Ollie?" Sage screamed, attempting to pull her brother away from the structure.

"Dandelion flowers the dragons are mad for them," Ollie said, continuing to remove flowers from a bag hidden under his cape and pressing them onto the wall.

As soon as Sky reached the cage, she hung upside down by her legs with her arms extended. Bastian walked away from the wall and then ran towards it, jumping to grab Sky's hands. He used her body to climb to the top of the cage. He was a heavy man; Sky had to use all her strength to keep them both from falling. As soon as they were up, Sage threw them their swords, and they jumped into the fighting ring just as the dragon was returning to finish off Gabriel.

Viviane smiled full of hope. She squeezed Marcus' hand tightly and murmured, "Three united as one, as expected. If they reunite, the realm will follow."

Sky jumped onto the ground, and shouted, *"Look at me! Fight me!"*

The beast pulled its eyes away from the fallen Ange'el and turned to face the Yi'ingo. She roared at the beast, demanding its full attention. The dragon launched one of its wings in her direction, and she used the opportunity to jump on it and climb the dragon.

Gabriel attempted to stand but fell to the ground, wailing with pain.

The audience was on its feet, screaming and cheering for the three descendants of Ahe'ey. Sky reached the neck of the dragon, which danced erratically, trying to throw her without success, while Bastian fought the dragon's tails, which were now regrowing quickly. Sky stood on top of the beast, preparing to deliver a deadly strike to the dragon's neck, but the monster unleashed one of its tails in her direction, whipping her body. The Yi'ingo was propelled into the air and slammed into the wall at full speed. She hit the ground unconscious.

"Sky!" Bastian screamed as he looked at the inert body of the Yi'ingo.

The Wali'ingooteer turned to face Bastian, all three tails fully regrown and ready to strike. Bastian simultaneously fought the tails and the mouth of the dragon. He used his strength to unleash powerful blows onto the beast and to cut off one of the tails. In another strike, the Ma'asai's sword pierced another of the tails, and as the dragon backed away, the sword got caught in its tail and flew from Bastian's hands. The dragon cornered Bastian, who was now unarmed with nowhere to run.

The dragon looked back at Sky, who was still down, and continued to move towards Bastian. The creature's pointy tails aligned with the Ma'asai's heart and the Yi'ingo's back. As the Wali'ingooteer pulled its tails backwards, ready to strike them, the creature turned its eyes towards Gabriel. The Ange'el was lying against the wall, bleeding heavily from his shoulder. It was a look of defiance, a look of victory, as it prepared to end Sky's and Bastian's life.

Rise, my love. Rise. Show them all your glory. Viviane spoke directly to her son's mind. She held her breath in fear and expectation. *Rise Ange'el!*

What happened next was impossible to predict, as the broken body of the Ange'el jumped to his feet and propelled himself onto the neck of the dragon. The audience gasped; many blinked their eyes, confused with the brief sight of wings in Gabriel's back. The Ange'el was sweating water and blood. He screamed in pain as he used his broken body to strike the dragon. He placed his sword behind the dragon's ear, at the spot where the beast had no skull to protect him. The Wali'ingooteer immediately froze and lay down, surrendering to Gabriel.

The crowd screamed:

"Finish him off!"

"Kill him!"

"Destroy the beast!"

But Gabriel stood immobile with his sword against the dragon's neck, looking at the queen and king. The dragon made no attempt to move. The Wali'ingooteer was defeated, and it was too intelligent to place its life at risk. Bastian helped Sky rise from the floor and she shook her head, finding her bearings.

The audience applauded and cheered. The Yi'ingo in the crowd screamed, continuing to demand the death of the dragon. Viviane took a deep breath of relief, opened her eyes and stood up. "This battle is over. The dragon has lost."

The beast bowed to the queen, acknowledging her words.

The golden cage was lowered into the floor until it disappeared. Gabriel sheathed his sword and slid down the dragon. The creature roared and bowed to Gabriel, who had just enough strength to bow back. The dragon's head reached towards the dandelion flowers, and its long wet tongue swooped them all up, while the creature's menacing eyes focused on Ollie, who retreated backwards in fear. Then the Wali'ingooteer extended its wings and took flight, heading in the direction of Ka'alama.

Gabriel was close to collapsing when Bastian and Sky joined him. Viviane cried as she watched her children come together.

"Are you okay?" Gabriel asked both of his cousins.

They laughed, looking at his sorry state. The Ange'el kissed Sky's hand and embraced Bastian with tears in his eyes. "Thank you." Then he looked at his son and smiled, and the boy rushed to his side and embraced him.

"You and your flowers saved my life," Gabriel whispered, kissing his head.

Bastian saw two Yi'ingo warriors rush towards Gabriel. They pulled him up by the arms and dragged him to a podium that rose from the ground and now stood facing the queen and king.

"Be careful with his shoulder. What are you doing?" Bastian shouted, watching Gabriel almost collapse in agony as the warriors touched his body. "What's going on? Let him go." Bastian moved in the direction of Gabriel.

"Stop, Bastian!" Marcus commanded, "Wait, my son."

Bastian remained unconvinced as the Yi'ingo locked Gabriel's hands in chains that dangled from a pole on the podium. The chains pulled his arms up, making him scream with pain.

"No!" Sage shouted as she ran towards him followed by Ollie. One of the Yi'ingo warriors stopped them.

"If you touch those children, I'll have your head!" Sky said. Sage and Ollie were released immediately.

"You ordered this?" Bastian looked at Sky.

She shook her head and shrugged her shoulders.

Blood was gushing from Gabriel's shoulder. They all looked at Viviane and Marcus, demanding an explanation. Bastian had his hand on his sword. Sky stood frozen as if trying to figure out what was going on. At this moment, Aria and Riley entered the room. They hadn't been allowed to watch the fight but were now joining Gabriel to celebrate his victory.

"Apollo!" Riley screamed, who was the first to see her father on the podium.

"Daaaddy!" Aria cried from the back. Ollie rushed towards them and hugged his little sisters.

"Children, come sit by my side," Viviane said. Ollie led Riley and Aria up to the stage, where the thrones stood.

A voice came from behind the thrones. "This test was designed to prove the bravery and courage of the contender to the throne. The rules were simple—fight the Wali'ingooteer in the arena alone and kill it. The rules have been broken, and I demand that the queen and king hold a trial so that we can decide the fate of this land and his fate." It was Amalia.

She continued, "I do not hide my agenda. I want to deny the crown to my grandson. He does not deserve it. He should be condemned to death as was his destiny before his cousins intervened in the battle. Sky should inherit the crown from Marcus and Viviane. Death to Sathian's shadow. Death!"

"Why do you fight so aggressively for the demise of your own grandson, Lady?" Bastian shouted.

"The four accusations I have against Gabriel are the following: One, that he is a coward, a mouse. He did not kill the Wali'ingooteer. He has proven time and time again that, in the most crucial moments when courage is required, he succumbs to his fears and lets others down."

Amalia looked at Sky as she spoke. "Two, he is weak and unworthy. He needed the help of both Sky and Bastian to win this fight. He is as inadequate physically as he is psychologically. He is less pure than Sky, whose good genes are showcased by her athleticism, health, and intelligence.

"Three, he is not committed to Ahe'ey. He cares not for our people or our land. Where was he when the war was devastating this land? What sacrifices has he made for our people? Four, he is a man and an Ange'el, just like Sathian, and like Sathian, he can manipulate our minds and bring doom to this land. Destroy him!"

Amalia shared her venom with passion and hate. Every word was projected with the confidence and strength of her convictions. She knew how to instigate her audience—she, the one who had lost so much, the one who had conquered so much, the one so filled with grief, bitterness, and rancour. The comparison of Gabriel to Sathian made half the arena stand up, cheering her in support and contaminating the others with hate and fear. Sathian was the monster that lurked in their nightmares, hated by the Hu'urei as much as he was hated by the other tribes.

"Have it your way, Amalia," Marcus said, his voiced filled with restrained frustration. "If you will stand for the accusation, I will stand for the defence. May the people of Ahe'ey be our jury."

"No. The law of this land states that decisions are made by the royal family, and, as you know, I have permission from my brother to vote on his behalf," Amalia said.

"Very well, can I have a show of hands before the trial of who believes that my son isn't worthy to be king?"

Amalia raised her hand. Sky took a moment, her eyes scanning the audience and then resting on Gabriel's eyes. As Sky's hand went up, her eyes sunk to the floor.

"You just saved his life and now condemn him to death." Bastian's face was red, and his anger fuelled every single muscle in his tense body as his veins popped above his skin, the betrayal stinging.

"I don't wish his death, but I can't support his claim to the throne. He's not fit to be the king of Ahe'ey," Sky projected her words so that they could reach the audience.

Marcus' jaw was locked tight as he looked at his niece. He took a deep breath and then addressed the audience. "We have a tie. If, by the end of this trial the tie remains, the people of Ahe'ey will have the final word. May the trial begin."

A THOUSAND LIES

CASUALTIES OF WAR

Gabriel could hear his little girls screaming and attempted to stand straight. He was barely conscious, and as he tried to move, waves of pain flowed through his entire body. But his children were his lifeline, reminding him he couldn't give up on life. He tried to focus on his father's voice and make sense of Marcus' words.

"I will start Gabriel's defence by asking him why he decided to let the Wali'ingooteer live. Gabriel, son, can you hear me?"

Gabriel struggled to reply. He was weak, too weak to respond. *What was the question?*

The Ange'el saw someone running in his direction; it was his Sage. Two Yi'ingo warriors moved to block her passage, but she continued, unfazed by the armed soldiers that stood between her and her father. The Yi'ingo unsheathed their swords, and Gabriel screamed, pulling against his chains despite his pain.

Before Sage could be stopped, Sky and Bastian had joined her, swords in hand, and Sky shouted, "Let her pass!" None of the Yi'ingo would dare to face Sky and Bastian. The women backed off and allowed Sage to pass, bowing to the royals.

Sage tore a piece off her dress as a bandage to contain the bleeding on Gabriel's shoulder. "Ollie, get us some water, please."

The boy ran and returned promptly.

Gabriel drank the water and felt his voice return "Thank you, my love. Take a seat; this will be over soon," he said reassuringly. Bastian and Sky now stood on either side of Gabriel, replacing the two Yi'ingo warriors.

"Son, why did you spare the life of the dragon?" Marcus repeated the question.

"My king, our ancestors created the Wali'ingooteer to help and protect us. They were designed to be loyal to their masters. When we became divided by war, our enemies used the dutiful Wali'ingooteer against us. The dragons were only serving their masters and their purpose. It was not their fault that Sathian decided to attack his own people." He paused to clear his throat and gather his strength. "For years now, the Wali'ingooteer have lived quietly and peacefully in the mountains until this one was called upon to test my bravery. I will not rule a kingdom that punishes the ones that fulfil their duties. I won't rule a kingdom that seeks revenge on other casualties of war. You asked me to lead this land in peace. Peace does not start with unnecessary death. The real monsters died many years ago. Today, we are all victims, even the dragons."

The audience's reaction was mixed. The Ange'el clapped and cheered, as did some of the Hu'urei. Most of the Yi'ingo and Ma'asai remained silent; they didn't share the compassion of the Ange'el. The Wali'ingooteer had been the cause of numerous deaths within their armies and many warriors were still grieving the loss of their friends and family.

Marcus spoke, "People of Ahe'ey, do not confuse his actions with lack of bravery. It would have been easier to kill the Wali'ingooteer than to stand trial."

"If Sky and Bastian hadn't intervened he would be dead," Amalia retorted.

"Ahe'ey does not need a warlord who fights and wins battles by himself. We need a leader who inspires others to act and follow his or her greatness, preferably without bloodshed. A ruler who unites us and encourages us to reach our full potential. A compassionate king. My son is such a leader."

"A coward is never a leader. There is no space for compassion on the battlefield," Amalia replied, full of conviction.

Gabriel felt his legs collapse under him. His entire body hung from the chains around his wrists, placing extra stress on his injured shoulder. The voices around him seemed to vanish in a fog. *I'm not a king. I don't want it,* he thought.

"We need to leave the battlefield! The war is over. We all lost." Viviane raised her voice as she faced her mother. Her words echoed across the arena.

Marcus held his wife's hand and continued, "Amalia repeatedly accuses Gabriel of being a coward. I would like to address this once and for all. Viviane will show you three distinct parts of Gabriel's life that will leave no doubt that he is the rightful king of this land."

Gabriel looked at his mother and begged her to stop with his eyes. She pushed a wave of love at him as she rejected his plea. He felt hopeless as Viviane prepared to unleash her power.

Apollo

Viviane closed her eyes and entered a deep trance. Her mind's eye connected to every Ahe'ey present in the arena and she prepared to show them scenes of a not-so-distant past. The images in everyone's minds were vivid and in full colour. A tapestry of historical moments in Gabriel's life, experienced by the Ahe'ey as if they were being witnessed first-hand. Smells, textures, and even emotional states were shared through Viviane's ability to connect with the minds of her people and exchange information. This was a skill that, of her generation, only Viviane had mastered. Before her, only her grandmother had possessed such a capability. She had shared with Viviane that the power to unlock it came from pure integrity of voice. It was a gift that would be lost in the moment it was used to manipulate the truth.

The Ahe'ey saw a little blonde girl; she was no more than six years of age, walking barefoot in what it seemed to be a war zone. She was speaking a foreign language that some of the Ange'el scholars would recognise as Albanian. She screamed for her mother and father and pointed at a collapsed building in front of her. Bombs were dropping from the sky and people ran in all directions, attempting to flee from the danger. Soon after, they saw Gabriel run in the girl's direction and pick her up.

She whispered to him in Albanian, "My mum and dad . . . "

"They sent me to take care of you," he murmured as he embraced her in his arms. At this time, a bomb exploded beside them. Gabriel hit the floor, using his body to protect the girl. He continued to speak to her in her language. "It's going to be okay. I'm invincible," he said with a smile.

"Like Apollo?"

Gabriel was surprised. "Yes! Like Apollo." The little girl smiled.

Viviane felt Gabriel's emotions as he recalled the first time he had met his eldest daughter. From the moment they met, he had known that she was a special girl. Highly intuitive, she had called Gabriel by the name of one of his most famous ancestors—Apollo—an Ahe'ey leader that had significant interactions with humans during his lifetime.

"I'm Sanije, but people call me Sage. Apollo is my favourite Greek god."

"I'm Apollo. Very nice to meet you, Sage." He winked at her, trying to keep her calm. "Can I tell you a secret?"

The girl's eyes expanded with curiosity.

"Apollo wasn't really Greek or a god."

She smiled, and he smiled back.

Several men with machine guns moved in their direction, shooting continually. "Can you keep your eyes closed for me, Sage?" The little girl complied and hid her face in his neck. Gabriel stood, picked Sage up with his left arm, and without letting go of her, he fought all six men with great speed and agility. The Ahe'ey at the arena were witnessing his exceptional skills in full health, and they had never seen anything like it, not even from the champions of Ahe'ey during the Games. His mastery of sword fighting and martial arts was outstanding, and his ability to avoid the bullets was unsettling even for those used to the powerful skills of the royals. In a matter of seconds, the men were all dead. He kissed Sage's head and ran.

Viviane looked at Sage, who was sobbing. The queen allowed everyone in the arena to experience what Sage was feeling in that moment. The human Ange'el was faced with the memories of the death of her family and rescue by her Apollo, a nickname that all his children had adopted from that moment onwards. She remembered how safe she had felt in his arms, how his large hands had wrapped around her body and head gently as they ran, how he used to tell her stories of her favourite Greek gods to soothe her to sleep, how he had encouraged her to develop her skills. His unshakeable confidence in her capabilities had allowed her to flourish in a new land, one that had initially dismissed and rejected the human child as an equal. In the eyes of her father, she had seen her own infinite potential and bloomed into one of the most skilful healers in Ahe'ey. He was her hero and her role model.

Preparations

The Pierre Hotel, New York

Morgan felt minuscule as she sat on a sofa by the large twenty-foot high arched window that filled the room with twilight. She'd read somewhere that the windows of the penthouse were replicas of the cathedral windows in the Versailles chapel. The place was fit for royalty, although she wasn't even sure that there were any royals left who could afford such a lavish home.

Morgan was watching the girls get ready for the ball in one of the many bedrooms of the penthouse. Scout and Quinn sat on a bed so large that it could easily sleep an entire family and their pets. Morgan observed the expressions of the two young warriors with amusement. They focused on the task as if they were playing a game of chess. Occasionally, Quinn would shoot her a glance, asking for some reassurance, and Morgan promptly returned a nod and a smile.

Morgan was startled by the fresh scars on Scout's upper arms, shoulders, and back. "What happened? Are those battle injuries? I thought the war was over?"

"Nothing much. They will heal; my blood is very pure," Scout said defensively.

"Of course," Morgan replied, attempting to connect with the warrior.

"Amalia's whip," Quinn said matter-of-factly. Scout's threatening eyes cut to Quinn, who shrugged her shoulders, frowning. "It's the truth."

"Why would she do this to you?" Morgan asked, startled.

"It's time to go." Scout jumped to her feat, but Morgan stood up and grabbed her hand.

"You look beautiful, Scout. Just perfect, but we have to cover those scars or they will call too much attention. We're trying to fit in, remember?" Morgan pulled a middle layer of tulle from Quinn's skirt and wrapped it around Scout's shoulders.

"What's wrong with my scars? Don't humans have them?" Scout's pouty, rosy lip sunk to the floor as her eyebrows arched in the opposite direction.

"There's nothing wrong with your scars, Scout. Unlike you, human women tend to be ashamed of theirs, so they cover them up. It's quite silly, but you need to become one of them today."

"Humans are ugly, with or without scars," Scout retorted coldly.

"Yet nothing is uglier than your words. Hideous."

"Should I lie to be pleasant?"

"You should look for beauty in kindness, joy, love, and friendship. Beauty is skin deep." Scout shrugged and turned away.

"You're wasting your time with her, Morgan," Quinn said as she put on her coat. "What animal is this?" She brushed her hand through the fur of her long white coat.

"It's probably fake," Morgan said.

"A fake animal?" Quinn asked in disbelief.

"Fake fur. Made artificially."

"This place is totally weird," Quinn replied, rolling her eyes and pulling her skirt up to attach her sword to her leg.

"You don't need your sword, Quinn."

"I won't use it. It's just there in case something goes wrong. We need to protect the code of the royal blood, right?"

"Right." Morgan replied, "But don't use it and keep it out of sight."

"Sure," Quinn assured Morgan with a victorious smile.

"You both look stunning. Off you go; your car is waiting." Morgan searched her memory. She tried to reassure herself that she had provided the girls with all the information and advice that they would need. "Stay out of trouble," she said, wishing she could go with them.

THE PARTY

Waldorf Astoria, New York

Quinn held her breath as they entered the Grand Ballroom of the Waldorf Astoria. The room soared at least four stories high. In the centre of the ceiling hung a large shiny chandelier that drenched the room with sparkling light.

Young people danced in the middle of the room. They were watched by others that sat at round tables set around the dance floor. Quinn felt as if the entire event was taken out of one of the old history books that she'd read back at Ahe'ey with her father. She missed him, and she was worried about the battle with the dragon. *It'll be fine, just fine*, she thought, repeating the words Gabriel used to reassure her every time she was scared. Quinn tried to focus her thoughts on her current mission; she was proud to be Morgan's guardian. She knew her father would approve, and she couldn't wait to go back and tell Ollie about her adventures in New York. *He'll be so jealous.* She smiled.

The men at the ball were all dressed in black, the colours of the Hu'urei. *Not a good sign.* They wore funny bows around their necks and seemed to treat the girls as if they were fragile and disabled creatures. Quinn blamed it on the girls' shoes; she'd tried some at the store, and it was clear that this was the likely reason for the girls' meekness. The air smelled of sweet flowers and vanilla; the sickly scent gave her a headache, and the stiff bodice of her dress didn't allow her breathe properly.

As Quinn looked around, she sighed. Even in New York she could barely find anyone non-Caucasian in the room. The women were all tall, mostly blonde and seemed to drop the Gs at the end of their words. Quinn had to work extra hard to listen in on the mindless chatter.

Quinn's Asian features didn't seem to be cause for attention. All eyes were on her Ahe'ey companion, who stunned anyone that had the misfortune to land their gaze on her. Scout was, without a doubt, the most beautiful creature they'd ever seen. Eyes widened, jaws dropped, and the chatter stopped as both men and women followed the young warrior as she walked across the room. At first, Scout hunched her shoulders and lowered her head, attempting to hide from the prying eyes, but soon she gave up, lifted her gaze and gave them a pose so regal that Quinn thought for a second that it was Sky and not Scout walking in front of her.

Secretly, Quinn quite liked her grumpy companion. She respected Scout's skills in the arena, and felt sorry every time Amalia punished the young warrior. Quinn knew that Scout had reasons to be bad-tempered; she didn't have a family to love her and protect her. She was all alone, living under the shadow of Amalia's terrifying rule.

"Hi! I didn't see you in the receiving line." A young man approached the two women with a wide, friendly smile on his face. He was no more than fifteen years old. His dark hair was held back by such a large amount of shiny gel that Quinn could see her reflection on his head. His adoring eyes were set on Scout, who towered over him in all her majesty and perfection.

"We don't speak English," Quinn said in perfect English, while Scout simply turned her back to him. His eyes travelled down to meet Quinn's suspicious gaze, and he extended his hand towards her.

"Pleased to meet you. My name is Thomas Mathews Joyce, but you can call me Tom. My uncle, Sir Charles, asked me to look for you and keep you company tonight."

Quinn raised her hand, covered by an elbow-length satin glove, and shook his hand. His eyes moved once again to her companion who turned to face them both. Her dress and perfectly arranged hair bun didn't soften Scout's cold, scornful gaze. She was as intimidating as ever. Quinn saw the poor boy shrink under Scout's mighty stare. He released a nervous laugh and attempted to fill the awkward silence with some light conversation.

"Have you set your eyes on a young suitor yet?" Tom asked Quinn casually.

"Suitor?" She looked up to meet his eyes.

"A rich, eligible bachelor to marry. Isn't that what this is all about? My sister looks like a kid in a candy store." He glanced in the direction of a bubbly young woman surrounded by a group of men dressed in military uniforms.

"Marry? I'm too young for that. I don't even know if I . . . I mean . . . I don't speak English." Quinn felt Scout's elbow hit her ribs and she winced with pain. "Ouch! You bastard!"

Several older ladies turned towards them with wide eyes and downturned, pursing lips.

"You seem to know a lot of English." Tom laughed loudly, managing to annoy Scout further.

Quite an achievement, thought Quinn.

The Yi'ingo warrior grabbed Tom's wrist and squeezed it.

"Where's your uncle?" Scout spoke softly but furiously.

"Get off," Tom said, trying to contain his pain. "I'll take you to him."

Scout released him, and he massaged his wrist as he guided them around people and tables to the opposite side of the hall.

"Someone should teach you some manners, young lady."

"We aren't ladies; we're warriors," Quinn replied just before Scout slapped her in the head.

"Sure, sure you are," Tom said dismissively. "Feminists, right?" He shot a glance at Quinn who replied with a puzzled look, shrugging her shoulders. "Well, today you are belles at the ball, rubbing shoulders with the crème de la crème of the next generation of the international elite. This event is attended by granddaughters of presidents, world leaders, and industry giants. So do try to behave, will you?"

"I'm the future king's daughter." Quinn couldn't help herself; she was proud of it. "After dad wins the battle with the dragon, he'll be king."

Tom chuckled and raised his eyebrow, "A princess? I see."

Quinn felt Scout's hand clasp firmly around her arm. "Stop talking."

"She's the princess and who are you? The Ice Queen of Tashkent?" Tom asked Scout jovially, but as soon as he looked into her eyes, he gulped and blushed.

"The one who'll break all your teeth if you don't move quickly," Scout spat her threat sternly.

"My uncle will come soon. You must wait," he said, frustrated. "Why are all pretty girls big bullies?"

"I'm not a bully," Quinn replied. He looked at her with an amused look on his face, and she blushed a little as he leaned in and used his index finger to move a blue lock of hair from her eyes.

"Come, Princess; let's dance." He grabbed her hand and pulled her closer to him. She instinctively reached for her sword, before deciding that the boy was harmless.

"I don't know how to," she interjected, placing her hands on his chest and pushing him away.

He released her immediately and said, "Come. I'll teach you. Just follow my lead."

"I want to lead."

"But you don't know how to dance. Come on." His arms reached towards her, and after some vacillation, she grabbed his hand and allowed him to lead. "You are a funny little thing, aren't you?"

"Nothing funny about me. If you wanna talk funny, we should talk about your greasy hair and that stupid bow." He chuckled and pulled her towards him. Her leg brushed against his, and he pulled back with surprise as he bumped her sword.

"What's that?"

"My sword," she whispered.

After a brief pause he replied, "Right, you're a warrior. I forgot."

"Yeah," she murmured, and he seemed to accept it at face value.

"So, are you Tatiana or Anya Allabergenova?"

"I'm Quinn, but don't tell anyone, okay?" she asked, pleading with her eyes.

"Oh," he said worriedly, "I must dash; it seems I must find some other girl with blue hair."

"It's me; I'm the one sent to meet your uncle."

"Okay," he said, looking even more confused, "that's fine then."

"We made up those names. I just want you to know my real name. Quinn, but you can call me Quinny if you want." She immediately regretted her unabashed enthusiasm as a cocky expression replaced his casual smile.

He smirked, "Do you like me, Quinn?" His eyebrow went up and he attempted to project an overconfident smoulder that made her roll her eyes.

"No, not like that," she said decisively. "I just don't have a lot of friends that are boys, and no human friends so . . . "

"You are the weirdest girl I know."

"Thanks," she replied, pleased with herself.

Once she'd learned the steps, Quinn stepped forward, once and then twice.

"What are you doing?" Tom asked just as she stomped on his foot.

"Leading."

"Girls don't lead."

"You're funny," Quinn said, chuckling. She quite liked Tom's sense of humour.

After a bit of a struggle on the dance floor, the girl realised he might not have been joking. She persisted, stepping on his feet a few more times as she battled for control. Defeated, he frowned and then he allowed her to lead. Tom ducked his head and looked around. She noticed that his face flushed every time someone looked in their direction.

"So, if you don't want to get married, what are you going to do with your time?" he said, finally getting over his embarrassment.

"Join the army and win the Games."

"Oh! What games?"

"I want to win them all, but I should have a good chance at archery because my size won't matter there."

Suddenly, a large bearded man stood by their side and Scout approached them shortly after. "Tom, you found them," he said.

"I did! This is Quinn. Apparently, the other names were made up."

"Quinn? Gabriel's daughter?" She nodded with enthusiasm. The man wrapped his arms around Quinn and lifted her off the floor. "Quinn, my dear. Your father told me everything about you. How is your training going?" The man's happiness was so effusive that Quinn couldn't help but smile.

"Very well, Sir."

"This is my uncle, Sir Charles H Mathews. And this is . . . ," Tom looked at Scout and waited for her response. The warrior stood coldly, refusing to oblige.

"This is Scout," replied Quinn. "I have a letter for you." She gave the letter to the man.

"Thank you Quinn. Would you like a cocktail, girls?" asked Sir Charles, placing his hands on the girls' backs and moving them away from the dance floor.

"We are here to pick up the package," Scout replied firmly.

"We'll take care of business in a second, my dear. It's important that you act like you belong here, okay?"

Scout nodded.

"Let's go to the Jade Room."

As Quinn passed by one of the dining tables, she extended her white gloved hand and picked up a leg of duck.

"You might want to take the gloves off first, Your Highness," Tom smirked as she wolfed down the duck. Quinn simply nodded and dropped her gloves on the floor as her puzzled companion picked them up with a disapproving look.

"This is awful," Quinn said, spitting out the duck and hitting his shiny black shoe.

"You have the manners of a truck driver, Your Highness."

"Warriors don't need manners."

"You'll never get a boyfriend if you continue to behave like that."

"I told ya. Not looking for one. Are you deaf or something?"

"Shut up human," Scout ordered from behind the couple.

"What's wrong with your sister?" Tom asked.

"She's not my sister."

"You must stop talking," Scout repeated.

"Yeah, I know. Sorry, I got overexcited," Quinn murmured apologetically.

They all left the Grand Ballroom and headed to another large room where cocktails were being served. Sir Charles handed the girls two tall glasses filled with some red fizzy drink. Quinn took a sip and immediately closed her eyes, struggling to cope with the tingling sensation inside her nose. She sneezed.

Sir Charles stood to one side, quietly reading the letter.

"I'm hungry," Scout stated as her stomach growled.

"Don't touch the food; that bird had been dead for days. 'Twas disgusting," Quinn replied, contorting her mouth.

"Ladies, here are your presents." Sir Charles handed the girls two cyan bags with large bows. The bags read *Tiffany & Co.* "Keep these safe and ensure you only open them at home. Do you understand?" The old man's sombre expression left no doubt about the contents of the bags. Quinn nodded.

"It's time to go," Scout ordered.

"Quinn, give my regards to your father." Sir Charles approached the girl and murmured into her ear. "Please tell him we miss him, and that we can't wait to see him again."

Quinn nodded and embraced Sir Charles, "I miss him too. Very much."

The old man handed her a card. "If you need anything, my dear, don't hesitate to call me. My Tom will escort you back to your hotel." The old man smiled and moved away.

"We don't need you. Go away." Scout said, looking at Tom with her usual aggressive disdain.

"I'm taking my friend Quinny home. What you do is none of my business." Tom grabbed Quinn's hand and started walking towards the door.

"I'm not helpless, you know?" Quinn scoffed.

"Clearly," he replied as he kept walking, holding her hand tightly.

"I can take care of myself," she said, frustrated.

"I know. I just want to spend some more time with you; okay, friend?"

"Yeah okay," she beamed as she looked back at Scout who followed closely behind.

The Price

Sky was trying to make sense of the images that were flashing through her mind. She was experiencing extreme cognitive dissonance between what she knew of Gabriel and the information that had been emerging over the last few days. The wings, the heroism, and the love she'd seen in him, all hidden from her, *why?* She felt guilt every time she looked at the Ange'el, knowing that her vote and voice could end his pain and even save his life. But her people had to come first—the safety of Ahe'ey relied on having the right ruler, a ruler who wouldn't abandon or disappoint them at the first sign of danger. The Ahe'ey needed a leader who was prepared to walk through fire for them, to sacrifice everything and everyone to keep Ahe'ey safe and enable it to prosper. He was no such leader.

Viviane's eyes glanced to Sky, her gaze cutting, then she closed her eyes once again, and Sky and the Ahe'ey saw a young Gabriel. He was no more than sixteen-years-old and his face reflected the young optimism in his heart. He was by a lake, talking with Marcus.

"My son, Ahe'ey needs a strong female leader to helm its rebirth from Sathian's flames of terror. The war on women has brought destruction to our kingdom for long enough. We need a Phoenix, a warrior queen to rise from the ashes and lead us to victory. Viviane and I will continue to rule, but we need a soldier that can inspire our troops into action. Sky is very young but has all the qualities of a military leader. She has the strongest warrior genes in the land. She is fearless, an outstanding fighter, and a child of royal blood with all the capabilities associated with it."

Gabriel nodded, smiling with pride. "Yeah, you should have seen her yesterday, climbing the tallest tree in Ange'el. She's daring, fast, resilient, and resourceful. I'll join the warriors to serve her and fight at her side. We'll—"

What happened to you? Why did you leave me? Jealousy? Sky's mind was spinning with a thousand questions.

"No. There is something that is holding her back." Marcus looked at his son with tenderness.

"What is it, Father?"

"You, my son. From the moment she arrived here, you kindly took her under your protection and taught her to fight, and to survive. She adores you; her connection to you is strong, and she sees you as her leader and her role model. While you are around, she will follow instead of lead. While you protect her, she will not flourish and become the warrior she was born to be. She believes you are more capable, when you have the potential to be equals."

"She's just younger than me. That's all. She's growing and learning every day. Yesterday, she beat me at—"

"We must separate you if she is to achieve her full potential and gain her independence. But first, you need to make her believe she deserves it; you need to make her rely on herself. She will not grow in confidence or capability while you hold her hand."

What have you done? Sky felt her heart sink to her stomach.

"But why can't I support her while she leads?"

"Gabriel, while you are her hero, she will not lead. While you stand beside her, others will not see her, even if you are both equally matched. The Ange'el's blood was designed to project greatness, trust, and charisma. Even before you have earned it with your actions and values, people will believe you deserve it because of your looks, because of your glow. It is an unfair advantage, and Sky is as susceptible to your light as anyone else."

"This glow, this shell. It's a curse." Gabriel's mouth twisted down.

"Only those who truly deserve it see it that way. I am proud of you, Gabriel." Marcus placed his hand on his son's shoulder. The boy's eyes refused to leave the ground.

The next scene to enter their minds was well known to Sky. It was the nightmare that had festered in her dreams for many years. She saw herself in the forest. She was fourteen years old, Gabriel was just beside her, and they were walking to the lake to swim. Back then, he had been spontaneous and unaffected, always smiling and teasing her. Sky felt her heart sink as she remembered her young companion. How much she missed his light.

The cousins saw four Hu'urei rebels appear from the middle of the trees, swords in hand and ready to attack. Gabriel saw them coming, paused to think, and held back, doing nothing as Sky fought and killed the first men. He stood there, motionless, watching her carefully.

Sky witnessed her younger self fight four huge Hu'urei simultaneously, and she was proud. *What a brave and strong little girl.* While she battled the last three attackers, Sky could now see that Gabriel was just behind a tree, following her every move. Behind his back appeared two other Hu'urei that he fought and killed swiftly and quietly. He stayed hidden as she sat alone in the forest amongst the dead bodies and cried. She wasn't sobbing because of the attack, but because he had abandoned her. He stood there hidden, crying silently, as she made her first step to becoming the Warrior Queen. They had never discussed it. His face said it all. It was the face of a boy devastated by what he had been forced to do, a young Ange'el who had just lost his best friend, a prince who had deliberately diminished himself in the hearts and minds of his people.

In the next image, they saw Gabriel wearing Ma'asai armour and putting on a helmet that covered most of his face. He looked identical to

Marcus, and no one ever suspected that he was there, in the battle. They saw him fight side by side with Sky and Bastian in every major battle, saving their lives on a multitude of occasions. The Ahe'ey saw the Ange'el prince kill a dragon who was seconds away from crushing Sky with his teeth. He left the battles early so that no one would ever know he was there. Gabriel and Bastian embraced at the end of a battle, showing that Bastian knew his cousin was there. For the first time in years, Sky understood why there was such a strong bond between the two men. She finally comprehended the blind faith and loyalty Bastian had for his cousin, the type of connection that could only be forged in war.

The images kept rushing through the minds of the Ahe'ey: Young Gabriel pulling out of the Games that he loved participating in so much. Sky's constant mocking and disdain. Amalia's rage when she learned that he had abandoned Sky in the forest to fend for herself against the Hu'urei. Oliver's frustration over asking his father to prove his courage, and Gabriel's response to his son. They saw Sky transform from a sweet but fearless girl into a cold, rage-ridden warrior queen. They saw Gabriel diminish and then disappear from Ahe'ey's public life and the hearts of his people. They could see the price that both had paid.

Sky shook her head to push all the images away from her mind. She closed her eyes for a moment and then looked at Viviane and Marcus. Her eyes were wet, full of fury, and her face red. She lifted her sword and turned in the direction of Gabriel. The audience gasped, expecting the worst. She screamed with rage, pulling her sword backwards ready to strike, and strike she did. With one single blow, she broke the chains that held him to the pole. She dropped her sword and grabbed him as he fell; they were both on their knees, holding each other tightly.

He whispered, "I'm sorry, Sky. I'm so sorry. I lied to you. I betrayed you."

She helped him stand up. They stood, and they embraced, crying, hurting, and grieving. After a few minutes, she composed herself, kneeled, and presented her sword to him.

"My king, you have my sword and my allegiance." At that moment, all the Yi'ingo warriors in the room kneeled, followed swiftly by their Ma'asai peers.

"Stand up, my sister, my hero." His voice quivered, revealing his fragile state. "I'm alive today only because of your courage, kindness, and loyalty. Ahe'ey is at peace because of the sacrifices you have made on our behalf. Stand up, sister. Please stand up. I beg you."

Everyone was up and clapping in support as Sky and Gabriel stood together, and yet Marcus asked them to take a seat. "We are not done yet. We have one more thing to show you."

Virtue and Sacrifice

Viviane looked at the pale face of her son and spoke directly to his mind: *Hang in there, Gabriel. It will not be long now. We need every single soul in Ahe'ey on your side.* Bastian was beside Gabriel, lifting him up by his left shoulder. Sky was by his right side, and Sage was giving him water and keeping his body cool with a wet cloth. Marcus looked at Viviane and nodded. She closed her eyes and went back into a trance, connecting with the minds of her people, and listening carefully to the feelings of her dear family.

The audience was now at the Met, watching Gabriel and Morgan fall in love with each other. Gabriel looked at his mother, frustrated and in pain.

"Why are you doing this to me?" he whispered, shaking his head in despair. He didn't want to go over those memories. He didn't want to share his inner world with the entire population of Ahe'ey. But he had no choice. The audience saw the attack at the Met; they saw their fights, they saw their reunion, and they saw him jump against a fast-moving car to save her life. At that moment, many in Ahe'ey realised for the first time the seriousness of Gabriel's wounds during his battle with the dragon.

"This is good," Bastian said. "This is good." But that was far from the end of it, as Viviane continued to share her son's heart with the world.

The audience felt how much he adored Morgan. They heard them make vows to one another. They saw them melt in each other's arms until there was no doubt in their minds that she was his world and soul mate. Viviane wept as she shared these images with the crowd. Her eyes were closed, her heart in pain from the punishment she had unleashed on her son. The next scene showed Marcus and Viviane talking to Gabriel and demanding from him the ultimate sacrifice, and his response.

"If anyone has any doubts that Gabriel has put Ahe'ey and humankind before his life and his love for Morgan, speak now." Marcus looked around and then repeated, this time shouting, *"Speak now; I dare you!"*

After a moment, Joshua got up and walked slowly down the stairs. He stood in front of Gabriel, put his hand on his left shoulder and said, "Cousin, you are my leader and my king." And then he did something even more surprising. He stood beside Sky. Suddenly, the Yi'ingo left her place without once looking at Joshua. There were some murmurs in the audience where the Hu'urei were seated.

"How dare she!" someone shouted from the audience.

Sky went to a Yi'ingo warrior and took her sword. She returned to Joshua and gave it to him.

He smiled and bowed his head to his half-sister. Josh turned to Gabriel and said, "Sir, you have my sword."

Everyone stood up cheering and clapping; the environment was electric. Half of Ahe'ey was celebrating, the other half embracing and crying. Then, Viviane delivered the final blow. They stood quietly as they watched Gabriel open the passage without the moonstone. They stood frozen as he said goodbye to his love. They stood stunned as they watched Gabriel transform into his highest self, the winged creature of light that inhabited his heart, an Ange'el, the most virtuous of all Ange'el.

This is you, my son. Accept it, Viviane spoke directly to her son's mind who was seeing his own transformation for the first time. She saw his confusion with her mind's eye. Her son was humbled, and overwhelmed by the revelation.

The people of Ahe'ey were silenced by the heavenly images in their heads. Their skin felt the energy that emanated from Gabriel. They opened their eyes to look at the broken prince covered in blood and sacrifice, and their hearts showered the Ange'el with love and respect. At that moment, both Viviane and Marcus, holding hands, turned to face Amalia and the rest of the elders that stood behind her, and they waited.

Amalia spoke.

"Thirty-four years ago, I swore to never again bow to any man. I saw the rape of my Ahe'ey sisters, my land devastated by war, and lost my own daughters and granddaughter to those dark times. I have seen all my grandchildren thrive, but I vowed years ago that no man would ever again take the throne. Today, I stand before the purest of all Ahe'ey, and he happens to be a man and my grandson. All that I have witnessed today has shown me that, above all else, he is the truest leader of this land. I have hope that he will be able to lead us in peace as well as my Sky was able to lead us in war."

Amalia walked to Gabriel and looked him in the eyes. Viviane felt her mother's apprehension. Amalia shivered as she observed his features; he had a perfect likeness to her nemesis, Sathian.

He is not Sathian, Mother, encouraged Viviane.

Amalia overcame her fear and kissed the Ange'el on the mouth. She then picked up Gabriel's and Sky's hands and brought them together, wrapping her hands around their hands. Many in the audience, including the queen, the king, and Bastian, understood the symbolic message. Neither Sky nor Gabriel realised what she was doing; they were both too overwhelmed with emotion. The audience clapped. Viviane felt compassion for Bastian. In his eyes, a shadow of sadness, a pinch of pain, a quiet resignation. He loved them both. He wished them well.

Every single leader in Ahe'ey surrounded Gabriel. Marcus and Viviane hugged each other, crying with joy and relief. Everyone was celebrating. The children ran to Gabriel. Oliver looked taller and proud. The Ange'el was barely able to stand, but he made a real effort to smile for them. The crowd rushed to pick up the Ange'el, to lift him up and parade him through the city. Sage attempted to stop them. The young woman placed herself between the mob and Gabriel.

"No. Back off. He's too weak," shouted the golden Ange'el, extending her arms. Sky and Bastian were about to use brute force to stop the mob when Gabriel lifted his head and spoke.

"Wait, my friends. I must now retire to mend my wounds, but I have a worthy representative who would love to celebrate with you on my behalf," Gabriel said, looking at his son. The crowd lifted Ollie, who seemed overjoyed to stand on behalf of his father.

Sage frowned as she watched the crowd take her brother. Joshua looked at her and said, "Don't worry, my lady. You have my word that I'll watch over him and will bring him back in one piece. No harm will come to Oliver."

Sage smiled and nodded, "Thank you, Josh."

"I'd do anything for you, sweet Sage," he murmured as he followed Ollie and the crowd.

Bastian supported Gabriel as they walked to the Sacred House followed by Sage and Sky. "You did it!"

"We did it," the Ange'el replied.

Sky put her hand on the shoulder of the younger woman. "You have a fearless heart, Sage."

Sage gave Sky a side hug. "I'm surrounded by great role models, my dearest kinswoman."

Viviane sat on her throne, numb, exhausted, ridden with guilt and relief. The first phase of their plan had been accomplished successfully. The queen and king knew that there was nothing more powerful and more inspiring than the public sacrifice and martyrdom of a pure-blooded Ange'el. The reaction of the masses was predictable, coated with a religious quality that transcended time and culture.

Over the millennia, Ange'el had been burned at the stake, nailed to the cross, hanged by the neck, impaled, drowned, lashed, and tortured. These stories, like the viral memes on the humans' internet, were like tsunamis—tectonic shifts that inspired impossible change and united those who could not be united. These were events that changed the course of humankind. The sacrifice of the Ange'el—their death, resurrection, suffering, and loss—moved mountains. It was a tool, to be used in desperate times; an instrument designed for maximum impact; a strategy that had been unleashed by mothers and fathers on their Ange'el daughters and sons as they reached the peak of their glow, of their power.

Viviane was heartbroken and exasperated every time she was reminded that, to advance their enlightenment, both humans and Ahe'ey demanded bloodshed. Martyrdom was required where logic and love should suffice. The symbol they worshipped was ultimately their doom. The cross, sword, muscle, blood, violence, war—all needed to be purged from the definition of leadership and heroism. *One day . . . but not today.* Today, blood had been spilled on the arena—her son's blood. Violence and pain had been unleashed on the best of them. Today, they had delivered an experience designed to bring all Ahe'ey together. Carefully planned propaganda. At the centre of their elaborate campaign, a pure Ange'el whose genes had been designed specifically to seduce the entire world.

The first goal of the rulers of Ahe'ey had been achieved; the land was once again united under the sacrifice of a leader who inspired change. There was no time to rest; they had a lot more to accomplish before the solstice.

HUNTERS

Scout left the taxi followed by Quinn and Tom. They stood in front of the private entrance to The Pierre's penthouse.

"Ladies, it was great to meet you," Tom said, shooting a wide smile at Quinn.

Scout noticed that the boy's teeth were unusually white. She wondered if he'd washed them with light-absorbing particles. *How odd.* Her stomach was still growling; she hadn't had proper food since they had arrived in New York. Everything in human land tasted like old rotten food and metal. She turned to face the park and began walking in its direction.

"Where you going?" Quinn asked.

"Hunting."

"Good plan, I'm starving."

"Hunting?" Tom followed the girls; his pitch escalated as they approach the park. "Let's go back. This place is dangerous at night."

"We'll be fine, Tom. See you later," Quinn replied politely.

"Get lost, boy." Scout turned around and pressed her boot against his stomach, pushing him away. Tom was propelled backwards; he had to work hard to avoid falling.

"You don't need to be rude, Scout," Quinn said, placing her arm around the gangly boy. "Sorry, friend. You should go now."

Tom brushed off his white shirt with his hands; his face was flushed, and his lips were pressed tightly together. He took a moment to compose himself.

"My grandfather told me to escort you home. I can't just leave you alone in Central Park at night, no matter how rude she is."

Scout was too busy searching for food to pay any further attention to the young man. She dropped her long white coat to the ground, gathered her puffy skirt and tucked most of it under the silver belt. The two young women handed their Tiffany's bags to Tom and scanned the area, looking for their prey. Not even their conspicuous white dresses prevented them from blending in, disappearing between trees and shrubs. In a matter of minutes, they'd found and killed a possum and a duck. As they returned to meet Tom, Scout saw him surrounded by two hooded figures, both holding knives.

"Give me those bags," one of the men ordered.

Scout looked at Quinn and raised two fingers on her right hand, waving it in a circular motion. It was a simple Yi'ingo war sign that meant full, overt attack, a manoeuvre set to intimidate and drive away the opponent. They dropped the hunting spoils, lifted their swords, and ran towards the hooded figures, screaming as loud as they could. As they approached, they engaged in a series of acrobatic jumps, cutting the air around them with their swords as they grunted and screeched like a couple of Wali'ingooteer in heat. Scout worked extra hard on her intimidation tactics; she worried that the silly dress and the neat, high bun on top of her head could undermine the fearlessness of her war dance.

She saw Quinn take her dagger, still coated in the blood of the possum, and clean the blade on the bodice of her gown, watching the attackers with a condescending feral sneer. Scout couldn't help but chuckle at the efforts of her tiny companion, and she decided to up her game. She pulled the silk band out of her hair, releasing her white hair over her shoulders as her purple crest landed in front of her eyes. She waved her sword in front of her, gritting her teeth ferociously.

The two attackers stood frozen, confused or scared by the strange

Yi'ingo war dance. The gowns, the blood, the swords, the fierceness and probably Scout's beauty all contributed to their surprise. The amazement was quickly replaced by fear as the two young women moved to attack. The thugs ran away fast. The warriors chased them for long enough to ensure that they wouldn't be back.

As Scout walked back, she used the tip of her sword to lift Tom's jaw off the floor. The poor boy was pale and distressed as he stood holding the bags and staring at the two warriors. The girls looked at each other and laughed loudly.

"You okay, Tom?" Quinn asked with a warm smile, resting her sword over her shoulder.

"Perhaps . . . it's best I go now," he shot a fearful side glance at Scout.

"Stay; eat with us," Quinn replied as she began working on skinning and preparing the possum.

"I'm not hungry," he said, but after a moment his tone changed, and he asked in a high pitch, "*Who the hell are you?*"

"It's none of your business," Scout murmured.

"Just girls. Start the fire, will you Tom?" Quinn asked, too busy with her activity to notice Tom's queasy expression.

"How . . . do I do that?" He asked, puzzled. Then he shook his head, raised his arms and spoke assertively, "You can't just start a fire in the middle of Central Park. It's forbidden."

"Never mind," Quinn said, cleaning her dagger on her puffy white skirt and walking away to search for wood, leaves and bark. In no time, they lit the tinder nest and had the meat ready to barbecue.

Scout looked at Tom with suspicion and asked, "Don't you hunt?" He shook his head. "Vegan?" He shook his head again. She scratched her forehead, attempting to make sense of the puny boy. The Yi'ingo spread out the two white fake fur jackets on the ground, released her sword from her leg and sat on top of the rug. She pointed to the other jacket with her dagger, telling him to sit. After a few minutes, Quinn came back with more leaves and sat beside him.

"Are you cold?" Tom took off his jacket and offered it to Quinn.

"Nah, thanks. I'm all right. Want some?" Quinn pulled off a roasted duck wing and took a bite. He shook his head as his mouth contorted in horror.

"I'm getting out of here. You gals are nuts, and I don't want to be arrested."

Quinn and Scout ignored him and focused on the food.

"What's your Snapchat handle, Quinny?"

She looked at him confused.

"Facebook?"

He was met with another blank stare.

"Do you own a phone?"

She shook her head, and his right eyebrow went up in disbelief. He pulled up a pen from his jacket's pocket, wrote something on one of the bags, and then handed both bags to Quinn. "Here's my phone number and email address. Keep in touch, will you, Warrior Princess? You're a good pal. Stay safe."

She reached out and hugged him, and Scout saw his freckly cheeks turn crimson.

He faced Scout and made a military salute.

"Ice Queen."

She stared at him coldly behind the purple mane that covered her eyes. She had never met such a fragile and meek boy, but he was kinder than most of the boys she'd met at Ahe'ey.

"'Bye Tom," Quinn said sweetly as they watched him leave.

The night was clear, and the snow that had fallen in the previous days had completely dissipated. Scout was still unsettled by the hustle and bustle of the town. Even in the park she could hear all the cars and buses. She felt like she was in the belly of a Wali'ingooteer.

The human kid seemed to be having a good time; she devoured the duck voraciously, still finding time to smile between bites. Scout had never understood the insurmountable energy and enthusiasm of her companion. In the warrior's mind, Quinn had no reason to be so happy, after all, she was a mere human, and an odd one too—little, lacking muscle mass; not to mention the funny-shaped eyes.

Quinn's unshakable confidence and misplaced self-belief were a mystery to Scout. After years of fights in and out of the arena, Scout knew there was nothing that could keep Quinn down for long. She admired the human's resilience, even if she thought that one day all that pig-headed determination would come at a price.

A figure appeared out of the darkness. The two young women jumped back and reached for their swords as the stranger used their coats to cover the fire.

"The NYPD is coming; we must go," said the woman.

Scout recognised the vagabond that had helped Morgan when they emerged out of the fountain. She could hear the hooves of horses in the distance; the beasts seem to be trotting in their direction.

"What's an NYPD?" Quinn asked.

"Guards. They protect the park, and you're breaking the law," Rita replied with urgency.

"We can defend ourselves," Scout's face was contorted with disgust for the raggedy old woman. Rita pulled the sleeve of her torn and soiled red top, uncovering a moon-shaped tattoo in the back of her hand.

"Let's go," Rita said, holding Quinn's hand and running towards the darkest area of the park. The young human happily followed the tramp and Scout had no choice than to run after them, frustrated with Quinn's trusting temperament.

"Who are you?" Scout asked as they reached a dark hideaway surrounded by thick shrubs.

"Just a friend," Rita's tone was warm and sincere.

"A human with an Ahe'ey tattoo?" Scout growled.

"Who says I'm a human." Rita teased, still smiling at the Yi'ingo warrior.

"Your face does."

"Where did you learn to be so cruel, Scout?" The Yi'ingo was surprised at the human's tone. The old woman expressed disappointment and sadness instead of anger.

"How do you know my name?" Scout demanded.

"You have a birthmark on your right shoulder plate in the shape of the moon. A gift from your mother, perhaps the only thing she left you when she disappeared after your birth."

Scout pulled her dagger and pressed it against Rita's weathered neck.

"Who are you?" she repeated forcefully.

"You two must stay out of sight. You're calling too much attention to yourselves. If you are caught and someone takes a blood sample . . . ." Rita looked at Scout.

"Sorry Rita, you're right. We've been careless," Quinn said, trying to clean some of the blood off her dress. "We were quite hungry."

"We don't need advice from some rotten human."

"Go home." The eyes of the old woman suddenly locked on Scout's scars. The Yi'ingo had lost the tulle that Morgan had wrapped around her shoulders during the hunt. "Who did this to you?" Rita's expression changed.

Scout saw a strange mix of anger and intense emotion flood the woman's face and eyes. The vagabond placed her right hand on Scout's skin and closed her eyes. For a moment, an image flashed through the Yi'ingo's mind: a younger woman, dressed in the attire of an Ange'el priestess. A large, blonde Yi'ingo man wearing royal regalia lashed her incessantly.

Who did this to you? Scout heard inside her head, and her unspoken answer was delivered promptly, unfiltered by pride or shame. A single tear rolled down Rita's face before she composed herself. "Go home, warriors."

"Thank you, Rita," Quinn said politely. Rita smiled at the teen and then turned to Scout.

"Stay close to the young king, Scout. The young royals are our hope." Rita reached out once again to touch Scout's scars as the warrior walked backwards away from her. The old woman clasped the Yi'ingo's shoulder and closed her eyes as Scout reached for her dagger.

"Release me, or you'll die," Scout barked, gritting her teeth.

"Go home," Rita said, opening her eyes, turning her back, and walking away.

"Your scars. They are gone," Quinn murmured. "She healed—"

"No. I told you. My blood is royal," Scout replied, shaken by the interaction with Rita. "Let's go."

It took them hours to explain to Morgan what had happened. The human was quite concerned by their sorry state. The blood and the rags made Morgan panic the moment they walked through the door. Scout lost patience quite quickly, falling half-asleep on the sofa as Quinn recounted the events of the evening for the fourth or fifth time.

Scout couldn't help but think of the old vagabond and the strange familiarity she felt towards the stinking human. She recalled Rita's words, *'Stay close to the young king, Scout.'* But she quickly dismissed them. The wings didn't fool her, Sathian's shadow had many tricks. If Sky didn't trust him, neither would she, and an old lady with bad breath wouldn't change that.

GRIEF

All he saw was great darkness, and all he felt was a tremendous pain. Pain inhabited his heart, crushed his soul and far exceeded the discomfort of his broken body.

Viviane and Sage used all their skill and love to mend his wounds; they cleansed his gashes and wrapped him in a cocoon of healing gels. He was left to rest in complete silence. Everyone, including the children, was asked to respect his privacy. Guests were discouraged and even forbidden. He woke up for short periods of time, was forced by Sage to sip some soup or juice, and then he simply closed his eyes again. His body would mend with time, but the sadness in his heart was there to stay. He had nothing more to give. He had no energy to fake a smile or to be courteous to those around him. Gabriel was now able to grieve while the others celebrated.

Soon, they would come and demand more of him. They would ask him to, once again, deliver on his word. The dragon was the gentlest of all tests when compared to a lifetime without her, a loveless wedding, and the weight of a crown that rightly belonged to someone else.

Sky's mind was racing through the memories of every single interaction she had had with Gabriel. He had taken her anger, her frustration, and her rage without ever retaliating. The Ange'el had looked her straight in the eye as she accused him of being a coward time and time again. In public, as in private, Gabriel had let her say what she had to say without ever attempting to stop her, without ever dismissing her. He had just taken it, quietly and respectfully, while others had tried to put a stop to it.

The Ange'el had always been supportive of her as Marcus and Viviane made her the acting ruler of Ahe'ey. He'd been grateful when she had accepted his children and treated them as family, and he had always paid deference to her, accepting and respecting her status. Gabriel had diminished himself for her; he had trusted her ability to lead. She remembered his words of despair at the gate: *"Do it, Sky! For mercy's sake, end my torment."*

It was the middle of the night, but Viviane was up and opened the door to her room at the Sacred House as Sky approached it. Sky's eyes pierced the older woman's flesh; there was so much anger inside her, so much resentment towards the high priestess. Viviane lowered her eyes and took a step back, allowing Sky to enter the room.

"Why?" Sky asked, her voice trembling. "Why did you do it?"

"I had no other choice. War and hate were ravaging our land. We needed a strong military leader."

Sky raised her voice. "You had two strong leaders! You didn't need to separate us and hurt us in the way you did."

"The land needed a female ruler, a role model of strength. You were too close to Gabriel."

"We could have led together."

"You were too close and about to go into puberty. Soon, you would have been in love with each other, and you would have been lost in the security he provides. You were starting to forfeit your agency, your ability to choose and decide for yourself. I could not afford to wait until you regained it. I did not have years. I needed Gabriel working outside Ahe'ey, and I needed you to lead, not follow."

Viviane attempted to approach Sky, who backed away, rejecting the connection. "Our gift comes with tremendous responsibility and sacrifice. No one else could have led that army, Sky, only you. Amalia and the Yi'ingo would have refused a king, and it was not the right time to focus on that battle. There were other, more important issues to resolve."

"You cursed me."

"You are my daughter, the daughter of my sister. I have loved you as my own. You know that our gift is our curse, Sky. As queen, as high priestess, and as a member of the royal bloodline, I need to put the interests of the world before my interests and the love I have for my own children. I need to ask you to do the same. I ask you, my Sky, to believe me when I tell you that every suffering you and Gabriel have endured, I have felt in my heart, and it hurts me twice as much as it does any mother experiencing the pain of her children. Do not turn your rage on me as I try to fix what I had to break. Please, allow this to be a time for healing and rebuilding. Let me be by your side as we move forwards into peace." Viviane glowed with love and harmony. Anyone else would have succumbed immediately to her truth. Anyone else but Sky.

Sky was disarmed by the queen's vulnerability, but she wasn't ready to forgive Viviane. "You have used us all like puppets in a game of deceit and manipulation. You didn't treat us as capable leaders that could help you shape the future of Ahe'ey. You cursed us; manipulated us. You made me lose the last hope I had in men."

"Yes, I did. You were forged by fire. Your rage was the only weapon that could defeat the monster that ravaged our land. Your wrath saved us. Your vexation, your hate, was the call to action that brought our army together. Your thunder and your storm saved us."

"All that was grounded on a lie." Viviane's excuses exasperated Sky. The warrior looked straight into Viviane's eyes rejecting the queen's pleas for redemption.

"I ensured that your warrior gene was fully expressed. A soldier works best when the line between good and evil is crystal clear. Gabriel gave you hope in men; he blurred the line." Viviane lowered her gaze and cleared a tear from the corner of her eye.

"You say you love me, and yet you've underestimated me and belittled my ability to handle complexity."

"You won the war because you did not vacillate. Not once. I took away your heart, and, with it, your sole weakness as a warrior. Now you have it back. Cherish it; use it to rebuild this realm. Show me that you are more than a soldier."

"I'll show you nothing! I won't move an inch for you. Never again."

"You will do it for him," Viviane said softly. "Your loyal and fearless heart will serve him as well as it served me."

"No. I'll stand beside, not behind him. I'll never again serve anyone blindly."

"Yes. Show me that you are more than a soldier," said the queen with a loving smile.

Sky grabbed the blade of her sword and squeezed it until she felt her warm blood drip down the palm of her hand and the sharp pain zinged up her spine. She welcomed the pain; it helped her cope with the anger, frustration and disappointment she had towards Viviane and Marcus. She turned around and left.

Whims and Dreams

It was the middle of the night. Morgan was wide awake, tossing and turning in his bed. The sheets had the soft fresh scent of soap and citrus, and on the bedside table lay a pile of poetry, history books, and science fiction novels. *1984* by George Orwell was on top of the stack. The opened book had an underlined passage: "If you want a picture of the future, imagine a boot stamping on a human face—forever." A dark, gloomy quote highlighted by a light worker. *Why was he brooding on so much darkness?*

She missed him, and she was worried sick about him. *Is he alive?* The last few days had been filled with revelations about the nature of her Ange'el. For the first time, she'd been able to see how much he'd loved her and how vulnerable he was around her. In her eyes, the god had become a man, yet her love for him was stronger than ever.

To keep her safe he'd exposed his power. To avoid controlling her mind, he'd revealed a bit of his world, placed his life in danger, and had broken the rules of his realm. He worked with and around her foolish whims. He had allowed her to speak at Central Park when he could have simply controlled her mind and ordered her to leave the country. When it came to her, he was weak; he was all heart, and she loved him for it.

Morgan finally understood Sky's reaction at The Pierre; the warrior was protecting Ahe'ey's secrets. The carelessness of her cousins enraged the Yi'ingo. The exposure of the Ahe'ey to protect Morgan could have a catastrophic outcome. As things started to fall apart, Morgan knew it was her responsibility to fix the mess she'd unintentionally caused. She realised that he needed her as much as she needed him, and that somehow gave her the strength to attempt the impossible.

She pulled up the laptop from the side table and reviewed the media files sent to her by the CIA. It took her a while to figure out how to download and decrypt the data. Matt had explained the rigorous security measures she had to follow, and after some initial struggles, she was finally able to view the photos and videos. She was happy with the result and was proud of Scout and Quinn for their solid performances.

Tomorrow morning she had to face her dragons, the worst of the worst, the darkest of villains, those who had no heart. She was being forced to play a game of deceit, a dangerous game. To clean her slate, she had to get closer to the tactics and strategies of her opponents, hoping she'd never turn into the thing she most despised.

The sample of royal blood had been destroyed; all copies of the genome were safe in her hands, and tomorrow she would attempt to neutralise the supremacist propaganda of Zanus and Co.

Yet, her heart was tight, crushed by intense pain, not because of tomorrow's event, but due to her fear that she'd lost him to a raging dragon. She held on to the little faith she had left, and focused her heart and mind on it. She lit a candle, closed her eyes, wrapped her arms around her legs, and rocked her body backwards and forwards with her head lowered and her eyes closed. The rhythmic movement of her body didn't clear the void in her heart and mind, but it relaxed her muscles and slowly enabled her to fall into a sleep-like state. She wasn't quite sure if she was dreaming or awake when she heard a voice inside her head:

"I love you."

It was him; it must have been him.

"I love you too," she replied, raising her voice for no reason. Morgan rolled to one side, placed her head on his pillow and slept soundly, reassured by his voice and his love.

Fighting Lies with Lies

They had rearranged the library so that the online viewers couldn't recognise Morgan's location. The girls had fitted a panel behind Morgan and moved all books and personal items away from the prying eye of the laptop's camera. Morgan sat behind the desk and placed the laptop on top of a pile of books, aligning the camera with her eyes.

She tested the split screen functionality of the broadcasting platform, ensuring that the viewers could see a special video on the main screen. In parallel, she would appear live on a small window in the top right corner of the webcast.

At Morgan's request, the CIA had commissioned a film, a collage of several photos and videos. This compilation included previously released footage of Gabriel and the Ahe'ey, but also new footage gathered or created by the CIA. They had managed to find several videos of Sky at Central Park as she and Bastian blocked a man from approaching Morgan. Other footage had been fabricated in the previous days and featured Scout and Quinn in a variety of made-up humanitarian rescue scenarios, showing off their physical abilities and fighting skills.

The two fearless young warriors had worked on a choreography that was quite impressive, even if it could not match Gabriel's royal ability. With a bit of smoke and mirrors, they'd put on a show that copied the style and might of the future king of Ahe'ey. Others of all races and skin colours were strategically featured in the photos and videos, and they wore fake Yi'ingo and Ma'asai hooded capes. The message of the video was clear: yes a movement exists and it includes mighty men and women of all races.

While Morgan waited for the start time of the live stream, the CIA staff uploaded the video compilation to all the most popular social media platforms of the web. The files, uploaded by fake user accounts, were backdated and tagged with the hashtag #ProtectorsOfTheNation. They were attempting to neutralise the white-supremacist propaganda with a mix of fact and fiction.

Morgan picked up her speech. She had extended the copy of her controversial invitation for the webcast. She reviewed all the new paragraphs that were highlighted in bold on the page, ensuring that they conveyed the right meaning; a final reassurance that her message was clear and impactful.

Then she sat, waiting for her audience to join. She looked at the viewer numbers and noticed that the number of attendees was rising. It quickly jumped from the thousands to the tens of thousands. Matt approached her from behind and looked at her screen.

"We are monitoring the bots of the extreme right; they're flooding Twitter with the hashtag and a link to the invitation to the webcast. It looks like they're rallying the troops. Soon it'll be trending, and your audience will rocket."

"Bots?" Morgan asked, puzzled by Matt's comment.

"Automated software that floods Twitter with messages using a hashtag, making it go viral."

Morgan hoped that the highly controversial statement that she'd released on the invitation's landing page would discourage the mainstream audience from joining. After all, her goal was to contain the racist propaganda. The live chat box of the webcasting event was running wild with messages from viewers.

"U finally saw the truth. From liberal witch to patriot. Well done 3!tch. #ProtectorsOfTheNation"

"Finally! Revenge for all the people killed by Muslims. #ProtectorsOfTheNation"

"#ProtectorsOfTheNation Down with brown, black, and yellow. Red, WHITE,

and blue all the way."

"They rape women and steal our jobs. We must take back our country. #ProtectorsOfTheNation"

Morgan gave a sigh of relief. No good-natured human being would stay to watch an event where such poison was being spewed in hundreds of messages.

The viewer count jumped to a couple hundred thousand people just as the longest dial of the library's clock landed on the hour. *It's time.* Morgan looked at Matt, and he raised his thumb. She cleared her throat, turned on the camera and started speaking.

"A few weeks ago I was subject to a horrific attack at the Metropolitan Museum, **an assault organised by Walter Zanus with the intent of blaming our Islamic communities and instigating fear.**"

Morgan looked up to face the anger on Matt's face. She hadn't told him that she intended to accuse Zanus.

"An assault that showed me the truth, that made me stand against those who attack our Western liberties. **Our liberty to be at peace with our neighbour, to be open to those who are different and to expect the best of our fellow human beings.**

"An attack by those who want to divide us, who work to make us fear anyone who's different. Those who spread hate, because divided, we are weaker; divided, we can be controlled.

"While we seek security, we'll never have peace, because the arms, the walls, the internet bubbles, the flags that are supposed to keep us safe, only work to separate us. They stop the dialogue and decrease our ability to learn and understand each other. They prevent us from seeing the value of diversity, the beauty in difference. They allow us to dehumanise what

we do not understand until we become numb to someone else's pain. Until the kidnapping of two hundred school girls in some remote part of the world receives less attention than Taylor Swift's latest boyfriend."

The chat box went wild. Life and rape threats, name calling, and other attacks flashed through the screen at the speed of light. They were quickly replaced by other messages even more unsettling. Morgan had to pull her eyes away as adrenaline rushed through her body.

"During the attack, I was lucky to be in the company of a man who is part of a global community of guardians trained to protect those who are most exposed to the worst evil in the world, the sub-humans. This group of protectors, who has been named by the internet as the Protectors of the Nation is, indeed, quite extraordinary. I've spent a few weeks with them, watched them train in martial arts and learned about their mission. I have decided to join their movement and have been given permission to share what I've learned and to introduce you to some of their leaders."

Morgan pressed play, and the video appeared on the main screen as her image moved to the corner of the live stream. The audience witnessed a fierce group of women and men of all races performing humanitarian acts of bravery and heroism.

"The Protectors of the Nation—their identity preserved by hoods; their anonymity a sacred right that allows them to guard us against those who challenge the natural order of the world. **The natural state of humanity, where we care for all living creatures with respect and dignity. Where we share what we have, and seek to understand and to connect with those who are different.** The supremacy of our great values is under threat—**our human values, our compassion and empathy and kindness.** And the guardians are rising once again to purify this land through fire, **the fire that burns in our hearts against bigotry, racism, chauvinism, fascism, power, and greed.**

Morgan's eyes landed on the audience counter, and she took a deep breath as she saw that the viewers were dropping quickly. She decided to turn off the chat box and reject the hate and violence that overwhelmed her screen and then her body.

"Their virtuous ideology will rise again; their hooded power will protect those who are worthy from those who are not. Those who seek to disrupt our social order will fall by the hands of our siblings: **our brothers and sisters from all races, creeds, genders, sexual orientations, abilities, socio-economic backgrounds, and levels of education. Our order is social—people and planet above all else.**"

Morgan raised her eyes above the screen to smile at the young women sitting on the sofa in front of her. Quinn's smile was brighter than the sun; she looked proud, *so proud*. The live stream was projected on one of the side walls of the library, allowing Scout, Quinn, Maria and the CIA staff to watch the event. A bottled storm filled Scout's eyes and the conflict in her mind was present all over her face and body. The young warrior crossed her arms in front of her body as her watery eyes met Morgan's.

The audience numbers continued to drop, until only five thousand people were now online. Morgan turned on the chat box and discovered some encouraging messages of support as the trolls abandoned the webcast.

"The devotion to our own will make us stronger, and we will not give up until our virtue, our morals, our values, messages and views are law. Our Knights will ensure that the eternal light rises again. Our circle and clan is bound by our special blood, the superior genes that unite us. **The human gene, shared by all races and creeds**. The right to the supremacy of the children of the sun is our civil right. **The supremacy of our humanity, which makes us responsible for all creatures on this planet living under the same sun.**

"**We, the people of all nations will work to turn the world into one nation, a united place that embraces and celebrates diversity.**"

The last scene in the video zoomed in on a circle of hooded figures holding hands. They all turned around to face the camera and pulled back their hoods so that the audience could discover a diverse group of people smiling. The backing track of the video was the melody of John Lennon's "Imagine". The unity anthem that had been playing in the background was suddenly more audible as Morgan finished her speech. The experience had been perfectly designed to connect and inspire. Morgan was silent, allowing the unspoken lyrics to flood the subconscious mind of her audience.

Matt placed a handwritten note on her table:

"Many extreme right sites are deleting videos and blogs about the PotN. Tweets are vanishing, and hashtag mentions have dropped by half. Tumblr is the exception. The kids love Gabriel. The video and the quotes of your words are trending there."

She nodded.

Morgan knew her work was done, that she had neutralised the racist propaganda that was going viral around the world. Neither Zanus nor any white supremacy group would ever again mention Gabriel and the Ahe'ey. The story would be buried in the depths of the internet, becoming just another conspiracy theory that would inhabit neglected websites featuring UFOs and Loch Ness monster sightings, stories that no one took seriously.

Her direct accusation towards Zanus would hopefully make him pause his attacks in fear of being caught. It wasn't a long-term solution, but it was the best she could do until she had clarity about the future of Gabriel, and Ahe'ey's ability and willingness to influence human affairs.

The worst of the worst were gone; they had disconnected from a story that didn't serve their interests, but perhaps there were others online. The kids from Tumblr that had been inspired by Gabriel's compassion and heroism rather than his gender and skin colour, those young people could benefit from a tale of humanity and hope. She thought about what she could tell them, and the obvious answer arrived swiftly to her mind.

She took a breath, feeling welling up inside her, and spoke straight to the camera as the video finished and the music faded away. "In 1957, two young lovers, both seventeen years of age, were forced to abandon their homes as a deadly volcano erupted in Faial—an island in the Azores archipelago.

"Eunice's family farm was covered in deadly ash. Her cattle died, choked by the acid fog and starved by the thick black coat of death that stood between them and their nourishment.

"Luis had left school the previous year to help on the farm. His parents couldn't afford a higher education for their son, and he had to give up on his dream of becoming a doctor.

"Eunice and Luis used to hide at the back of the Capelinhos lighthouse at night. They challenged the parish's priest and old town folk with their unapologetic desire for each other. Their naughty escapades are still the base of folk tales told at Peter's— the oldest and most famous pub in Faial, a place frequented by sea travellers from all over the world.

"The young couple were the first to sight the underwater eruption that emerged just in front of the lighthouse in the middle of the Atlantic Ocean. For days, weeks even, they witnessed the destruction of their homes by a force beyond their comprehension. The little they had was gone, but their bond and love for each other only grew stronger with the escalating calamity.

"Broken, homeless, but not defeated, they followed the other 1500 immigrants that were welcomed to Massachusetts, by then U.S. Senator John F. Kennedy. JFK helped Congress pass the Azorean Refugee Act, opening an exception in border policy to welcome the displaced victims of nature's wildest forces.

"Grateful to the country and people that had helped them in a time of great need; Eunice and Luis joined the UNICEF's humanitarian team in Boston, and have since worked tirelessly to protect children's rights in the USA and around the world.

"In the Eighties they left their adopted nation when they were offered UN leadership roles based in the UK. During those years, they had the opportunity to visit their country of birth. And they were met with a surprise as they hiked to Lagoa do Fogo—the crater lagoon of São Miguel, another Azorean island.

"They came across an abandoned little girl, roaming alone on the sandy shores along the rim of the Fire Lagoon. It was love at first sight; apparently, I smiled and giggled as they approached me. Eunice and Luis did their best to find my parents but were delighted not to have to part with the *fadinha do lago*, the little lake fairy that came into their lives on a foggy morning as they visited the mouth of an old volcano."

Morgan smiled as she remembered that day. She realised that her life was rich with synchronicity, meaningful coincidences that she struggled to comprehend. Sometimes, she felt close to assembling the puzzle. But, like a special dream at the moment one drifts out of sleep, the meaning was gone, lost in the second she would reach out to grasp it.

"My name, Morgana, was born of their love for a long tradition of popular tales depicting strong and capable priestesses of the lake; the last echoes of a matriarchal tradition centred on life and earth instead of death and power. My parents always believed in magic; the magic of hope, humanity, and science.

"My father was taken from us during the Christmas of 2010 in a suicide attack outside the UN Food Programme distribution point in northwestern Pakistan. Keeping the spirit of her soulmate alive, Eunice rejects the fear, violence, and hate of the fundamentalist groups working to divide us. She continues to work tirelessly as the UN high commissioner for refugees, a responsibility she bears with humility and pride."

Morgan realised that her mother was probably worried sick about her. She made a mental note to write to Eunice and her team as soon as the event was over.

"I, Morgana, the so-called world leader that some want to protect from the evil immigrants, am a proud daughter of humble refugees that were forced to leave their home, a man and a woman who are role models of civic duty, hard work, kindness, and gratitude; a couple that represents the growing number of displaced people in the world, people that strive for human dignity and the compassion of strangers in a foreign land. All that you said that I am, if I am what you say I am, is fruit of their labour and of the generosity of the good people of Massachusetts.

"I dedicate my life and my work to my parents and will continue to work hard to pay it forward. They are the real heroes in human history, unmatched by the feats of any Marvel fictional character.

"Some of the videos we've released appear to show superhuman beings whose feats save us from the worst of the worst. Yes, some of the capabilities of my friends are impressive, but they are just like you and me. They are flesh and blood, mortal, fallible, capricious, and kind. They have fears as much as they have dreams. Just like you, they have to decide every day how they are going to use their time to make the world a better place.

"No superhuman being is going to land on Earth to save the day. The destiny of our planet and all its beings relies solely on the big and small decisions you, as individuals, make every day about how you treat your neighbour, what you do with your time, how you vote, what you eat, and how much waste you produce. We are counting on all of you to show up and save the day, in every small and big way that it needs saving."

Morgan felt a pair of arms embrace her neck from behind, and then she saw Quinn's loving smiling face pop up beside her head on the screen. The girl kissed her on the cheek and waved to the audience. Morgan smiled, waved to the camera, and ended the webcast.

Morgan looked up beyond the laptop's screen and met Scout's eyes. For the first time since they first met, the young warrior welcomed Morgan's gaze with a shy smile.

"Well then. Our work is done," Morgan said as Maria approached her with open arms.

Sacred House, Ange'el

A day had passed since the trial when Sky stopped by, during the cover of night, and let herself in. She sat on the bed, held his hand, and stayed there for a while trying to conjure the few healing skills she had learned while at Ange'el. Looking at her cousin's face as he slept, she wished with all her heart that she could take his pain away.

Sky remembered the gentle boy who used to be her companion during her youth. He had always worn an open, genuine smile, and he was trusting and supportive in all his words and actions. His ability to build up the people around him was still evident in the happiness and confidence of his children. She remembered the day they had been told that Gráinne, her mother, had died and her sister had disappeared. She had been devastated by the loss and Gabriel had held her as she cried, grieving for her lost family. During the night, the Ange'el had visited her, and they climbed the tallest tree at Ahe'ey to look at the stars.

"Every year, seabirds and butterflies leave the shores of Africa as their ancestors have done for millions of years. They fly in the direction of our old homeland. For many, it's a fatal flight as what they look for is no longer there. The collective consciousness of the universe hasn't yet adjusted to this new reality, and so they fly to their deaths, encouraged by the shadows and voices of their ancestors. Footprints of past lives that continue to exist beyond these physical bodies. Gráinne is inside you and inside me and all around us. Her knowledge, her spirit and her soul will never leave us. Remember that, Sky. Know that in your heart."

They had sat on the highest branch, her back resting on his chest as they looked up. The ten-year-old girl believed her cousin's reassuring words. Even back then, he had his Ange'el glow, a glow that washed away fear and grief.

"It's rare, the times where our collective consciousness betrays us as it does those birds and butterflies. It's there to connect us with all the knowledge available in the cosmos, and when we pay attention, we listen to it in our hearts." He had such a strong influence over her—his quiet confidence, his generosity, his ageless wisdom.

She kissed his forehead as he slept. *I should have known better*, she thought, angry at the time they had lost and regretting so many unkind words.

RESIGNATION

Bastian walked into Gabriel's room just as Sky kissed the Ange'el. The Ma'asai wasn't expecting to see her there as he checked on his cousin during the evening while Sage slept.

"How is he?" Bastian asked, noticing the way she caressed Gabriel's hand with infinite tenderness, a softness that Bastian had never experienced from his Yi'ingo lover.

"Peaceful," Sky replied, her eyes still set on the Ange'el.

After a moment of quiet sorrow, she got up and they both walked outside to the veranda. Bastian felt an unfamiliar sombreness settle over him. His eyes expressed dignified resignation as if predicting a future that, in his mind, was now inevitable. He tried to conjure a bit of his old self—how he could use an overconfident smile right now.

"You should have told me. I can't believe you let me—" Her eyes admonished him with a single glance.

"I didn't know everything."

"I saw it with my own eyes. You two fought side by side during the war. All these years. You lied to me."

"Gabriel asked me to conceal it from everyone. He made me promise, but he never explained why. I assumed that his lack of visibility was leaving the path to the throne clear for you. In that way, I was a willing accomplice."

He moved closer and reached to touch her arm. She rejected his gesture as if she were waving away an inconvenient fly. He recoiled like a wounded puppy, crossing his arms in front of his chest and stepping away from her.

"I don't understand how I never noticed him fighting by our side."

"Gabriel and Marcus wore the same armour and always fought as far as possible from each other. With the helmet and a little bit of help from Gabriel's Ange'el capabilities, they looked identical."

"How I've behaved towards him. What I've done. I just want to" She looked crestfallen, an unfamiliar expression of guilt pulling her features down.

"You were both victims of the games played by our rulers, and he knows this. He never whispered a single word against you. I must admit I never understood the real root of your anger until the trial. Why didn't you tell me what happened in the woods?"

"He and I were all that you had. I didn't think you needed that burden. I've always known how much he means to you."

He held on tightly to her words as a meagre proof of her love for him. *Some sort of love, any sort of love.*

"That attack in the woods . . . I can't even begin to imagine how you must have felt. You loved him and looked up to him. It must have been devastating."

Her silent answer came from the agony in her eyes. He saw them, the two beams of fire screaming: *Yes, I loved him. Yes, it killed me inside.*

"I made him pay. Every time I had a chance." She looked back at the sleeping Ange'el, full of regret.

Bastian wasn't used to seeing Sky express remorse and guilt. He couldn't help himself; he felt a pinch of jealousy, one that he fought promptly and decisively.

"I promise that there's nothing but love for you in his heart."

She nodded. He watched her as she left. She was too busy dealing with her pain to realise that he needed some reassurance, that he was trying to overcome his own emotions—sadness, loss, resignation. Bastian was working hard to let go of his feelings to benefit the people he loved most. Sky's abrupt exit was another signal that he had lost her to his best friend.

Morgan could hear the blades of the Yi'ingo's swords clashing mid-air all the way from the library. Maria and the CIA staff had left the penthouse, and the girls were training in the giant living room. The sound echoed across the rooms, and the furniture shook as if an earthquake was fast approaching. She worried for Gabriel's expensive furnishings and artwork, but she was too busy managing Matt to walk over and stop the ruckus.

"You've betrayed our confidence. Our investigation is exposed because of you." He walked over to her, moving close. Too close. She thought of Sky, what she would do, and Morgan stood her ground, head held up, eyes firmly set on him.

"I did not. I didn't mention the CIA."

"Zanus will retreat. You've warned him." His index finger aggressively pointed at her face.

"I made sure he stopped killing people."

"We had a chance to put him in jail. You've destroyed it. When he's president, he'll kill many more lives."

"He'll never be president."

"Naïve fool. I know your type: you drive expensive electric cars and drink green juices with your gay friends in the rich suburbs of affluent cities. You live in a bubble of yoga and happy thoughts, completely detached from reality."

Yes, I guess I do. I do, she thought before she came back swinging.

"We won't save lives by letting him murder people so that we can catch him."

"It's the price we pay to keep the world safe. We've protected you."

"Many others have died."

"We are running an investigation. We do what we can, but sometimes people die."

"I pity the world that has people like you in charge." She immediately regretted her attack. She knew she was reacting to what he'd said in previous conversations. She didn't trust him; she feared him almost as much as she feared Zanus.

"Wait until you have Zanus in charge." He paced the full length of the room. "Where is Gabriel? I must speak to him." Matt's tone was firm, his expression hard.

"I told you; he's away. He'll return after the winter solstice," Morgan said with conviction, looking him straight in the eyes.

"I'm tired of all your lies." His eyes were set on her like a predator waiting to strike. "Today's show, all fake. It shows you don't have Gabriel's power to support you."

His overt aggressiveness was back; she knew immediately that she was in trouble.

"No, I don't. But he is powerful, and he will be back shortly."

"You have bullied the CIA into helping you spread your liberal propaganda. A campaign that shows you've got nothing. Your threats are full of hot air."

"Nothing has changed; he and his people will soon return to partner with you."

"His people? How many more like him? *I need proof!*" His fist hit the desk, and the laptop jumped in the air, hitting the desk with a hard clang.

"I have none." Her heart pounded hard against her chest.

"Those girls, the ones we filmed. We found footage of them at the Waldorf. What was in the bags they collected from Charles Mathews?"

She closed her eyes, scolding herself for underestimating the CIA's interest in Gabriel's affairs. She scrambled for answers.

"Gifts. Jewellery."

"Don't lie to me. The man is a key entrepreneur in biotech and genomics, and a friend of Gabriel. What were they up to?"

"Ask him."

"We've searched the offices and labs and found nothing. Show me the contents of those bags."

Suddenly, Morgan realised that it was likely that the CIA, not Zanus, had hacked Sir Charles' company and the Ange'el Foundation. Matt's right hand went to his pocket; she predicted the worst.

"Those bags are none of your business."

"National security *is* my business. The activities of an enhanced human with paranormal abilities *are* my business." Matt pulled a gun from his pocket and pointed it at Morgan.

"Shoot me; go on. You'll get nothing from me. Nothing. You'll kill me, and he'll come after you." Deep inside she was terrified; her heart raced and pearls of sweat rolled down her back. Yet, she held her head high and her face wore confidence and determination as a shield against his bullying.

"If he cared, he would be here now," he said as he pondered on her reply.

"It's your risk to take." She didn't back down.

"Morgan. The vase. We didn't mean to break it." Quinn raced through the door, sword in hand, as Matt turned to point the gun at the girl.

"Quinny, stay back. Drop your sword," Morgan screamed, grabbing Quinn's attention with the urgency in her voice.

"Drop the weapon," Matt ordered. The teen did no such thing. She gritted her teeth, raised her sword, and prepared to attack the man.

"Quinn, please. Put the sword down." Morgan pleaded with the young woman.

"Give me the bags or the girl will die."

"She's Gabriel's daughter; you hurt her, and he'll kill you."

He dismissed her words, a small smile tugging at his lips.

"Sure. I want the bags now!"

Morgan looked at Leonora Carrington's painting—*The Giantess*. The famous artwork hung above the mantel of the fireplace. Behind it stood Gabriel's safe, where she had stored the bags. She stood up and walked to the safe swiftly.

"Morgan, stop; I won't let you do this. I'll attack him if you do," Quinn shouted.

"Quinn, drop the sword. Please. Your life is invaluable. Please, Quinny. Trust me and do as I say." Morgan looked at the girl and spoke full of tenderness, "And trust your father. Okay?"

Quinn hesitated for a few moments, and then she dropped the sword as Morgan opened the safe.

Morgan had placed the bags beyond sight. In front of them stood piles of banknotes and some jewellery boxes filled with old expensive earrings, bracelets and necklaces. She took two of the boxes, opened them, and extended her hands towards Matt. The gold, pearls and diamonds sparkled in the light.

Matt grabbed Quinn's hair, pulling the girl towards him and placing the barrel of the gun in her head.

"The truth, or the girl dies."

"Please stop," Morgan begged. She tried to keep her eyes on Matt, even as she spotted Scout quietly approaching him from the back. Morgan turned to the safe and grabbed the two Tiffany's bags. She faced Matt, holding the bags up in front of her.

"Let her go and I'll give you the bags." Morgan walked half way towards them and dropped the bags to the floor.

Scout attacked the moment Matt lowered the gun to pick up the bags. She kicked his hand, making the gun travel in the air, and then she pushed her sword through his thigh. The man went to his knees screaming in pain as Quinn kicked him in the groin and then used her elbow to strike his face.

Soon, Scout had her foot on his back and her belt around his neck. The Yi'ingo pulled hard, choking him as his hands lashed out at her. Morgan picked up the floor lamp and hit him in the head with its heavy metal base. He fell to the ground, unconscious.

"Is he alive?" Morgan asked as Scout used her belt to tie his hands behind his back and Quinn did the same to his feet. Morgan quickly realised that neither of the girls cared much for the man's well-being. She placed her hand on his neck and felt a strong heartbeat. Sighing with relief, she picked up the two bags off the floor.

"My queen," Scout said, bowing her head towards the door.

Morgan lifted her head to find Viviane and another Ange'el woman standing at the entrance to the library. After a closer inspection, Morgan recognised Rita's features. The old woman glowed, her face and body were clean and fresh, her hair rusty-brown and wavy, and even more surprisingly, she had a full set of white teeth shining between her full lips. She looked as old as Viviane and the symbols in her garment indicated she held a high rank within the Ange'el.

"Lady Viviane, Rita, I'm so glad you're here." Morgan stood up and walked in the direction of the two Ange'el.

"Do you love my son?"

"Lady!" Morgan bowed to the queen. She welcomed the glow of the Ange'el and immediately asked after the welfare of her love. "Is he alive? Did he win the battle?"

Viviane nodded, "Do you? Do you love my son?"

"Apollo won! *I knew he would!*" Quinn jumped with excitement and slapped Scout on the back. The Yi'ingo stepped away from Quinn, flicked her mane of hair to the opposite side of her head and refused to show anything but contempt.

"More than life itself. Is he well, Lady Viviane?" Morgan was anxious for any news.

"He is fine." In less than a second, Viviane showered the four women with the scenes of the battle and trial. Quinn raced to Morgan's arms; they both sobbed. Scout's expression softened as if a great fog had lifted from her eyes.

"You were not supposed to leave Ahe'ey," Viviane admonished Morgan with her eyebrows.

Morgan was overwhelmed with the sounds and images that had flooded her mind. She was trying to predict the future implications of the trial and took a while to respond to the queen.

"We've had some complications that we had to deal with."

"Yes, I can see that." Viviane looked at Quinn and spoke, "Young lady, your father is worried sick about you. The passage is open; go to him. Race to Bethesda; wait until no one is around, set your mind to Ahe'ey and touch the water. Go."

"Go now? Alone?" Quinn asked as her puppy eyes shifted to Morgan for guidance.

"Juno will escort you," Viviane replied.

The woman Morgan knew as Rita bowed to the queen and then smiled to Scout. Morgan saw Scout's jaw drop and her face turn white. She was puzzled about the warrior's reaction, but the queen kept talking: "Take Morgan's bags with you and give them to your father. Only to your father, in confidence. Do you understand?"

The girl nodded.

"Go now." Quinn hugged Morgan and took the bags.

Morgan squeezed the girl tightly and spoke, "Go to your father's room, change clothes and find a hat or a hood. Remember that you are now famous and you must hide that blue hair and cheeky face."

"Yeah, I'm famous. Dad will be proud." Quinn grew taller as she spoke.

"Quinn, tell your father that if he sets one foot at Lake Do'oras I will close the passage forever." Viviane delivered the threat gravely.

Quinn gulped and then nodded. The teen turned to Scout, smiled, and said, "Thanks, friend. We make a great team," and then she left, followed by Juno.

Scout prepared to follow Quinn when Viviane pointed her index finger in her direction and spoke.

"Stay!"

"Do you know what's in the bag?" Morgan asked Viviane.

"My son may work hard to avoid my mind's eye, but he underestimates how well I know him."

"Is his life in danger? Will he be punished?" It was a plea disguised as a question.

"He will be if he continues to challenge my orders. Do you love my son?"

"You know I do," Morgan replied, exasperated with the queen's repeated line of questioning.

"And yet you leave him at a crucial time."

"I'm more useful here. I can't fight dragons or challenge your ruling. My presence at Ahe'ey would only cause us both pain."

"You need to come back with me now. Everything depends on it."

"Like what? I don't understand. Why should I come back when you force him to marry another? Has he chosen a queen?" Morgan's heart twisted.

"He will not; we will most likely have to choose for him."

"Who?" Soon after she spoke, Morgan realised she really didn't want to know the answer.

"Sky and then Scout are on top of the list. The pure, and the least impure of all others."

Scout's eyes opened wide; she blushed, and her head lowered so that she could hide her face under a wave of purple and white hair.

Morgan's anger erupted in flares of hot lava and toxic fumes. "You treat them all as if they're cattle. How can you do this to them?"

"You speak of what you do not know. If you love my son, you will follow me now. His future depends on it."

"With all due respect, I've seen what you do to your own children. I've seen the 'advanced' civilisation you lead." Morgan caressed Scout's back and then moved the girl's hair away from her neck to uncover some of her scars. She was surprised to find that they were all gone. "This young woman was lashed mercilessly. That is your kingdom, my queen." Morgan's tone was as cutting as her eyes. "Here, I'm helpful to him and to my people. Here, I can make a difference."

"You and my son have the same weakness, the same naïve idealism. You are foolish Morgan, very foolish. You may have won a battle, but you have also increased the size of your opponent's backlash."

"And I'll be here to face it and to fight back."

"Girl Scouts don't win wars. You can't win a battle without accepting collateral damage."

"I can try."

"You think by proving that minorities are as strong and capable as white men, they will make space for you all. You believe that this war can be won by reason. *It cannot. It will not.* It may indeed help the minorities rise, help them and others accept their worth, but don't ever assume that those in power, those who hold the status quo, will make way for you. The more you show your strength, the further you rise, the more threatened they will become, and the harder they will fight to push you back down. Systems of privilege are not defined by merit, skill or worth. They are established by command and control. They rely on oppression, not logic." Viviane spoke with conviction and sadness.

Morgan took a moment to think, attempting to refute the Queen's arguments. Deep down, she knew that the Ange'el was right.

"What are you saying? That I should just accept the status quo? That I should do nothing?"

"Story-based systems of oppression, the ones that use stereotypes to limit and divide, are some of the most peaceful ways to retain power. You take that away and you get war and violence."

"Is that why you erased your men's history?"

"I did not, but yes, it is. A population sedated by self-doubt is easily contained and controlled. History is identity, pride, and power; it connects you to others and makes you stronger. Take it away and you are nothing. Your history books are filled with white male achievement; ours are rich with women's feats. History is a tool—edited, controlled, and erased by those on top. To overcome systems of oppression, you need more than idealism and good values. You need to play a sophisticated game of chess."

"And your children are your pawns."

"Yes, they are, and so are you. There's no other way."

"What you've done to Sky—" Morgan was full of compassion for the teen girl abandoned in the woods.

"I have no regrets. Her rage saved Ahe'ey."

"You took her heart and *burned it*; you almost killed your son."

"I unleashed his power. I showed him and all Ahe'ey what he is capable of."

"The price we pay for your games is too high."

"Your actions are no different than mine. You designed an illusion; you edited history. You fought evil with lies and manipulation. Look in the mirror before you judge me."

"If what happened today inspires one single girl to be strong, I've done my job."

"Everything about today was a lie, an illusion. Scout is not a normal human girl, and Quinn is not as powerful as you made her out to be. You spend your life telling imaginary stories to young girls, swapping crystal slippers in children's tales with swords. My son tells his children they can become as capable as an Ahe'ey. You both push a reality to others that you refuse to accept when it comes to your own potential. So, who is right? Is it as simple as changing a story, providing inspiration, changing a belief? Or are you manufacturing lies and raising hopes without merit or justification? Are men bad and women good? Are men strong and women weak? Does race matter? Genes or beliefs, which is it?"

"I don't know," Morgan cried, overwhelmed with all her own doubts. "*I don't!*"

She had worked so hard to protect Ahe'ey, to contain the crisis, and now as she faced her actions she wondered if she was any better than

Zanus, fabricating news to fight his fake news. In the battle for truth and honour, he won, as none was left.

"No! I won't allow men like Zanus to drive hate and destruction. I won't be a victim." *A deer.* "If I have to play games to defeat him, I will."

"Then acknowledge your glass house and keep your rocks to yourself," Viviane admonished, her beautiful dark eyes piercing Morgan's skin.

"My lies are lies for good. They are white lies, designed to inspire and empower."

"A belief held by every liar as they edit reality to suit their interests. Do you want to find out? Would you like to see definitive proof of who's the winner in the battle between nature and nurture, story and genes? I can show you."

"Tell me," Morgan demanded.

"Come with me, and you will have your answer."

"I'm needed here."

"I give you my word you will return when you wish to come back."

"What do you want, Lady?" Morgan was confused. Why would Viviane want her back at Ahe'ey when she had destroyed her future with Gabriel?

"I want what you want, child. I am on the side of light and love; I have simply been around for longer. I have seen the best intentions cause the most damage. I've seen human idealism crushed by greed. Sometimes, to bring light to others, we must walk into the shadows. Come with me."

"Have you changed your mind about your son and me?" Morgan asked, full of hope.

"No, I have not. Gabriel will marry an Ahe'ey."

The queen's words crushed Morgan spirit.

"But the genome is safe and on its way to Ahe'ey. Please, set him free. Please!"

"You do not understand. A ruler can only walk a few steps in front of her people. Government and laws are never far from what its subjects think they want. All my people worship the pure blood that roams through his veins, no matter what they say or what tribe they come from. The existence of a royal family allows them to hold on to the shadow of a distant past, the heaven they lost."

"You said it before. It's just edited history to keep people sedated, to oppress the masses."

"A reality I have inherited. My subjects complain about the power of the royals, not because they want to abolish royalty, but because they want to be part of it. Scout is lashed for being different, yet she despises those less pure than her and those who are just like her."

Scout listened attentively to the words of the queen, wincing.

"She does not fight her bullies because, deep inside her heart, she wants to be just like them. People create their own prisons and dictators. Their reality."

"Excuses. You wash your hands from your mother's abuse and blame the people. How ridiculous. Your hands are as red as hers."

"Perhaps they are, but some genome on a hard disk will not make a difference. True change must come from the people. We, the royals, are their Hollywood celebrities, their escape, their chance to dream. They must be the ones rejecting the glamour, the dreams of supremacy. They must demand a fairer world for all. I promise you I bring light, not darkness. Come with me child. Let me show you the truth."

Morgan vacillated. Her feelings for the queen encompassed equal amounts of love and hate. After a few moments, she nodded.

"Very well, be prepared to leave in twenty-four hours. I have to clean the mess you have made."

The queen kneeled and placed her hand on Matt's head. His body jolted, and his eyes opened wide. He had a blank stare on his face as if he was in some sort of a trance. Viviane looked at Scout, and without a word exchanged between the two, the warrior used her sword to cut the belts from around his hands and feet. The man stood up, and both he and Scout followed Viviane as she left the room.

As Morgan stood alone in the library and the adrenaline started to vanish from her body, there was only one thought on her mind—he was alive and tomorrow she was going to see him. That was all that mattered.

HER CHOICE

Brothers

Sacred House, Ange'el

Bastian found Gabriel awake and in bed. The Ange'el's upper body leaned against the headboard, supported by several pillows.

"The light of the Ange'el is gone. Who dared to steal it?" Bas spoke tenderly as he approached his cousin.

Gabriel had his head down, and stared blankly at his hands.

"How are you?" Bastian asked.

There was no response, no acknowledgement, nothing. This was completely out of character. Gabriel always went out of his way to make everyone feel welcome, no matter how he felt inside. He'd always been polite and thoughtful, and never allowed his emotions to get in the way. Today, his expression was numb, exhausted, devastated. The Ange'el didn't hide his pain, not even from Sage, who was by her father's side.

Bastian signalled the young woman with his eyes, asking her to leave the room. He sat on the bed beside Gabriel and pulled a small flask out of his pocket. "Have one with me, brother. I think today even the most wholesome of the Ange'el can have an exception." The Ange'el looked at the flask wearily, then had a drink.

"Well, at least now I have a chance," Bas said.

Gabriel looked up with quizzing eyes.

"You look much uglier without your glow. Today, I win in the looks department. It's about time. Don't you think?"

The Ange'el attempted a hint of a smile.

"Oh come on; don't smile or you'll ruin it for me."

Gabriel began laughing and crying simultaneously, but all Bastian could see in his eyes was a devastating pain.

The Ma'asai opened his arms and embraced his cousin. "What have they done to you?"

They spent the night drinking. Bastian used his best material; he even tried some unusual self-deprecating humour. The farmer knew his cousin's smiles were forced, mostly to keep him happy, but he settled for that outcome. A forced smile is better than no smile at all.

"Is the passage open, Bas?" There was a touch of desperate hope in the Ange'el's voice.

Bastian shook his head, "Only after the coronation of the new rulers. They'll be fine, Gabriel. Use this time to rest and mend."

In the early hours of the morning, the slightly inebriated Bastian became unusually sombre and spoke, avoiding Gabriel's eyes. "You know . . . you and Sky are my family. I couldn't have survived the loss of my parents without you by my side. I adore Sky. I would, you know, be with her if she . . . . But recently, I have come to the conclusion that I'll never be good enough for her. She was raised to be the queen of this land. It's her ambition, and I want her to have it."

"To have what?"

"The crown."

"So do I Bas, but I gave my word. I don't know how to—"

"Her happiness means everything to me. I know you love each other . . . ."

Gabriel looked at his cousin with a puzzled expression.

Bastian continued, "I'm giving you my permission to ask her to . . . you know. I know you would never think of it because of me, but . . . I think you should . . . if you want to and if she wants to." His eyes were still focusing on the floor, his stomach twisting. "I'm not undermining your love for Morgan. I know it's insensitive of me . . . but . . . you have to marry an Ahe'ey, so marry our queen, the queen we both love."

Gabriel's eyes opened wide, and he was suddenly fully present. He looked at his cousin; his eyes expressed worry, his lips, bemusement. "What happened to your unshakeable confidence, Bas? Is Sky's recent bad humour getting to you?" Gabriel smiled and placed his hand on Bastian's shoulder. "You know whom I love, and whom she loves."

"Yes, but things have changed, and if someone is going to be a queen, it should be her."

"We'll rule together, regardless of who wears the crown. When it comes to Sky, there's only one person she loves. Don't you know how much she adores you and how much she needs you? As for me, all I can hope is to one day recover her friendship."

"You are as blind as a bat, Ange'el. You were her first love, possibly her only love."

Gabriel positioned his face so that Bastian had to look at him. "Don't succumb to the force of her hurricane—look beyond it. In the eye of the storm, you'll find an emotional creature both desperate for love and terrified by it. She fights you because she loves you."

"Yeah, exactly! She fought you all her life. As for me reaching the heart of the storm . . . I don't stand a chance."

Gabriel touched Bastian's arm. "Sky is too bright to let you go. Let her come to you. She's just scared. Give her time."

"Consider her for your wife, Gabriel. I love you both."

Gabriel chuckled, "Two men, drinking, deliberating on which one should a woman marry—the most feral, independent, and headstrong woman in the world. I think there's something wildly wrong with this picture. Don't you think?"

This time, it was Bastian who made a half-baked attempt to smile.

Suddenly, Gabriel's body tensed, and he tried to stand up. As soon as he put pressure on his broken leg, he grunted in pain. He sat back down and took a deep breath, looking around for something.

"What are you doing?" Bas asked.

"My cane? Where's my cane?" The Ange'el was smiling even as he struggled with the pain.

Bastian looked around for the cane, handed it to Gabriel, and helped him stand.

"You shouldn't be up just yet."

Gabriel ignored him and walked to the door. Before he reached it, the door opened.

"Apolloooo!" She yelled as she ran into his arms. "I'm back! I'm back! And I'm famous. Really famous."

Gabriel dropped the cane and wrapped his arms around Quinn.

"Dad, you defeated the dragon. I knew you would. I'm famous now. I helped Morgan get the code of the royal blood. I have it. It's for you." She handed two bags to her father and turned to Bastian to give him a hug.

"Code? Blood?" Bastian asked confused.

"Shhh, it's a secret. Morgan stole the royal blood, and Sir Charles used a machine to decode the secrets. We got it from him during the ball." Quinn talked non-stop. Her excitement burst out of her body with her words, hand gestures, and expressions.

"Morgan stole our blood?"

Bastian looked at Gabriel, startled by the news. The Ange'el confessed his crime silently without interrupting his daughter. Bastian knew he was probably ahead of her, seeing her memories with his mind's eye as he listened to her words. Gabriel's peaceful smile reassured the Ma'asai, who was left to ask Quinn all the questions already secretly answered by the Ange'el.

"So you all fought the director of the CIA?" Bastian asked, looking at Gabriel with wide eyes.

"Uh huh! Too easy." A cocky smile hung from her lips, and then she continued her story. At some point, Gabriel got up, kissed Quinn's forehead, picked up his cane, and limped towards the door.

"Where are you going?" Bastian asked following him. "You can't—"

"Dad. Stop. Apollo!"

Gabriel turned to face his daughter.

"Viviane will close the passage if you set foot on the lake." She walked towards him and wrapped her arms around his waist, placing her head on his chest. "She said so. I'm sorry."

He leaned his back against the frame of the door, closed his eyes, kissed Quinn's head, and replied, "Never mind. I've missed you Quinny. I've missed you so much."

Unlikely Friendship

During these difficult and turbulent times, Sage had decided to keep her family close to her. She asked Ollie to move back to Ange'el to spend more time with his family. The boy was more than happy to respond to his sister's request. The last few days had been intense and quite unsettling, and all of them were craving the familiarity and tranquillity of Ange'el.

The children were all gathered outside having breakfast. Aria sat on Ollie's lap eating pieces of bread with honey; her tiny sugary fingerprints were all over Ollie's shirt. Quinn was beside them doing squats. She carried Riley on her shoulders as the youngest counted the number of squats out loud.

Sage saw Aria throw the bread to the floor and hide her sticky face on Ollie's chest.

"Josh!" Ollie said. "Join us. Would you like some breakfast?" Ollie caressed his little sister's hair. Aria was restless due to the stranger's presence.

The Hu'urei stood awkwardly by the apple tree.

"Hi, Joshua, how are you?" Sage said, smiling. Josh's visit surprised her but she was happy to have the opportunity to thank him for his kindness during the trial.

"I'm fine, sweet lady."

Quinn's eyebrow raised, and she shot a quizzing glance at her older sister who could feel heat spreading across her cheeks.

Josh continued speaking, unaware of the not-so-subtle exchange between the sisters.

"I visited my daughter and thought I should stop by to inquire after your father and ensure that you are all well." The large rugged man spoke to Sage with great softness.

Quinn snorted between squats, almost dropping Riley on the ground.

Sage admonished her sister with her eyes and replied, "You are very kind. We are well, and my father is recovering slowly. Most of the flesh wounds are gone, and the internal bleeding has stopped. We are just waiting for his bones to mend. Please, have a seat with us. The bread is still warm."

"No, I don't want to disturb your peace of mind. I just wanted to know you were all in good health and high spirits. May I also compliment you on your courage during the trial, Lady Sage? Your father must be very proud of you."

Sage blushed even more.

"Quinn, you're back!" he continued, turning to the young warrior, who was biting back a grin.

"Yeah, I'm back, and I'm famous now."

"Famous? I see," Josh kept talking, trying to contain his snickering smile. "Still planning to beat Sky at the Games?"

"Yeah, but I'm behind with the training. Dad's sick and I heard Sky is in a terrible mood. She's stopped running the Yi'ingo training sessions. Why do they always do this to me?" She rolled her eyes theatrically, and Sage smiled at her sister's antics.

"Not everything is about you, Quinn," Ollie admonished his sister.

"Quinn and Ollie, stop by at Hu'urei after breakfast and we'll train together. I don't have your father's skills, but I'm good with the sword and always happy to help you beat Sky in the arena," he said, winking at Sage.

Soon after, Sage accompanied Quinn and Ollie to Hu'urei, and the teens spent the morning training with Joshua. Quinn had told Sage that she should stay away. Apparently, Josh and the Hu'urei were less fun when the Ange'el was around.

"No swearing, burps or farts. Around you they all act like the weakling boys at the debutante ball," Quinn complained to her sister.

Yet, Sage was too anxious about her family's safety, and she was quite intrigued by the big-hearted leader of the Hu'urei.

As Quinn, Ollie, and Joshua trained in the arena, others joined to watch and cheer. It was a rare occasion and the builders seemed happy to have visitors. The rough and raw Hu'urei did appear to change their behaviour as the humans arrived. They were more polite and considerate than usual. Some of them confessed that they'd never seen a human before the trial, particularly a non-Caucasian human. Sage wasn't expecting so many Hu'urei to join them around the arena. The builders amused Sage with their over-the-top attention. They marvelled at the one they called "the beautiful and courageous lady healer of Ange'el".

The teens seem to feel at home there. Marcus had trained both Joshua and Gabriel to fight and the two had similar approaches to the way they taught. It was also good for Quinn and Ollie to befriend a half-human Ahe'ey. Gabriel, Sky, and Bastian had perfect and accurate movements, complete symmetry, and superhuman strength, which were both an inspiration and a cause of frustration for any aspiring human warrior. Joshua had more human characteristics. He was still tall, strong, and unusually gifted but also had a bit of a gut, a few scars that had never completely healed, and a small bump on his nose. He was kind yet impatient. His sense of humour was coarse and lacked the fine manners and sophisticated habits of his pure-blooded cousins. The two teens particularly enjoyed learning new curse words.

"Come on, Ollie, you can beat the old arse!" they shouted, followed by loud laughter.

Then someone else joined them at the Hu'urei arena, an unexpected visitor who left everyone nervous and on edge.

Healing Begins

Sky walked alone and unarmed into Hu'urei land. The crowd standing around the arena parted in silence at the sight of the unlikely visitor. Joshua was fighting another Hu'urei to demonstrate to Ollie and Quinn a battle technique. The sudden silence from the audience made him look up to see what was going on.

"I am told that some here conspire to overthrow me in the Games," Sky projected her voice and it echoed throughout the forest. She held her body straight, her head high and her expression calm and self-assured. She looked at Quinn as she spoke, and the girl's eyes expanded with excitement.

Sky had never been in Hu'urei land for any reason other than to fight, pick up criminals, or communicate new mandates from the king and queen. This was the first time she'd been there alone and unarmed. In these lands, many hated and feared her. She'd killed many kinsmen of the Hu'urei and had often spoken with disdain of the entire tribe.

Some were starting to see her in a new light after experiencing her journey at the trial; they praised her for handing a sword to Joshua. The Hu'urei had been forbidden to handle any weapons outside the Ahe'ey arenas since the war ended. Her gesture to Joshua had signified a small but significant step, a message of renewed trust, and now she was here to build on that. Yet, a lot more would be required for the deep wounds between Yi'ingo and Hu'urei to mend completely.

"The rumours are true," Joshua said, after a moment of surprise. "We can't wait to cheer your defeat as our new champion kicks you off your golden pedestal." Quinn was small in comparison to Sky and Joshua and she looked up like a proud child receiving attention and praise from her parents.

"If you're going to teach the girl to defeat me, you'll have to improve your technique." She picked up Ollie's sword and, with her right hand, signalled Joshua to attack her. "You see, Quinn, they can be taller and stronger than a woman, but there is something that they don't have— light feet, speed, and flexibility." She demonstrated it by dancing around Joshua quickly, moving closer, and striking her sword onto his, only to change direction before he attempted to retaliate. She gave an acrobatic jump over him so that she could strike, but he was ready and grabbed her feet, making her fall to the ground. Sky rolled on the sandy gravel with the grace of an acrobat and was up in no time.

Joshua laughed when she ran towards him and kicked his chest, putting him on his back. The tip of her blade pressed against his heart as she smiled.

Josh got up slowly with his palms towards Sky. He shot a defiant glance at Quinn, and said, "One thing you shouldn't learn from the high-ranking Ahe'ey is to be overconfident and arrogant. It's a god's weakness that can be exploited by any hardworking human.

"Yes, winning is a great confidence booster. You should try it some time." Sky retorted, handing the sword back to Ollie.

"What brings you here, Warrior?"

"Walk with me." Sky walked towards the forest, followed by Josh.

"I praise you for the way you handled the test and trial. An impartial and courageous stance." Josh spoke slowly, as if he was measuring the consequences of every word.

She stopped, looked him straight in the eyes and spoke.

"I came to the realisation that I've been fighting a war that has been over for some time. I don't have the forgiving heart of my cousin Gabriel. The fire in my gut comes from the pain of losing my family at the hands of your people."

His response was immediate and decisive: "Not my people, my dead ancestors."

She could see the tension escalating in his body. Blue veins popped out of his blood coloured skin.

"She was my mother too," he continued without looking at her.

Sky ignored his statement, dismissing it as soon as he'd unleashed it. She was ready to drive peace at Ahe'ey, but she wasn't prepared to accept Iblis' son and Sathian's grandson as family. She raised her chin and went straight to the point.

"Gabriel called upon me before the trial and asked me to refocus my work on the outside world. I can't do that without first assuring the stability of Ahe'ey. As a gesture of good faith, I would like to invite some of the Hu'urei to join our defence forces. I assume some will have the warrior gene. You clearly do not," she sneered, unable to hold back the shot. "In return, I ask you to accept any Yi'ingo that wish to learn your crafts and skills. In time we will extend the offer to other tribes."

Sky was determined to have the integration plans ready and rolled out before the coronation. She wanted Gabriel to be able to focus on opening the gates and guiding Ahe'ey to fulfil their purpose.

Joshua looked down at his hands for a moment, eyebrows pensive. He replied, "It's an honourable proposal, but one that may cause further rifts. No matter how hard we all try, some problems will arise—fights, disruption, further deaths."

"I accept the risk as long as I have your word that you will work with Bastian and me to resolve them. I can't guarantee the Yi'ingo will behave, but you have my word that I'll be an exemplary leader on this matter."

Joshua nodded.

"Join Bastian and me at the temple this afternoon so that we can formalise these plans to present to Viviane and Marcus."

"Lady Sage should join us," he said.

Sky thought it was an odd suggestion coming from the Hu'urei. She stared him in the eyes until his gaze sank to his shoes.

He coughed. "The presence of the young Ange'el will bring out the best of us at this critical time."

"Very well," Sky responded, with some concern for Sage. The human Ange'el was too innocent and kind to be the object of Josh's interest. He was a crude man; his coarseness and temperament were a good match for any Yi'ingo roaming the forest at night looking for sex. But Sage had been raised under the loving protection of great men—Gabriel, Bastian, and Marcus. She had never been exposed to the runt of the litter, and she'd be blind to his darkness.

"Thank you," Joshua bowed.

"She's too good for you. Keep your hands off her," Sky said as she turned her back to leave.

"Yes, the human is too good for me," he murmured.

REFORM

Alone in his room, Gabriel tried on a new exoskeleton. He held his breath in a foolish attempt to contain his pain as he twisted and turned his body to fit the apparatus. Earlier in the day, Sage had challenged his plans to leave his room with the help of the device. She'd protested with great conviction, asking him to rest for a few more days. At the time, the Ange'el had agreed to stay in his bed, but now he was going crazy in his room thinking about Morgan. He needed to get out and be involved in something productive.

Sage had left to join the others at the Temple of Lights for the reform kick-off meeting. Gabriel used the opportunity to call Bastian with his mind's eye. He recruited his cousin to help him escape from his daughter's loving detention. Bas admonished the Ange'el for his rebellion but, soon enough, was helping Gabriel fit the exoskeleton. Then they walked out together to meet the others. As they reached the temple, they could hear Sky and Joshua shouting at each other.

"My men will never accept this half-baked proposal," Josh declared, sounding appalled with something.

"It's a start!" Sky retorted, matching his enraged tone of voice.

Gabriel and Bastian looked at each other, silently communicating, and slowed down, letting the two argue for a minute.

"A plan that denies them leadership positions outside Hu'urei for five years? An affront!"

"We need time to regain trust. You can't expect things to change overnight."

"You had a decade—" Josh took a few steps in Sky's direction, both hands pressed into fists.

She placed her hand on the hilt of her sword. "There have been too many violent incidents lately."

"The men are angry and frustrated. They react to your low and unjust expectations. On the day you accept them as responsible members of Ahe'ey, they'll honour it." Josh took a step back and raised his palms towards her, trying to defuse the situation.

"You're getting ahead of yourself. Your aspirations are too ambitious."

"Is this about the reform, or—"

"One and the same," she replied decidedly.

"Perhaps you two should take a break. Where's our Sage? She should know better than to leave two Wali'ingooteer alone." Bastian tried to lighten things as he walked into the room, followed slowly by Gabriel.

"Bastian. My king." Joshua bowed, still breathing heavily.

Gabriel bowed to his cousins. "Not yet Josh, not yet." He considered his response carefully and then he spoke. "People tend to perform according to the expectations placed upon them. I prefer to raise the bar and support them to reach it."

"We aren't talking about children. These are angry men, forceful and dangerous men," Sky replied, berating the Ange'el with her eyes. Her hand was still steadfast on the grip of her sword.

The debate between the Yi'ingo and the Hu'urei continued uninterrupted for a while. They spoke at each other, showing resentment collected over a lifetime. Gabriel watched and listened; he knew the two needed to have it out and he placed his hand on Bastian's arm, asking him to stay out of it.

Josh's voice was hard, filled with grievance. "Men that you have been undermining and disrespecting openly for years. We've been trying our best to live honestly under a cloud of distrust and hate."

"Not an excuse for violence. Two Yi'ingo dead and several injured by five rogue Hu'urei just last week."

"Do you also keep count of the murder of innocent Hu'urei? Men killed instantly, without a trial, at the hands of your warriors. How can I appease my men's anger? I have nothing. By now they have more than enough reason to instigate a full-scale mutiny."

"When you excuse their actions, you fuel the violence." Her anger was escalating fast and her body was as rigid as the stone pillars of the temple.

"We have paid the price for what our forefathers did. No more. Enough!"

"Have you forgotten the violence and hate that men drive on this planet?"

"I can't speak for all men; I can only vouch for mine."

"Besides, you told me that conflicts would be unavoidable in this transition, that your men are angry, and now you want us to rush and put them in positions of power."

"They are no less deserving than any other Ahe'ey."

"I need time to assess this myself."

"Why? They are my people. I'm their leader. Hold me accountable. I was raised by the same man that raised you, Bastian, and our future king. Why don't you, for once, trust my judgment?" Joshua's tone was non-confrontational.

Sage walked into the room and immediately shot an admonishing gaze at her father for being up and about. Gabriel smiled at her and used the opportunity to interrupt the argument with a question, "Do you think they are ready, Josh?"

Josh looked at Sage, smiled, and his entire body softened. "Yes, sir, they are. They are inspired by you and your kind family and by my sister's renewed trust in them."

Gabriel met Sky's eyes with a smile. The Yi'ingo refused to react as

Josh continued speaking.

"These are good, loyal men. They may be rough around the edges and aggravated by the current situation, but I have never seen them this ready to rise to meet your expectations. They are ready to follow you, my king."

Gabriel's gaze was set on Sky, an unspoken question in his eyes.

"I'll think about it," Sky spoke, her voice battling to exit her firmly pressed lips.

The Ange'el smiled and bowed to the Yi'ingo. "Josh, I need your men to deliver to Sky's expectations and have the same respect for her that they have for you. I know she'll respond in kind."

Joshua nodded.

"It took you one smile," Bastian whispered, "just one. I hate you sometimes."

Gabriel was too focused on strengthening the bond between Sky and Josh to respond to his cousin's comment with more than a casual smile.

The work continued all afternoon. Gabriel was delighted to see Sky, Sage, Joshua, and Bastian together and was impressed as they shared their plans for an integrated Ahe'ey. The Ange'el's words were encouraging and full of praise for what they'd achieved, and yet he knew that soon he was going to push them further. But it was the first day, and he was grateful to Sky for building the bridge that would bring peace to Ahe'ey. Gabriel smiled at her; it was an open, unguarded smile.

She bowed, awkwardly attempting to return his warmth.

THREE HEARTS

Sky took a break from the discussion and moved away from the others. She was struggling to cope with Bastian's foul mood. The Ma'asai continuously stomped his foot on the floor at a fast rhythmic pace. His activity shook the table and surrounding furniture and released a nervous energy around the room. He crossed his arms over his chest, and occasionally rubbed his face and massaged his neck. His eyebrows almost touched over his nose, such was his grumpy disposition. Sky had no idea what had gotten into him. His short and sharp replies to her questions had left her frustrated and annoyed.

She took a deep breath and walked towards Gabriel. The Ange'el stood alone, his glow gone, and he was immersed in his own thoughts. He leaned against a column at the inner courtyard of the temple while the others discussed logistics related to the distribution of the Ma'asai farms. She stood beside him, watching as several Hu'urei spread a fresh coating of light-absorbing particles over some of the art in preparation for the coronation.

She was silent and lost for words, vacillating about how to proceed. Their relationship was as fragile as it was tempestuous. For so many years, her words had been barbs designed to unleash maximum pain. She wasn't sure how she could transition from those sharp attacks to casual conversation. His eyes set on her with a welcoming smile, and after a moment of silence, he kindly found a way to engage in conversation.

"I'm a bit overwhelmed by all this pomp and circumstance surrounding the coronation. I neither have the charisma nor the talent to be the centre of such an elaborate scheme." Warm, open, and self-deprecating, he knew how to melt the wall of ice between them, and she relaxed.

"The people need a reason to celebrate. It's the perfect opportunity to reset the past and give them all a fresh start under your leadership."

"Under our leadership. I need you by my side."

"You have my unconditional support. I . . . " she stopped, attempting to find the right words. "I'm sorry." Her eyes sunk to the floor in front of her.

He took her hand, looked at the fresh scar on it and kissed it. For a split of a second, his eyes flashed with some feeling as he touched her skin. "I was weak to obey my parents despite the consequences for the ones I love."

She shook her head, "You were just a young boy—"

"Who sacrificed the life of a young girl. I betrayed you once, and now, I betray you again. I'm weak, and my weakness hurts those I most love." His lips quivered as he looked at her scar. It was as if he could see what caused it. Perhaps he could. Of course he could.

"We are but puppets." She paused for a few seconds and shot him a side glance. "I punished you, time and time again."

He smiled, "I deserved every lash." His thumb grazed through her wound, slowly healing it, "But if you want to make me happy, then please forget the past, sister. All I want is to put it behind us."

"It's done. I'm a strong leader and the best soldier. I may be useless in times of peace, but I'm proud to stand by your side. My warrior genes are at your service."

"No. Your skills go much beyond the sword. You, my Sky, are a queen."

"A queen without a crown," she replied with a pinch of resentment.

They stood side by side in silence. He wrapped his long fingers around her wounded hand and closed his eyes. The mighty warrior allowed his energy to soften hers. She peeled back all the layers of anger, fear, resentment, and hate that she had accumulated throughout the years. She allowed herself to experience the magic of vulnerability and trust for a moment. He washed away the scars on her skin and her heart.

"I'll be back later. There's something I must tend to." Bastian excused himself loudly, exiting the room abruptly.

"What's going on with him?" Josh asked Sage, who shrugged her shoulders.

"Bastian!" Gabriel shouted, but the Ma'asai ignored him and left. The Ange'el seemed distressed; he rushed his fingers through his hair, shook his head and murmured, "You foolish heart. You misunderstood."

"What the hell is going on?" Sky asked.

"Sister," said the Ange'el.

"Yes?"

"Speak to him?"

Gabriel's opaque request puzzled Sky. "Do you know what's wrong?"

He nodded with a knowing smile, and she waited for more information. She got none. "Are you going to tell me?"

He shook his head. "Go," he encouraged her softly. "Listen beyond his selfless, misguided words."

Sky ran after Bastian as he left the Temple of Lights. She was smiling, happy with the renewed bond she had with Gabriel and with the progress of the negotiations.

"Bas, wait!"

He looked back and stopped.

"Where are you going?"

"I just need some time. I'll be back later. Okay?" He refused to look her in the eyes.

"I'll walk with you."

"It's best you stay here and continue with your . . . negotiations."

"Gabriel's got it. I trust him."

"Indeed." He started walking faster.

"Hey!"

She walked by his side. As they reached the forest, she grabbed his hand. He stopped, and she stole a kiss. He kissed her back, but his expression was sombre and his eyes unusually hostile. She could see that something wasn't quite right. She kissed him again, and this time her hand travelled down his body, making him jolt with desire.

"Stay with me tonight?" she asked, looking into his eyes and touching him between his legs.

He stared into her eyes, and she saw the turmoil inside his.

"Will you? Stay?"

He wore his obvious desire awkwardly. He was unable to hide it, but unwilling to own it. He finally nodded and walked beside her in silence for a while.

"Are you going to tell me what's going on?"

He took some time to reply. They headed in the direction of Yi'ingo. As they approached the village, he stopped and grabbed her hand.

"Sky, I love you. I want you to be happy." He lowered his eyes, and she pulled him towards her and kissed him. "Wait," he said as she looked at him, confused. "You were born to be the queen of Ahe'ey. That's your destiny, and I know you love him. Now that you knowI just want you to know I would understand if you would decide to"

"To what, Bastian?"

"To marry Gabriel," he whispered in despair, looking straight into her eyes. "To marry your first love. Perhaps even . . . your only love."

She stopped, said nothing, and took a while to decide how to respond. For the first time in a long time she looked at Bastian, really looked at him. She remembered the energetic little boy who had followed his older cousins everywhere they went. A typical Ma'asai, he would often stop to smell the flowers and watch the insects. At the age of six, he already knew the name of every plant and root in Ahe'ey. He was more interested in life and nature than in death and war.

She recalled how his beautiful body had flourished rapidly during puberty. Plump muscles generously filling his chest, arms, and legs, transforming him into a tower of power and strength. He had become a warrior by duty, not choice, and yet he had become a courageous war hero, respected by his people who owed him their safety and their lives. His overconfident varnish had magnified his charm and hidden his weakness—his inability to be with himself. Solitude reminded him of the boy waiting for his missing parents, worrying and despairing—the boy who had once lost everything that was dear to him; the boy who would do anything to ensure the well-being of the ones he loved.

Humour, charm, and good looks had veiled his anxiety with a layer of cockiness that was now part of his identity. The mask had become the man once he was fighting side by side with Sky and her Yi'ingo. There had been no space for emotion or weakness on the battlefield. He'd needed to show them that he was worth their trust under a cloud of scepticism from the female warriors. So strong was the character he had created that few still remembered who he really was. Gabriel had provided Bastian with a solid harbour for stormy weather. Sky had occasionally allowed him to be vulnerable, but more often than not, she had punished him for it because his weakness reminded her of her own.

Now, as she looked into his eyes, she rediscovered the man behind the mask. She grabbed his hand and started walking, leading him. She walked in the direction of the Games arena. The large building emanated blue-and-gold light as the sun disappeared over the horizon.

The light-absorbing particles shone all over the structure like the starry sky. As they stood in the middle of the arena, they could see the walls and the stone audience stands glowing. All around them were paintings of the Games, the strong, beautiful bodies of men and women engaging in battle. Prominently featured in those paintings were Sky and Bastian, two of the greatest champions that had ever lived.

There was no other place that better summarised who they were. One of the paintings showed them fighting each other with smiles on their faces, enjoying every minute of the battle. They engaged in competition and physical mastery while savouring every moment of the experience.

He looked at her and whispered, "Are you trying to remind me that you are stronger than me in battle? Rejoice now; I'll take your title in a few days."

She remained quiet, enjoying the beauty of the building and the paintings of the Games, and gathered her words. She looked into his eyes, put her hand on his face, and kissed him. Then, she went down on one knee, took his hand, kissed it on the inside, and whispered, "Sebastian, will you marry me?"

As he lifted her up, he kissed her, hugged her, and kissed her again. "You . . . want to marry me?" His eyes were open as wide as his heart; both filled with surprise and delight.

She nodded.

"You don't want to marry him?"

She shook her head, wearing an amused smirk on her lips.

Sky moved closer and whispered in his ear, "I'll give my life for him today and every day. You, my Bastian, you will be my future husband. If you'll have me?" She paused, lifting her eyebrow and smiling.

"Yes. Yes! Of course, yes." He wrapped her in his arms and lifted her off her feet.

"I love you Bas, and wouldn't exchange your love for any throne. Your willingness to give me up is the most beautiful gift I've ever received. You've been my partner in crime, my brother in arms, my lover and friend. We've fought loneliness, dragons and men. Your constant love and companionship are the bedrock of my existence."

His face, like the sun, beamed with hope and happiness. She took turns mocking and loving him, and his laughter echoed across the stadium as she called him an oversized horny peacock with underwhelming fighting skills.

They stayed there for a while, lying in the middle of the arena and looking up to the stars. It was a good day, a great day. She may have lost the crown, but she'd found hope. She was now sure of the love and loyalty of the two most important people in her life.

All three young royals knew how fragile and precious their bond was, and how easily it could be destroyed by the forces that enslaved their lives and blood. Today was a good day, the best day. The day where three hearts beat as one, in sync, caring for each other as human beings, beyond blood. Selfless, loyal, loving hearts. They'd been targeted by evil enemies and betrayed by kinsmen and women who claimed to love them, but now they had each other. The three children once hidden in the forest were reunited at last, and Sky was determined to keep it that way.

Collapse

The Pierre Hotel penthouse, New York

Morgan sealed the final letter and placed it with the others on top of the desk. Ten messages of reassurance were addressed to her family, friends and colleagues. She left a note to Maria asking her to post the correspondence. She thanked the CEO of the Ange'el Foundation for her support and explained that she expected to be back in New York in a few weeks. She also advised Maria to keep a strict media blackout until Gabriel returned, unless Viviane had told her otherwise.

Then, she searched the web for news about the webcast; she'd been following the press coverage throughout the day. As expected, none of the far-right sites had mentioned the event. Past articles about The Protectors of the Nation were deleted without explanation. Many of the videos posted by the white supremacists featuring Gabriel and the Ma'asai had vanished from YouTube and Facebook.

The media created by Morgan's team and the CIA were flooded with comments accusing the posters of sharing fake news and being a mouthpiece for Islamic propaganda. She scrolled through news feeds, reading the key headlines.

"Walter Zanus trolled by human rights activist Morgan Lua."

"Female martial arts experts shut down Zanus' divisive antics."

"Presidential candidate's hate campaign annihilated by rogue vigilantes."

"A group of superhero wannabes with some serious Bruce Lee skillzzz."

"Zanus plots an attack on girls' rights activist in order to blame Muslims."

"Feminist Trojan Horse Emasculates Zanus."

"Rebels against white saviour propaganda."

"Girl Power Queen Bee Schools the KKK."

"The handsome philanthropist and his army of vigilantes."

The articles, all featured on low-reputation, high-traffic sites, mostly mocked Zanus. The clickbait headlines made the stories go viral on social media. Morgan was reassured that no one seemed to be following a superhuman angle in the news coverage.

On Tumblr, the adulation of Gabriel continued to escalate, but now the theme was one of diversity, inclusivity, and humanity. The villain was indisputably Zanus, and his caricature on social media was accurately bizarre. A man that relied heavily on hubris and propaganda was ridiculed and satirised by the incessant online chatter of the progressive youth. Yet, the mocking failed to call out the vile and malignant nature of the object of their ridicule. Morgan worried that the satire worked to normalise Zanus' antics, and while the world laughed at his expense, the devil plotted his next move.

"Turn that on." It was Viviane. She walked through the door pointing at the TV. "Turn it on, now," she repeated with urgency. Viviane's glow flickered, making the lines on her forehead visible. Scout came in the room following the queen. Morgan got up and pressed the power button on the device.

"...the death toll of the confirmed terrorist attack has climbed to twenty-five, but the number of casualties is expected to rise over the next few hours. To recap, we have some breaking news. Girl activists from all over the world were travelling by bus to the United Nations in New York to speak to government and UN agencies about their work. This was a follow-up session from the Girls Speak Out event held on the eleventh of October, during the International Day of the Girl.

"The bomb exploded less than half an hour ago, just as the bus reached its destination. A few minutes before the explosion, a small flying drone dropped several Islamic flags at the main entrance of the UN building. UN Secretary General Hussein A. Aboulatta will issue a statement in the next hour."

Morgan's knees went to the floor as a sob wracked her chest. Chinelvie, Liling, Ana, Josephine, Fatima—she knew them all, her girls, the girls on that bus. She was their mentor and friend. Her heart was jumping off her chest and yet she refused to breathe.

"The backlash," Viviane said, and Morgan looked up, sobbing, her mind screaming.

"This can't be his doing?!" It was a statement and a question; a possibility that she'd considered and discarded immediately. "The murder of school girls to advance his platform of hate and division? No, he wouldn't dare—"

As if on cue, another news update showed up on screen. "Walter Zanus just issued a statement heavily criticising the US government for what he calls an irresponsible border policy and a catastrophic national defence strategy. He is travelling to the scene of the crime to pay his respects to the families of the victims, and will be holding a press conference at 10 am EST."

Viviane looked at Morgan, who rejected the queen's compassionate eyes.

"Why didn't you stop him?" Morgan spat her words, and she felt herself sink into insanity, the madness of deep loss, regret, and despair. "Why?"

"I am not omniscient."

The empathy in the queen's eyes only served to aggravate Morgan's fury against herself. She stood up and walked quickly towards the door. Scout stepped in front of her.

"Let me pass," Morgan demanded, but Scout looked at the Queen who seemed to be driving her actions. Morgan attempted to push through. "I must go to the UN; I must face him."

Scout embraced her, firmly but gently, as Morgan battled against the warrior that towered over her.

The queen spoke, "Nothing can be done now, Morgan. There will not be another battle today. Today we lost. This war will be long; we must not react foolishly. We will prepare; we must unite Ahe'ey under the right leader, and then together we strike at Zanus and others like him."

"This is my fault. This is all my fault. Hope sponsors the event. He did it to attack me. It was his revenge." Morgan kicked and punched the strong body that held her captive.

"Shhh," whispered the Yi'ingo giant with an unusual softness in her voice. "Stop fighting me, Morgan."

"I did this. I killed them." Morgan was delirious with regret but her strength was fading as she pushed against Scout.

"No, my dear child. No." Viviane's tone was maternal and loving. "What happened today was set to happen, sooner or later. Zanus knows his only path to power is through a divisive campaign of terror. You just accelerated an inevitable sequence of events."

Morgan was distraught; her tiny body wasn't able to cope with so much grief and guilt. The girls' faces flashed through her eyes, and she sobbed, screamed, and mourned. She'd personally mentored each one of them. "They're dead because of me! I undermined his power. I forced his hand." She held onto Scout, pushing her tearful face into the Yi'ingo's chest.

"Enough. We have to go," said the queen, placing her right hand on Morgan's head.

Morgan closed her eyes and felt her body collapse onto Scout's arms.

A New Era

That evening, they were all invited to dine at Yi'ingo to celebrate the engagement. Despite being weak and exhausted, Gabriel was delighted with the news and keen to celebrate with his cousins.

The Yi'ingo had organised special food for their vegan guests and had decorated themselves with colourful body art, feathers, and lots of golden accessories. Even Sage was wearing blocks of gold and red on her face and body, courtesy of her Yi'ingo friends.

Gabriel sat beside Sky and Sage. Joshua and Bastian sat in front of them. Gabriel found solace in the smiles, laughter and kind words exchanged around the table. It was an incredible sight for anyone who knew the recent history of these tribes.

Sky was a glamorous and charismatic host. Adorned in gold, with her head held high, she excelled in her role as a powerful royal and role model. She walked the tight rope between cold detached governance and discreet kindness.

"How come you only have four toes on your left foot Josh?" Sky said without looking at her half-brother.

"I have ten perfect toes, like everybody else," Josh looked down over his large belly to check his feet.

"How can you possibly know this, if you haven't seen them in years?" She had a devilish smile on her lips as she looked down at Josh's gut. "Soon we'll run out of wild deer because of the appetite of this Hu'urei."

It took Josh a minute to recognise the playful mock, and once he did, he placed his hands on his gut and laughed.

"What else can a man do for pleasure at Hu'urei? We eat, drink, fight,

"

and laugh."

"Clearly the first two take the highest priority. You're in danger of falling on your front and not being able to get up in the next Games."

"One day, someone will beat your mighty arse, you cocky cockatoo. All skin and bones. It'll happen."

"No one with a gut like that. Want some more deer, Josh?" She used her sword to stab a large piece of deer and place it in front of Joshua's nose.

Josh looked at Sage and softened his tone. "Lady Sage, you should teach the Yi'ingo some of your wonderful manners. They have the grace and the politeness of wild boars."

"Never mind her, Josh. Eat some more," Sage encouraged cheerfully.

Gabriel noticed that Sky watched Sage with concern.

"A lady like you, sweet Sage, could turn a barbarian into a saint," Josh said, beaming at Sage.

The young Ange'el looked at Josh. In her eyes was the authentic, unguarded sweetness of one who had experienced a life filled with love. "What a man does with his life is his sole responsibility. Good or bad, the accountability lies only with him. No woman can save him, and no woman can break him."

At that moment, Sky's grave look turned into a loud laughter. Gabriel smiled at Sky reassuringly.

"You are the most beautiful of all roses, my lady," Josh said, humbled and besotted with Gabriel's eldest daughter.

"Thank you, sir. But I'm not a rose. My father raised me to be a ginger plant." Sage exchanged a knowing smile with her father.

I did, I learned this from . . . . Who taught me? Gabriel searched his mind in vain.

"Ginger?" Josh said, raising one eyebrow.

"Eat, Josh," Sky commanded, placing the deer on his plate. "Sage and I'll roll you all the way back to Hu'urei at the end of the night. Your . . . grace will be unmatched."

The exchange of pleasantries continued for most of the night as Sky's warriors became more relaxed in the presence of the handful of Hu'urei that had accompanied Josh. They took Sky's playfulness as their own and the Hu'urei responded in kind. Gabriel knew that the wounds between the tribes were deep and would take many years to heal, but he was hopeful that these were the first signs of a united and peaceful Ahe'ey.

At the centre of this tectonic shift was the relationship between Sky and Gabriel. Beyond the cool and commanding demure of the royal Yi'ingo, there was an unspoken bond and a renewed intimacy that had quickly developed between the two cousins. This new, deep relationship was no longer a threat to dearest Bastian, whose sunny smile hadn't stopped beaming since he had arrived, and whose voice and laughter were louder than ever.

Yet, what was most surprising was how Sky had taken upon herself to protect and guide Gabriel into his new role and responsibilities, a turn of events that had him both grateful and heartbroken. He was assuming a role he didn't want, one he didn't feel suited for or worthy of; a role that belonged to her, a position that she had been born to fulfil. She'd placed him at the centre of the table, had deferred the toast of the night to him, and ensured that her people treated him with the deference worthy of a king. She did all that without ever losing her might, dignity, and immense power. While his parents dismissed her has a soldier, unable to move beyond her hate; all he saw was a queen growing into her own after walking through fire. A mighty queen, and the rightful queen of Ahe'ey.

Later in the evening, Joshua came to Gabriel's rescue. A large number of Yi'ingo warriors surrounded the Ange'el, who was still quite frail. The women sought his favour with the hope of becoming his future queen. Gabriel was overwhelmed with all the attention. He indulged them when they asked him to demonstrate some of his fighting skills but was quite uncomfortable with their physical Yi'ingo-style advances. He tried to deflect the harassment by focusing on his technique with the sword.

"Warriors!" Joshua said. "Give the man some space. I think he would be safer and more at ease locked in a cage with the Wali'ingooteer." Everyone laughed. The Yi'ingo moved on, but not before they kissed him and rushed their hands over his body one more time.

Gabriel smiled at Joshua. "Thank you, Josh. I was way out of my depth."

"I'm the one who must thank you, Gabriel. I'm grateful for all your kindness and the kindness of your young family. I regret not accepting your friendship sooner."

Gabriel patted his cousin on the back. "We've been through a lot, Josh. I'm happy that we can leave the past behind us and encouraged by what we can achieve together."

"Are you, really, sir? Do I have your trust?" Joshua watched him closely as Gabriel nodded with a smile. "Sir, the day may come when I'll test the depth of your confidence in me by asking you that you entrust me with your most precious treasure."

Gabriel looked at Josh in the eyes, reading his mind, and smiled. "It's not my approval that you should seek, cousin. All my treasures are capable of shaping their own futures. I trust them and their hearts. As for mine, it tells me that you are an honourable man who I'm proud to call a friend."

"I would expect you to reject the grandson and son of murderers and rapists," Joshua spoke without rancour.

The little light in Gabriel's eyes vanished. "May I be the last one to have to sacrifice my love because of the past."

Sage approached them, hugged her father, and said, "Come and dance with me, Apollo." She grabbed Gabriel by the hand and guided him to the dance floor.

The heir to the throne glowed as he danced with his daughter; her hair touched his face as they moved ever so gently to the sound of an old ballad that told the story of their lost homeland. All eyes were on them. He closed his eyes, enjoying the moment and taking a break from all the attention. Father and daughter had the same calming energy and soothed one another on the dance floor, forming an Ange'el cocoon, invisible to those around them.

"Apollo," she whispered, "I . . . have something to tell you."

Gabriel looked at Sage with a tender smile and replied, "Trust your heart, my love." He kissed her hand. The future king signalled Joshua to take his place. The Hu'urei bowed as Gabriel walked away, overjoyed with Sage's happiness.

The Best Seed

Quinn stood by the balcony of the Yi'ingo's royal home and began telling Sky all about her adventures in New York. She was so proud of her achievements and was excited to share them with her hero.

"You should have seen it, Sky. I ran up and over the wall and did a backflip and landed on my feet. They filmed it with cameras and—"

"What have I done to deserve such humiliation and disregard?" Amalia's bitter voice sent shivers down Quinn's spine.

"Have I upset you, Grandmother?" Sky asked, surprised.

"Leave us!" Amalia barked at Quinn, her mouth twisted with disgust.

"Go join the others, Quinny. Enjoy the party. I'll join you in a few minutes," Sky said calmly.

Quinn was furious with Amalia's tone. She flipped her body towards the door and rolled her eyes once her face was out of sight. She walked back inside the house but decided to stay hidden by the door of the balcony to listen to the conversation.

"Who gave you permission to accept a marriage proposal?"

"I didn't. I proposed to Bastian, and he accepted," Sky said firmly.

"Why? Now that you can have the king, why settle for less?"

"So now Bas is less?"

"It has been several millennia since we had an Ahe'ey that unlocked its wings. The Ange'el has good genes. We cannot allow him to wed with a mixed-race woman. You love him. You always have. Don't you want to be queen?"

Quinn's heart raced as she listened to the hateful words of the bitter old woman. She was inspired and fired up by Morgan's views, and she was offended by Amalia's racist opinions. Plus, Apollo couldn't marry Sky; he loved Morgan. What a mess!

"I'll support my king and will rule by his side as his military leader. I don't need the crown. I want my life back, and I'm recovering it from the strong hold you've had on it for all these years. If you want to be part of my life, Amalia, I suggest you adapt quickly and support our plans for reform." Sky's voice didn't waver.

"How dare you speak to me in that tone, child. Have you forgotten the sacrifices I have made to save this civilisation from the devastation unleashed by Sathian?"

"No, I haven't, but remember that I too have sacrificed everything. I've made my decision. Please don't be cruel to Bastian. He's your grandson, and I've never seen him this happy. Leave him his joy. Don't poison his mind with worry."

"You are a child. You know nothing of the responsibilities of power. This decision is not yours to make."

Quinn shrank behind the door as she listened to the words of the queen mother. Every word was delivered like one of her lashes—forceful, brutal, and deliberate.

"Was I a child when you asked me to lead the Yi'ingo army? Was I a child when I led them into battle, facing head-on the men and the dragons that killed my mother and sister and raped my kinswomen? Was I a child when my best friend was separated from me so that disappointment and anger could crush my heart? Was I a child then? Am I a child now?"

"This conversation is not over. You and Bastian are being irresponsible and are jeopardising the future of the bloodline. I will not have it. I'll speak to Angha and—"

"Leave, Amalia. Perhaps one day you'll stop looking at me like a womb to be traded and controlled. Come back when you care about my happiness." Sky spoke without any hesitation or guilt. She freed herself from her grandmother's sharp claws.

"You will marry Gabriel."

No, she won't. Quinn couldn't hold back her objection anymore. She peeked her head from behind the door and interjected in Amalia's command, "We have the code, the code of the royal blood. Sky and Apollo don't need to marry."

"What did you say, pet?" Amalia walked in the direction of Quinn and grabbed her by the hair.

"Morgan st-stole the ro-yal blood and we . . . we got the code here at Ahe'ey. They don't have to marry. They really don't. Morgan's a hero." Quinn attempted to release her hair from Amalia's tight grip.

"Release the girl," Sky said. "She's just a child."

"My daughter. Where's my daughter?"

"Probably back from New York," Quinn replied, fighting with Amalia's hands, which continued to pull her hair.

Amalia pushed Quinn out of the way and rushed through the door without saying another word.

Sky looked furious as she extended her hand to Quinn and pulled her to her feet. The teen took a few moments to compose herself.

"Phew! You'd make a terrible stepmom." Quinn grinned mischievously.

Sky shook her head and her frown turned into an amused smirk.

"What is this code you talk about?"

Quinn took some time to explain to Sky what had happened in New York and the Yi'ingo left with urgency to find Gabriel.

Bastian approached Gabriel who was sitting in the corner of the room, observing Sage and Joshua.

"Our baby girl is all grown up," Bastian said, sitting beside Gabriel.

"It seems that love is in the air," The Ange'el replied, bumping shoulders with his cousin.

"How are you?"

"Happy for you and Sky. You both deserve the world."

"It's time for you to stop taking care of everyone else and think of yourself."

"I'm fine, Bas."

"In the last few weeks, you've jumped in front of a fast-moving car, fought a dragon with a half-broken body, and attempted to commit suicide by opening the passage without the moonstone."

"I wasn't committing suicide. I was—"

"You're not fine. You're putting the needs of everyone else above your own, and it's time to stop. Go find your love and bring her back. You must demand it from your parents."

"You know I can't. I gave my word; I said I would marry a high-ranking Ahe'ey."

"We must make your parents acknowledge that things have changed. The Ahe'ey people adore you; you're their leader, and because of the trial, they now know you inside and out. No one at Ahe'ey wants to separate you from your love. You've inspired the Ahe'ey to change and to reform, and yet your parents ask you to stick to old traditions that don't serve you."

"It's due to my parents that I have gained this place in people's hearts —"

"No, it's not. It's due to who you are—a king of kings, the most honourable man I know—a fact that was hidden from many because of your parents." Bastian was frustrated. He wanted to shake his cousin out of his passive acceptance of his parents' mandate.

"My parents' guidance and leadership have kept this land safe. Their priority is Ahe'ey, and as a father myself, I can only imagine how it must feel to rule against the happiness of your child in favour of the land and its people. I don't doubt my parents' affection for me, and if they are asking me to let go of what is most dear to me, I can only imagine how important this must be to Ahe'ey as I know my grief is their grief and my happiness is their happiness." Gabriel watched Sage dancing with Josh as he spoke. "And I hope never to be in their place as I may not have the courage to hurt the ones I love so dearly, not even for the sake of my people."

"You are hurting them, you blind dummy. I fear you give your parents too much credit."

"I'm biased when it comes to Morgan. I lose track of my duties, put the security of Ahe'ey at risk. I was careless in New York, too careless. She's my life, my love, and my soulmate. I must trust my parent's guidance and wisdom, and hope that maybe one day they'll release me from this punishment."

"I don't wanna see you hurting like this."

"Go join your bride. Seeing you so happy and in love fills me with joy. I'm fine. I'll be fine."

"If you attempt any other stupid suicidal numbers, I promise I'll kill you myself." Bastian put his hand on Gabriel's arm and held it firmly and reassuringly just as Sky approached them.

In a sudden turn of events, Gabriel gasped; his eyes opened wide, "I must go." He rushed towards the door with his broken pace. Bas and Sky looked at each other puzzled.

"Leave this to me," Sky said as she got up to chase the Ange'el, and then she stopped for a brief second and looked back at Bastian.

"Go, please gooo. I was an idiot. I love you . . . and him. I love you both."

He watched her as she raced to catch Gabriel.

WHITE LIES

Forest, Ahe'ey

Scout walked through the dark forest holding Morgan's hand. The human walked quietly; the numbness in her expression didn't hide her grief. Scout felt quite protective of her fragile companion. The tiny creature looked as if she would break at any second. The human had been kind to Scout; even her admonishments had seemed to be unleashed from a place of interest and care. No one had ever really cared for the warrior before.

Scout's mother had abandoned her at Ange'el soon after her birth. Juno was her mother's name. She shook her head, pushing away a tiny hope coated by thick layers of fear and anger. That woman wasn't her mother, and if she was, then she didn't deserve one minute of her time.

Viviane had asked Scout to take Morgan to Yi'ingo. She'd ordered them to stay at Angha's old house until the queen sent further instructions. Angha's and Gaia's former home had been abandoned since she'd died and he'd left to live at Sma'aragdus with the dragons. Their tree house was located at Yi'ingo but away from the town centre. It was remote enough to give Morgan some privacy and allow her to grieve in peace. Keep her away from my son, Viviane had ordered.

They stopped just outside the village; Scout led them into the closest stables. She'd decided it was best to continue their journey by horse. Morgan was weak and barely responded to Scout's requests to walk faster.

Scout gasped as she stared at the formidable silhouette of Amalia's stallion leaving the stable. The creature reared just in front of where she stood, covering the sun with its head and mane. The queen mother spoke, looking at Morgan.

"How dare you come to my land to steal our most precious royal blood!" Amalia jumped off her horse and slapped Morgan on the face so hard that she fell to the ground. "You do not know your place. First, you attempt to claim the heart of our purest son, and now you betray us." Amalia kicked Morgan in the stomach twice as Scout jumped in between the two women. Morgan spewed blood from the corner of her mouth and gasped for air as she curled her body around her gut.

"My queen, please stop, please. The human destroyed the blood sample and brought back every copy of the royal code." Scout kneeled to help Morgan stand up. The queen mother pulled back her whip and delivered a lash onto the warrior's back. Scout wailed and fell on top of Morgan, using her body to protect the human as Amalia prepared to unleash another lash. Several Yi'ingo warriors gathered around the queen.

"Get out of the way or you will perish with the traitor," Amalia roared.

Scout turned around and pulled up her sword, facing the full wrath of the queen mother.

"Scout, don't!" Morgan screamed, her voice weak with pain.

In response to Scout's gesture, the Yi'ingo warriors unsheathed their swords and moved towards Scout and Morgan. More warriors arrived at the scene, and many others descended from their treetop homes, alarmed by the voice of their leader. It felt to Scout like the entire population of the village was closing in on them.

"Scout, my friend, this is my battle. Stay back," Morgan said as she slowly rose, moaning with pain, her hands placed over her stomach. The human pulled Scout back by the arm, stood in front of the warrior, and faced the increasingly large group of Yi'ingo that stood by their terrifying leader. "I took the royal blood, and I returned with the map to your genes. My gift to Ahe'ey."

"You will die for it."

"Then do it. Do it now. You'll be doing me a favour," Morgan whispered.

Scout moved forwards to stand next to Morgan, looked at the human's face, and there, she found only insanity.

"You broke our rules and betrayed us," Amalia barked.

"I bring an end to the slavery of your people, you . . . you bully."

"You stupid creature, the code is nothing without the live blood." Amalia unsheathed her sword as Scout moved to protect Morgan.

"Stay back, Scout," Morgan said.

Several warriors surrounded Scout. Morgan placed her hand on Scout's blade.

"No violence, my friend. Please." The Yi'ingo warriors disarmed Scout and grabbed her by the arms as she kicked and screamed.

"He's too good for you. How dare you come to Ahe'ey and steal our jewels." Amalia lifted her sword, ready to strike the human.

Suddenly, Scout saw a change in the expressions and postures of the warriors. The Yi'ingo sheathed their swords, lowered their heads, bowed, and took a step back. Amalia's eyes opened wide, her expression softened, and she lowered her sword. Scout looked back to find him—the royal Ange'el prince, on top of his horse; his eyes set on Amalia and her sword. His glow. Wow.

The sunlight hit his eyes, and they shone like beams of blue-green light. He shook his head as if he was clearing his mind. The future king jumped to the ground just in front of Morgan and walked in the direction of the queen mother.

"What is the reason for all this?"

Even Scout could see and feel his almost imperceptible anger. His jawline was tight and his breath fast and shallow.

"The human stole our blood; she must die. It's our law."

"Morgan didn't, I," Gabriel was interrupted before he could finish.

"Yes, I did. I stole it. It was me," Morgan confessed from the top of her lungs. She attempted to stand straighter even while she clearly struggled with pain. "Don't try to defend me, or lie for me. It's done. They know the truth."

The Ange'el turned to look at Morgan for the first time. His eyes went to her hands, still wrapped around her stomach; they travelled to the bruises on her face, and then finally, to her eyes. Scout had never seen so much love contained in just one gaze. His control over his anger seemed to be quickly coming undone. The frown, the tight fists, the locked jaw emerged as physical signals of his inner struggle. His body leaned towards the human, only to quickly retreat as she continued speaking.

"You are very kind Gabriel, but it was me. All me. Scout and Quinn saw it. They saw it all." She looked at Scout, and her intense eyes demanded the Yi'ingo's confirmation.

Scout vacillated, her expression reflected her silent protest, but Morgan didn't back down. The human pressed Scout with her eyes and Scout nodded.

Gabriel shook his head; his disapproving frown made Scout stammer.

"No ha-rm w-as do-ne. We brought the co-de and . . . and we des-troyed the blood."

Gabriel was unfazed by Scout's truth and Morgan's confession. He was having none of it. He turned to Amalia. "Lady Amalia, I was the one who—"

"The human abused our trust and must be punished," Sky's voice echoed from behind Morgan. The warrior queen leapt from her horse and looked straight into her cousin's eyes. "The human must be punished, and, after the coronation, the new king and queen should decide her sentence." Sky turned her eyes to Scout as she uttered the word "queen" and she bowed to the young warrior. The Yi'ingo warriors responded to Sky's small gesture by immediately releasing Scout.

Scout perked up her body, raised her chin and nodded. She knew her warrior queen well and immediately understood her plan. The young warrior inflated her chest and did her best to imitate the majesty of her leader. As if by magic, half the Yi'ingo took a step back. Scout placed her hands on her hips and narrowed her eyes, scowling at her audience.

Amalia sheathed her sword. She seemed to be satisfied with her granddaughter's suggestion.

"Do you agree my king?" Sky said coolly, raising an eyebrow. "My kinnggg?" Sky reminded Gabriel of his new power in front of her army; she was a seasoned ruler, one who knew how to lead her people and influence her grandmother. Scout and many other Ahe'ey had been spared from the terror of Amalia's whip because of Sky's diplomatic skills.

The Ange'el took some time to reply; he seemed so shaken by Morgan's state that he struggled to make sense of his cousin's plan. Scout could see the spark in his eyes as he slowly unveiled Sky's true intentions. When he did, he simply raised his eyes and nodded.

"Scout," Sky commanded promptly, "escort Morgan back to Ange'el and guard her carefully. Stay with her at Ange'el until the king decides her fate." Sky handed the lead of her horse to Scout. The young woman bowed, mounted the horse, helped Morgan climb behind her, and galloped away as fast as she could.

"Your back . . . ." Morgan whispered.

"Just a scratch. I'll survive, my blood is . . . I'll be fine. Hold on tight."

It was a clear and warm night. Ollie and Marcus were at the farm, inspecting the crops. Ollie had skipped the party at Yi'ingo to meet with his grandfather, a rare treat due to the king's schedule and commitments. Ollie loved to spend time with the royal Ma'asai and learn about farming, biology, and ecology. The luminous insects and plants provided just enough light for them to be able to walk safely through the fields.

"You are a true Ma'asai my son. Nature loves you and thrives under your care."

Ollie cleared his voice and prepared to share an idea he'd been working on. He was proud and excited to be speaking about it with the king.

"I believe I can double the yield of this farm in the next two years. I have a plan that I'd like to—"

"We do not need it," Marcus interrupted Ollie. "We have enough produce to sustain Ahe'ey."

The boy was surprised by Marcus' short and sharp response. The boy frowned and persisted.

"But wouldn't it be nice if we had some extra? We could store it and take the pressure off our farmers and make things more efficient."

"It is a fair and intelligent suggestion, one that has been put in practice by many men before you. One that is the beginning of a long path of decisions that leads to the destruction of our planet."

Ollie was attached to his idea. His pride was at stake and Marcus' answer only served to ruffle his feathers.

"What an exaggeration. I didn't suggest that—"

"I heard you." Marcus interrupted once more.

Ollie was now furious with the king. He bit his lip, trying to avoid an ill-tempered reply.

"You want to produce more and store the surplus. You want to make our lives easier and more convenient. These micro decisions have huge implications to our planet. You just need to observe the outside world carefully."

"What do you mean?" Ollie felt the heat on his face as he became increasingly frustrated. He had worked hard to impress the king, and now Marcus was shooting him down and didn't even let him finish explaining his proposal.

"Today, humans measure the success of their nations by something they call their gross domestic product, the GDP. It measures the surplus of resources that a nation is able to produce. This toxic indicator of a nation's success measures the conversion of natural resources into commodities. A thriving living forest does not contribute to the GDP unless it is cut down and sold as timber. A small farm that just sustains a family does not produce anything; a freshwater well that sustains a community for free does not contribute to the success of a country, but the packaging of water into plastic bottles to be sold in vending machines does."

"But that's not sustainable; they'll deplete the Earth." Ollie wiped his clammy palms on his tunic. He was starting to realise the faults in his plan and he felt ashamed of himself.

Marcus nodded and continued, "In this world that is measured by its surplus, forests are destroyed, packaging is created and disposed of in the ocean, humans mindlessly extract and destroy nature."

"I wasn't proposing that." As soon as he said it, Ollie realised that his pride was getting in the way. He remembered his father's words: There are more important things than my pride or your pride. He realised he was more concerned about defending his own image than learning and adding value. He worked to let go of his ego. He leaned in and listened attentively. "What should we do?"

"It is important that we can track what we consume all the way to the farm, that we can identify the happy, healthy chicken that laid the egg, that we know which tree grew the apple. We don't need warehouses or boxes or cans to store what we eat because we harvest just what we need when we need it, and we do not waste it."

"But what happens when our population becomes too large, and we're not able to sustain them with the current methods of production?"

"Then we should have fewer children. This planet does not have endless resources. The old Ahe'ey civilisation had to make this decision too. We increased our life span and limited our ability to bear children."

"Is there something we can do to change things in the outside world?" Ollie was a little jealous of his sister's visit to New York. Quinn's incessant boasting about her feats made him want to step up and do more to help his father.

"Yes, there is. Your father and I will be counting on your help and leadership when the time comes."

Ollie became slightly overwhelmed, "I'm not sure if I'm as strong as Dad. I . . . I wouldn't cope with what you have put him through."

"You are stronger than you think you are, Ollie, but no one will ask you or anybody else to endure Gabriel's tests and destiny. What we have asked from your father proves he is the right leader of Ahe'ey. It was important to ensure that everyone was on his side."

"No one doubts it now, not even the Yi'ingo."

"No one but Gabriel. He has convinced everyone else but himself." Marcus paused and turned to face an unexpected visitor.

"Father! What brings you to Ahe'ey?" The Ma'asai seemed surprised to see Angha emerge from the forest. The elder rarely left the mountain.

Ollie was intimidated by Angha's stern features. The old man had curly white hair that reached the middle of his neck, his icy eyes were greyish blue, and his eyebrows heavy and cruel. His lips were thin and pressed together tightly. He wore Yi'ingo colours, which reminded Ollie that he was the last of the Yi'ingo males.

Angha looked at Ollie with curiosity and then he replied to Marcus. "I am here to speak to your son. Where is he?"

"Have you met Oliver? He is Gabriel's son and a fabulous Ma—"

"You know my thoughts about bringing these dirty creatures into Ahe'ey. What's wrong with his skin?" Angha spoke with cold detachment. "Where is your son? I must speak to him immediately."

Ollie was mad, his jaw clenched. He had to reply; he just had to say something. His father had taught him that in case of injustice, silence is complicity. The boy searched his mind for a good answer—something smart and cutting. He couldn't find any. He was too intimidated and his mind blanked.

"What . . . What's wrong with your skin?" The outburst was sloppy and awkward, but at least he had spoken out.

"Oliver, please forgive my father's manners. He has been living amongst the Wali'ingooteer for far too long." Marcus admonished his father with his eyes.

"Be grateful you are his pet, or you would be dead by now, boy." Angha's expression was menacing and his words ice cold.

"What do you want, Sir?"

"Where is Gabriel?"

Ollie decided to reply to Angha. He refused to be intimidated by the horrible man. "My father was at Yi'ingo with Sky, but by now he's probably on the way to Ange'el to see Aria and Riley before they go to sleep." Ollie felt his voice pinch up.

"What do you want with Gabriel?" Marcus asked.

"You begged me to use the Wali'ingooteer to prove your son's worth. I answered your request, and soon, we will crown him the next king of Ahe'ey. It is time for him to return the favour." Angha turned around and left.

Ollie felt a chill go down his neck as he watched the wicked old man leave.

LIGHT

Morgan allowed herself one moment of joy. To see him alive and well, to be near him once again, even at such a perilous moment, was everything. Everything. Amongst all her pain and the sight of the deep and raw wound on Scout's back, Morgan felt a pinch of hope. She knew she was surrounded by unlikely friends—women who worked to protect her and support her. The bond she had with Sky and Scout seemed to overcome all the forces that pulled them apart.

Morgan had noticed the renewed bond between the royal cousins. The trust and complicity between Gabriel and Sky were palpable. They made the most striking couple in the history of humanity. She was happy for them, and no matter who would be the bride at the royal marriage, she felt connected to all of them—to Gabriel, to the two Yi'ingo and to Bastian.

Her priorities had changed; she needed Ahe'ey's help to defeat Zanus, to avenge her girls. And to achieve it, she needed Gabriel at the throne of Ahe'ey. If his marriage to Scout or Sky was the price she had to pay, then it was a worthy price to defeat evil. She grieved for the murdered girls; her hate for Zanus was as powerful as her love for Gabriel.

Morgan held onto Scout tightly, trying to avoid the Yi'ingo's wounds. She felt faint, so faint. By the time they arrived at the Sacred House, Sage was waiting for them at the door, and Gabriel galloped just a few metres behind them. Her love had arrived before they had time to dismount the horse. Gabriel took Morgan in his arms as Scout leapt to the ground. Morgan melted into his healing embrace. *How I missed you, my love.*

"Apollo, your shoulder. Be careful." Sage whispered while she squeezed Morgan's hand and smiled. "We missed you, Morgan."

"I'm fine," Gabriel said. He then turned to Scout and spoke softly: "Warrior."

"Sir."

"I'm in your debt. My daughter Sage will care for your wounds and Quinn will be by your side shortly. You are our guest of honour, Scout. "

"I'm not supposed to leave her side, Sir. Sky said so."

"I'll take good care of Morgan."

"Yes Sir," Scout said, resigned as Sage held her hand and guided her inside the building.

"Come, Scout. Let's have a look at that back. My sister told me all about your adventures in New York. I'm so proud of both of you."

Morgan wished the journey would never end; she missed those arms and that body and that feeling of heavenly bliss that she found every time she looked into his eyes. She couldn't bear to part with him once again, and although she worked hard to hide her feelings from her Ange'el, she knew it was an impossible task. The pain in her stomach was bearable in comparison to the sting she would feel the moment he left her side.

He walked silently until they reached her pavilion. He placed her on her bed, took her shoes off, and covered her with a blanket. She remembered that day in New York when he had carried her to her room at The Pierre. He was healing me when I kissed him.

"Gabriel, you must open that gate, and you must become king. Zanus, he—"

He kissed her forehead. "I know. I will. Rest."

"He killed all those girls, the monster. He must pay. I want him to suffer, to die."

"We will defeat Zanus." His tone was calm and neutral.

"Torture him. Take his eyes, cut out his ears."

Her desire for vengeance seemed to overwhelm him. He sat beside her and wrapped her in love, a love so pure that it almost conquered her hate, but her grief defied even the most powerful of the Ange'el. His body flinched as if her darkness had unleashed physical pain on his body.

"Those feelings are beneath you, my love."

"I need your people, your army, and your power. Promise me you'll be king." Her words tasted like poison; their cost was too high. She saw it in his eyes, he felt it—the sting, as she traded his love for power and revenge . . . to save her people. But he had done it before her; he had put humanity ahead of their love. Now they were evenly matched and united in their quest.

He nodded. "I give you my word that all Ahe'ey will be at your side as we defeat Zanus, but purge vengeance and hate from your heart; I'll have none of it." Sombre and determined, he wrestled with her hunger for revenge, so she turned on him.

"Who are you to talk? You stood quietly while your cousin stewed in it for years." She regretted her words and reached to grab his hand.

He lowered his eyes for a moment and then took a deep breath. He placed his hand first on her eyes to close her eyelids and then on her stomach. As she closed her eyes, she felt a rush of well-being shoot through her entire body. She pictured herself floating in the air, surrounded by stars. She could see him, a breathtaking, translucent winged creature made of light and stardust that floated in front of her. His turquoise eyes were set on her, full of love, empathy, compassion, devotion, and understanding of all things past, present, and future. His hand was on her stomach, absorbing her pain, healing her wounds. She could feel it, and she could see it—the darkness in her body absorbed by his own body, unsettling his light for a few moments.

His glow embraced her, and they danced within it, holding each other tight as if it was the last time. It was the last time, one final time. He dissolved her rage with unconditional love. Their dance formed a spiral of white starlight in the sky. They slowly moved down the spiral, the light fading away, the magic dispersing as the image of her room became more vivid and real. He was there sitting beside her, touching her stomach. He caressed her hair and she fell into a blissful, peaceful sleep.

A Shadow of the Past

He sat by Morgan, holding her hand and guarding her dreams against any darkness or unrest. He desperately held on to those last moments of proximity. He appreciated her features and shared with her the last pinch of hope and vitality he had to offer. When he left, he cursed his fate. His heart stayed with her.

He walked into the Sacred House and slowly climbed the stairs on his way to Aria's and Riley's room. Before he reached the top of the staircase, he felt a dark and twisted energy approach him. He looked down to find the powerful presence of an older man just a few metres from him.

What happened next was both unexpected and unsettling. As the Ange'el turned to face the old man, he felt his visitor's intense surprise, followed by his fear, panic, hate, and horror. And in the middle of the tsunami of emotions, Gabriel found himself becoming the object of the man's lust. A dark, sadistic desire, different from the many others he'd experienced in his lifetime. Gabriel shook his head and rejected the deeply disturbing images that flowed towards him.

"Angha? Is that you?" Gabriel hadn't spoken to his grandfather since he was a child.

Sathian's seed! Angha's soul screamed in deafening silence.

The Ange'el heard it with his mind's eye. He sensed his grandfather's struggle. The old man tried to control himself, but as the Yi'ingo looked at the face of his old enemy, his heart raced, adrenaline shot up through his body, and Gabriel felt it all.

"Grandfather? Are you okay?" Gabriel asked as he walked down the stairs and attempted to place his hand on Angha's shoulder.

Angha took two steps back, still coming to grips with Gabriel's resemblance to Sathian. "You look like—"

"I know. I'm sorry. It's not my wish to revive your worst nightmares." Gabriel pulled his hands back, his palms facing Angha as a sign of peace.

"Your mother risked our safety by allowing you to stay at Ange'el and to be initiated into their mysteries."

Sathian's seed? Gabriel stood quietly, waiting for Angha to calm down, the question running through his head. His heart raced well ahead of his mind. His body had answered the question before his mind caught up with it.

"I am reassured by the news of your wings, but my gut struggles to move past the evil shadow that you carry in your appearance."

Gabriel wasn't sure how to reply to the Yi'ingo. The Ange'el was still deeply shaken by the obvious truth that now stared him in the face—that face they shared.

"Walk with me outside, son. There is no privacy at the Sacred House."

As they wandered through the garden, Gabriel could feel the Yi'ingo's turmoil. Angha's uneasiness and distrust were hitting the Ange'el like a thousand paper cuts. They mirrored the messages and feelings he'd experienced from Amalia, Sky, and so many others. For most of his life, the Ange'el had listened to every single hateful thought directed at him. He held their suspicion and fear in each cell of his body. Angha's trepidation fed the Ange'el's deepest insecurities. The gravitational pull of the dark abyss where he held all his fears and uncertainties yawned before him, now impossible to conquer.

"I am here to ensure that you marry your cousin and put a stop to her ridiculous engagement to Bastian."

"Bas and Sky will be happy together." Gabriel took a deep breath; the objection was easily answered. The decision was clear and permanent.

"Their happiness is irrelevant. Your seed must fertilise a pure-blooded egg. We vowed to keep our bloodline pure. You have an obligation to your ancestors."

"The bloodline is safe with Sky and Bastian."

"You have better genes." Angha's face was red, and his voice guttural. He spoke as if the words he was uttering burned his tongue. Gabriel didn't understand why.

"I won't marry Sky! There's nothing—"

"She must rule by your side. No one else should take her place on the throne."

"Sky and Bastian will rule by my side until the time that we can shape a democratic system."

"You challenge me and your ancestors, undermining our history and our great civilisation. Your reform plans are dangerous and irresponsible. You Ange'el always believed you were above our rules."

"I'm doing my best to honour our past and to move us towards the future."

"You will listen to your elders and will marry my granddaughter! We know best. She will be the queen of this land. You may have your wings, but I still control the dragons."

"Is that a threat?" Gabriel raised his voice, his eyes focused on Angha, warning him to mind his words. The Ange'el could feel the Yi'ingo's darkness; he could taste the dangerous insanity of a broken mind. In his own mind, he saw Angha unleash unimaginable abuse on his body. Was it? My body? The images were so dark and disgusting that he had to close his mind's eye to the pure evil that poured out of his elder's mind.

Angha placed his hand on his grandson's neck and squeezed hard. "It is a fact! One misstep and I will show you and your human pets who holds the real power in this land. I am watching you!"

Gabriel felt Angha's dark lust for him, and his stomach turned.

"Be careful, Angha. Today, I choose to blame your words and actions on my physical resemblance to Sathian, but it's the last time I'll take such threats so lightly." Gabriel walked away, deeply unsettled by the encounter.

He stopped by Aria's and Riley's room and kissed them as they both slept soundly. When he reached his room, he removed the exoskeleton and collapsed on his bed with exhaustion. He'd been putting pressure on his broken bones for most of the day, his shoulder wound had reopened, and all his vitality had been used to heal Morgan's wounds. Angha's darkness had been the final nail in the coffin.

The Ange'el regained consciousness for just a moment in the next day, but this time Sage used more than words to force him to heal. His daughter kept him sedated for a few days; he wasn't quite sure for how long. He could hear his mother's voice guiding his daughter's hand in his forced internment.

YOUNG BULLY

9 December 2014 - Ange'el

Morgan woke up to find Scout sleeping on the chaise longue beside her bed. She quickly realised that her pain was gone and that the red and blue bruises on her stomach had disappeared. She walked over to Scout and noticed that the young warrior's upper body was wrapped in bandages.

"Scout darling, you should be recovering in your own bed," Morgan said as she got up.

"Sage told me I'm good to go. I'm strong . . . unlike you." Scout jumped to her feet. "You better?"

Morgan nodded, ignoring the Yi'ingo's boasts. The memories of the recent events returned to her mind and hit her like a fast-moving train. She sat on the bed staring at the blank wall.

Scout grabbed Morgan's hands and pulled her up. The young woman embraced her, wrapping her arms around Morgan's waist.

"Thank you for having my back, Scout." Morgan looked up and attempted a grateful smile. "Literally."

"My back heals faster."

Morgan couldn't have predicted what happened next. The Yi'ingo lowered her head and kissed her on the mouth. Scout's lips and tongue were wilful, hungry, and intrusive. Morgan took some time to make sense of the turn of events.

The Yi'ingo took her passiveness as encouragement, and her hand went up to fondle Morgan's breast. Surprise, shock, and anger took over Morgan's mind. She pulled back abruptly, pushing Scout's body away from her.

"Nooo."

"Kiss me," Scout said, pulling Morgan's hips towards her. "Be mine, and I'll take good care of you. I'll protect you."

"Scout, I don't like you in that way." Morgan had to work hard to see beyond her friend's lack of tact. She managed her anger and tried to recognise the affection that had manifested as overt sexual harassment.

"You find me disgusting." The statuesque creature slumped her shoulders and pouted like a spoiled schoolgirl.

"No, not at all. If a man had kissed and touched you forcibly like that, what would you have done?"

"I know you find me disgusting. Everyone does. I'm a monster." Scout released Morgan and sunk into the chaise longue, crossing her arms in front of her chest.

"You must stop being a bully. Apart from that, you are perfectly normal, intelligent, and desirable."

"So? Lie with me." She stood up again and gave a step towards Morgan who retreated away from her.

"I don't like you in that way." Morgan's voice was filled with compassion.

"But I'm much more beautiful and pure than you. Why wouldn't you desire me?" The confusion in the Yi'ingo's eyes reminded Morgan that the girl was a product of her Ahe'ey upbringing.

"Because what is most attractive is skin deep."

"Are you saying I'm ugly on the inside?"

"What you said was ugly."

"But it's true! It doesn't stop me from lusting for you. It's weird; you are growing on me. I find you strangely attractive." Scout's greedy eyes scanned Morgan's body up and down.

"That's because, despite your awful manners, you aren't shallow." Morgan felt naked and vulnerable. Her trust and goodwill towards the young warrior were quickly dissipating.

"Yet you reject me." The pout was back now, enhanced by tears that threatened to roll from Scout's desolate eyes.

She's just a kid, a strong kid. She needs rules and direction. I won't give up on her. "I'm in love with someone else, Scout. You know this. Everyone knows this," Morgan said, overwhelmed with the idea that her most intimate moments had been shared with all of Ahe'ey.

"Sure, who doesn't desire a pure-blooded Ange'el. Even I want to f" Scout stopped in the middle of the phrase as Morgan's eyes locked on her like sharp spears. Even the insensitive Yi'ingo could feel the pinch of Morgan's wrath. "You talk about depth, all high and mighty, but you lust after the most beautiful of the Ahe'ey. Hypocrite much?"

"I don't love him because of his looks. I've met many handsome men and never felt like I do for him."

"Yeah, sure. Who are you trying to fool? There's no one like him in your world. We're all wired to seek the best genes. His temperament has nothing to do with it." Scout rolled her eyes and walked towards the door.

Morgan realised that she was falling for Scout's provocations. Just a young wounded pup with a crush. She's barking for attention, Morgan thought, remembering the intensity of her own feelings at Scout's age. Morgan felt empathy for her friend. Scout had been subject to bigotry and bullying throughout her short life. She'd been raised without the guidance of a loving adult. No wonder she's confused about my friendship and affection.

"Scout!"

"What?" The Yi'ingo stopped; her doe-eyed expression speaking louder than her words.

"Thank you for having a crush on me, darling. I like you too. You're a great friend."

"You love, and I have a crush. Am I so easily dismissed like a child sent to her room without a meal?"

"I'm not a meal, and you can't love me. I'm ugly, remember?" Morgan said, smirking.

"Look who's shallow now."

As Scout left the room stomping her heavy boots, Morgan quickly fell into mournful darkness and despair. She spent the day with the schoolchildren at the Sacred House, listened to the teachings of the Ange'el, and observed the kids as they learned and played. Throughout the day her heart broke for the young Ahe'ey every time a teacher explained that some of them wouldn't be able to pursue their abilities and dreams because of what they had between their legs. This world, so different, yet strangely familiar, is as broken as mine.

Sathian's Seed

Angha paced nervously around his rock-carved home. Outside his living space at Sma'aragdus, the dragons followed his moves. The Wali'ingooteer hissed and roared, unsettled by their master's outward rage and by the scent of Angha's adrenaline.

Angha was aware that the virtue and honour of a royal Ahe'ey could be washed away by great heartache or overwhelming temptation. Angha knew this not just because of the history and actions of his cousin Sathian, but because of his own past behaviour. He had sunk into the darkest of conduct; he had committed the gravest of sins, and he had been responsible for the madness of his cousin and the terror that the Ange'el had inflicted on the women of Ahe'ey.

Many years had passed, and Angha had believed that his hate had vanished with the deaths of Sathian, Gaia, and his children. He thought his heart had healed. He had hoped that his rage, his deviant lust, his shame, punishment, and grief had gone. He had vanquished all those feelings from his system. Yet, they returned at the moment his eyes set upon the majestic and ethereal Gabriel, the future king of Ahe'ey. The raging tempest had returned the second he realised that Gabriel was Sathian's grandson.

Sathian had played one final hand, and against all the odds he had won—his grandson was going to be king. Angha screamed, unable to contain his revulsion and rancour for the two men who shared that one perfect and provocative body. The dragons howled and grunted, joining their master in a symphony of terror that echoed deep inside Ka'alama's belly.

My granddaughter must rule this land. He will undermine the bloodline to benefit his dirty pets. He will destroy us. I must destroy him.

<h1 style="text-align:center">Good Intentions</h1>

10 December 2014

Bas was happy, deliriously happy. He had never truly believed she would be his. Sure, he knew she'd be likely to take his seed and his hand in marriage if he was her only choice. Now she had options, and her other option was the perfect Gabriel. Yet, she had chosen him. He was happy, deliriously happy, but he wouldn't be totally happy until his best friend was happy too. So he focused his efforts on the happiness of Gabriel. Her name was Morgan.

The young royals continued to work on the reform plans. This time they assembled at Joshua's home in Hu'urei. Josh had decided to host one of the sessions as a gesture of goodwill and openness towards the new king. Sky had invited a handful of high-ranking Ahe'ey from all the tribes to join a discussion about the proposed changes.

Without consulting his broody best friend, Bastian stopped by at the Sacred House to invite Morgan to join them. He explained to her that they needed her perspective and input on the reformed plans. The Ma'asai hid a second and more pressing motivation. He was committed to reuniting Gabriel and Morgan, and to challenging Viviane's and Marcus' orders.

Bastian found Morgan to be gaunt and grief-stricken, but she agreed to help the Ahe'ey with her experience from the outside world. They left a moody Scout behind at Ange'el; the girl wasn't happy to let Morgan out of her sight.

"I should be able to protect the lady. Don't you think, Warrior?" Bastian retorted with some frustration as the Yi'ingo used Sky's orders to try to convince him that she should go with them.

Morgan travelled to Hu'urei in silence, immersed in her own thoughts.

Her gloomy mood charged Bastian's resolution that something had to be done to stop the suffering of his friends. Poor Morgan seemed inconsolable because Gabriel was going to marry someone else. I must bring them together, he deliberated with great conviction as they reached Joshua's home.

The sharp and severe frost of the Hu'urei's home fuelled Bastian's rebellious mood. The absence of nature unsettled the Ma'asai as he accompanied Morgan through the corridor, making way to the main saloon.

The design and features of a Hu'urei's house mirrored the outstanding architectural and construction skills of their owners. Stone was the material of choice. The builders shared the taste for elegant simplicity with the Ange'el. Yet, the lines at Hu'urei were edgier. They excelled in creating cold, clean spaces enhanced by asymmetrical design features.

No paintings hung on the walls, as if they wanted to reset their past and create a blank slate. Their art, mostly sculpture, was modern and abstract and yet managed to depict anger, rage, and loss through the use of blacks, intrusive lines, and contorted metals. The Hu'urei architectural soul celebrated paradox—the strength and roughness of the stone, carved until it was smooth, elegant, and dangerous with incredibly sharp edges.

The reform group had gathered around a table. Gabriel sat in front of Sky and Josh with his back to the door. Four trusted companions, one from each tribe surrounded Bastian's cousins. The royal Ange'el was speaking with passion and conviction: " . . . I'd like us to take this further. I want us to abolish royalty and its privileges during the first years of my term as king. All Ahe'ey should have access to knowledge and take part in the decisions related to this land and its people. We will repeal any law that infers that one race or group is superior to another."

Madria, Sky's second-in-command, sat beside Gabriel. She cleared her voice and spoke, "But the high-ranking Ahe'ey are more intelligent, live longer, and due to this, they are more experienced. Our genes integrate our values. Is this not enough justification for those less capable and less virtuous to delegate their power and decisions to us?"

Big Magnus, who stood behind Sky and Josh, joined the voices of dissent. "There's a reason why these rules exist. The treasures locked in our blood could destroy the world if left in the wrong hands. Only high-ranking Ahe'ey can protect it."

"A small group of people shouldn't decide the fate of a treasure and a curse that can impact the world so greatly on behalf of so many," Gabriel replied. "We need all of our people. Their views matter."

Josh scratched his bearded neck. "Cousin, even I think this strategy is too risky. The pure bloodline needs to be protected from greed and abuse. The story of my grandfather and father show us how dangerous it is to—"

"To leave so much power, unrestrained, in the hands of a few. We'll structure a democratic governance model with checks and balances. Opposition is crucial to" Gabriel stopped talking in the middle of a sentence and turned his body to face Morgan and Bastian.

Bastian saw his cousin crumble in front of his eyes, and he quickly realised that his plan wasn't well thought through. The Ange'el went silent, and the entire room froze; all eyes set on Morgan.

Sky shot a disapproving glance towards Bastian. He didn't need Ange'el skills to read his lady's mind. A wave of guilt and uncertainty hit the Ma'asai as the tense and sombre mood sucked the oxygen out of the room.

"Morgan! Come, join us at the table." Sky moved over, making room for the human.

Morgan spoke as she walked around the table to sit next to Sky. Her face was sombre and her tone unapologetic.

"The tribes will respond to your actions more than your words. This land is the stage of deep racial and gender discrimination. Everywhere I look I see oppression, intolerance, and violence. A class system driven by genes? Access to roles in society limited by gender? Homophobia? If you are serious about bringing light to humankind, you must clean your own house first."

"And forced marriages based on descent," Bastian added, soon regretting his words when he saw his cousin's discomfort.

Gabriel's eyes screamed with sorrow. "We are doing all we can to reform Ahe'ey as soon as possible, Morgan. All your points are valid and are being addressed even before I take the throne." His reply was reassuring, and his demeanour contained.

"The Ahe'ey couldn't wish for a better leader." She lifted her eyes to meet his. "I too have lost faith in democracy. Too many casualties and compromises. Perhaps a benevolent, powerful ruler is what the world needs." Her mind seemed to have travelled to a faraway place.

"The darkness of grief prevents you from seeing the light." The entire room was caught in his sweet tenderness towards the human. "We will reform; we will defeat hate, and we'll do this with the full participation of both our people and your people."

Morgan remained indifferent to the Ange'el's reassurances. Bastian felt great compassion for the lady with the broken heart. Even Gabriel seemed to be publicly acknowledging her pain. Bastian's human friend seemed so different, so hurt and confused. He had to speak out.

"We aren't going far enough. I object to your sacrifice." Bastian couldn't resist.

"What would you have me do?"

Few had ever experienced Gabriel out of balance. His outburst emerged with no filter. It came straight from his heart: "Do you remember what happened the last time a royal son of Ahe'ey pursued his own interests and passions, elevating them above his people's needs? Haven't you seen the wave of destruction caused by self-serving desires? As Sky pointed out recently, have we forgotten that the devil was once the most virtuous of Ange'el?"

Sky was about to interject, but Morgan spoke first.

"Marry whomever you like; just keep your word. Rule. Open the gates. Defeat Zanus." Her tone was neutral and her face numb.

Bastian looked at Gabriel, puzzled by his words and Morgan's response. "Gabriel! Are the wings not enough of a clue?"

With his mind, Gabriel admonished Bastian. Neither Gabriel nor Morgan needed their wounds publicly prodded by the blunt object that was Bastian's perseverance.

"I'm incapable of objectivity about . . . I must leave it to those who have a track record of placing Ahe'ey's needs before their own and the needs of the ones they love." Gabriel dropped his head and squeezed the tips of his thumbs as he spoke.

"They are wrong, Gabriel. They are wedded to old traditions that no longer serve their people. If you don't trust yourself, then trust me." Bastian had gone too far. Morgan had tears in her eyes while Sky admonished him with her frown. Madria and Magnus looked away awkwardly, unsure how to react to such an emotive debate.

"Excuse me," murmured the Ange'el. Gabriel looked at Bastian angrily and walked out.

"He has no idea of his own virtue. I fail to understand how this is possible," Bastian said. He was exasperated by the turn of events.

Joshua replied, "It's easy for Gabriel to compare himself with Sathian.

He's the third wheel of three royal children. He grew into manhood as the hated outcast of his generation. He's trusting his parents because they have proven to be unbiased. They certainly had no reservation in sacrificing their son for the benefit of Ahe'ey."

"He's no third wheel. I'll stand firmly by him and for him," Bastian said, leaving in pursuit of Gabriel.

Bastian walked outside the meeting room into the corridor to find Gabriel in the arms of his father.

" . . . he came to see me," Gabriel said. "He was out of his mind."

"I will speak to my father," Marcus replied.

Bastian saw Gabriel vacillate. The Ange'el left something unsaid, lowered his head, and then turned to face Bastian.

"Congratulations on your engagement, Bas," Marcus said, extending his hand to his nephew.

"Thank you. It was . . . unexpected," Bastian said, shaking Marcus' hand. "Uncle, can we talk?" He avoided his cousin's eyes.

Marcus nodded. "Sure. What about?"

"The royal marriage."

"You will be wasting your time," Marcus replied assertively.

"Father, Bastian and I must go now." Gabriel pulled Bastian by his arm towards the main door.

"I went through the reform plans this afternoon. I am proud of what you all have accomplished in such a short period," Marcus replied before he entered the main saloon.

Gabriel stopped and put his hands on top of Bastian's shoulders. "I need some fresh air. I hear the Hu'urei arena is well stocked with some high quality fighting sticks. Want to give it a go?"

Bastian took a deep breath. It was exactly the escape that both of them needed. The two men walked towards the arena, took off their tunics and entered the ring. The Ma'asai was reminded that his cousin was still recovering as he noticed the exoskeleton that wrapped around Gabriel's body.

The noise echoed throughout the forest as their sticks came together in the air. Bastian fought using his full strength and power, and he grunted at every blow. Every strike had the impact of his entire body weight. The Ange'el's lean body defended each blow without flinching, and it was in those moments that he demonstrated his power. Bastian's strength didn't seem to affect him. Gabriel stood tall, showcasing all the elegance and grace of the Ange'el.

The future king was more precise and fast in his attacks, rotating the sticks and dancing around Bastian. Neither of the men had chosen to put on any armour; they anticipated each other's moves and avoided full contact between stick and body. It was a battle of muscle versus agility, heart versus brain. Gabriel's superiority was obvious as the heir to the throne simulated blows to Bastian's head and body. Once in a while, he used the sticks to make Bastian fall.

Bastian got mad; he flew through the air towards Gabriel using his signature battle move, a flashy manoeuvre that made crowds stand and cheer at the games. The blonde man looked like lightning striking the earth in all its destructive glory. Gabriel dodged him in the last moment, rotated around himself, and used the stick to almost hit Bastian on the back of the neck, stopping the motion millimetres from his cousin's head.

"You continue to let your emotions cloud your judgment, cousin," Gabriel said, extending his hand to Bastian, who was still kneeling in the place he'd landed.

"Something you should practice more often, my king. Perhaps you should use me as a role model." Bastian used the power of his entire body to project his shoulder and elbow onto Gabriel's stomach. The

Ange'el wasn't expecting the blow and shrieked in pain. Gabriel used his stick to trip Bastian and simulated a hit to his head. The Ma'asai got what he had asked for—emotion surfaced in the actions and expression of his Ange'el cousin.

"I can't afford to lose my balance. Bastian, for heaven's sake, have some compassion. Please stop. I beg you, cousin. I fight myself every day. It's eating me inside. I don't have the strength to fight you too. Not you."

Bastian threw his stick to the floor and placed his hands on his cousin's shoulders. "I can't stop. Someone has to watch your back and be on your team. You clearly are not." As Gabriel walked away, shaken by the exchange, Bastian shouted out loud, "How can you let her suffer like that?"

"She's mourning for the death of the girls."

"What girls?" Bastian asked, puzzled by Gabriel's response.

The Ange'el shot an exasperated glance at him and walked away.

"Dead girls? Why does no one tell me anything?"

Sky and Morgan left Joshua's home together. Sky wasn't quite sure what she could say to the little creature. The Yi'ingo recognised the rage in the human's eyes. Rage was something Sky understood. She always felt connected to those at a breaking point, those unwilling and unable to accept more pain, those ready to fight back.

The Hu'urei's suspended bridges allowed people to travel along the rooftops of the buildings and experience the magnificent views from above. The ground was left to nature—a patchwork of edible gardens and wild forest. The presence of the two women was unsettling to some of the men. Some watched with curiosity and others with nervousness as they spotted the warrior queen on their land. They walked towards the stables to fetch Sky's horse.

"A lot was achieved today," Sky said as she monitored the groups of men gathered on some of the rooftops as they walked by.

"Sky, behind you!" Morgan yelled.

Sky was confused. *How can she know what's behind us?*

The Yi'ingo turned to see an imposing red-haired man running in their direction with a knife in his hand. She recognised him as the man who had harassed Morgan in the forest.

The Yi'ingo kicked the attacker in the groin, and then kicked again at his hand, making his knife fly in the air. The man grabbed Sky by the neck, lifting her off the ground and reaching for her sword. Morgan stood up, picked up his knife from the ground and stabbed him in the shoulder. As he groaned in pain, he released Sky's neck as she rotated around herself and thrust her elbow into his face, knocking him out of action.

Morgan, still holding the knife, ran towards the unconscious man and pulled the weapon up above the man's heart, ready to deliver a deadly blow. Sky grabbed Morgan's wrist. The human used all her body to fight the Yi'ingo's mighty grasp. It was useless; Sky had more strength in one hand than Morgan had in her entire body.

"We are done." Sky squeezed Morgan's arm just enough to make her drop the knife.

Several men were now running in their direction.

"Prepare to run," Sky said as she watched at least a dozen men rush to meet them.

"Are you okay?" said the first Hu'urei to arrive on the scene. Sky unsheathed her sword as he approached them. "It's okay, my queen. We're on your side."

The man tied the hands of the attacker behind his back. The Hu'urei smiled at Sky like a schoolboy with a crush. The unlikely demeanour of the man piqued the Yi'ingo's curiosity.

"Would you like us to deal with this situation, or would you like to take him to Yi'ingo? Sky?"

Sky was still in defence mode, her hand on her sword, her eyes piercing through every Hu'urei around her, looking for any sign of further attacks. She pulled Morgan closer to her.

The man finished tying the attacker's hands, stood up and then raised both hands, palms facing Sky. "My queen, he was acting on his own."

Sky raised her eyes and looked at him. "What's your name?"

"Atticus!"

Sky took a moment, considering her response and scanning the postures of the men who surrounded them. There was no aggressiveness in their eyes. Only fear. They knew she could take them. If she had to she could take them all.

"Atticus, deal with this criminal and ensure that he is punished for his actions. Keep this event contained. We don't need the news of this attack to spread throughout Ahe'ey. It'll fire further disorder and delay our integration efforts. I'll assume this man was acting alone."

Atticus bowed in agreement, surprised and delighted by Sky's words.

"Yes, my queen. Thank you. Thank you for trusting us to deal with this thug," Atticus replied.

"What happened here?" Joshua shouted as he arrived by foot. His eyes went straight to Morgan and the blood on her hands and dress.

"Arku attacked these women. Sky has asked us to deal with the situation with discretion," Atticus said.

Joshua looked at Sky with a smile and bowed his head.

"Very well. Do so; lock Arku in jail while we plan his trial. Lady Morgan, are you okay? I'm sorry for this. How are—"

"Not my blood. His blood." The human stared at Arku with disdain.

"Excellent. Are you hurt?"

Morgan shook her head.

Sky left the Hu'urei to deal with the criminal and escorted Morgan to Ange'el. She continued to watch the groups of Hu'urei on their path.

"Predators. All of them," Morgan murmured, her eyes narrowed as she stared aggressively at the men.

Sky turned to look at Morgan raising an eyebrow, "All of them?"

"They kill, rape, pillage. Worst, they stand passively watching others take and destroy what doesn't belong to them. Murderers."

"Some of these men are just—"

"All men. Power and control, that's all they care about."

"You don't really mean that. Do you?"

Sky recognised the conflict and confusion in her friend's expression.

"I do . . . Sometimes I do. When I think about their history of violence, I do. Maybe it's in their nature." Morgan placed her hand over her mouth as soon as she spoke it.

Sky knew that rage consumed, that fury couldn't be reasoned with, that pain wouldn't be healed with words. She understood Morgan's contradictions. She too had seen the best and the worst of men. She walked silently, escorting her human friend home, allowing Morgan to be with her wrath. Sky knew that wrath empowered even the most fragile and tender-natured soul to take a stand. Rage could be a window out of darkness and despair.

As they reached the pavilion Sky simply said, "Today a lioness was born." She smiled at the human, bowed her head, and then galloped towards Yi'ingo.

HER GAME. HIS MOVE.

"He's . . . he's my—"

"Yes," Viviane replied as she turned to face her son.

He felt Sathian's dark legacy crush him in a single blow.

"Is Father aware of—"

"Spare him, Gabriel. Nothing good will come of it." There was no glimpse of warmth or love in his mother's eyes.

"You push me to be king when you know the devil shared my genes."

"I have set the rules of the game. How you play, it is up to you. You must decide what will rule your life. Are you a slave to your genes? Take the throne, and you will prove you are not."

"You ask me to prove I'm not a slave to my genes by marrying a high-ranking Ahe'ey?"

"My game. My rules. Your turn."

My queen, please speak to me as my mother. I need you now. His voice failed him.

"I am. I've pre-selected fifteen high-ranking women. Spend time with them."

He left, holding his heavy heart in his hands. The turmoil had turned into exasperation and then anger. He wanted to rebel, to fight, to challenge her, but he was trapped and he was alone.

INVISIBLE CAGES

A Glimpse into the Future

11 December 2014 - Ange'el

The soon-to-be king was coming to grips with a new reality. A reality where he could no longer walk freely in Ahe'ey without being engaged by crowds of admirers that demanded his time and attention. He'd attained a celebrity status unlike any other in the history of Ahe'ey; he was a god, their god. He'd inspired them and touched their hearts. They all wanted a piece of him in a time when he had little to give.

Most of the energy coming his way was nurturing and positive. The humble Ange'el was a kind, dedicated leader, taking the time to speak to his people and understand their needs and concerns. He showed how grateful and flattered he was by all the kind words. He was bathed in love. Gabriel was tireless and promised himself that he would never take this attention for granted and would always use it to drive a positive impact in the world.

Some of the scrutiny was more intrusive and uncomfortable. Some young women, in particular, were quite obsessive and forward when it came to the heir to the throne. He tried to be polite and keep his sense of humour as women objectified him and preyed on him in lust and obsession. He never uttered an unkind word or a rude gesture, but deep inside, it was taking its toll. They knew him too well and relentlessly used their insights from the trial to make advances on him, attempting to replicate some of the most precious moments he had had with Morgan.

In the weeks before the coronation, Vivianc had ordered Gabriel to meet many of the high-ranking single women of Ahe'ey. She asked him to select a future queen. With a heavy heart, he met with each suitor to the throne. He was still keen to know each one, asking questions and connecting with them based on their interests and ambitions. The untrained eye would only see the welcoming posture, glow, and kind expression, but the dark circles around his eyes and the forced smiles were evident to those who knew him well.

He held the meetings away from the Sacred House, as far from Morgan as possible. Bastian's strong opinions meant Gabriel couldn't rely on his cousin for support during this difficult time. Sometimes, between meetings, he would go as far as throwing up, his body rebelling against his mind, telling him exactly what his subconscious thought of the entire affair.

Gabriel had to summon all his skill to get through the dates without upsetting his suitors. The other Ange'el attempted to connect with his mind. They knew too much, and they pushed too many buttons as they searched for his inner thoughts and feelings. The trial had left him exposed and vulnerable. The Yi'ingo were physical creatures, quite forward in their claims on the Ange'el. Some were sexually voracious and aggressive in their advances. Gabriel walked the line between graciously backing off and assertively blocking overconfident claims to his body.

The Ange'el was meeting another suitor, the young Yi'ingo warrior called Scout. The small feathers hanging from her left ear danced in the air as a gentle breeze caressed her features. Her poise impressed Gabriel. She walked in with the confidence and certainty that she had nothing to lose or to gain by having this encounter; she looked calm and self-assured.

"How are you, Scout?"

"Fully recovered, sir." She bowed.

"Good. I remember you well from the time you studied at Ange'el. You were always one of my favourite troublemakers."

"Erm . . . I was hoping you'd forgotten, sir. I promise I don't go around trying to convince the Ange'el to change their ways and eat meat." She grinned.

"Well, if I remember correctly, your methods didn't include persuasion or influence. You tricked them into eating a vegetable pie that contained a little more than vegetables." His expression was playful; he teased her with his eyes and lips.

"I just assumed that once they'd had a taste of it, they'd understand how mind blowing it really is. Lady Viviane has never forgiven me for that experiment."

"Do you continue to cause trouble at Yi'ingo?" he asked curiously.

"A bit, yeah. I think if it weren't for Sky's protection and my father's genes, Amalia would have killed me by now."

"Why is Amalia displeased with you?"

"Let's just say I don't see eye-to-eye with Amalia when it comes to the roles and responsibilities that are imposed upon the high-ranking Ahe'ey."

"I hope you'll be happy with the reform plans that are being discussed with the tribes."

"They're okay, but you have a long way to go. Sorry . . . I meant," Scout paused to find the right words, "that it's generally going in the right direction."

Gabriel laughed, "You don't need to mind your words with me warrior. I'm here to serve you. I'm interested in your fierce and unfiltered opinions."

She rolled her eyes and looked up to meet his eyes, "Yeah. Sure."

He couldn't contain his amusement. "If you aren't careful, you'll end up an advisor to the king of Ahe'ey."

"Is the future king a fool? He should know that I challenge everything and everyone."

"Precisely. The future king would be a fool not to seek your counsel."

He was tempted to dig deeper into the mind of the spirited warrior, but decided she deserved her privacy. "So tell me, mighty warrior, why do you want to be my queen? It seems an unlikely choice based on what I know of you."

"Well, sir—"

"Please, my name is Gabriel."

"I'm told I have the purest blood after the royal ladies. It's my duty . . . I guess," Scout said with a cold detachment.

"Tell me the truth. Will you, Scout?"

"You see, sir . . . Gabriel . . . The truth is that Amalia will kill me if I don't mate with a high-ranking man. I . . . I like women; I'm what humans call a lesbian. I'm a failure in Ahe'ey."

Gabriel was impressed with the forthrightness of the young woman. It was a rare occasion when an Ahe'ey had the courage to come out as homosexual. It was a dangerous move. "I'm sorry to hear this. You, my young friend, are not a failure. Have you spoken to Sky or my parents?"

She shrugged her shoulders. "They turn a blind eye to Amalia's bullying. After all, they are the guardians of our lineage. It's not in their interest to lift the childbearing burden from any fertile young woman of royal descent. I'm hoping you see it differently."

"You can rely on it. So, you put your name forward to be queen so that you can help change these rules?"

"Me? Nah. I've no skill or patience to deal with rules and laws."

"I'm still unclear on what brings you here."

She looked at him and then hid her face behind her crest.

"Scout, you know I won't judge you or betray your trust, don't you?"

"Yeah. I do. Someone told me that a good leader protects those that are different, and you have a lot of different people around you, including your insufferable daughter." She smiled defiantly.

"I hear you saved my daughter's life. Thank you."

"She saved mine first. It was an eye-for-an-eye sorta situation."

He smiled, amused at her choice of words. "Looks like you've had an eye-opening experience. Why are you here, Scout?"

She took a moment, her foot playing with a small round rock. "I know that you love another, and that love will never fade. I'm not allowed to love whom I love and . . . she won't have me anyway."

In his mind's eye, Gabriel saw Scout kiss Morgan, and everything became clear. Scout continued, unaware of the Ange'el's insight.

"It'd be a good arrangement if we joined in our sacrifices for Ahe'ey. I'm willing to bear children for the bloodline and you, if you'll have me, as long as you understand that it would be just for that—"

"Scout, you don't have to sacrifice yourself. I promise that under my ruling, we'll drop any barriers that are stopping you and others from having a fulfilled life. You don't have to marry me to achieve it."

"I'm not here because of my desires. I'm here for you, my king. If you are willing to sacrifice your love for the sake of the Ahe'ey bloodline, who am I not to contribute with my womb? We're both broken, aren't we? You're broken because you love a human; I'm broken because I love a woman. Perhaps two wrongs can make a right?"

The same human woman? He avoided the growing urge to invade her mind. This sting in the gut, is it jealousy? He'd never felt it before.

"If that's the message that you are receiving from my sacrifice, then I'm sending the wrong message. There's nothing wrong with you. Follow me, will you?"

They galloped towards Lake Do'oras, and just before they reached the gate, they turned to the forest until they arrived at the two crystal capsules. He guided her to the door of one of the capsules, turned to her and spoke.

"A long time ago, we had evolved passed the gender binary that is pushed by our rulers today. Our desire and sexuality were not shackled to a need to procreate. We connected; we loved; we enjoyed sexual ecstasy. We were male, female, both, none; it didn't matter as long as we were worthy, authentic, and kind. We lost it all when the sea claimed our land and most of our people. Suddenly, our survival relied solely on the spreading of our pure seed. So our ancestors deleted our past, the vestiges of our evolution. They purged the love and the lust that men had for men and that women had for women. They erased the creatures that had transcended a single gender identity and orientation. Here you will have a glimpse of our past and our future. Here you'll find that all that you are is just right."

"What's inside?"

"Art and history. A vision of a better world, hidden here by the survivors of the flood."

"Are you joining me?" she asked as she approached the sliding crystal door.

He shook his head, "I have something I must do." He reached to grab her hand and kissed it. "Scout, thank you for your offer and generosity. I'd like you to be part of my team."

"Why do you want my opinion?"

"Your unique experience and point of view are important. A ruler must surround himself with diverse voices to make the best decisions."

"You speak just like her," Scout said, and he smiled openly, a touch of emotion overwhelming his heart.

"Will you, Scout? Be part of my team?"

She nodded and he continued, blushing a little:

"She's amazing, isn't she?"

"Divine, sir. Divine."

Scout's eyes focused on the Ange'el in that moment when he was most vulnerable. He knew that look, a person turned into a predator by his Ange'el glow. She moved towards him, placed her hands around his body and pulled him towards her until her front was glued to his.

"You know, Gabriel, you're the first man I desire."

His eyes didn't flinch as her hawkish gaze focused on him. Her warrior gene—the predator, the hunter—had her eyes locked on her prey. She moistened her plump lips with the tip of her tongue.

"It's not me; it's the glow." He paused and then, without moving, he spoke assertively, "You should learn to keep your hands off what doesn't belong to you, Warrior." The moment she stole a kiss from Morgan flashed in Scout's mind as he admonished her.

"Jealous, Sir?" Her hands pulled him towards her, forcefully. "A Yi'ingo will always be a Yi'ingo." She smiled.

"No Scout. Don't take. Learn to ask; learn to respect," he spoke to her as if he was admonishing one of his children.

"Sure." Her eyes turned into slits and she caressed his back with the tip of her nails. "I'll keep my hands off your sweet love if you keep your mind's eye off my head. Deal?" She held her head high and spoke, wearing defiance in her eyes.

"The lady makes a valid point," he smiled and nodded.

She dropped her hands, bowed, and walked into the capsule.

Gabriel could still experience her ecstasy despite the artworks' deafening voices. Joyful overwhelming emotion flooded Scout's mind and body. Then he kept his word and focused his attention elsewhere. He needed to see Morgan. He had to see her.

Morgan was leaving the Sacred House when Gabriel walked through the door. She took offence to his glow and his beauty. She rebelled against his mournful eyes. She disliked everything about him. She knew where he had been; Scout had told her about his recent activities. The thought of Gabriel and Scout destroyed her, even when her rational mind screamed the raw facts. She liked the warrior; the girl wasn't to blame. But Gabriel, he needed a wake-up call.

"Is it done?" Her eyes, mouth and tone of voice, all cutting. "Have you assembled them like cattle and picked the one best suited for breeding? What are you doing?" She looked at him, her tone coated with harsh exasperation.

"Morgan I—"

"Have you lost all sense? What message are you giving to your people?"

"I'm doing what I can," he murmured, lowering his eyes.

"No, you're not."

"They'll close the gates forever. Don't you understand? You asked me to be king."

"You're submitting to bullying. You're colluding with those who stand for racism and bigotry." Her entire body leaned forward as she shot her words in his direction.

"That's not fair. When I'm king, I'll reform—"

"When you're king, you've achieved it by rejecting everything you have stood for. How can you champion nurture by marrying genes? How can you promote love by ignoring your heart?"

"I'll do it, so no one else will have to."

"Spineless. Sacrifice or fear? What drives you, really? Be a man. You're not Viviane's child anymore. Grow up." She was unrepentant in her attacks.

"Things are . . . complicated."

"Actions speak louder than words." And looks, she thought, rejecting the magnetic pull of the beautiful sorrow that stood in front of her. He was so lost, just a shadow of his old self. "I don't care about your glow, your genes, your wings, your battle skills, or how many dragons you defeat. I loved you because of what you stood for. And right now, I despise you. Hate you. You stand for nothing."

"I have to compromise to drive change—"

"Some things you just can't compromise."

"Morgan, I love you; I know this is hard. This kills me too." His eyes were full of compassion.

"You think I'm speaking about us? That this is about me?" Her pitch kept climbing towards the dark place where oxygen is as rare as gravity.

I see your pain. I share it. I . . . I'm not marrying Scout.

Did he speak it? It didn't matter; she replied with the same strength of conviction. "Good, she's too damn good for you."

"You're hurting. I"

"I don't hurt because I've lost you. I grieve because you've lost yourself. Once, I wanted to be yours and you mine, but right now you don't deserve me."

I never did, his voice echoed inside her head.

"Argh. That. What you're doing right now. That doesn't just hurt you. It . . . it almost destroyed Sky. It undermines every boy and man at Ahe'ey. While you fear your power, you are telling boys they are monsters. Every time you fail to lead from the front, you are letting them down. You neglect to show them how a great man leads, what they can aspire to be. You allow others less honourable to set the bar. Why do you let Sathian define manhood?"

"What about him? What he did. There's something you don't k—"

"Be a man Gabriel. Stand proud and confident of who you are."

"Don't you see? That's how it starts. Is that what you want? The brutal hand, clasping the Sabine's flesh in Giambologna's statue. Zeus, under the cover of the night, forcing himself on Danaë. Your most beloved art, all symbols of crooked manhood. Is that what you ultimately want of me? One missed step and I'll—"

She slapped his face with the entire strength of her body. It stung, his understanding of her deepest and darkest contradictions. How dare he utter them out loud in daylight. How dared he shame her like that. She was part of the culture and the art of her world, a world controlled and edited by men, a culture that objectified women. She did her best to escape the gilded cage—the symbols, the art, the history. But, they chased her. It wasn't her fault, it was the men, the crooked men.

Exactly! She heard inside her head, and his eyes told her he was listening.

"I'm sorry. I'm sorry," he murmured, turning his back to her and rushing his hand through his hair. He seemed out of his mind with despair. Her anger quickly washed away as she looked into the soul of the winged creature that desperately flew against the cage, his body crashing against the golden bars. The heavenly cloud of white feathers, lost during the inner battle, slowly glided towards the floor. Sathian, his cage. The history of men, his cage; her cage.

Morgan recalled Viviane's words: "Remember that there is strength in vulnerability."

"Nooo, my love. No." Her voice softened. She spoke with urgency. "Be Gabriel, fully Gabriel, unapologetically Gabriel. Without fear of the shadow of a past that's not yours to own. Don't hide behind someone else's bloody ledger. Create your own history, story, legend. Show the world what it means to be a man. A good man, the best of men."

He turned around to face her and took a step towards her. Morgan stepped away from him and turned her back, preparing to leave.

"Prove the world wrong, Gabriel. Lead."

"I gave my word," his voice quivered.

"You were held to ransom by those you most love," she replied, moved by his suffering. "Do me a favour, Gabriel. Spend a day with the schoolboys at Ange'el. Watch them play, watch them learn. Just . . . watch them." *If you won't do it for yourself, you'll do it for them.*

Morgan walked away. She hated him; she despised his weakness; she couldn't stand it; she . . . she tried her best to hate him, to gather all her frustration and build a wall. This wasn't about her, about them. Not just about them. Her wall of pride was falling apart again; perhaps she was biased, blinded by his rejection of her, but some of what she'd told him was true. She was sure of it.

He doesn't need my adulation; he needs my strength. Her gut fought against her mind.

"Have you seen Gabriel?" It was Bastian walking towards her, slightly out of breath.

"I just left him; he went into the Sacred House. We . . . fought. I . . . gave him hell." To Bastian, she confessed the regret she'd attempted to discard a few moments before.

"It is time," Viviane said as she approached Morgan in the Ange'el garden.

Morgan was too immersed in her own storm to attempt to make sense of the queen's words. Viviane continued, "Scout is waiting for you at the pavilion; you are to depart immediately. She will take you up the mountain to a place of worship, and there you will see the light."

"What do you mean, Lady? I'm in no mood for your games." Morgan was ready to unleash her frustration on the queen.

"You wanted to know the truth. You shall have it. Go now."

It was a command, and it travelled deep into Morgan's mind. Her anger remained, but her feet promptly followed the will of the mighty Ange'el. Morgan returned to the pavilion. A pair of leather trousers and a matching tunic had been placed on top of her bed and, on the floor, some boots. Morgan recognised the Yi'ingo outfit; she knew the Ange'el never wore animal skin.

Scout popped her head through the door.

"You'll need to put those on. The Ange'el adjusted them to fit your weird body shape and size." Scout's tone was casual, the message awkwardly delivered, but Morgan knew that the barb was unintentional. "We'll be climbing Ka'alama; most of our journey will be by foot. The vegetation is thick and the bush unforgiving."

The girl was cheerful, her smile was unguarded, and Morgan had never seen such a joyous spark on the Yi'ingo's eyes. Scout's meeting with Gabriel had brought light to the young woman and Morgan was left to battle the unavoidable resentment that clouded her mind.

"I'm going to get the horse; I'll be right back." Scout left with a spring in her step as Morgan burst into quiet tears.

The absent-minded young warrior whistled merry songs as they galloped on one single horse through the Yi'ingo forest on their way to the mountain. Whatever had happened between Gabriel and Scout had lifted the heavy shield of grumpiness that had been the trademark of the purple-haired girl.

Morgan placed her face on Scout's back and tightened her embrace. She refused to feel anything other than friendship for her young companion.

"Do you know this place we are going?" Morgan asked as they abandoned the horse and started the hike up the mountain.

"I have escorted Queen Viviane there a couple of times. It's just a fountain inside an inverted tower; an empty well. Pretty boring."

"So, what are we supposed to do when we get there?"

"I don't know; that's up to you. My job is to take you there and back in one piece. Easier said than done. If you continue to walk at this snail pace and stumble on every other step, we won't get there before nightfall."

Morgan followed Scout up the mountain. The long-legged Yi'ingo had to constantly stop or slow down, rolling her eyes as she waited for the human. Morgan had to jog to keep up as Scout pushed through the woods like a feisty locomotive. With her right hand the Yi'ingo used her sword to clear the dense bush that surrounded them. Her left hand held onto Morgan's, pulling her up the hill. As they reached the Mu'urnu lagoon, Scout took off her boots and jumped head first into the pristine waters. The light cyan surface of the water reminded Morgan of his eyes. His reflection vanished as Scout emerged to the surface.

The Yi'ingo had come into her own in just a few hours; she wore her sexuality without shame or fear. The shape of her firm breasts, perked up to the sky, pushed the leather tunic that covered them. Freedom and defiance were present in every contour of her body as it moved under the water. Never had Scout been more beautiful; her skin glowed from within.

"Come," Scout said, splashing Morgan with the cool crystal water.

"What happened to you? You've blossomed," Morgan asked with a smile.

"Gabriel, he —"

"No, no sorry, don't tell me. I can't . . . ." She took off her boots and clothes, and then dove into the lake. She kept her head immersed for as long as she could. When she finally came up to take a breath, she simply changed the conversation.

"How long will it take for us to reach the place?"

Scout didn't reply right away; she paused as if she was assessing her friend's state of mind. In return, Morgan used all her skill to push out a reassuring smile.

"The Heart of Ahe'ey is just half an hour away from the mouth of Sma'aragdus." Scout pointed to a dark hole just above them on the mountain.

"Smargdus? That's where the dragons live. Right?"

"Yeah. My father watches over them."

"The famous Angha. Are you going to visit him?"

"I've never met him before. I'm just a bastard, one of many." There was no sign of resentment in Scout's tone, just resignation.

"Too much time hanging around Quinn?" Morgan teased.

"They're only interested in my womb."

"You my darling, are a courageous, kind and loyal friend. It's his loss to miss out on your accomplishments."

"You and the Ange'el prince are cut from the same cloth. You support people, make them thrive."

"No. My people . . ." I'm death. My people die. "I need great Ahe'ey like you and Gabriel to ensure that no one else suffers in my land."

"Anything you need, tiny human Ange'el. I'm here for you," Scout shot her a smile and flipped her wet hair to the other side of her head.

"I'm no Ange'el," Morgan shrugged her shoulders.

"Whatever you say, pretty lady. Whatever you say."

Gabriel stayed hidden behind a tree, watching the children play. Joy, laughter, playful creativity, and curiosity filled the school garden with the vitality and innocence of those who hadn't yet been touched by disappointment. Then he saw him, a young boy, no more than five or six years of age. The child walked alone towards a nearby shrub, focusing on something that Gabriel couldn't see. The boy's long black hair extended to the middle of his back and he wore it lose and wild.

The child squatted in front of the shrub and used a dark veil of hair to cover his activities. Gabriel was curious and used his mind's eye to see what the boy was seeing and thinking. A sparrow still covered with the feathery fluff of youth seemed to suffer from an injury on its wing. The small creature jumped and flapped its good wing in ongoing bursts of effort. The endearing clumsiness of the bird was a sign of the creature's exhaustion as it fought for its life.

The young boy looked back, his eyes touched by fear. He scanned the playground, looking for his tutors, and sighed with relief, as none were outside. He placed his hands around the little creature and closed his eyes, his unlawful action hidden by clumps of wild black hair.

Within seconds both wings flapped as the child released the sparrow to fly up to the top of the tree. Gabriel's inner joy gave him away; the boy turned around and his eyes met the gaze of the future king. The child had the Ange'el's gifts; his mind's eye was strong and powerful. Gabriel saw the terror flash in the boy's face as their eyes met.

"Please. Please don't tell. I know it's wrong. I won't do it again. Please sir?" Gabriel walked towards the boy, kneeled and took him in his arms without saying a word. Their minds connected. Much was said as their mouths stayed firmly closed. Young Micah nodded and smiled as he jumped to the ground and ran towards the other children.

As Gabriel left the school's garden, he experienced a sudden flashback. He had to stop and lean against the wall of the Sacred House. A cloaked man approached four-year-old Gabriel who sat by a creek at the Ange'el garden.

"That butterfly, bring it to me. It will give me joy," he said. First, the man touched the boy in the space between his eyes using his index finger, then he extended his arm and opened the palm of his hand to the sky.

Young Gabriel focused his eyes on the butterfly, and the creature flew into the man's palm.

The hooded figure spoke: "Well done." The man turned to face Gabriel, placing the butterfly on top of the boy's shoulder. "One day you will claim the throne and the ring. Then, you will show them who we really are, my son." Gabriel looked up into the man's face and he saw himself, his beardless face as an adult. A shiver went down the Ange'el's spine and his gut twisted and turned.

The future king remembered him, the princely man who had visited Gabriel as a child—his secret friend. He recalled the adulation that he had felt for that man.

"I am now going to erase the conscious memory of our time together, son," The man said at the end of each visit touching the boy's forehead. Gabriel had never asked why. He trusted the fun creature that fed his curious mind with knowledge.

Sathian had taught him to improve his powers. Gabriel was so talented that, years later, when Ange'el men were forbidden to use their gifts, Viviane had decided to protect her son's powerful skills. She sent him to New York so that he could flourish freely away from the shadow of Amalia's sword.

He was twelve-years-old when he had last seen his grandfather. At that time, the young boy no longer welcomed Sathian with an open smile. He was now old enough to recognise the deformed face of evil. The devil appeared at the hideaway in the forest while Sky and Bastian slept. Gabriel was summoned outside by the powerful mind of the terror. But before the boy succumbed to the calling, he grabbed his sword and faced his kinsman with defiance.

"Don't be silly; have I ever hurt you?"

"You touch them; I'll kill you."

"I'm not here for them. Not today, maybe some other day. I'm here to say goodbye, son."

"You're a murderer." Gabriel felt the weight of his sword increase until he could no longer hold it up. He wrestled with Sathian's powerful mind. The boy knew it was a mind trick, but he lost. He dropped the sword and was forced to listen in silence.

Sathian ignored the boy's accusations and spoke: "This is my last and most important lesson." He pulled a rose and a ginger root from his bag and spoke about both—the beauty and thorns of the rose, and the nutrients of the ginger root. At the end, he spoke with sadness in his eyes. "Grow your roots even when everyone around you praises your flowers. Love and recognise the plants with strong roots. Nurture them and they will, in turn, feed your heart and soul."

I liked him . . . I . . . adored him. Even at that moment, when I knew what he had done, I . . . I cared for him; I listened to him. The devil was once my friend and companion. The devil guides my hand.

"Hey, we must speak." Bastian said as they crossed each other at the corridors of the Sacred House.

Gabriel ran past his cousin without saying a word. He sprinted into the woods, disappearing for many days and nights until the best tracker in the land would finally find him.

Morgan tried to cobble together the images, scents and sounds that she'd experienced in the heart of the mountain. She battled to find a path through the dense mist that had descended on her mind. The fog stifled her ability to think, to remember, and to connect the dots that she knew could be connected.

The statue of the angel, the fountain, the arrow that moved as she touched the water. Her hand, a child's hand. Whose child? The memories, a sense of déjà vu: his face, the silver eye patch, the lake of fire that gave birth to a curly-haired fairy. The mist inside her head; she couldn't shake it. The answer was crystal clear, and yet, it was inaccessible to her. His face, his loving face, holding the girl: Aria, Morgan, or Fay?

Echoes of history repeating itself. The cycles in time that form an ever-expanding vortex, spinning at the centre of the place where darkness becomes light, and light turns into darkness. Consciousness ever expanding even as history repeats itself. From hate to love, from love to hate. Learning fuelled by contrast; necessary growth pains that move humanity up the twirling funnel. An eternal dance, death and destruction followed by life. We must stay in the light . . . We won't stay in the light forever . . . We will emerge from darkness once again…

She grabbed her head with both of her hands and clutched her hair with her fingers; her forehead pressed against Scout's back. The fog, the thick fog inside her head. They galloped into the Ange'el village and quickly arrived at the Sacred House. She jumped off the horse and ran up to find the priestess, the queen, the Lady of the Lake.

The lady was waiting in the main courtyard of the Sacred House. Above them, the Eye of Ahe'ey enhanced her glow. Viviane spoke, and her words echoed inside Morgan's head.

"In those books, those empowering stories that you share with your girls, the heroine is trapped. She pushes against the shackles that hold her back; the wounds in her flesh are self-inflicted. She ignores the key to the chains that she holds in her pocket. She's too focused on the unfairness of her status, too busy fighting an oppressor who is taking full advantage of her self-enslavement.

"The readers scream at her, at the heroine in the book. They all know it; they had guessed it from the first few chapters. They become exasperated as they watch her fight for a right that had always been hers. They watch her battle powerful forces; they see her contradict herself at every turn. Yet she has heart, courage, and determination. She is worth their time and patience.

"The readers shout, frustrated; she gives away her power at every chance she gets. A blind fool, trapped by stories that have shaped a reality that need not be hers. Her muscles and bones did not grow; they did not know they could. Her capabilities did not flourish; how could she be what she did not see in others? Her vitality, attacked by the poisoned food, water, and air. Soulless plastic, lack of nourishment, disrespect for the food chain.

"The lesson she had been teaching all her life was the lesson she had to learn. Now the revelation comes at the highest price."

Morgan sobbed. The mist dissipated in her head and the truth was too overwhelming to be confronted so quickly.

"You had an entire life, my love," Viviane whispered.

Morgan experienced equal amounts of pain and exaltation. Her aunt glided towards her and embraced her. In her mind, she saw a baby's hand playing with the curly copper locks of a female warrior. In the woman's face, she recognised Sky's eyes and nose, in the rebellious curls she recognised her own untameable locks. Gráinne.

"My sister died to liberate you from his claws. She opened the passage and paid for it with her life. Now you return home my Ange'el. My Fay."

Morgan held on to Viviane in a tight embrace. Much was shared in silence, a hundred shades of love and joy. The queen filled Morgan with the happy memories of her mother and father. Their love was strong, their complicity endearing. She thought of him, her love.

"Price?" Morgan asked.

"Claim him as yours by right of birth and become part of everything you fight against."

"What?"

"Or give it all up—Gabriel, the throne, your power; the power you need to defeat Zanus."

"What . . . What are you doing? Why are you doing this?"

Morgan was too overwhelmed to be able to think straight. She wanted to celebrate the news and connect with her family, yet the queen worked to shatter the joyous moment.

"What do you want from me? What, exactly, do you want me to do?" she asked, confused.

"My dear child. My work is done. What I want is not important. The world belongs to the young, the ones who will live with the consequences of the choices that will be made in the next few years. They are not my choices. The elders can and should advise, educate, share history and experiences, but it is up to you—my children—to fully own your next move and accept its consequences."

"I don't understand. You . . . You've bullied, manipulated, controlled your subjects and your children's lives. How can you stand there and tell me this is none of your business? How can you wash your hands now when he's trapped by your orders?"

"Is he? Trapped? He has a choice and so do you. My game, my rules, your move."

I'm an Ahe'ey, a royal Ahe'ey. She was coming to grips with the impact of the revelation.

"Yes, you are."

If I marry him, he will be marrying my genes.

"He will not, but that is not what the Ahe'ey will see. They will worship the fairy tale and happily conform to the rules of the bloodline."

Morgan sobbed, her chest jumping in small convulsions. She was drowning in soul-wrenching misery. "So . . . we are slaves to our genes. That is what you brought me here to learn."

"Are we? Look at you—small, weak, helpless, lacking the powerful skills held by those who share your blood."

"I'm not helpless," Morgan objected as she cleaned her nose with her sleeve.

"You are, when compared to your cousins. You are the poster child of limiting nurture. Your genes, child, are pure, the purest. Yet, look at you. Frail, so frail."

"What do you want from me, Lady Viviane?"

"I want you to think about your options, and I want you to make the right choices. I have set the rules of the game; I have compressed a lifetime of learnings and suffering into just a few weeks. A set of controlled experiences that allowed my children to learn what you would have learned during your entire life. I have taught you that life is messy, that there is no black and white, that for every choice there is an unwanted consequence. I have shown you contrast and suffering and loss. I am done, my sweet love. I am done. All of my four children are ready to take the lead. Your turn, Gabriel's turn, Sky's turn, and Bastian's turn."

"Why did you choose to tell me now?"

"Because as a human, you saw his flaws; you overcame your pride and insecurity and you challenged him. You saw beyond his magnificent glow."

"I need to think. I need time—"

"Join the Ange'el apprentices here at the Sacred House. Take a vow of silence until the solstice. Listen, learn, meditate, and serve. Take time to process this revelation. And remember, whatever you decide to disclose will have implications for everyone around you."

Morgan submitted to the advice of the queen. Her days were spent in silent reclusion, away from her lover's mind's eye.

The Weight of Leadership

16 December 2014

Sky tracked Gabriel's footprints across the forest. After a while, she could easily predict where he was heading. She found him on the highest branch of the tallest tree at Ahe'ey, the place they used to visit in their youth. When she reached the top of the tree, she sat behind him and did exactly what he used to do when she needed reassurance. She put her arms around him under his arms. He said nothing, but the comfort of his cousin's embrace was enough to break through his façade. She could feel the movement of his chest as he cried. His agony burst from inside his soul in a steady stream of salty tears. He placed his hands on top of her hands and held them near his heart. There they sat for hours without uttering a single word.

The sky was clear, and they could see the entire island and the sea beyond the dome. The sun was setting and the birds chirped as they were starting to settle in the trees around them. Although the Ahe'ey had introduced many of the fauna and flora when they settled on the island, one could still spot some of its native birds, like the longtail and the albatross. Ahe'ey was a well-planned and man-made ecosystem that was hidden from the world under a permeable dome of invisibility. Only water and gas could cross its invisible wall. Due to this, migratory animals had adjusted to stay within its borders. The technology that enabled the dome and the portal by Lake Do'oras had been lost as the ancient Ahe'ey land had sunk into the sea. This small island, an ancient outpost of the former civilisation, had been transformed into the main home of all its survivors.

The Ange'el allowed Sky to feel what he was feeling. He shared his soul with his cousin, reminding her how much he respected her and how grateful he was for her leadership. On top of the highest tree at Ahe'ey, Sky listened to his fears and aspirations. Gabriel was reminded of the fragile situation of his people and how much knowledge could be lost in just one moment. He felt the weight of the responsibility that was about to shift onto his shoulders. He reviewed the history of the queens and kings before him, looking for clues and lessons that would enable him to rise to the occasion. He was grateful to the strong Yi'ingo warrior who now held him in her arms, who had been asked to rule a land at war in her teen years after losing all the people that she most loved. She had sacrificed everything she had to lead Ahe'ey to peace, and he was grateful that she was going to be by his side as he ascended to the throne.

The bond they shared had completely deleted almost thirty years of separation and distrust; there was nothing that could separate them now. Brother and sister watched the sunset, embraced—a true partnership, two leaders who matched each other in strength, valour, and honour.

Sky and Gabriel, like their parents and grandparents before them, understood the weight of leadership, its responsibilities and sacrifices. They shared the torments of decision making, where there was no way forwards that didn't have significant costs associated with it. Yet, each flawed decision, taken with the best intentions, had the power to corrupt and distort the humanity and purity of their vision and values. In their nightmares lived a demigod who decided to fight inequality and racism by raping women. Power corrupts, and hell . . . hell is filled with good intentions.

At the first signs of twilight, Sky finally said what she had come to say to him. "Before we go, I need you to turn around and look at me, Gabriel."

He did. They both stood on the branch of the tree. The turquoise in his eyes reflected her features as he touched the braids in her hair.

"You aren't Sathian. You'll never be him. You're the leader Ahe'ey deserves. I trust you with the lives of all my people. But, let me set you free from your fears. I . . . I may not be good at many things,"he was about to interject, and she put her finger on his mouth"but I'm your best warrior and the commander of your army. If you or anyone else becomes a threat to Ahe'ey, I'll prioritise the security of our people. I will obliterate any threat," she smiled. "I will resist. I will lead the revolution once again. Rule. It's an order. I'll hold you to the highest standard, and I'll take your head if you fall short of greatness." She saw his eyes light up as he placed his hands on her shoulders and squeezed them.

"Give me your word, warrior. Your word!"

"You have it. My word," Sky said looking straight into his eyes, "I'll kill you if you ever turn into a Sathian." She raised her dagger and pressed it against his neck. "Rule Gabriel. Stop containing your light; we need all of it. I'll defend us all against darkness. That's my destiny."

He smiled and embraced her.

She gave a nervous laughter. "Only you would respond to such a threat with a glowing smile. Don't you believe me?"

"Quite the opposite. I do."

"Can we go now? It's time you visit a distraught Ma'asai who's driving me crazy with his everlasting grouchiness. Seriously, you need to fix it."

Sky stayed at the farm for long enough to see the men embrace. Then, she left them as they exchanged words of affection coated in sickly sweet honey. Men. She rolled her eyes, smiled, and walked away, strutting across the forest.

Her Word, His Sentence?

Viviane went down to her knees, her body pulled backwards, her head followed, and her raven hair sliced the air in a circular motion. Precognition was a skill she had not yet learned to master fully, so when a burst of the future came to her it triggered a strong physical reaction. Her mind and body collapsed under the weight of the potential outcome that had just been unleashed somewhere in the world. A current event that, like the first fallen piece of a domino chain, would likely lead to a series of future events. Her body convulsed, and the grief broke her, even before the images flashed through her eyes.

Her son, kneeling on the ground; his bare body covered with bloodied gashes and cuts. His neck, hands, and feet in chains. Gabriel's eyes, one cyan, the other emerald, lit from the single source of light at the top of the cave. Was it Gabriel? So much rage in his heart. His green eye cried blood as Sky pressed her sword into his neck.

Darkness washed away the images in the Queen's mind's eye, and then the empty blackness was replaced by another scene, the one she feared; the one she rejected. The body of her son collapsed on the stone ground in a pool of his own blood.

"What have you done?" the queen sobbed as she tried to locate her children with her mind's eye. "What have you done?" she repeated as she watched them come together in a loving embrace on top of the highest tree in Ahe'ey.

Solstice

21 December 2014 - Temple of Lights, Ahe'ey

Ten days had passed since he'd last seen her. Gabriel closed his eyes and concentrated on his breath. Around him, several Ange'el helped him prepare for the coronation. They fitted him with a cyan-and-silver tunic, a light and shiny chain mail armour on top of it, and breast and shoulder plates. On his chest was the insignia of the Ange'el—the moon and the stars. His light beard had been perfectly trimmed, and his hair was being braided and adorned with tiny silver beads.

The preparation for the coronation was underway. The event coincided with the winter solstice and the opening ceremony of the Games. It was the biggest event of the last two centuries, and the entire population of Ahe'ey was involved in the activities.

He was dizzy from all the attention and anxious to push through the whole affair as quickly as possible. The people demanded pomp and circumstance. These events, festivals, and games had the power to heal and unite the people. They were shiny affairs and, just like Gabriel, they'd been carefully designed to glow and to emote a sense of wonder and loyalty. Throughout his life, the Ange'el had despised his power, a cheap privilege that took zero effort to attain. Yet, now he was about to embrace it and magnify it a thousand times. He understood that his people needed light, and he was prepared to unleash it . . . even if reluctantly.

Gabriel had met Amalia just an hour before to confess his crimes. He had kneeled in front of his kinswoman and explained the crucial role played by Morgan, Scout, and Quinn in the safeguarding of the bloodline. He'd declared full responsibility for the risks he had taken with the royal blood and submitted to her judgment with humility and penitence. The queen mother had simply said, "For a quarter of a century, I have honoured and protected the sanctity of our blood; genes whose powers are only expressed in those who truly deserve it. The miracle of your wings has affirmed my blind faith in the bloodline. I will not reject what I have worshipped. Your wings outrank my orders. Your wisdom and virtue outshine my age. Rule son."

As Gabriel recalled his conversation with Amalia, he worried about her blind faith in the royal genes. After all, it was just a code designed by humans, and code could be flawed.

Viviane entered the room at that time. "Only those who seek perfection spend their time looking for flaws. They can either be paralysed by them or travel on an endless path of self-improvement, a journey where they learn and grow." His mother beamed love, light, and hope. Her cyan dress had a train that wove along the floor as she moved. Light beads covered her dark hair, and her sleeves touched the floor on the sides of the train. "You make me so proud, my son."

Gabriel kissed the queen.

Marcus came in just a few seconds after Viviane. "This is going to be the biggest celebration of all time. I have never experienced Ahe'ey so vibrant. How are you, my son?"

"I am well, Father. Happy to have you both here."

They walked to the main balcony of the Temple of Lights. On either side of the balcony stood stone angels with silver wings. The creatures held moon and sun icons high above their heads. Below, they could see dozens of women and girls walking into the building. It was a hopeful day for them all as Gabriel had committed to choosing a bride. He lowered his head and closed his eyes for a moment. Focus on your breath. Slow down. Breathe.

As he prepared to speak to his mother, she put her hand on his mouth.

"There is nothing more to be discussed, my darling. You will need to choose your own path. We have done all we can for you and Ahe'ey."

Gabriel looked up, his eyes set on Viviane's platinum crown. He was once again reminded that she was a ruler first, and a mother second.

The children came running through the door. Gabriel lifted his head with a forced smile to greet them. Aria and Riley wore matching white dresses with moon- and star-shaped blue patterns that sparkled in the sun. They twirled around the room, excited by the event. Viviane had asked them to lead their father as he entered the Throne Hall for the coronation ceremony.

Quinn walked in, proudly wearing a formal Yi'ingo apprentice uniform. The leather was adorned with crimson and gold phoenixes and made her look older. Gabriel noticed she had a fresh moon tattoo just above the thinner end of her right eyebrow.

"So that I always remember to be as brave as my Ange'el dad," Quinn explained as she kissed Gabriel.

Ollie's green Ma'asai kimono had sun-shaped golden patterns. His outfit was like his grandfather's, but in a chartreuse tone that contrasted with his dark features. His long dreadlocks were tied back, and at the side of his neck was a fresh moon-shaped tattoo and the four stars of the Ange'el.

"Dad, I want to study economics. Will you teach me?"

"Of course."

"That's what we need to fix first, in the outside world. Right?"

Gabriel looked at his son, put his hand on the boy's shoulder, and smiled, proud. Oliver was the most vulnerable of his older children and the one most likely to attempt to hide it, yet in the last few weeks he'd matured into a fine young man. He was learning to be quietly confident and self-assured.

Sage arrived together with Sky, and they looked like frost and fire. Sage was wearing a long, glimmering white priestess tunic tied at the waist by a silver-and-blue belt. Her blonde hair sparkled as the golden locks travelled down her back. Sage's ethereal aura and lightness contrasted with Sky's solar storm. The Yi'ingo wore a tight, skin-coloured dress. The gown was adorned with the beautiful designs of golden and crimson phoenixes. The texture gave the illusion that the birds had been painted directly on Sky's naked body. She was fully covered, and yet the dress showcased her figure and enhanced her curves. The Yi'ingo wore her golden winged helmet and flat sandals that laced up her long legs. Sky's statuesque body and strength contrasted with the human's featherlike fragility. Both women laughed as they entered the room. The bond between them was strong. Gabriel was delighted to see his cousin so carefree and relaxed, as if a heavy weight had been lifted off her shoulders.

Quinn rushed to greet Sky.

"How is my new Yi'ingo apprentice?" Sky asked.

"I'm well, thanks. You look beautiful, Sky. But . . . it's a bit much." Quinn paused and pressed her lips together tightly. Then, she continued, "And too . . . ."

"Too what?" Sky asked puzzled.

"Girly." Quinn's eyes opened wide, feigning innocence.

Sky put her hands on her hips, flipped her hair, and lifted her chest dramatically

"I'll see you tonight at the arena, warrior. This girl will make you eat some dust."

Quinn chuckled and replied, "First, you'll have to change, or you'll catch a cold. All this glamour, I don't get it. It's like that silly party in New York. Just give Apollo the crown already. Let's start the Games.

What a draaagg."

For a moment, Quinn's quirkiness made Gabriel forget his troubles.

Bastian walked in wearing his golden armour. He made his way in the direction of Gabriel and was about to say something, but as he walked past Sky he did a double take.

"Wow! You look stunning, my lady," he exclaimed before he composed himself. Then, he cleared his voice, smiled, and spoke, "It's time, my king."

Gabriel closed his eyes and concentrated on his breath. It is time.

THE CEREMONY

Gabriel stood quietly, listening to the crystal violins that played in the background. The door to Throne Hall opened, and the audience stood up to welcome the new king. Riley held her little sister's hand, and they both started walking in front of their Apollo.

Gabriel looked at Aria with pride. The little girl was walking into a room full of strangers with a big smile on her face. Both girls walked decisively, but once in a while, they looked back at their father, smiling, seeking reassurance, and providing him with support. Inspired by the courage of his young daughters, Gabriel raised his head and stood like a king. He unleashed his full glow and enraptured everyone in the room.

The Ange'el walked towards his parents who sat at the thrones. The rectangular room was filled with the happy faces of members of all tribes, who had made an effort to mingle beyond faction or rank. He found himself surrounded by love and support, and as he walked he bowed to his people.

Just behind him followed Sky and Bastian and Sage and Josh—the leaders of each tribe walking together behind their leader—proud, happy, and grateful for all that they had accomplished together. Each one of them carried a banner with the insignia of their tribes. It was no small sign that a human and a Hu'urei were part of the royal party; it was a strong indication of reform.

Throne Hall had space for the one thousand Ahe'ey citizens that had been selected based on their contributions to the community. All Ahe'ey wore their best outfits; colour, sparkle, and sophistication filled the hall and spilled out to the amphitheatre at the grounds of the temple. There were thousands and thousands of people waiting for the new king to arrive.

Gabriel saw Quinn and Ollie standing next to the thrones. They both seemed quite eager for the event to begin. The elders of Ahe'ey sat just behind the queen and king with one notable exception—Angha was conspicuously absent from the important event. Gabriel felt his heart jump in his chest every time he thought about his conversation with the old man.

To clear his mind from Angha's darkness, he scanned the room admiring the artworks. Paintings of historical figures, extinct species, and mythical creatures decorated the four walls of the hall. A large frame stood on the wall to the left of the thrones. It depicted Marcus killing Sathian, and behind the image of the king, there was a dragon ready to attack. The wall to the right of the throne showed a painting of Sky and Bastian fighting a Wali'ingooteer. And on the wall opposite the thrones, stood Viviane's image. Her hands faced the sky as she commanded a cloud of dragons to fly towards the mountain.

A new artwork adorned the area above the thrones. It showed a winged creature kneeling on the sand by the lake, touching the shimmering water. Light emanated from the Ange'el's body; he was translucent, ethereal, and stunning. He looked straight at the audience, and his eyes, touched by turquoise, were mesmerising. It was difficult for Gabriel to recognise himself in that painting. He had never seen such creature or experienced his own glow.

For the first time in the history of that land, Gabriel was represented in their art. Yet, the same face adorned two paintings. One was distorted by menace and rage, and scarred by the absence of one eye. It represented all that is dark and evil. The other symbolised light and virtue and showed the face of a leader, the face of a king. Gabriel took a deep breath, overwhelmed by the expectations represented in the art.

Every step towards the throne was an opportunity for Gabriel to leave behind his self-doubt, his introversion, and his fear of failure. He glanced one final time at the painting of Sathian, and as he did he remembered the words of encouragement of his cousins, and he recalled Morgan's plea. *I choose light*, he thought as he continued walking in the direction of the throne.

He became calm and more centred as he stood in front of the king and queen, surrounded by the people he loved so dearly. *I miss you, my love*, he thought as he searched for her face amongst all the loving faces that surrounded him. His mother had told him that Morgan had refused her invitation to be present at the hall during the coronation. Morgan had told the queen that she didn't want to affect Gabriel's peace and happiness during such an important moment.

As Viviane stood up, took her crown from her head, and placed it on his, Gabriel vowed to "serve all the creatures of the Earth, honouring his responsibilities, forever grateful for the privilege that had been entrusted to him."

At that moment, Sky, Bastian, Sage, and Joshua pulled a string on each one of their banners and unveiled a new insignia. All four banners showcased a design that incorporated the Phoenix, the Sun, the Moon, and the Dragon, the same design inked on the body of their new king, a surprise from the leaders of each tribe, a sign that they were now united under one banner and one king. Gabriel smiled and bowed. He was proud and humbled by the gesture.

Ollie and Quinn approached him and replaced his armour plate with another bearing the new insignia. Gabriel was, at first, unsure of what was going on as the two eager teens pushed and tugged his body plate a bit too abruptly. They were too excited about the surprise. Bastian laughed out loud at the scene until Sky's elbow hit his rib cage. "Shhh!"

As the audience celebrated and his mother and father stepped away so that he could take the throne, he bowed to them and walked towards the door. This king had neither temperament nor reason to sit on his throne. He was going to be with his people, and as he moved, others followed.

Gabriel walked to the balcony of the Temple of Lights followed by his family. Thousands of Ahe'ey gathered around the amphitheatre, cheering the new king with great joy and affection. To everyone's surprise, many of the Hu'urei had enhanced their usual black and grey outfits with a touch of colour, raspberry pink. It reflected the happiness in their faces.

Gabriel left his family at the plateau and walked down the stairs of the Temple until his eyes were at the same level as the eyes of his people. His body relaxed a little as he walked amongst them. He spoke as a man, just a man, speaking to thousands, yet speaking to each one. His voice wasn't loud; he didn't have to shout to reach each soul. His Ange'el heart could connect intimately with each and every citizen of the lost land.

"It is my greatest privilege to serve you. I inherit this responsibility, not from divine right like the medieval kings in history, nor for being an established leader in this land with proven worthiness. I'm here due to my blood, designed to heal, with the potential to destroy. I am nothing but a citizen of Ahe'ey, humbled and honoured by this great responsibility that you have placed on my shoulders. I promise you I will not fail you, my sisters and brothers.

"We live in extraordinary privilege. Our land, our biology, and our knowledge are jewels that we must cherish and celebrate as they are as special as they are rare. We must learn to share them and make it our mission to elevate the quality of life of every child and every living being on this planet. It is a bold ambition, but one that we will conquer with determination and perseverance. For, while I accept our fallibility, frailty, complexity, and contradiction, I trust our honesty, our virtue, our valour, and our heart.

"I'm here at your side, not above you. I'm as excited and scared of what we have to accomplish as you are, but I give you my word that together we will heal our land and share our gift with humankind. By your side, I will honour our founding mothers and fathers and their vision of a civilisation that shines so bright it brings light and hope to humanity, and purpose and joy to our people.

"My tears are your tears. My joy is your joy. We will take care of our beautiful world, celebrating the miracles of art and science but refusing a culture that rushes our experience and turns every blessing and every moment into a disposable asset as our life and our time are all we have to give. There's nothing expendable about the patchwork quilt of meaningful moments that make up our existence.

"As we proceed together on this journey, resetting our past and refocusing our future, we must remember to be brave in our ambitions and unleash the hunger of our passionate hearts as we will never win unless we stand to lose."

At that moment he saw her, sitting amongst the Ange'el novices. He took a moment to recover from the glorious aftershock of her smile. He allowed his eyes to rest on hers and then he bowed; his heart and gaze filled with gratitude and devotion.

"I'm so proud of you Gabriel," he heard inside his head, "But promise me you won't read my thoughts today," she asked. He nodded, and his inner light wavered; he assumed she wanted to hide her pain.

The Ahe'ey cheered for the young king, and he absorbed their emotions and thoughts with great humility. They connected with his passion, ambition, strength, and utter vulnerability. In the people's minds, the reluctant leader was a beloved leader, a true leader, the only leader that could bring the tribes together and guide them to fulfil their purpose.

"Today, as your king, I am unveiling my gift to you. I have been working with friends to sequence and store the genome of the seven direct descendants of the royal bloodline of Ahe'ey. The secret of our past has been unlocked and it now lives beyond our perishable bodies, putting an end to the dynastic rules and to the restricted freedoms of our foremothers and forefathers.

"We will close, once and for all, this chapter in our history where we fought to control the wombs of our women, where we dismissed love for the benefit of biology. No more. Never again. Our gift is safe until the time we can share it. It is now time to unlock the treasure of possibility that can only be unleashed through bold, unrestricted aspirations."

Some of the Ahe'ey celebrated the news immediately; they embraced each other and clapped with enthusiasm. Others tried to make sense of Gabriel's words, recalling Amalia's rules, and debating the validity of the solution. But even the most conservative amongst the Ahe'ey shared a sense of quiet optimism. Above all else, they trusted their new king.

The sun was setting, and the sparkle on the outfits and bodies of the Ahe'ey was starting to emerge. The crowd was elated, screaming his name, celebrating, and dancing.

He smiled with grace and renewed optimism as his people celebrated his vision. He raised his right hand, asking them for a moment of silence, and a wave of calm propagated across the thousands of Ahe'ey. He was about to speak, but he was distracted by Bastian, who ran down the stairs towards him and grabbed him by the arm.

"Your people want to see you, my king." The Ma'asai dragged Gabriel half way up the stairs.

The people cheered and laughed at the friendly interaction between the cousins. Bas returned to his place at the balcony beside Sky, leaving Gabriel to face the audience. The sound of the Sacred House's bell echoed across the forest beyond the amphitheatre.

The first sign of dusk was the signal for the next stage of the ceremony. Dozens of young women lined up at the top of the stairs just below the royal balcony; amongst them Scout. Her white gown didn't soften her rebellious expression. Her hair, belligerent eyes, and height made her stand out from the group.

The audience was now dead quiet. In other times, this would have been a happy moment for the Ahe'ey. Many kings and queens had officially selected their partners on days like today as the people of the land celebrated the happy event. Not today. Today, silence spread throughout the audience as the moon claimed the place of the sun in the sky. The final solar beam took with it the audience's last smile and laughter. They stood quietly with their eyes set on him; the entire land knew his struggle.

Gabriel's head was down as he prepared to address his parents. He knew what he had to do; he had spent days weaving together the right words. He looked at the faces of the women that stood above him at the top of the stairs; his expression was full of love and empathy. Then, he turned around, looking for her face amongst the crowd, until he found the eyes that could soothe his heart. There, he found only love—no judgment, no resentment—just pure, unconditional love. Her dark hair was unleashed in a thousand waves and fell loose down her shoulders like a fountain of dark chocolate running down the beaming silver-cyan surface of her gown.

Marcus took off his crown, walked down the stairs and placed it in the hands of his son. Gabriel held it with his left hand and raised it high above his head. He faced his mother and spoke decisively, "I gave my word that I would fight a dragon, become king and choose a queen. Those promises I can and will keep." He stopped, turned around and spoke to the crowd. "I will choose a queen. A queen selected by merit, not marriage or birth. A queen who will not marry me; a queen I will not marry. The rightful queen of this land." He looked up, set his eyes on Sky, and smiled. His right hand reached towards the Yi'ingo, asking her to join him as he walked up in her direction. The entire audience stood up and cheered. The Yi'ingo roared with joy supporting their fierce leader.

Gabriel felt the overwhelming enthusiasm of his people. He was so proud of his cousin. In a short period, Sky had gained the trust and respect of the Hu'urei.

"Yeah!" Bastian's fist pumped the air above him while Josh turned to his half-sister and kneeled. All the Hu'urei followed Josh, and soon all four tribes kneeled in support of the future queen.

Viviane and Marcus stood quietly, carefully watching things unfold. Sky took some time to react. Her eyes, filled with pride and desire, were set on the gleaming crown. She walked towards Gabriel, but as he tried to place the crown on her head, her right hand went up, palm facing him, and she shook her head.

"No," she said, simply.

"You deserve it Sky," he pleaded, "and we need you."

Amalia came forward on the balcony and prepared to intervene, but Viviane stopped her by making a hand gesture and asking her to wait.

"Yes, I know," Sky's eyes gleamed with confidence as she spoke, holding her head high. He looked at her, confused, and she continued, "I once gave my word to a future king; an Ange'el afraid of his own power and the supremacy of the crown. A king that feared the corrosive nature of power; a man about to accumulate too much of it.

"He made me promise to hold him accountable. To guard Ahe'ey against evil. To always put the safety of our people above my affection for him. To oppose him, and even kill him if I had to." He smiled and nodded as she spoke. "And although I know this will be a particularly boring and uneventful job, if I'm going to speak truth to power, I cannot, I will not ascend to the throne.

"You, my king will never need my opposition, but opposition you shall have. A strong critical eye, watching every step you take and challenging you and your mighty power. No one is better qualified to do this job than I." Her smile was both joyful and adversarial. She looked back, shot a glance at Bastian and used her thumb to point back at the Ma'asai. "He certainly is not." Bastian chuckled, and everybody followed. "I, on the other hand, I have an outstanding track record. Don't you think?"

"Indeed," Gabriel said. He raised his eyebrows and opened his eyes wide. But he couldn't hold on to his dramatic response for long. His lips quickly turned upwards, and his eyes glimmered, giving away his playful joy.

Laughter and banter travelled across the audience.

"I'm not an Ange'el, but I can predict a lot of pain in your future, my king," Josh shouted, teasing. "Sister, welcome to the rebellion," he said lightly.

"So shall it be." Gabriel held Sky's hand and kissed it. "I kiss the hand of resistance; the hand of a leader blind to my Ange'el glow." He unsheathed her sword and held it by the blade below the phoenix-shaped grip. He raised the golden bird to touch his lips. "I kiss the sword of justice; may it test, challenge and, if necessary, resist and withdraw my power. I'm grateful for my cousin's defiant fellowship." She nodded and turned around without bowing, returning to her place beside Bastian. As Gabriel followed Sky with his eyes, he met his mother's horrified expression. He wished he had the power to read the queen mother's thoughts.

Gabriel stood, holding the consort's crown, his finger skimming over each crystal embedded in the golden circlet.

"It looks like that I won't be able to keep my promise." He placed the spare crown on the stairs and then looked up to face his suitors. "There is another promise I won't keep. You, my kinswomen, you are all fine, accomplished, and honourable Ahe'ey. You deserve the world and a partner who loves you above all others. I cannot be such a partner; my heart is already taken. It was conquered long ago and sings joyfully in its captivity. One day I hope to marry the one I love, the only one I love, if she finds in her heart a way to forgive me." He turned to face the audience and looked into her eyes, full of regret and hope. "And if you, my people and my parents, don't accept me as I am, then . . . " his hand went up to his crown, and he took it off, placing it on the stairs beside the consort's crown. "I cannot lead change if my actions fail to match my words."

The two bands of power lay on the ground beside each other as he turned to face his parents. He kneeled with his head down. "Release me from my promise?"

"No," Viviane's voice echoed across the amphitheatre. The audience gasped, reacting to the decisive tone of the queen mother. "You have given us your word, and you will marry a daughter of royal descent." She was calm and spoke softly. The whispering of the crowd reminded Gabriel of the sound of a beehive. It was deafening, and he felt the weight of all their minds, mouths, and eyes as they focused on him.

A voice cut through the deafening noise. Someone chanted in fierce defiance within the group of aspirants to the throne. The purple of her crest gave her away even from a distance.

"Morgan! Morgan! Morgan!" The warrior screamed as loud as she could, looking at Viviane and Marcus. She marched down the stairs in front of thousands of people. Another voice joined her, and they shouted in unison. It was Bastian; his baritone voice filled the air with Morgan's name as he walked up to stand next to Scout. Quinn led a procession of all her siblings, shouting, almost singing.

As the full moon was rising behind the Temple of Lights, a chorus of voices joined them from all corners of the amphitheatre until all of Ahe'ey, including the aspirants to the throne, had joined them in fierce rebellion. It was their gift of love to their king. Gabriel's eyes were full of water as he bowed to Scout and Bastian, who stood side by side, leading the heavenly choir. They both smiled, with their best irreverent, childlike faces. One by one, the crowd stood up to be counted, challenging the rules of the bloodline. United and defiant against the shackles of their genes.

Morgan's eyes stayed with him. Her love burned so intensely that self-combustion was a possibility she almost welcomed. To perish now would be to die deliriously happy; she couldn't imagine another moment that could possibly reach such heights of unadulterated joy. His eyes, she missed them; she wanted to dive into them and cool down her insatiable yearning for his being.

She watched Sky strut down the stairs. First, the Yi'ingo extended her hand to Gabriel and asked him to stand. Then she picked up his crown and placed it on his head as the audience continued to shout Morgan's name. Sister, my sister, Morgan smiled. Sky, the Phoenix whose power needed no crown, whose majesty needed no title. Love. Morgan had so much love for this lioness with the golden heart. She saw Sky make her way through the audience to reach her.

The Yi'ingo extended her hand as Morgan looked up at the gleaming figure who stood between her and the sky. She held her sister's hand, and they walked up to meet him. The audience's joyful roar vibrated in every cell of her body. Morgan pulled Sky's hand towards her and stood on her tiptoes to hug her sister. She squeezed the Yi'ingo with all her strength and whispered in her ear, "Thank you, sister."

Sky smiled, unaware of the deeper meaning behind what had been spoken.

The young king walked slowly in her direction. He held her hand and placed it close to his heart as he spoke, looking into her eyes. His voice was coated with humility, and his glow flickered, such was the vulnerability of his condition.

"In your eyes, I am home.

"In your eyes, I thrive and become fully alive.

"In your eyes, I want to spend my eternity.

"In your eyes, I see the best of me.

"I see the fountain of all your intelligence, wit, grace, strength, and honour.

"In your eyes, I see my future and my history.

"Lock your eyes in my eyes and dance with me for all eternity.

"Marry me, my light, my love, my soulmate. Marry me?" He whispered it; his wavering voice anxious for her answer.

Self-combustion, it'll happen at any second now. So much love, so much joy. This is how it feels to be fully alive or to die of pure bliss. Morgan had to work very hard to stop herself from jumping into his arms and screaming "yes" from the top of her lungs. She paused, cleared her voice, and considered every word she was about to unleash on her love and on the people of Ahe'ey.

"Over three hundred years ago, Mary Wollstonecraft dared to write the following, 'I love man as my fellow; but his sceptre, real, or usurped, extends not to me, unless the reason of an individual demands my homage; and even then, the submission is to reason, and not to man.' To marry you Gabriel would be to submit to reason and to love. I'm worthy of you and you are worthy of me, and nothing would make me happier and more fulfilled than to pay homage to my darling king."

She felt his joy propagate through her mind and body in the form of a jolt of well-being. His glow was so bright that she had to squint her eyes to see his smile. As he leaned in to kiss her, she stopped him.

"Wait. Wait my love. I haven't finished." She lifted his hand and kissed it. Then she turned to look at the audience. "I am proud, so proud of you today. I'm overjoyed that you, the people of Ahe'ey, have chosen a healer and a teacher to be your king. In my world, the best of us are the ones least recognised and rarely compensated. Our nurses, carers, and educators—the unselfish people that add the most value to our communities. Today, you have chosen one of them to be your king. He may have the skills to defeat dragons, but at his core, he prefers to heal, to teach, and to empower others.

"I am proud, so proud of you today. You have championed love above race, status, or blood. In accepting me into your family, you have made an honourable choice to welcome a stranger. A human that many, less virtuous than you, would consider inferior or unworthy. You chose to accept difference into the heart of your most beloved family. Thank you.

"I wish I could stop this story here. I wish I could just accept the hand of this virtuous man, and celebrate your kind gesture. Unfortunately, I can't. But, as I proceed with this story—our history—I want you to acknowledge and celebrate your choices. Because what you will learn today won't invalidate your gesture and kindness towards me.

"I have realised recently that nothing good can come from lying, even if our intentions are worthy and our goals virtuous." She noticed Gabriel's confused expression and caressed his hand, attempting to reassure him. Trust me; I'll never hurt you. Never. Then, she raised her eyes; Viviane's eyes were already set on hers. With her mind, she asked the queen mother to disclose her identity.

Fay

The queen mother walked towards her children. Her long dress slid down the stairs. The shimmering silver train looked like the restless sea as the light of the moon touched its surface. She stood beside Morgan as she spoke to her people.

"There is no greater agony than the suffering of a ruler who must place the well-being of their kingdom above the happiness of her own children. Marcus and I have conspired for years so that Ahe'ey could reach this happy moment. It has cost us our hearts and our blood as our actions, although noble and pressing, have pierced the flesh and the souls of the ones we love. We brought them pain beyond measure and demanded their sacrifice." Viviane looked at Gabriel, Sky, Bastian, and Morgan as she spoke.

"Many years ago, we lost a young flower button from our land; a button that was forced to flourish without the nurture of her people and the comfort of her home. Proving that we are a product of our environment as much as of our genes, this flower, who holds in her roots all the capability of the royal lineage, has not yet bloomed to her full potential. The potential to heal, to see, to connect, and to lead as a powerful, high-ranking Ange'el, a daughter of Ahe'ey.

"This flower has returned to us in recent times. I recognised her from the moment the light touched her face in my presence as she carries with her, on her face and in her eyes, the soul of her ancestors. The wit, wisdom, and delight of her mother. It was obvious to me that the two that were meant to be, had crossed continents and seas to find each other. How could they not be drunk with love and passion when body, mind, and soul had such a powerful bond?" Viviane felt the confusion and anxiety in her son's mind.

Gabriel looked at his mother, waiting for further validation that he had understood what she was saying. He yearned for more words, more clues. More, please, more . . . .

She heard him with her mind's eye.

She continued speaking, "It was all I could wish and desire—my children reunited, my niece returning home after a lifetime of separation." She heard his silent gasp.

"Recently she touched the water at the Heart of Ahe'ey. The arrow that only moves for a royal Ange'el moved for her. As happy as I was to have found my niece, as delighted as I was that my son had found his love, I was certain that the unveiling of this information would damage the plans for the reform that Marcus and I had been striving towards. We wanted you, our people, to demand revolution. We wanted change to be led by you. A story of royal love would only sedate you into acceptance of the current world order. We needed change, we needed reform, and nothing and no one could threaten the revolution that we were conspiring and instigating in the background.

"We quickly realised that the best way to show you how unfair our laws were, was to show you their love and demand their separation. We withheld Morgan's royal descent from you. We justified our demands in the same way that generations of rulers before us had asked their children to sacrifice their choices to benefit the bloodline. Today, at this moment, you have made a choice; a choice to allow a mere human to marry a king, the right choice, the choice to free us all from the shackles of dynastic ruling.

"And now that you have spoken in unison and have liberated us all, I can unveil that Morgan is not a mere human. She is our Fay, the daughter of my sister Gráinne and the sister of our Sky."

A sob escaped Gabriel's mouth. *I should have known. Fay, our Fay.*

Bastian placed his arm around Gabriel's shoulders, while Sky hugged her little sister, lifting her up in the air. Morgan laughed and cried simultaneously as she was engulfed by the body of her tall, strong sibling.

Morgan's mind was overwhelmed by the happy sobbing of thousands of hearts. The Ahe'ey's joyful cry was profound and uncontrollable. A wave of emotion circled amongst the people as they celebrated the return of their precious royal daughter. For them, it was personal, as if Morgan represented all the mothers, daughters, and sisters lost in dark times. They shouted from the audience stands.

"Gráinne's daughter!"

"The royal baby girl!"

"Their pure blood brought them together."

"It was written in their genes."

"Make her queen; her blood is pure!"

Their words, like arrows, destroyed Morgan's joy. She looked up to discover the heartbroken expressions of Quinn and Ollie; the faces of those who had lost their biggest human ally. The two teens who celebrated the moment where the Ahe'ey had placed a human above their blood, only to see it vanish in minutes. Morgan realised that the pure gene was the Ahe'ey's Holy Grail, a symbol, a brand too powerful to be abolished in just one day.

She saw Amalia walk down the stairs and pick up the consort's crown. Her grandmother, the woman who, a few days ago, had been prepared to kill her, now reached to place the crown on her head.

Morgan walked backwards, slipping on the stairs and falling into Gabriel's arms. She looked into his eyes and dived into his sea of hope and understanding. In that safe space, she confessed her next move and she found nothing but resolute support and unshakable loyalty. We're leaders; we're role models; we'll lead by example with our words and actions. Who had said it? She wasn't quite sure, her voice was his, and his heart was hers. His mind, her mind; two become one.

She tasted his lips, and then ran the tip of her nose down his neck. She inhaled his magic healing scent, and then she battled to stand on her own two feet. It was a fierce battle against herself. It's almost impossible to leave heaven of one's own free will. She stood up and extended her hand in the direction of Quinn and Ollie and asked them to join her. The two distraught teens moved to stand by her side as she placed her hands on their shoulders.

She avoided Amalia's gaze and found comfort in the cyan sea of her lover's eyes. "My Gabriel. My love. I have fought all my life against those who tried to tell me that gender, race, stars, gods, or genes controlled my destiny. They told me that I had no say in the matter. That who I am, what I like, how much I achieve, were predetermined from the moment I was conceived. Yet, look at me and my sister; look at the accomplishments of these young people. Genes are not destiny."

"Genes are not destiny!" Quinn shouted from the top of her lungs.

"Hurrah," Scout replied from above, leading all her companions who clapped in support.

"Thanks Scout. You're my favourite bastard," Quinn replied, blowing Scout a kiss.

Morgan giggled and continued speaking. "To marry you right now, under the shadow of our blood, would be to weaken our bond, and to dilute all that you are and all that I am. I refuse to accept that I love you because I'm programmed to love you, and I hope with all my heart that you too love me beyond my genes.

"To marry now when my past is unfolding, when I'm just learning who I am and what I am capable of, would be a disservice to our love. We have all our life together to marry, and when we do, there will be no doubt in anyone's mind that our love runs deeper than blood, and runs stronger than family ties.

"So, no, my Gabriel. I won't marry you today, and I won't marry you tomorrow. I won't marry you in all the days that we will be together as I don't plan to leave your side ever again. I won't marry you until the day I can prove to the world that I don't love you for your blood or your sceptre. I love you because you are deserving of my homage, my fellow and my king."

Morgan turned to face Amalia, "As for the crown, I don't want it; I don't need it. My power, these children's power"she squeezed the teen's shoulders"doesn't come from crowns or genes. It comes from our desire to make the world a better place." The eyes of the old queen scanned Morgan's features; she looked like she was still processing Viviane's revelation.

Amalia softened her expression and spoke, "You are headstrong, just like your mother."

Gabriel nodded and smiled with the intensity of a thousand full moons. He looked completely overwhelmed by emotion and joy. Amalia embraced Quinn and Ollie and then walked towards Gabriel, placing her hands on his face. She kissed him as he wrapped his arms around her. For a brief moment, he hid his face in the curve of her neck to hide his emotion. He kissed her again and again as the people of Ahe'ey cheered and clapped with exaltation.

Behind the royal couple, Bastian gave Scout a high five before he turned to hug his own love and spin her in the air.

POWER

Viviane glowed as she looked at her children, allowing herself to savour the sweet taste of pride. Then, she turned to her husband, placed her hand on his face and kissed him. "We are done, my treasure. We are done," she whispered before she turned to face her people. "It was always our wish to see the love of Gabriel and Morgan consummated.

"And it was our desire to show our four children how strong and worthy they are, as they were able to overcome their fears and to sacrifice their needs to benefit humankind. They have showcased their valour; together they are worthy leaders. No doubt should lurk in their conscience as all pride, pretension, and weakness have been stripped away in this soul-breaking test that they have conquered. My gift to you, my children, is a lifetime together as leaders of this land, knowing that you are loved and that you are worthy of your position, not because of your blood, but because of your valour."

Marcus spoke, "My children, my people, do not resent our actions, for they made you all rally and demonstrated your virtue and valour." He looked at Bastian with affection.

Viviane continued speaking, "I follow in my son's footsteps, and I will respect his desire to redistribute power in this land—the absolute power that I held for so many years. To my son, I gave the crown, the helm of this kingdom. May he use his Ange'el gifts to lead the world with great compassion."

Viviane lifted her hands and removed her moonstone ring, the key to the portals between Ahe'ey and the outside world. "This," she held the ring in her hand, "I give to our mighty protector, the one who will work to keep Ahe'ey and the world safe from harm." Viviane walked towards Sky and placed the moonstone on her niece's ring finger. Sky's face was touched by surprise as she bowed to her aunt. The Yi'ingo was sombre, acknowledging the responsibility that was being trusted with her.

Then, Viviane pulled the quartz ring off her middle finger, forever breaking the link that imprinted the key to the library on her genes. "Fay, Morgan . . . this is yours, child." Viviane walked towards Morgan and held her hand. "You, who roamed the Earth in search for knowledge all your life. You, who have continuously shared your learnings with passion and devotion. You, who are so hungry for answers and always sought to ask the right questions. You, my child, are the rightful owner of this most precious gift." Viviane felt Morgan's hand tremble as she pushed the quartz ring into her niece's index finger. It was the only finger large enough to hold the jewel.

Marcus walked towards Bastian and stood by his side as Viviane spoke to her nephew. "I have nothing to give you, my son, because all that you need you have stored inside your heart. You, my beloved child, you will continue to play the most important role in this family. You hold your cousins together with your blind love and faith." Viviane allowed her worries to surface in her eyes. "I feel it in my gut, that a storm approaches and the wild wind gusts will work to tear them apart." Viviane's eyes pointed to Sky and Gabriel. "Bastian, my son, your heart and your love must continue to be the foundation that keeps this family together. Even when everyone else works to pull it apart."

Bastian nodded to the queen mother. Viviane saw the spark in his eyes as he finally understood his place amongst the two titans.

The young king embraced his best friend. "Thank you, Bas." Then the Ange'el looked up and signalled to Joshua to join them.

Viviane closed her eyes for a brief moment admonishing herself for her omission. Then she spoke, looking at Josh with a smile, "Join us, my son."

The large man held Sage's hand. He was initially flustered by Viviane's omission, but the Hu'urei was quick to let go of his grievance. Josh and Sage walked down the stairs followed by Riley and Aria. The Hu'urei turned to Morgan with a smile, "Sister, welcome home."

"Thank you Josh. Yes, I am finally home." Morgan smiled, surrounded by her loving family.

The new royal Ange'el glowed in all her glory; she floated in happiness by the side of her love as she watched the joyful faces of his family, her family. The daughter of Ahe'ey had finally returned home, and she was ready to defeat Zanus.

EPILOGUE

EPILOGUE

Games Arena, Ahe'ey

Morgan sat by Gabriel in the royal box of the Games Arena. He held her hand, caressing it with his thumb. The opening ceremony of the Games had begun. The warriors paraded through the arena wearing suits of armour that shone under the moonlight. The champions led the group; Sky, Bastian, and Marcus were in front. Their armour was covered with the emblazoned victory laurels. The novices were at the back, and Morgan could see Quinn's smiling face. The young warrior waved to her family. She seemed ecstatic to be the first human to have ever qualified to take part in the Games.

Sky broke off from the group and went to the middle of the arena. *"You!"* she roared, pointing her sword at Gabriel. "Yes, *you!*" She was doing her best version of mighty Sky—defiant, intimidating, aggressive. She projected her voice and power throughout Ahe'ey.

Gabriel smiled.

"No more excuses, Ange'el. Come down here and join us. Let's see what our king is made of." She rolled her sword in her hands and gave him a mischievous smile. "Come on, where is your couraaggee?" The audience cheered. The warriors beat their swords against their shields and stomped their feet on the ground.

Morgan saw Ollie's eyes open wide as he looked at his dad, who was now standing and removing his cape and crown, never breaking eye contact with Sky, a gesture of friendly defiance that no one had ever witnessed coming from the king. Gabriel kissed Morgan and jumped off the second-floor balcony into the arena.

"No geentle anymore," Aria said, pointing at her dad. The little girl was sitting on Viviane's lap. Everyone laughed.

Before Gabriel joined Sky, Bastian, and Marcus in leading the parade, he hugged his daughter and picked up Scout's hand, raising it up in the air as the audience clapped enthusiastically.

Morgan smiled as she looked at the raised hands of her lover and Scout. She lifted her eyes to look at the clock face that stood in the highest tower of the arena. It was nine o'clock in the evening. As she focused her gaze on the dial of the clock, she remembered her dream. Sathian washing her hands with the tears of the weeping angel. Suddenly, she had the answer; she knew how to unlock the door to the Heart of Ahe'ey. Morgan turned to face Viviane preparing to share her insight but was interrupted by the sound of the gong that told Sky and Gabriel to move to the centre of the ring. The warriors took their positions as the audience screamed with excitement.

"My call sign is Apollo," he said confidently, winking up at Sage. "Let the Games begin." Gabriel and Sky unsheathed their swords waiting for the second gong.

Morgan felt a shiver down her spine. She looked up at the night sky as a dark shadow covered the light of the full moon. As she raised her head, expecting to see some clouds, she saw them, the dragons. A threatening cloud of hundreds of Wali'ingooteer flew in their direction.

THE END

Before you go . . . If you liked this book, consider writing a review. Much love, Jamie

APPENDICES

Appendix I – Map of Ahe'ey

Appendix II – Royal Family Tree

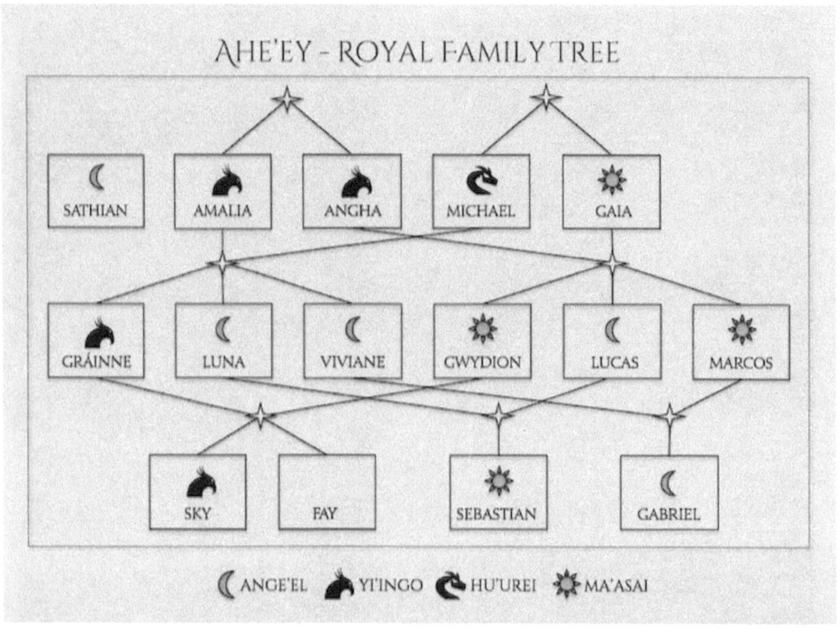

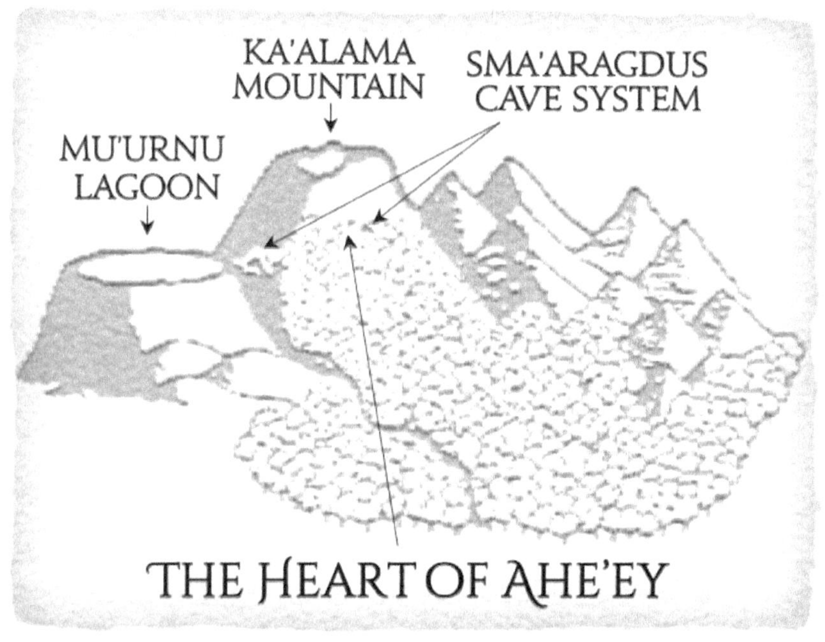
MU'URNU
LAGOON
KA'ALAMA
MOUNTAIN
SMA'ARAGDUS
CAVE SYSTEM
THE HEART OF AHE'EY

Appendix IV – Characters' Ages

Characters' Ages in 2014

Amalia - 254 years old

Angha - 213 years old

Marcus - 134 years old

Viviane - 112 years old

Gabriel - 46 years old

Sky - 44 years old

Sebastian - 40 years old

Morgan - 34 years old

Joshua - 33 years old

Sage - 21 years old

Scout - 19 years old

Oliver - 14 years old

Quinn - 14 years old

Riley - 7 years old

Aria - 2.5 years old

1754 to 2014

1754

Michael is born

1760

Amalia is born

1801

Angha is born

1802

Amalia and Michael marry

1804

Amalia and Michael become queen and king of Ahe'ey

1808

Sathian is born

1812

Gaia is born

1870

Amalia gives birth to Gráinne

1872

Angha and Gaia marry

1873

Gaia gives birth to Gwydion

1874

Gaia gives birth to Lucas

1876

Amalia gives birth to Luna

1880

Marcus is born

Sathian marries Sabine

Sathian becomes the leader of the Hu'urei

1882

Sabine gives birth to Iblis

1902

Amalia gives birth to Viviane

1920

Gráinne and Gwydion marry

1932

Luna and Lucas marry

1935

Amalia and Michael close the Passage of Ahe'ey

1960
Viviane and Marcus marry

1968
Viviane gives birth to Gabriel

1970
Gráinne gives birth to Sky

1974
Luna gives birth to Sebastian

1980
Fay is born
Iblis kidnaps Gráinne and Fay
Sathian kills Luna and Lucas
Ahe'ey civil war starts
Viviane and Marcus become queen and king of Ahe'ey
Amalia leads the Yi'ingo army to war
Gabriel, Sky, and Bastian are hidden by the Ange'el

1981
Gráinne gives birth to Joshua

1982
Gráinne dies
Fay disappears

1983

Michael and Gwydion die in battle

Marcus kills Sathian

1984

Sky leads the army and become Ahe'ey's ruler under martial law

Gabriel opens the Bethesda passage

Gabriel starts working outside Ahe'ey

Gaia dies of grief

1986

Viviane and the Ange'el subdue the dragons

Angha moves to the Sma'aragdus caves with the dragons

Iblis and the rebels flee to the southern mountain range

1999

Sage arrives at Ahe'ey

2004

Sky kills Iblis

The Hu'urei rebels are mostly defeated

The war ends

2005

Oliver arrives at Ahe'ey

2007

Quinn arrives at Ahe'ey

2008

Riley arrives at Ahe'ey

2014

June - Aria arrives at Ahe'ey

21 November - Morgan arrives in New York

22 November - Party at the Metropolitan Museum of Art (full moon)

26 November - Morgan wakes up at Ahe'ey

6 December - Test and trial

21 December - Winter solstice (full moon)